Tunku Halim was born in 1964. He lives nomadically but is a frequent visitor to his country of birth, Malaysia.

His previous books include several short story collections, his latest being *7 Days to Midnight* (2013), two novels, *Dark Demon Rising* (1997) and *Vermillion Eye* (2000), and the novella *Juriah's Song* (2008). His non-fiction books include *A Children's History of Malaysia* (2003) and a biography of his late father *Tunku Abdullah — A Passion for Life* (1998).

His first book with Fixi Novo was the bestselling mid-career retrospective *Horror Stories* (2014), which won the Popular-*The Star* Readers Choice Award in 2015 as well as the MPH Best of 2014 award. It has sold over 30,000 copies in its first 3 years, making it the bestselling Malaysian English fiction book of all time.

His subsequent books for Fixi Novo are the novels *Last Breath* (2014) and *A Malaysian Restaurant in London* (2015).

FIXI NOVO MANIFESTO

1. We believe that omputih/gwailoh-speak is a Malaysian language.

2. We use American spelling. This is because we are more influenced by Hollywood than the House of Windsor.

3. We publish stories about the urban reality of Malaysia. If you want to share your grandmother's World War 2 stories, send 'em elsewhere and you might even win the Booker Prize.

4. We specialize in pulp fiction, because crime, horror, sci-fi and so on turn us on.

5. We will not use italics for non-American/non-English terms. This is because those words are not foreign to a Malaysian audience. So we will not have "They had *nasi lemak* and went back to *kongkek*" but rather "They had nasi lemak and went back to kongkek". Nasi lemak and kongkek are some of the pleasures of Malaysian life that should be celebrated without apology; italics are a form of apology.

6. We publish novels and short-story anthologies. We don't publish poetry; we like making money.

7. The existing Malaysian books that come closest to what we wanna do: *Devil's Place* by Brian Gomez; and the Inspector Mislan crime novels by Rozlan Mohd Noor. Look for them!

8. We publish books with the same print run and the same price as those of our parent company, Buku Fixi. So a book of about 300 pages will sell at RM20. This is because we wanna reach out to the young, the sengkek and the kiam siap.

CALL FOR ENTRIES.

Interested? For novels, send your synopsis and first 2 chapters. For anthologies, send a short story of between 2,000-5,000 words on the theme "KL Noir." Send to info@fixi.com.my anytime.

HORROR STORIES 2

TUNKU HALIM

Published by
Fixi Novo *which is an imprint of:*
Buku Fixi (002016254-V)
B-8-2A Opal Damansara, Jalan PJU 3/27
47810 Petaling Jaya, Malaysia
info@fixi.com.my
http://fixi.com.my

All rights reserved. Except for extracts for review purposes, you are not allowed to duplicate or republish this book, in whole or in part, without the written permission of the publisher. Although to be honest the idea of pirated books is kinda cool and we'd secretly take it as a compliment.

Horror Stories 2
© Tunku Halim 2016
www.tunkuhalim.com

First Print: October 2016

Cover and layout: Teck Hee
Consultant: Izaddin Syah Yusof & Alyssa Mohamad

ISBN 978-967-0954-61-5
Catalogue-in-Publication Data available from the
National Library of Malaysia.

Printed by:
Vinlin Press Sdn Bhd
2 Jalan Meranti Permai 1, Meranti Permai Industrial Park
Batu 15, Jalan Puchong, 47100 Puchong, Malaysia

Acknowledgements are due to the following for permission to reproduce stories which appeared in the following publications:

All the stories in *7 Days to Midnight* were previously published by MPH Group Publishing in 2013.

The novella *Juriah's Song* was published by MPH Group Publishing in 2008.

"Something Called Mamsky", "Birthdays are Deathdays", "Haze" and "Monkeys!" were published in *44 Cemetery Road: The Best of Tunku Halim* (2007) by MPH Group Publishing. "The Hidden Shore" and "A Summer Quartet" were published in *Gravedigger's Kiss: More of Tunku Halim* (2007) by MPH Group Publishing. "Pig Heart" was published in *The Woman who Grew Horns and Other Works* (2001) by Pelanduk Publications.

Contents

✕

INTRO   9

---

7 DAYS TO MIDNIGHT (2013)   13
   SATURDAY: Shrine   14
   SUNDAY: Kyoto Kitchen   33
   MONDAY: The App   49
   TUESDAY: Goodnight, Mama   68
   WEDNESDAY: Clear Blue Sky   94
   THURSDAY: In the Village of Setang   111
   FRIDAY: Midnight   135

JURIAH'S SONG (2001)   149

EARLIER STORIES   237
   SOMETHING CALLED MAMSKY (1999)   238
   A SUMMER QUARTET (1999)   256
   BIRTHDAYS ARE DEATHDAYS (1997)   279
   HAZE (1999)   285
   MONKEYS! (2001)   294
   THE HIDDEN SHORE (1997)   300
   PIG HEART (2001)   331

INTRO

Wonderful to see you here in this second volume of *Horror Stories*. Even if you've never read the first volume, the tales that tremble in these pages await you with pleasure.

You'll find here not only some of my favorites, including several knife-wielding ones, from the past two decades but also *7 Days to Midnight,* my short story collection from 2013. As we were somewhat estranged then, I didn't write an introduction to that volume, so this is a good opportunity to talk about them.

I wrote that book while living in Taroona, a suburb in Hobart, Tasmania which is rather distant now because I'm writing this in a condo in KL. As I look out at the city's hazy skyline, I recall those long walks on empty beaches, with an Antarctic-like wind chilling my face and sometimes, if I was lucky, there would be a pod of sleek dolphins playing among the waves. That seaside suburb was the setting for one of the stories: "Clear Blue Sky".

So, for me, as I listen to the traffic below and the humming of the ever-circling fan above, things have certainly changed. I've spent the past two years mostly traveling, for I've chosen not to have a home.

Technologically, the world has changed too since I started writing. And it will continue to do so. A story such as "The App" would have been incomprehensible a decade ago. But, in contrast, history and myths are mostly unchanging and the narratives "In the Village of Setang" and "Shrine" draw heavily from them.

As *7 Days to Midnight* is a slim volume of only 7 stories, the idea was to have you read a story a day and so to finish the book in a week. And if you did that, then you would be able to see a ghost!

Of course, that isn't true.

You can see a ghost at any time!

I know of someone who has the uncanny ability to see ghosts anywhere. There would be one hiding in her wardrobe or watching TV beside her. You must tell me if you've had your own spooky encounters.

Because of my writing, I'm often asked if I've ever experienced anything supernatural. I often reply: "That's a trade secret".

But, since we're being so candid with each other, I can tell you that "Something Called Mamsky", perhaps the first story I'd ever written, is based on my experience at university in England. It was perhaps one of the scariest nights of my life.

You'll also find my novella, *Juriah's Song,* within these pages. That horror-love story, written 15 years ago, is also inspired by true events, including a rocker who wanted me to write about a haunted guitar.

Within *Horror Stories 2*, you'll find "Pig Heart" which is the first and only play I've written. If you're a theatrical producer, I look forward to being invited to its premiere. Front row seats please!

Whatever your tastes, I hope you enjoy these stories. They were written over a period of 20 years but always written with you in mind. So let us now slip away together, to some quiet place, where we can spend our time alone.

Start turning the pages and we'll go to many places, you and I, perhaps even to a beach, far far away. A deserted beach at midnight where a sharp knife awaits.

Take the greatest care.

Tunku Halim
Kuala Lumpur
August 2016

7 DAYS TO MIDNIGHT

SATURDAY:
SHRINE

"THOSE BRITISH PLANTERS FOUND IT. Discovered the grave maybe a hundred years ago—when they were clearing the jungle."

Yvonne had short silky hair, bright questioning eyes beneath pale blue eye shadow and a gold stud through her nose. A necklace with a silver frog locket with emerald eyes sparkled from her smooth pale neck. She was a journalist at *The Star* and, like me, in her early thirties.

"What about the gravestone?" I asked that Saturday afternoon as I drove in my old Hyundai. "Must be at least a hundred years old."

"More than that, Malik. Maybe four or five centuries old. Because of its age the locals turned it into a shrine. They thought this was a grave of some holy man or even a shaman ... oh, here's the turn off."

"I didn't see a sign."

"That's 'cause there isn't one. It's the first left turn after the mosque."

The busy main road became a narrow snaking line of bitumen and the hurtling cars disappeared from view. We were suddenly alone, surrounded by wild grasses, coconut trees and fruit stands propped up by timber that now lay rotting. Squat brick houses scattered themselves before us.

"We call a shrine 'keramat'," I said.

"Yep, that's right," nodded Yvonne. "A keramat."

"Even we devout Muslims still visit these shrines. We beg for favors, we make blessings and we leave offerings for the spirit."

Yvonne crossed her tight jeans that squeezed her fleshy thighs. Even though her oversized blouse refused to hide the weight she had recently put on, her dimpled cheeks, the smooth curve of her neck, still brought out a desolate yearning in me. Once, in the darkness of a nightclub car park, I had kissed those full lips. The next morning her text said it could never work. I replied "Ok" and neither of us ever mentioned it again.

"We Chinese visit these shrines too." Yvonne dug noisily into her handbag. "We light incense and pray there. So race and religion don't matter. The supernatural, it transcends all that."

"Very true," I said. "Everyone, no matter what religion, believes in ghosts."

Yvonne chuckled. "You Malays believe in our Chinese ghosts and we, well we believe in yours!"

A goat peered from beneath a banana tree, its bitty horns dull and blunt beneath the afternoon sun. It shook its head up and down as if agreeing with my colleague. Its eyes were bright and sharp and its nostrils flared. As we drove past, I searched for it in my side mirror but it had vanished.

"Why does the paper bother with these follow-up stories anyway?" I muttered. "The police have finished their investigation. The villagers have been interviewed. And they send us out here on a Saturday!"

"Our readers, they're hungry for more," Yvonne said as she lit a cigarette. "It's not just about two mysterious deaths. They wanna know about the keramat."

"I don't get it though. People are robbed and murdered in KL all the time. Just because two people are found dead at a shrine in some tiny village, suddenly it's big news. Just because there may be some supernatural link."

"Ah, Malik, that's 'cause our readers love the supernatural. Normal crimes are so boring. The supernatural gives added favor. Like lobster instead of chicken in your pot noodles!"

I laughed and told her she was weird.

Bitumen soon gave way to dirt and the road turned bumpy. The car occasionally brushed against a wayward tree branch or clumps of wild grass. Jungle pressed upon both sides. Tall trees and tumultuous undergrowth surrounded us.

"I don't like this," I muttered. "Are you sure we're not lost?"

"Don't worry, city boy," Yvonne said. "This is the way. I was here last week. Or have you forgotten my story on page 2?"

"It was a good one," I said, grinning. "Spooky!"

Moments later, the jungle gave way to a rubber plantation. Trees stood in rows and rows into the distance like dark sentinels on a deserted battlefield. A timber house on wooden stilts suddenly sprang out, followed by another and another.

"Stop at that corner," said Yvonne. "We can walk to the shrine from here."

I stopped the Hyundai beneath a spindly coconut tree, beside a fallen bicycle. I grabbed my camera bag from the back seat, shut the car door and was jolted by the embracing shrill of insects. Yvonne had lit another cigarette and was already walking ahead in her white track shoes.

Beneath the humid heat of the afternoon sun lay a village deserted. As we trudged along the dirt road which had been parched and cracked for the lack of rain, I sought out faces in the houses but saw none. Usually villagers would sit on terraces chatting; their children would play in the dusty compounds. Even the chickens that pecked the earth had vanished. And where were the cats that leapt in and out of the monsoon drains?

"Where are they?" I called out. "All the kampung folk?"

Yvonne turned to me, flicking ash on the track. Her nose-stud glittered. Her frog locket seemed to squirm beneath the bright sunlight, its green eyes glowing warily.

"When I was here last week," she said, "I interviewed an old lady. In her raspy voice, she told me her family would be leaving the next day. That everyone would be fleeing the kampung."

"Why? Because two people were found dead?"

"No, because evil had come."

I stared at her open-mouthed, my throat dry.

"It started when those two foolish rubber tappers went and broke the shrine. Split the thing right down the middle. No one knows why they did it. The villagers think this was what killed them. Since then the kampung folk had seen strange shadows, weird noises round the rubber estate. They stopped going to the keramat because they were too afraid."

"But that's no reason to leave."

"There's more. The old woman crept right up to my ear, you know, and whispered that something had come to the shrine. Attracted by its power. By the offerings made by the villagers. She had no doubt this something was evil."

"What is this *something?*"

"Something ... unspeakable. Her voice, you should have heard her, it was rasping away in the folds of her throat. I could hardly understand her. All the while the poor thing was trying to hide her face with her selendang with one hand. Her other hand was clutching mine so tightly. I can still hear what she whispered. She said it killed those two men. A boy and a girl had also disappeared a few days after. And a baby ... it was found dead in its cot."

"Allah! What is this thing?"

She stared back at me and grinned. "This thing, it's supposed to be ... a vampire."

"Yvonne, don't play games. What the hell then are we doing here? The villagers have fled. So should we!"

"Don't worry. It's just what the old lady said, okay? These poor villagers are so superstitious. They believe all those horror DVDs they watch. We need to drag them into the twenty-first century."

"Is that why you came back? To follow up with this ... this vampire story?"

"Yes, it's more interesting to read about than two mysterious deaths. I wanted to find out about how the villagers are coping ... but it looks like they've all gone."

"Maybe we should head back."

"No. I'm gonna do a story on the deserted village. That'd be so cool. And you've got to take your photos of the shrine. It's not far ... follow me."

Yvonne turned, crossed the dirt road and took a trail that led down a slope into the rubber estate.

I hesitated. The villagers had reason to be superstitious. Their beliefs had protected them for thousands of years. But if I didn't follow my colleague she would soon be but a small shadow up the trail, engulfed by trees. Then she would be gone.

"Come on, Malik!"

I trotted into the rubber estate and caught up with her. A dank coolness touched my face, my armpits. The insect voices turned quieter, as if they were slowly dying, and except for the scrape of our shoes, all lay silent. Then I smelt insecticide and thought I understood. I felt a dry tickle in my throat as if chemicals were already poisoning my cells.

Yvonne walked in silence. The rubber estate continued to draw us into its deepening shadows so that the tip of Yvonne's flittering cigarette glowed. I glanced about searching for possible answers, yet not knowing the questions.

The trees had been planted in ordered rows over the rises and falls of the terrain, their scraggly silhouettes stretching out as far as my eyes could reach. Deep cuts had been made into each trunk. Wooden cups, placed there to collect latex, dangled from them. Most had overflowed with liquid; some had splattered to the ground like spilled milk. Why hadn't the workers been doing their jobs? Surely they hadn't fled too?

Yvonne turned onto a narrower trail which wended its way steeply between clumps of wild grasses and several trees which, from their lack of foliage, appeared disease-ridden.

"This way, Malik!"

The path now led downwards, past a dilapidated hut probably used for storage or to shelter the workers during heavy rain. Then it curved around several mounds. The late afternoon sun glinted from behind the upper branches.

Yvonne glanced around as if to get her bearings, then she left the path and scrambled up a hillock. I struggled to catch up with her and, without warning, was buried in shadows. I heard Yvonne breathing hard from her exertions. The mass of foliage, the ancient trees and their entangling vines told me that we had entered all that remained of a vast jungle.

Then, my eyes were drawn to a sullen paleness.

There, on the ground, about three feet in height was ...

... the keramat.

As I stepped towards it, I caught the faint smell of rotting—of leaves and perhaps ... the flesh of something dead. I expected to see a decomposing civet cat on the ground but only a plethora of twigs and tangling thorny undergrowth stared back at me.

Yvonne's face was pale and pinched. She clasped her metallic frog locket in one hand as if to hide it from the shrine.

"Look at it," said Yvonne, pointing. "You can see that it's ..."

"... broken," I whispered.

It was as if someone had taken a mallet and smashed it. The stone was split right down its middle. Bits of rubble were scattered at our feet.

"It's as if the thing has exploded," said Yvonne. "Why would those two rubber tappers want to smash it?"

I shook my head and stared at the wounded stone.

It was gray and narrow and seemed too tall for a normal gravestone. It climbed upwards in three sections, each curved like a tiger's claws.

I stared about us, searching for the best location to place my tripod. The keramat was on level ground. It was likely the highest part of the rubber estate. Such places were supposed to be holy like Mount Meru, the holy mountain of Hinduism. The religion of the Malays before they embraced Islam. This was the sort of place a shaman would be buried. The British colonials, respecting local beliefs, had not interfered with the jungle around the grave.

Yvonne squatted and, as if in contemplation, she slowly ran her index finger over her bottom lip, then she delicately touched the grave.

As I stood next to her I could see upon the worn stone that curious leaf-like shapes had been carved into it. Then I blinked and in the dappled light, hiding within the shadows, I swore I could see faces. Not only faces, but faces within faces, small and large, and each one staring at me. Were the faces pleading or were they full of wrath?

"Touch the stone," whispered Yvonne.

"I don't want to."

"Just touch it, Malik."

Gingerly, I placed a finger on it.

A numbness ran down my finger and up my arm. "It's cold," I gasped.

"Not cold, Malik. It's ... bloody freezing."

I yanked my finger away. Yvonne was right. The stone was freezing like a block of ice. I rubbed my arm to warm it up.

"I can't explain it," said Yvonne as she stood up. Her face was pale. "And what's that?"

I followed her finger. Upon the apex of the grave, just where the stone had been split, sat a small grotesque shape. It appeared to be two miniature cobras intertwined into a ball. It was as if they were suffocating something or keeping whatever it was tightly bound.

"Not sure," I said. "Didn't you see all this when you were last here? Didn't you touch the stone?"

"No, the police had cordoned off the area. No one could get close. The bodies were over there and there." She pointed to two spots on either side of the grave. "They were covered with plastic sheets ... Anyway, you should start taking your photos. It's getting late."

"What about that gravestone? It shouldn't be so cold."

Yvonne crushed her cigarette under her shoe and crossed her arms beneath her breasts. "Just take your photos quickly and we'll get out of here."

I nodded, put down my bag and set up my tripod. I didn't like the shrine. I couldn't understand its unnatural coldness—as if all the life, all the energy had been stolen from it. When combined with the old lady's story of the vampire, its eeriness, despite the coolness of the jungle, brought sweat to my brow. As I was swiveling the camera into place, I heard a crack.

I turned but saw nothing. Then a shadow darted behind the trees. Then it was gone. I glanced at Yvonne. She was staring in the same direction.

"It's getting late. Hurry up." Her voice trembled.

"What was that?"

"Nothing. Just take your photos and we'll go!"

I brought out the flash. I took five or six shots. The successive washes of light from the flash were all too brief.

"All done?" asked Yvonne.

I nodded and quickly packed my gear.

When I turned to face her again, she was gone.

Yvonne would have had to walk past me to head back down the trail to the car. That meant she could only have gone in the opposite direction—away from the village.

Why did she want to do that? My instincts told me to flee too. To run back to the car and drive away.

But what about Yvonne? I couldn't leave her behind. I swallowed hard.

Not knowing what to do, I hurried after her.

The trail led steeply downwards. I hurried past a clump of bushes, which pricked at my arm, its leaves striking my face, and then I was back out among the rubber trees. But this area was more neglected, and the terrain undulated like the spine of some gigantic creature. Clumps of bushes and tall grass threatened to swallow the track.

"Yvonne!" I shouted. "Where are you?"

But there was no reply. Only the faint shrill of insects. As if they were fading into some other world where they would be safe from humankind.

"Yvonne!" I called again. "You've gone the wrong way. Come back!"

Maybe she could no longer hear me. Or could she have stumbled and hurt herself? Perhaps she was unconscious.

I pulled out my mobile phone to call her. There was no reception. And why would there be out here in this forsaken place?

"Shit ..." I whispered. Where the hell was she?

I trotted down the path, still calling out. The track inclined steeply and, in my desperation, I sprinted down towards a clearing.

Then my body flipped over. My feet were flying. A daze of sky and the tops of trees flashed by as my mobile phone leapt from my hands. My back slammed hard into the undergrowth.

I gasped in pain. It was as if someone had kneed me hard in the back.

Moaning, I slowly turned onto my front.

And then I saw it ... the thing that had tripped me over.

At first I thought it was a bundle of clothes. But how could I trip over it? My shoes had struck something solid. But not solid as a rock or a branch. The terrible truth lay in its shape.

It was a body.

From the size of the torso, I knew it was boy. He wore blue shorts and a faded T-shirt. I crept forward and his face emerged to meet mine. His was pale and bloodless, eyes wide open, mouth gaping.

As I tried to get to my knees, I nudged a bulk on my left.

I turned ... and lost my balance.

"No!" I cried.

It was the body of a young woman. She was thin and wore a simple white tudung. Her eyes were closed and her skin was smooth. Her mouth was twisted as though trying to contain an unspeakable agony. Her sarong was muddy and one blue plastic slipper dangled off her dark toe.

I staggered away, grasping the branches for support. It felt as though my legs would collapse.

I turned as the branches and leaves grasped for my face and, somewhere buried deep in the undergrowth between jungle and rubber estate, my mobile phone began to ring.

"No," I gasped. "No, no, not this ..."

I couldn't deny the tragic reality that a boy and a woman, maybe his mother, could be found dead in a rubber estate. What I denied was the sight further down the trail in the clearing. I blinked, hoping this was a nightmare I would wake from. But my eyes did not lie. This was too horribly real.

Bodies were scattered beneath the trees, slumped or curled up or splayed wide as if awaiting a butcher's knife. Some were men, some women, many were children. There were more than a dozen bodies. None of them moved upon the dry earth. All dead in the clothes they wore: sarongs, blouses, jeans, headscarfs, T-shirts. A little girl who was propped against a tree wore a face splattered with latex. An elderly woman, perhaps the one Yvonne had spoken to, lay sprawled face down, a clump of her white hair dangling out from her selendang. Her batik sarong was pulled up to her knees so that I could see the long veins in her thin dark legs.

Holding onto the branches, I hauled my way along the trail. This undeniable trail of death. The bodies were scattered on both sides of me as I drew myself along. Still my mobile phone inexplicably rang. The Bossa Nova ringtone I had recently downloaded belonged to another world.

A cloud drifted over and the shadows turned darker and deeper. It was like dusk, yet I could still clearly see the corpses and the scars on the rubber trees.

I stumbled pass a middle-aged man who was incredibly still wearing his songkok, even though his head was draped back over a fallen log. His dead eyes stared agonizingly up at the trees. It was as if the killer had attacked from above. Despite the half light, I could see small wrinkles about his eyes and a birthmark upon his cheek. One hand clutched at his heart, one finger snared in the breast pocket of his polyester shirt.

"What happened here?" I whispered. "Who killed all these people?"

I whirled around and dark faces—boys, girls, women, men, the elderly—stared back at me from their crumpled clothes as though demanding answers.

"I don't know," I moaned. "I don't know who killed you all ..."

"Don't you?"

I froze.

The voice was hers. But it was not quite right. It was completely wrong.

Slowly, I turned around.

Yvonne stood beside a rubber tree, her stony face cast in shadows.

I realized my mobile phone, if it had sounded at all, had stopped ringing.

"Don't you know why these people are dead?" Her voice was icy.

"Because they ... they refused to leave the village," I said as my mind spun trying to figure out what was wrong with her. "After the shrine had gone bad."

Yvonne laughed. It was impossibly high-pitched. I had never heard her laugh that way before.

"Why ... what's so funny?"

"Because, Malik, the shrine—it was *always* bad."

"What?"

"The people who made offerings, who came to pray, were casting spells to hurt others. The shrine, it attracts bad people. And their enemies were hurt—illness, car accidents, cancer, unexplained deaths. For those who came to merely pray, to seek blessings, I just ignored them."

"You—what do you mean *you* ignored them."

"It may look like one but it is no gravestone. It is a *binding* stone. To imprison me deep within the earth ..."

"What in God's name are you talking about, Yvonne?"

"And I was so imprisoned for three hundred years until the binding stone was discovered. And from everywhere, the malicious ones came and knelt before me. Even though I was trapped in the earth, I still could cast spells for them ... cast bad spells for bad people who wanted to do bad things ..."

"Yvonne, please stop this ..."

"Over the years, more vengeful pilgrims came, each seeking greater evils. This made the binding power of the stone weaker. In recent months, hordes of them knelt before me. Until, eventually, when the two men came seeking revenge on a debt collector. Then I emerged right through the center of the stone. Cracking it!"

"You killed them?"

"Yes ... I was hungry. I killed these people too."

"Yvonne, you're bloody crazy, you need to ..."

"Every single one of them. They came with their holy books and prayer mats and religion. They wanted to cast me out. So I killed them. When that was done, I summoned the rest of the village. I sent out a sweet fragrance from the rubber estate. And when they came in their dream-like state, not able to resist my call, I slaughtered them. I bit their necks and slurped their blood!"

Then, very deliberately at first, her head began to turn as if casting an evil look behind her. But instead of stopping, the head continued to move—oh, a neck-breaking twist it made, but how could it?—until it faced backwards!

Still, Allah believe me, it rotated in this impossible way—slowly spinning all the way around—until her eyes were fixed on me again. But this time deep lines were cracked into her contorted face and she was deliriously grinning. As she did so, there was the delicate sound of ripping and the flesh around her throat bloomed red.

"No!" I gasped.

I stepped back, tripped over a branch and fell. Still I stared up at her. But this monstrosity was not Yvonne.

The head now began to jerk upwards as if trying to escape its confines. Up and up it violently pulled as it shook, its dark hair lashing to and fro. There was an awful ripping sound as the head suddenly lifted—pulling at, dragging out the pink flesh of the trachea—then out, out flopped the bright red lungs.

"What the hell ..." I gasped.

I had not even in my most horrific nightmares encountered such a creature.

Then this perversion trembled violently and, without warning, it spun upwards and with a deep ugly squelch—like a baby being born—out tumbled the bulging stomach followed by a long trail of gray intestines. This was no baby but a slimy gruesome serpent.

For a second, Yvonne's body stood quite motionless. Then her frog locket, as if it could no longer bear the disembowelment of its mistress, slipped down her blouse and landed beside her white track shoes. I felt its emerald eyes peering mournfully up at me. Then, like a butchered goat, the ripped-up body trembled before collapsing in a bloody heap.

Hovering above it, before my unbelieving eyes, like a cast of one in a theater of lunacy, the grotesque thing floated. The demon's head stared, leering almost proudly. Yvonne's nose stud looked like a nail that had been hammered into her contorted face. A face that seemed to hide faces within faces.

The serpent-like demon swayed in the thick hazy air. It seemed to be doing some sort of despicable dance where the silent music wafted from hell. Blood trickled down the coils of guts and tapped onto the earth. The pungent odor of rotting flesh filled my nostrils.

I didn't realize it, but I was crawling on my back, moaning incomprehensibly while trying to get away. Trying to retrieve my sanity.

It felt as though a hundred cold corpses were caressing me.

I pushed past the man with his songkok, the one with the birthmark on his cheek. Instead of fear, his face seemed to be filled with pity. I realized my cheeks were wet with tears.

The unspeakable thing slithered its way towards me. There was the soft sound of squelching. Blood still dripped off its tail, its rectum, as it approached. It smelt of shit and a thousand dead things.

"No!" I screamed. "No! No! No!"

Then, in this nightmare of nightmares, the red lips on that head parted. And I saw them: long fangs, white as milk, sharp as a cobra's, sprang out from the blackness of that mouth, glistening in the shadows.

The demon drifted downwards, so close now that I could touch its blood-splattered hair, run a fingernail inside the cracks in its face. As for its body—made of slimy lungs, stomach and raw intestines—it dragged over the ground and its very end, its tail, Allah forbid, curled around my left foot!

The head drew closer, as if it wanted to kiss me. Its long coarse hair draped itself around my neck. The fangs dripped saliva on my shirt. Its eyes were burning as though they held the flames of hell.

"Ah, Malik," it whispered in a cold, dry voice that no longer pretended to be Yvonne's. "You only had to try harder and we could have been lovers. But I will now feast."

Out of the corner of my eye, the man beside me still stared, one hand entangled in his breast pocket. But now I saw that his other hand, the one that dangled to the ground was holding a book—our holy book.

Just as the fangs plunged for my neck, I turned, grabbed the Koran and shoved it into the head.

The thing shrieked. It was an awful piercing cry that shook the leaves and shuddered the sky. The demon shot over me and fell into the undergrowth, writhing and screaming.

I got up. Not believing what I had done.

Then I ran.

Away from the scattered corpses. Away from the screeching demon.

I jumped over the body of the boy, the one who had tripped me over. I dashed up the slope, not even hesitating at the broken gravestone. No, not a gravestone but a binding stone. The one that worked for three hundred years until bad people came in their hordes with their evil desires. That undid the binding.

I ran past my camera bag with all its expensive equipment. The rubber estate could keep it. My mobile phone too. I just had to get out alive.

I sprinted down the slope.

The demon shrieked. I glanced backwards and tripped.

I cursed as I got up. Pain tore through my ankle.

I stared up the ghastly hill that could never symbolize Mount Meru. I half-expected the demon to be soaring down after me, its intestines dancing, blood speckling the dry earth.

I tried to ignore the pain and stumbled on. My footfalls were heavy in my ears. I went past the mounds and the rubber trees. Past the cups that dangled from the trunks to collect latex. Cups that overflowed because all the workers were dead.

My ankle throbbed painfully and my legs had slowed. I couldn't make them move faster. My breath came in heaves. Cold sweat covered my T-shirt.

"I'm coming for you!" it cackled.

The voice didn't echo from the other side of the hill—but from the dilapidated hut that stood beside me. The one used for storage or as a shelter during heavy rain. How could it get there so quickly? Could the perversion manifest itself anywhere it chose?

"No ..." I gasped. "It can't!"

I needed my own shelter now. From the fury of hell itself. From the possibility that I was going mad.

Again it cackled. This time on my right.

I stopped and turned, expecting the head to be floating at my throat, with fangs ready to pierce it. But I only saw rubber trees, lining up in obedient rows into the distance.

I wiped the sweat from my eyes and tried to recall a prayer. Any prayer ...

... there is only one god but Allah, there is only one ...

... but my memory had forsaken me! How could it? When I needed it most?

"I can't stop now ..." I moaned.

I stumbled down the track. The tree trunks and foliage became a shadowy blur. My breath was tight in my chest. Blood rushed through my head.

There was not far to go now. I was sure of it. I just had to make this turn.

My heart soared. I was right!

I could see the dirt road and the village up ahead.

Suddenly, sunlight broke through the trees. The cloud had passed. The track was lit up in sunshine.

Breathing raggedly, I pushed my legs hard, trying to ignore the pain, telling them to keep moving as I struggled up the track.

Towards safety. Towards the real world. Away from the nightmare. Away from hell itself.

I could see the car now. It was shining in the sun.

It wasn't far. I could make it!

I hobbled as fast as I could. Hoping, praying that nothing would grab me from behind. With each step I took, I felt my hopes rising.

Then I stumbled out of the rubber estate and was bathed in light. The air tasted wonderfully fresh. It was as though the rubber trees that had kept me prisoner had suddenly set me free. Insect shrills filled the air, as though calling out in celebration.

A bird chirped a beautiful melody.

My car gleamed beside the coconut tree, the fallen bicycle, waiting for me.

"Alhamdulillah!" I whispered.

I glanced behind me. There was no demon following. No head and intestines dancing up the track. There was nothing but rubber trees. It was even peaceful here.

Perhaps it was just a nightmare. Or just my mind gone temporarily mad. It didn't matter. I had survived this.

I fumbled for the remote. For a second I thought I had dropped it. Then I felt its familiar shape. I pressed the button and the side lights blinked.

I heard myself sigh.

I opened the door and jumped in.

"Hello, Malik," said Yvonne. "I've been waiting for you."

Her frog locket. It was missing.

Sunday:
Kyoto Kitchen

THE GUN SITS SNUGLY in your jacket pocket. If you see him, you'll shoot him point-blank. Right between the eyes.

You tell yourself this. Over and over. Never mind the so-called fact that he was hanged a year ago in Taiping prison. His body fell through the trapdoor, the sudden jerk breaking his neck or, better still, strangling him to death. You wish you'd seen his legs dancing salsa-like beneath him.

But you'd fled the sweltering traffic-locked city by then ...

You wonder if he pissed in his pants.

You zip off your jacket, sling it over the wooden chair and sit down, quite aware of the gun and the spare magazines nestled heavily within. The restaurant is ill-lit. There are seven small tables, all empty. A small ceramic cat bounces from side to side next to the cash machine. It is painted white, has red ears with one paw raised.

Its big cold eyes burn.

You flip the laminated menu over. *Wallaby Yakiniku.*

Thinly sliced wallaby pan-fried with seasonal vegetables in sauce made with sake, fresh ginger and garlic.

"What you like?" asks the waitress in a light-blue uniform with a brown stain on the collar. She has short messy hair which reminds you of seaweed. The mole on her forehead reminds you of a hole in the head. Her name tag says *Mei*. She should have another on her neck, you decide. The one that says *Made in China*.

"Chicken Katsu," you say. It is, after all, five dollars cheaper. "And Japanese tea."

She scribbles the order, wrinkles her nose and saunters away.

You haven't shaved nor had a shower for days. You slept last night in these same clothes on the sofa, the television blaring its way through old soaps, adverts, news breaks and game shows.

Or was that the night before?

Outside the window, across the one-way street, is a supermarket and an ATM. Beside it, is a second-hand clothes store with an overweight, middle-aged blonde woman arranging multicolored dresses on a metal rack outside. A man with spectacles, wearing a dark-blue beanie walks a black poodle. An assortment of people wander by beneath lumbering gray clouds.

Your reflection in the glass is ugly: crumpled jumper, dirty brown hair, sunken face, hooded eyes. You drop a couple of pills into your palm and dry swallow them. You tap the empty bottle on the table.

A car rolls by, an industrial beat and an acidic voice spewing from its open windows.

Rap is crap. That's what Jenny used to say, her blue eyes lighting up.

"Watch your mouth," you'd reply. "Just say it's *rubbish*, okay?"

But now you know the undeniable truth.

Everything is crap.

It's chilly and you regret taking your jacket off. The furniture is dark brown and there's a framed poster of Mount Fuji on a wood-paneled wall. It's faded and so are the two red lanterns hanging above your head. There's a stale smell of garlic and beer. This restaurant is exhausted like an old woman who refuses to get out of bed.

Mei appears with a pot and tea cup. A Japanese pop song crackles from hidden speakers. The woman's voice is desolate and off-key. You tug a paper napkin from a metal dispenser, then pluck a pair of chopsticks from a plastic container. Your elbow bumps against the gun's barrel.

Yes, it's there. You feel safe with it. It keeps you company beneath the mattress as you lie awake at night in the bedsit, your thoughts churning.

Becky. Jenny.

They're whispering in your head. You're whispering back: *If I see Gazali, I'll shoot him dead between the eyes.* That's what you tell them. Over and over. You really will, even if your bullet just flies at fleeting shadows.

You've seen him spying from office windows, then vanishing like tinted smoke. Glimpsed his mustache behind the chanting Hare Krishna woman passing out leaflets. Caught him mingling in his khaki uniform at a corner outside a department store, then disappearing just as the green man appears and pedestrians hurry across the ever-busy bitumen.

Once you'd even seen him across the aisle at JB Hi-Fi pretending to look at CDs. He had his beret and a smirk on his face. But when you looked up again, heart pounding, he was gone.

You've never believed in ghosts. But what you saw on YouTube changed your mind. Often, you'd find yourself hunched over a screen in the city library. You glanced at the row of craning necks, like sheep to the slaughter, worshiping the machine. They, like you, need to surf. Go anywhere, just so you don't have to think.

As usual, you googled: *"Jalan Duri" Murder.*

Jalan Duri ... Thorn Street.

Sure enough, up jumped the search results. The first two were the English-language newspaper articles which you'd read countless times. You knew them by heart. Then there was the blog about how the house was now vacant, unsaleable and unrentable. Everyone knew about what had happened and no one dared live there. You had read that one too. It was riddled with spelling mistakes. But then there it was.

Something new.

A YouTube video.

Entitled *Jalan Duri Mystery Lights*. You stared at it, biting your lips, feeling in need of a double shot of Jim Beam. You put on the headphones and clicked. At first there was only a black screen, the sound of shuffling and someone mumbling. Then the house, in a shaky night shot, slowly came into focus.

A modern Californian-style bungalow.

That's what the agent said when she rented it out to you. Her business card read: **Elaine Choo, Reapfield Properties, Kuala Lumpur.**

"Everything's new inside," chirped Elaine that afternoon beneath the searing sun beside parked cars and neighboring front gates. "It's just been painted and it's close to the shops and restaurants. There's a small swimming pool at the back. I'm sure your family will like it."

They did, especially your wife, Claire.

In the night-shot video, the two-story bungalow with its rendered walls, its tiled roof and arched windows, was surrounded by hazy spherical lights. There were five of them, pulsing and steadily circling above the swimming pool.

It could have easily been a hoax. Still, your heart was beating rapidly in your chest like a caged bird. You struggled to breathe as you clicked back to the search results.

Then you noticed the second video. It was called *Jalan Duri Ghosts*.

"Chicken Katsu," says Mei as she slips the meal in a red-lacquered Bento box before you. "Everything okay?"

"Fine, fine," you mumble.

The sweet savory smell turns your stomach. The pale egg draped over the crumbed dead meat is like brain tissue oozing out. You sip some tea to calm yourself.

You close your eyes and the second YouTube video plays in your head. It's always repeating, ever since the day you saw it.

The digital read-out says 2:21a.m.

The image, saturated in yellow, is shaky. It pans to the left, over the top of the familiar iron gate, before darting to the right. Then it halts at a dormer window upstairs. The window to your family room. A light inside glows. Staring out are the three unmistakable figures.

Three dark, lonely figures.

Each shorter than the next, reminding you of Babushka dolls. Each fitting neatly into the other.

Becky. Jenny.

The tallest is the Filipino maid, *Maria.*

The camera zooms out. The grainy image slides down, trembles on the road, then pans up along the iron grilles, before focusing on the large padlock and chain. Then it jerks upwards.

Hands tighten against your throat. Your heart pounds like a hammer in your chest. He is there. Always there. His cheeks pushing sickeningly against the grilles, twisting his head one way then the other as though he was trying to escape through it, or to decapitate himself.

There's no doubt who he is. His mustache. His cropped greased hair.

Gazali.

Hello, Tuan.

"You bastard!"

That was what you screamed in that library the first time you saw it.

Heads spun at you.

Then you smashed a fist into the keyboard. That was when the stumpy librarian escorted you out of your seat, past the hall with its flapping community notices and out the automatic sliding door into the cold air.

"I'm sorry, sir," she said in her curly brown hair and loose green sweater beneath that purple sky. "We can't have you in here."

"That's okay," you stammered. "I'm sorry about the keyboard."

Stumbling away beneath rustling trees, you then spied, lit by a dim pool of light from a street lamp, a figure wearing a beret beside a butcher's, watching you. You had seen him often enough in your nightmares, glimpsed him in shops and crowded streets, but here he was, standing so erect, shoulders back, as though proud to be your acquaintance.

Which is why you now carry a gun and two spare magazines.

The Chicken Katsu is getting cold. It sits like a severed hand on sticky rice. The thick brown sauce is coagulated blood. There's a miserable slice of tomato interlaced with cucumber to resemble a flower. But this flower can only be made of cancer cells.

You never enjoyed Japanese food, Claire and you, not until you worked in KL. Life was pretty good. Your girls were happy. Becky, eight. Jenny, twelve. They were at the international school and they had made new friends.

But after what happened, Claire withdrew into the unreachable depths of herself. And why wouldn't she? You had returned to the city where you were born. The idea was for a fresh start.

But silence built upon silence, until it was screaming at you both. You no longer had sex. No longer ate together. You only stared at the TV and chased beer with Jim Beam, too drunk to walk out the door, let alone go to work. Then one day you found her handwritten note. It said:

I have to go. Life together is too hard. Sorry.

It is all too easy to pick that moment when life collapsed all around you. It was at a Sunday lunchtime function at one of KL's five-star hotels when Claire's mobile rang.

It was the police.

The inspector wouldn't say what it was about but he insisted you both had to go to the station immediately. So you quickly drove your Volvo into the congested city center and parked illegally at the front gate. As both your footsteps rang upon the external metal stairs to the inspector's office, you felt the sense of dread grow.

The office was hot and cramped. A printer whirred. There were several ancient-looking computers, and an air conditioner coughed and rattled. There were two men there. One was busy writing at his desk.

The other man got up, buttoning his dark-blue jacket. He had a chubby face and the pocks on his cheeks seemed to crawl like large ants.

"We've received a phone call," he said, eyeing you up and down. "Your neighbor, I think he's from Iran, he phoned and said that your security guard has stolen your car."

"That must be Claire's car!"

Claire drove a small Honda which she used to go to the neighborhood shops or to visit friends.

"Why would he take my car?" Claire gasped. She clutched her red handbag protectively against her stomach. "Maybe he didn't steal it. Maybe it was some kind of emergency." Then she cried out, "The children!"

"This security guard," said the inspector, scratching his neck. "He left your gate, also your front door, wide open."

"What? What the heck are we doing here then!"

"Don't worry," said the inspector. "Our men are already there."

You wound your way through the traffic with dreadful thoughts churning. Claire called the school and everyone she knew but no one could tell where the girls were.

When you got home, the electric gates stood wide open. Three police cars were scrummed at the front gate and uniformed men loitered in the driveway. One was taking photos. A couple yakked on mobiles. One was smoking and flicking ash into the swimming pool.

They couldn't find Becky or Jenny. Maria was missing.

They wouldn't even let you into the house.

The bungalow with its red tiled roof and arched windows stared with mistrusting eyes. You stood in the garden, a tightness gripping your chest. You felt like collapsing and held Claire's shoulder for support.

Then you staggered back into the blistering street, pass the police vehicles, and leant upon the car's hood, breathing hard, the sun pounding your head, sweat trickling down your back.

Your mobile began to ring as news of their disappearance spread through the city. Everyone was trying to be helpful, everyone offered their ...

Hello, Tuan.

You look up and jerk back. There is Gazali, with his thick mustache, sitting in the restaurant in front of you. He's in his beret and khaki uniform. There are dark stains on one sleeve.

His eyes dart to your empty pill bottle. He scrutinizes you for a second before glancing at your bento box as if he's working out its contents.

Then he grins at you.

Morning, Tuan.

It's after twelve but who cares whether it's morning or afternoon in the realm of the dead? *Perhaps*, you think, *he's still on KL time*. That was his habitual greeting each morning before you slid into your car, before your driver eased you out into the leafy bungalow-filled streets. Gazali would salute, press a button and the electric gates would swing shut.

You'd been there nine months, when it happened.

Eating Japanese, Tuan?

His voice is soft and ingratiating and seems to hum its way through his thin chest like a lawnmower. There's a waft of cigarettes and body odor.

You slowly reach for the gun in your jacket, your eyes never leaving his. Sweat trickles behind your ear.

You don't care if he's real or not. He's been following you, haunting you ever since you saw that YouTube video, but you've never seen him this close. Yes, you now know, ghosts exist and you're going to shoot this one ...

I have something to tell you, Tuan. Something important.

You withdraw your arm. You will wait and see what he has to say.

"What?" you whisper. "What's so important?"

It's this, Tuan. Either you're insane, I'm insane or we both are.

You realize he's only in your head. Gazali spoke some English, halting and broken most of the time, but here he is speaking fluently, although still with his Malay accent. Yet, right now, the difference between what is real and what is not doesn't seem so far apart.

"What do you mean, I'm insane? You're the mad bastard ..."

No, no, Tuan. Sure, I did what I did ...

"You did what you did? You killed my maid, then you ..."

It was love, Tuan. But Maria rejected me. So I sat there in the guardhouse, knocking my head against the wall, pinching my stomach until it hurt so much. All just to forget her.

"I don't care about your sob story, you murderer!"

All you have to do is find me and hold me ... and kiss my tear-filled eyes. That's what I said to her, Tuan, but she wouldn't listen. Then, that afternoon, when she was hanging out the clothes, I came from behind and put my hands around her throat.

Oh, she was so soft, so small. And her skin, so warm. I pushed my face into her hair. It smelt so sweet, so pure. I squeezed my fingers tightly, with all my love. Maria's necklace, her crucifix became entangled in my fingers as if trying to protect her. But, by Allah, I still squeezed and squeezed, until we were both kneeling on the grass. We had become the truest of lovers.

"You bastard ... you mad bastard!"

Your hands are trembling. But he's close and you know your shot won't miss. His eyes grow wide, they're chasms into madness. You'll let him talk for a moment as you fight to clear your mind.

In the end, we were both lying on the grass beneath the hanging laundry. I held onto her beneath its shade, whispering in her small ears. Oh, our bodies fitted so perfectly together. The sun was hot and high above us. Then came a gust of wind and the wet clothes were flapping, dancing for us. It was beautiful, believe me, Tuan. Then I looked up and saw your girls staring at me from the window upstairs ...

"You ... you were supposed to protect them ..."

They fought hard, Tuan. Your elder girl, she cut my arm with a knife.

You jerk at the sound of sudden footsteps. It's Mei, balancing a plastic bowl on a tray. She slides the bowl on the table.

"Miso soup," she says. She frowns at you but there's a glint of fear in her eyes. "It comes with the Chicken Katsu."

You say nothing and she hurries away.

You slap the bowl. It crashes.

The puddle of soup, bits of dark green nori and tofu scatter on the wooden floor.

I'm very thirsty, Tuan. What a waste. The miso looked good. I've never had Japanese. Not once in my life ...

Yes, the first time I saw Maria was when I went to ask for a glass of water. She was mopping the floor in a pale yellow dress. I could see the look on her face. It was so intense that it seemed that the ceiling fan's blades were slicing up her very thoughts. I felt a brilliant light pouring into my heart.

"I don't want to know about it. You said you had something important to tell me."

Ah, Tuan. You see, after I killed them, I knew I had to get away. But I had to get rid of the bodies. So I prised open the manhole and threw their bodies into the septic tank. It smelt awful in there. Maria went in first, then your daughters ... the elder one first.

You thrust the barrel against his forehead. Your finger tightening against the trigger.

"I don't care if you're real or not," you snarl. "But I'm going to shoot you!"

Wait, Tuan. Let you tell you what I came here to tell you.

"What is it, you bastard?"

Your daughters. They're, they're with you. They follow wherever I go ...

"Bullshit!"

How can ghosts haunt other ghosts, Tuan? I just want peace now. I want ...

His eyeballs slide horribly towards the window and he raises his arm, his index finger trembling.

Standing limply on the pavement, their foreheads almost touching the glass, are two thin pale-faced girls.

One is taller than the other. They both have shoulder-length brown hair. You recognize them straight away.

Becky. Jenny.

They're dressed in the same clothes you last saw them that morning. Becky is wearing a white cotton dress. Jenny, who had caught the soccer craze since the World Cup, is wearing the outfit for the Brazilian team.

They stare at you, their eyes expressionless.

"Becky, Jenny," you whisper. "You can't be real ..."

Your girls are covered in muck. Their locks of brown hair dangle wetly upon their foreheads. Dark splotches run down their cheeks like leeches and soil their drenched clothes.

With a death-like thud, Becky slaps her palm on the glass. It leaves a black splotch. Misshapen it is, like a map of some demonic island. Her hand is filthy. Her nails dirty. Her mouth slowly opens and closes, like a limp suffocating fish, as if she is trying to tell you something. Her eyes are pleading ...

Becky, your daughter who is eight—who *was* eight, she would be ten now—has small tears welling in her eyes. Tears which you want to kiss away. Jenny, your older girl, your firstborn—her face a hundred times sadder than you've ever seen—reaches one limp hand towards you, her fingers curling, slowly uncurling ...

Oh, dear God!

Sobbing, you stagger from your seat and stumble past the empty tables, almost bumping into Mei who is holding a rag at her chest. The two red lanterns hanging above the window are like blood-stained heads in nooses.

And the ceramic cat. It no longer moves.

You fling open the restaurant door and lurch outside.

Cold air hits your face.

A red scooter whooshes past.

Irrasshaimase! Mei calls out. *Welcome.*

Or you think that's what she calls out. Why would she say that anyway?

Is it a welcome to madness?

Your two daughters turn, heads swiveling. Their limp bodies shuddering towards you. Their eyes are dead. Dark water pools about their bare feet.

They have whispered to you through your days. You see their weeping faces in the night, but now, they're here ...

Their hands reaching for you.

"Becky! Jenny!"

"Yes, daddy," they call back in a dead monotone.

You don't care if they're dead or alive.

"I'm here, my darlings. I love you!"

They stop right in front of you. Awful raw sewerage wafts from their limp bodies.

Becky touches you on the chest. You gasp and step back. "Daddy ..."

Her touch is horribly cold.

A woman screams. It's the blonde woman across the road, frozen next to the clothes rack.

You look down and realize the gun is swaying in your hands.

Heavy, solid, loaded.

You turn to your two girls. But they're gone.

There's just the empty pavement. Not even the dark puddles remain.

Where are they?

You search through the restaurant's window. There's your table, the bento box, the pot of tea and the empty pill bottle. But your girls aren't there.

There's Mei, staring at you, her body quite still. Her lips are twisted and the rag is pulled tightly in both hands like a rope. She's a mannequin in a psychotic establishment. The lantern-like heads in their nooses sway from side to side. They are chuckling at you.

Then you notice the wooden signboard above the front door.

Kyoto Kitchen.

It's painted in thick black brush strokes.

You twirl around. A gawking crowd has formed across the street. Their fingers point. Their eyes fearful.

"Becky! Jenny!" you holler. "Where are you?"

Then you see him darting across the road.

Gazali!

Fleeing like the murderer, like the coward he truly is.

You had hired him to protect your family; instead he murdered them. Killed your daughters. Your darling daughters. Destroyed your reason for living.

"Gazali!" you bellow.

He stops before he gets to the opposite pavement.

Gazali turns. His beret is clutched tightly in his hands as if he is trying to rip it apart. His cropped greased hair glimmers in a shaft of sunlight. His drooping mustache bounces almost imperceptibly.

But you see everything.

The two elderly woman beside him. The blonde woman with one hand supporting herself on the clothes rack. A man with an army jacket. A teenage boy carrying a Target plastic bag. An Asian woman with a pram.

They're all glaring at you as if you're the criminal. Even the baby with a pink bib and pacifier has small burning eyes. They're staring like idiots. Mouths stupidly open.

Gazali calls out to you. His voice echoing above a four-wheel drive trundling past.

All you have to do is find me and hold me ... and kiss my tear-filled eyes. That's what I said to Maria, Tuan. If only she came to me ...

"Where are they, Gazali?! Where have you taken my girls?"

Gone, Tuan. Gone for good. I'm free now!

"This is bullshit!" you scream.

You raise the gun.

A van screeches. Someone screams. There's the sound of a plane overhead.

A car honks twice. Grinding music blares from it.

"Rap is crap," you whisper.

No, Tuan!

You squeeze the trigger. You shoot Gazali. Right at his chest.

But he's no longer there. The blonde woman clutches her stomach and collapses into the clothes rack.

"Where the hell is he?" you yell. "The bloody murderer!"

The crowd screams. Some flee into the supermarket. Most get in each other's way. Gazali, the coward, is hiding among them. You know he is.

You shoot again. And again. And again.

The pram overturns. There's the sound of breaking glass. Blood splatters the wall like graffiti.

Bodies collapse.

You're running amok. You know you are.

But the feeling is delirious.

And, dear God, for once you're laughing!

Yes, really, truly laughing.

You stumble across the street and, standing among the bloodied bodies, you look for him.

He isn't there!

Perhaps he's run into the supermarket. You grin and reload your gun.

The automatic doors slide open and the screaming truly begins.

Monday:
The App

SAM'S NEW SAMSUNG GALAXY ST changed his life. He'd had many other smartphones before, replacing them every year, but this one was different. It was brilliant for it moved between apps seamlessly, managing messages and contacts incredibly intuitively, doing stuff super quick too and with a seductive elegance.

It looked snazzy cradled in his hand, like a pretty girl draped upon his arm. This was good for he hadn't dated a girl in years. He thought his head too scrawny for his body, nor did he like his bulging nose. So attracting the opposite sex was tough.

He'd been exploring the Samsung's myriad features for several days when one evening, after watching several steamy YouTube videos, he noticed an app that wasn't there before. He certainly didn't remember downloading the thing.

It had an odd name: *You Lite*.

What was it doing here? He tried deleting it but the thing just seemed to hang on to its ephemeral existence. As it was getting late, he went to bed without thinking anymore about it.

The next day was Monday and he took the 7:42am train to work. As usual the carriage was filled with harried commuters. Most were engrossed in their smartphones, either texting, playing games, Facebooking, reading ebooks or listening to MP3s. A few just stared blankly into the tight spaces between each person.

Sam was lucky to get a seat. With time on his hands, he decided to check out the obdurate app. He tapped it. There was a pause, then up came the welcome screen and, to his surprise, he was looking at a grinning photo of himself. That was really curious. Could the app have taken a photo of him without him knowing? Yet he didn't recognize the background and he was wearing a white T-shirt that read *You Lite*. Very strange. Perhaps it just did some clever photo editing there.

Beneath his photo, a caption read: *Your Ultimate App.*

Yeah, he'd heard such claims before. He didn't even know what this one was supposed to do. Well, at least it was free. For the moment anyway. It'd probably, like many free apps, try for his credit card details after the end of the trial period.

Sam tapped the "Go" icon. Immediately, on a luminescent red background, leapt the words in brilliant white: *How are you today, Sam?*

Fine, he typed back.

How did the app know his name? Maybe it went into his Settings and found it there.

That's good, what are you doing today? came the reply.

Sam wondered if this app was like that old ELIZA computer program which processed natural language. Users were often tricked into thinking they were interacting with another person. This app was likely an updated and highly sophisticated version of it.

Off to work, he typed, wondering how it would respond.

App: *That's good, but rather boring, don't you think?*

An unexpected reply. Perhaps it used some sort of random phrase generator.

Yeah, but I've got a pretty assistant, he entered with a grin.

App: *What's her name?*
Sam: *Louise.*
Is she single?
Boyfriend.
Bad news, Sam. Have you heard of BMW?
No.
Best Man Wins. Do you like her a lot or just a bit?
A lot.
When you get to work, take a photo of her.

You Lite was certainly the oddest app he'd ever come across. Sam forgot all about it until after lunch. He had just been speaking to a client about some bonds that had just become available on the secondary market when Louise bent over at her desk across from him and begun to adjust the strap on her shoes. She had short brown hair and silky legs that glowed into his eyes.

He whipped out his Samsung Galaxy ST and took a shot. It made a loud click.

"Did you just take a photo of me?" said Louise, looking up at him with her gray eyes, her head at an inquisitive but rather attractive angle.

"Oh no," quipped Sam, thinking fast. "Of course not. I wouldn't want to shatter the lens on my new mobile. I was just testing out a new app."

"Oh, I see," she said with a smile. "I thought the company was looking for a new model. You know for our adverts."

Sam liked her good humor. He liked her face too. Her smooth skin. Those long eyelashes. She had a slight frame and smallish breasts. He'd often do nothing but think of her. She was in her early twenties and he was twenty-seven. They'd make a nice couple.

Except that she had a boyfriend. His name was John and he was in construction. He'd met him a couple of times. He was tall, full of himself and talked endlessly about cars and boats.

Just then Brian, his immediate boss and senior vice president, strolled past yakking on his mobile. He had slick black hair, round metal glasses, red braces and an annoying bow tie. He gave them a quick but disapproving glance.

"Oh yeah," Sam said in a loud voice. "I've got this report for you to look at."

He passed Louise a file and turned back to his computer.

While on the platform waiting for his train back home, Sam felt his mobile twitch in his trouser pocket.

It was You Lite.

She's pretty, was the message.

Yeah, he typed back.

App: *I mean it. She's a 10.*

Sam: *I know.*

You should ask her on a date. Boyfriend. BMW.

I'm not that good.

They'll break up tonight.

You're kidding.

Ask her out tomorrow, Sammy.

He slipped the mobile into his pocket. He didn't like being called Sammy. He had to admit that this app was brilliant. It was as if he was texting a real person. He knew that computers were incredibly powerful and could store huge amounts of information. Several years back, a computer called Watson had even beat the reigning champions in a popular quiz show. You Lite was probably accessing a similarly powerful server somewhere but its ability to pretend to converse with him without a single mistake was amazing.

The train was delayed and Sam got home late. He sluggishly climbed up the two flights of concrete stairs to his apartment, microwaved a Chicken Oriental, cracked open a beer and ate mindlessly in front of the television. He took off his suit, showered and went to bed.

✕

"Will you have dinner with me tonight?"

Louise looked up at him from her desk, her eyes registering surprise.

Sam's throat went dry.

Why did I do that? he thought. *She's going to say no!*

But that was unlikely. She would use some typical excuse: a netball game, movies with friends, maybe dinner with her parents. *Some other time perhaps, Sam*, she'll say. So no hurt feelings. It kept office relationships cordial.

He decided that it was a stupid thing to do to listen to the app. Why should she want to go out with him when she had John? John with his cars and boats. But he had seen her earlier, blowing her nose into a tissue. He knew she'd been crying. So the foolish notion came as he ate his sushi roll: *if not now, then when?*

He could see her thinking. Her long eyelashes trembling beneath the fluorescent lights.

Then she said it and he could hardly believe it.

"Sure," she said. "Thanks for asking."

"Great, Louise. That's wonderful."

"I don't know if I'll be good company though. John and I broke up last night. But it'll be nice to go out."

"I'm sorry to hear that. I didn't know. What sort of food do you like?"

"How about Korean? You know, that one round the corner?"

At dinner, Louise said that she was Facebooking on the bus back home, when up popped a photo of John with another girl. They were in each other's arms, naked on a red leather sofa. The girl was holding a whip. All her friends had seen it. John said it was a fake photograph but she refused to believe him. Sam was delighted with this news. He sympathized with her and tried being as caring as he could. They agreed to dinner again in a couple of days. They'd go to the Italian around the corner.

Sam grinned all the way on his train ride home. Not even his fellow passengers, its shaking carriage or the irritating hissing of its doors opening and closing bothered him. He held onto that warm glow in his head. So this was what happiness felt like. He slipped into bed, blissful thoughts slipping in and out of his brain.

During the night, his Samsung beeped.

What the hell!

He knew he had turned the damn thing off. It had jerked him out of deep sleep.

It carried on beeping, each one getting louder, until he grabbed it, almost knocking it to the carpet.

He expected to see the alarm clock app which he must have mistakenly set but, no, it was You Lite.

It had a message, flashing on the shiny red background: *You forgot to say thank you.*

He typed in, *thks*. Then collapsed into bed. The next day, he forgot all about it.

At the Italian restaurant, they ordered a bottle of white, mains and dessert. They chatted, joked and laughed. Sam was surprised at how well they got on. Later, they strolled arm-in-arm through the now quieter streets, illuminated dimly by decorative street lights. Then passed a cathedral lit dazzlingly against the night sky. Autumn leaves covered the pavement and they kicked them around playfully as they walked, the fallen foliage rustling and nestling against their shoes.

While waiting with Louise at her bus stop, the two kissed. Sam didn't know how it happened. It just did, without thinking.

The best things happen this way, he thought.

And, by far, this was the best thing that ever happened to him. The two embraced as the humming traffic echoed from some other place, as the lights from the surrounding buildings winked, as the brownish-red leaves trembled in their bare branches as if not daring to fall.

Sam and Louise were lost to the city and the world.

For the next few days, the two of them saw each other every evening after work. It would usually end up with her spending the night at his flat or him staying over at hers. They didn't tell anyone at the office that they were seeing each other except that Sam thought that his boss, Brian, had grown suspicious.

Intimacy is hard to hide.

During dinner at Subway several nights later, while Louise was on Facebook, he felt his mobile twitch in his pocket. He pulled it out. It was You Lite. He'd forgotten about the app for the past few days.

App: *Brian does suspect.*
Sam: *Suspect what?*
You and Louise.

Shit.

A career-buster.

"Everything okay, Sam?"

Louise was staring at him.

"Oh, it's fine," he said.

"You just looked so worried."

"Oh no, it's nothing. It's just this app doing strange things."

"I've got one like that. It's a silly game that keeps freezing every time I get near the high score."

Sam forced a laugh. He was worried about his job. Without it, he couldn't even afford the rent on his cheap flat.

They finished their drinks and spent the night at Sam's.

The next day, they took the train to work. Louise would usually slip into the office first and he would follow five to ten minutes later. By now, the two of them had started discussing moving in together.

After his nine o'clock meeting that morning, Sam checked his emails. And there it was, as promised: one from You Lite.

There was no message but several attachments.

It revealed that several risky bonds from a Chilean company which Brian had sold to clients had gone bust. Instead of giving them the bad news and losing their business, he had been paying them coupons using the bank's money.

Then his mobile beeped. It was You Lite.

I know. Watch for my email. Go to the President.

Why?

Recommend that the bank take over these bonds.

Huh?

Read my 2nd email.

He had missed that one as it was buried among the torrent of spam. This email had an attachment analyzing the company. It predicted that it would, within days, be taken over by a global mining corporation and that new shares would be issued to current bondholders. The share values would rocket because new technologies made these mines highly profitable.

Sam took the analysis, which he presented as his own, to the President. At a late night meeting, the company's senior management agreed with Sam, bought over the bonds, and the bank made millions.

"This is bullshit!" snarled Brian, his eyes blazing behind his round glasses. "I know you did none of that research. You're not qualified or bloody clever enough to do it."

Brian's face twitched with anger. He had just found out that he'd been fired only to be replaced by Sam.

"You're finished, Brian," said Sam. "I hope you've packed up. I'm moving into your office tomorrow."

"I don't know who the hell's been helping you. I'm going to find out where those reports came from. I have contacts with analysts. I'm going to expose your relationship with Louise too. You're not going to get away with this!"

"Time to go, Brian. Looks like security's here to kick you out. And I've always hated that stupid bow tie and braces of yours."

Brian stormed back into his office before the grim-faced security guard could get to him. The guard followed him in to watch him pack his personal things. Minutes later, he escorted Brian out of the building.

Just then You Lite beeped.

Don't worry about him.

Brian sped off in his white Porsche, his mind whirling. He didn't know where he was going. He barely saw the other cars, the pedestrians and buildings. They were but an aching blur in his head. He decided that he was going to get even no matter what it took. The angrier he got, the faster he drove.

Just as he got onto the highway, Brian realized how stupid it was to be so incensed. Whatever had happened, had happened. He might not be able to get another job in finance but there was other work he could do. He could even start his own business. He certainly wasn't short of funds.

But he'd get even with Sam first. The bastard must have got help from outside. He had to deal with that. Finding out where the analysis came from was Brian's priority. No one was allowed to cross him and get away with it.

He felt his breath quicken at the thought of Sam. He pushed hard on the accelerator.

Just as he was navigating the turn off, his iPhone burst out screeching.

It was so loud, it sounded like a jet engine in the confines of his car. Instinctively, Brian brought both hands to his ears.

The Porsche spun out of control.

"Nooooooo!" he screamed.

But the sound was so loud, he couldn't even hear himself.

The car smashed through the barrier and ploughed into the rocks below. Brian was dead well before the car exploded.

Over the next two weeks, Sam spent an increasing amount of his time hunched over his smartphone. He spent hours every day with You Lite. Louise complained but being a self-confessed Facebook addict, she resigned herself to updating her status even more often.

He had installed an updated version of the app. It included a speech recognition mode so he no longer had to type his messages to You Lite. He just had to say them and the app would write back its reply. It made things a lot more convenient.

"I bought the apartment," he said.

App: *Glad you took my advice.*

"You sure it's a good investment?"

Good location. Great design.

"Just collected my new BMW."

Best Man Wins, Sammy.

Sam chuckled.

He didn't mind being called 'Sammy' now.

He no longer wondered about his app, gift horses and all that. It had done wonders. Nor did he dare to think about how it managed to do these incredible things. He was certain now that it wasn't just software in a smartphone. And if it was linked to anything, it wouldn't be to a powerful server sitting in a building somewhere, but it had to be connected to something.

Or someone.

That thought sent dark shadows spiraling in his mind. So he pushed it aside. But it left a coldness in his gut.

He had to focus on the positive. You Lite had given him Brian's job. Although it was a pity that Brian, who must have been so upset at being fired, had killed himself. The app also recommended share purchases and Sam, together with his best clients, had made several killings. His app was a dream come true. So there was no need to ask how or why, was there?

You Lite was his best friend. It gave him all kinds of advice: which team would win the game, which clients would give him trouble, which horse to bet on and even which tie to wear to a meeting. He had fired a clerk because the app said that she was not up to the job.

Sam and Louise now dined at the best restaurants. They had designer furniture, accessories and clothes. They were now invited to the best parties and openings. They'd been on a luxury seven-day cruise. They lived in a brand-new apartment that overlooked the city's skyline.

All was perfect in Sam's world ... except for the dreams.

Sam had the same dream every night.

It began about a month after they moved into their new apartment. In it, his Samsung would beep louder and louder. He would fumble for it and the message from You Lite was always the same.

Now you are mine!

He would jerk up in bed, breathing hard, sweat on his forehead.

Louise would be sleeping soundly beside him so he knew his mobile hadn't actually gone off. He always checked, just in case, and it would only be the same black lifeless screen staring back into his eyes.

The Bose clock radio would usually say it was one or two in the morning. The city lights would shine dimly through the blinds into their bedroom. The Versace lampshades, the Persian rug, the ten-thousand-dollar watercolor Louise fell in love with, seemed to mock him in the half-light.

Tonight though, his throat burnt, so he quietly crept to the kitchen. His head throbbed, his stomach was coldly knotted, his limbs quivered and he needed three glasses of water to slake his scorching throat.

How could he feel so terrible when life was so good?

He stood alone trembling before the sparkling white counter top, among its shiny Miele appliances Louise was so proud of, and vomited.

Sam spent the rest of the night hunched over a toilet bowl.

"What's wrong, baby?"

It was Louise wearing a big frown and a new white nightie. Her hair was disheveled.

"Nothing, darling," he moaned.

She touched his shoulder. "You must have a bad tummy bug. You haven't been well this past week have you?"

"I'm okay," he said. "Just leave me alone, okay? I'll be fine."

"Sure, but tell me if you need anything."

"Okay," he grunted before vomiting again.

Sam staggered from the toilet bowl, washed his face and stared at his haggard face in the mirror. He hardly recognized himself. He was pale, thin and his eyes were pink. He leaned his forehead tiredly on the glass. He felt so ill, he almost wept.

When it was bright outside, Louise made him some coffee and toast, which he didn't touch, and went to work without him. He promised he would see a doctor. She texted him several times that morning to see how he was. He replied that he was fine even though his vision now began to swim.

The doctor didn't think that much was wrong with him. Perhaps a touch of the flu and exhaustion. You Lite thought that too, so it was probably a correct assessment. He got back to the apartment just after twelve, made a lemon and honey drink, took the prescribed pills, switched his mobile to silent and went to bed.

He dozed off.

A loud beeping shook him out of bed. It was You Lite.

He fumbled for it to turn it off.

The luminescent red on its screen glared into his eyes.

Rise and shine, Sammy.

"Why in God's name did you wake me up?"

I can think of all kinds of reasons.

"You're a bloody ..."

Here's one ... now you are mine!

The text was there: white and quite unmistakable.

Now you are mine!

"What the hell!" he cried.

This was no dream. This was real. *Why was You Lite doing this?*

Then the realization struck him hard.

His app, his so-called best friend, was not what he thought it was. Yes, it brought him a life he could only dream of: riches, a great job, a beautiful girlfriend, a fantastic apartment and that new-model BMW.

But You Lite was doing something else. It was making him sick. So terribly ill that he felt that his soul had been crushed. Or was it his vanquished soul that had caused this illness?

He didn't know. He didn't care.

Right now, all he knew was that the app had to go. It would never come back into his life no matter what promises it offered.

He stumbled to the window.

He slid it open.

The sound of traffic and a cool breeze rushed at him. He shoved the mobile out of the window.

It would be a long drop. Down twenty-eight floors to the pavement below. The Samsung could shatter to a thousand pieces and You Lite with it. It could go to its demented hell of ones and zeroes. It was a double- crossing fiend. The word 'frenemy' came to him and he wanted to laugh.

"Goodbye, you bastard!" he cried.

And then he did laugh.

At last, at last, he would get rid of it. He would be free.

He would get healthy again and, together with Louise, they'd have a wonderful life. He would never need the advantage of this app. He'd do everything by his own wit.

"Goodbye forever, you bugger!"

But his fingers, they wouldn't work.

They couldn't release the mobile.

"Let it go!" he gasped. "Let the damn thing fall!"

But still his stubborn fingers held onto the infernal thing.

Then, very slowly …

… *his hand turned!*

The red screen like a raging demon was facing him.

The thing was so bright it hurt his eyes. He couldn't turn his head away for his neck muscles wouldn't respond. The screen's intensity grew so bright that it pierced right into his brain.

He staggered back. His arm extended before him.

For a brief second, he saw himself wearing a white T-shirt with the words *You Lite* printed on it. He was winking and giving himself the thumb's up.

Then the red screen exploded in his head.

Now you are mine!

Sam stepped back, screaming.

He tried to get away from it, this evil thing in his mobile. But he couldn't because he was holding it. He crashed into a lampshade, knocked over the painting and tripped onto the rug.

"Let me go!" he yelled. "Please!"

Now you are mine!

The words filled his brain, over and over.

Now you are mine!

The deep voice, its endless echo brought a void into his head. He felt his soul being sucked into it.

"Now you are mine!"

The damnable phrase, repeated over and over, pulled him further away. Into a cold, shiny place where he felt only numbness.

Just as blackness swamped him, Sam realized that the words were leaping from his own tongue.

Then he blanked out.

When Sam woke up, he didn't know where he was.

He tried turning his body, but couldn't. His hands wouldn't move, nor would his arms or feet. No part of his body would respond.

He felt nothing either. He was neither hot nor cold. There were no physical sensations. Not even the movement of air in his lungs.

Although he couldn't turn his head, he could make out the familiar shapes of the stainless steel oven, the tall fridge, the curvaceous designer taps, even the polished blue kettle. He realized that he was lying on the kitchen bench and the lights from the sleek pendant lamp above, the one they had recently installed, only confirmed it.

Again, he tried getting up but still his body was frozen to the spot.

Instead of panicking, he tried to think clearly. Why couldn't he move? Perhaps it was some form of sleep paralysis. But what was he doing on the kitchen bench anyway? Did he sleepwalk here?

Then he heard footsteps. Followed by whistling.

They grew louder.

A shadow crossed his vision.

Whoever it was then stepped back, opened the fridge and pulled out a carton of milk.

Sam blinked.

He gasped, but no sound came. He couldn't believe it.

He was looking at himself!

He was dressed in jeans and a red polo shirt with his hair neatly combed.

But no, this couldn't be him. This had to be some impostor.

Then the figure turned and glanced at Sam.

"Ah, it's you," said the impostor. "You're up. You've been asleep all day. Well, you've been ill, haven't you, my friend?"

"What the hell!" cried Sam.

But nothing came out of his mouth.

"Ah," said the impostor, sticking his face forward. "You're quite right to be upset."

"Who are you?" Sam said, but again no words came out.

The impostor laughed. "Don't you recognize your own best friend, Sammy?"

No, he couldn't believe it!

This just couldn't be.

"I do like all these new clothes you've bought, especially those designer suits. Love the apartment too. What? Don't have anything to say, Sammy?"

But the horrible truth was staring Sam right in the face. The damn thing was wearing his clothes and talking to him.

You Lite.

The impostor was You Lite!

You Lite reached for Sam and suddenly Sam felt himself lifted in the air. It made him giddy. He wanted to vomit but nothing came.

This impostor that was once an app safely locked away in a smartphone was grinning. But it was not safe even there. No, the thing was especially dangerous then, for it had seemed so harmless. Now it was grinning cruelly.

It should have made the blood rush to Sam's head. But Sam felt none of it. He could feel no part, nothing of his body. But he felt anger and hate enter his brain.

And then Sam caught a reflection in the stainless steel oven.

He thought he would see himself and his double, confronting each other face to face. But what he saw was insane.

There was just the impostor alone, holding a Samsung Galaxy.

He was talking to the thing.

"Time to sleep, Sammy," said You Lite. "Louise should be home soon. I'm really looking forward to that. She's a lovely girl. I've wanted her from the time you snapped that photo of her. I'll take her out for dinner. Maybe we'll go to that Korean restaurant where we had our first date."

You Lite chuckled.

"Well, it really is my first date with your girl, isn't it? I may switch you on, so you can see it all. I'll leave you on mute, of course. Can't have any interruptions at our romantic dinner!"

You Lite did a little spin in the kitchen. It was a horrible movement that made Sam nauseous.

The impostor laughed.

This had to be a dream. But Sam knew this was no dream. He knew what had happened. His life was now a living nightmare.

You Lite whistled as he strolled into the bedroom.

"Oh, I'm going to enjoy your life, Sammy, especially your gorgeous Louise. As I always said, and you should remember it: BMW, Sammy, BMW."

Then the app clicked a button.

And for Sam, it all turned black.

As for You Lite, his life in flesh and blood had just begun.

Tuesday:
Goodnight, Mama

IS A WOMAN NOTHING MORE than sinew, blood, bones, phlegm and excreta? Is her beauty, as they say, only skin-deep? Strip off that lush lickable layer and where lies loveliness in that raw flesh, my friend?

When you lay beside your wife, feeling the steady beating of her heart beneath your warm hands, listening to her silken breath in the stillness of night, do you not curse her inevitable old age, her face shrunken, her back bent, her eyes rotten? Do you not feel your guts squirm when she's a shriveling corpse laden coldly in your arms? That beautiful, once-breathing person now a decomposing stinking sludge of blood, skin, marrow and bones?

I have never thought of such ills until this detestable day.

My beautiful mother was crossing the street in sunglasses and floral dress beneath the concrete piers of a monorail track when a bus lost control and smashed into her. A large crowd gathered around. A man who worked as a nurse in the General Hospital was attending her wounds when the ambulance shrieked its arrival. He shook his head when the paramedics sauntered over. She had no chance. They slotted her mangled body into the ambulance, leaving the wrecked bus and the gawking crowd behind.

On arriving at the hospital, they pulled open the back door and ...

She was gone!

That was the story anyway, but who would believe the two paramedics who were most likely on drugs? Bodies don't just vanish on a Tuesday afternoon in our busy city. Especially those of accident victims whose organs are likely damaged and not worth harvesting. Perhaps she wasn't dead. Just badly injured. Somehow, in the jammed-up traffic, she must have stumbled out of the ambulance and scurried away, swallowed by the city. Perhaps she had help.

I had to find her. But where to start?

I searched everywhere. Examined every possibility. Finally, I found myself at our vacant high-rise in Mont Kiara which we had not been able to rent out for years. The country no longer had as many expatriates as before. The apartment, like so many others, stared out emptily at the cityscape … unlived, unloved, unwanted.

The front door, its lacquer grossly faded, opened too smoothly. As if its empty rooms had been waiting. Stale, warm air pressed against my face.

In the lounge, the off-white curtains were half-drawn. From stained walls, faint rectangular blotches were all that remained of where paintings or family photographs once proudly hung. Where were these paintings now? Where were these families? A shattered lightbulb hanging from a broken fitting reminded me of broken dreams. Of accidents and death.

The droning expressway traffic penetrated my deep breathing. Then, as if in accompaniment, the call to prayers echoed from a newly-built mosque. Seconds later, a shrilling high-pitched voice joined it. It was from the old, smaller mosque just across the road beside a half-abandoned construction site. The two voices merged disconcertingly, competing yet conspiring in the heat of that late afternoon.

Through the drifting dust motes I eyed a stack of brown newspapers beside the balcony door, some scrunched up and scattered like dead animals on the floor.

Several had fresh dark stains. I didn't dare touch them. But I was sure now that she was here. Coldness trembled in my lungs.

I spun towards the open-plan kitchen, expecting to see my mother splayed and bloodied on its white tiled floor. But it was empty.

With its stained cupboards, greasy rangehood and blackened stove, it took the semblance of a dark servant squatting in a corner, eyeing me sulkily, yet licking her lips at the thought of what is to come. A spider scurried on the dusty benchtop and darted into her long hair. A tap or perhaps her flaring nostrils dripped, the incessant tapping joining the chorus outside.

Down that way, came her ugly whisper. *There's a surprise for you.*

I blinked. There was no squatting servant. Just an empty kitchen, unused for years. My imagination. The mind playing tricks.

Slowly, I turned to the corridor. If Mama was here, this is where she would have gone. I moved cautiously, my footsteps vibrating horridly up my spine. Darkness sought me and cobwebs like delicate fingers caressed my cheek.

Halfway down, an odor slid around my neck, embracing me in a warm fetid breath. It reminded me of a narrow alleyway between shophouses strewn with rubbish and smelling of rotten vegetables. A place of rats, discarded needles and other unspeakables festering in its blocked-up drains. But that wasn't quite it.

It smelt of something dead.

Or slowly dying.

Past the bathroom, which was small and empty, I spied the open door leading to the second bedroom. This room's single window faced a gloomy wall no more than five feet away. It peered down twenty-two stories, falling into a narrow air well. Once, I leaned into the funneling concrete and hot, stagnant air blew up into my face. I wondered who else eyed this same glorified hole. Who spat down it or what refuse was thrown there?

I cautiously glanced into this bedroom now. Except for the built-in cupboards, the dusty floor and a dead cockroach nestled beside a skirting board, it was empty. But it was never empty. There was always a presence there that I never liked.

At the end of the corridor stood the master bedroom. The door was shut. This room, I knew, had a large window that gazed over the city and, far beyond it, limestone cliffs surrounded by green hills. It was the only redeeming feature in this otherwise depressing condo.

But why was the door shut when it was usually open?

My heart lurched at the possibilities. I wanted her to be there. But at the same time, I didn't.

My poor dear Mama ...

Just as my fingers touched the doorknob ... I heard it.

An awful mewling.

A cat being hanged? Its limp battered body swaying from the groaning ceiling fan? Its blood dripping like that leaky tap, puddling on the parquet floor?

No, not today. Today I doubted I would have such luck.

My heart romped in my chest.

Mama was here!

She had been crushed by a bus this morning. They had found only her broken sunglasses in the ambulance. She had survived.

What kind of state was she in? But what if ...

I didn't dare think of that possibility. But my father had told me things. Awful, awful things.

A gecko called out a shrill warning ...

With my heart now pounding in my head, I pushed the door. It swung silently open before thudding against the doorstop.

Summing up my courage, I stepped into the room.

Instantly, the odor hit me.

That sweet rotting smell. Meat gone off. Bloody meat crawling with maggots.

As if announcing my arrival, there came again the two voices from the mosques. One new. One old. One higher-pitched than the other. They jabbed my ear drums. Swirled angrily in my head as the traffic hummed.

I almost swooned in the stifling heat. The sun blazed upon the full-length windows. The curtains, of a faded purple hue, were drawn closed. And, in its harsh, unforgiving light, I saw ...

A figure crouching behind the curtain!

She had heard me and was now silent. Unmoving. I didn't dare breathe. My legs were trembling. *Why did I have to be here? Why was it down to me?* The figure shifted, rippling the curtain.

I swallowed hard.

There ... it shifted again.

I wanted to flee. But I made myself hold my ground.

"Mama ..." I said. But it came out in an awful whisper. I scarcely recognized my own voice. "Mama, is that you?"

The figure *mewed*. A sound that slipped into the room as though from far away. From some awful place no one should ever know about.

"Please come out," I whispered. "Please ..."

But I didn't want her to come out. I wanted her to stay squatting behind that curtain to never show me her face. Because I didn't want to know. I didn't want to be here and face this madness. But what if she was just injured and needed help?

But still. The horrid possibility made my legs quiver.

Yet I had an obligation. A responsibility.

And we cannot escape our responsibilities, can we?

I had promised my father that I would take care of Mama. So it was up to me...

Sweat dripped down my face as I stepped towards the curtain. I winced for the smell was now terribly strong. Awfully rotten.

The curtain trembled. A ripple like a frightened gecko darted up to the pelmet.

I heard a low cough. Then, from behind the purple material, a bony bloodied hand reached out for me.

"We really must do something," snapped Zainab. "This situation cannot continue. I think your wife has gone crazy."

"That's not true," said Rafiq, staring at his podgy eldest sister in her tudung and flowing loose clothes. "Just because she eats alone on the kitchen steps doesn't mean she's crazy."

"But she doesn't talk to anyone. Why is she like that?"

"You know it's because of the accident. She cannot face me or our family for that matter, with that scar on her face."

Rafiq's marriage to Norainah had been arranged. But three weeks before the wedding, as his fiancee fried banana fritters, a can of condensed milk tipped off the shelf and fell into the wok. Hot oil scalded her cheek and she fell to the floor screaming.

His family had asked him to call off the wedding, but Rafiq refused. He would keep his word. Beauty, he philosophically decided, came from within. But he hadn't taken Norainah's feelings into account.

Rafiq shook his head, tears welling in his eyes. "I don't know what to do. It's been five weeks now since we've been married. She hardly eats. She's become so thin. It cannot continue like this."

"Then you must divorce her."

"I cannot do that."

But sometimes Rafiq thought it was exactly what he wanted. His new wife would mostly hide herself in one corner of the house behind the mosquito net, so that no one could see her. She would not allow him to touch her. She didn't believe that he wanted her in his life. Norainah refused to speak. Rafiq felt her sorrow and was determined that the marriage could work. Surely they could still find happiness together?

His sister's face was grave. "I know of someone who can help you."

"Who?"

"The pawang from Kampung Guning."

"The pawang? What would we want with him?"

"I've heard stories. Things he can do. I will go with Amin to see him. It will take a day's walk to get to his village. If he can help, I'll bring him back with us."

"How can he help here? Anyway, I don't like their ways."

"You have no choice. The district nurse has already visited your wife. She can offer nothing. If you want to help Norainah, you must get help from this pawang. I can leave tomorrow if need be."

"I'm not sure about this."

"I will go and talk to him first, that's all. What harm could it do?"

So three days later, Zainab and her husband, Amin, returned with the shaman.

He was tall with deep-set eyes. Despite being in his seventies, his back was straight and rigid like an army officer's. His thin face was framed by long white cloud-like hair. He arranged his black plastic slippers neatly on the recently-swept ground and climbed the five timber steps into Rafiq's father's house.

The shaman, Zainab, Amin, Rafiq's father and Rafiq discussed the matter quietly as they sat cross-legged on mats. They pulled the timber shutters shut, so that the only light came slanting through the louvers. In this gloom, they agreed what had to be done. Rafiq was asking the shaman if he had done this before when he found his voice was caught like a dead beetle in his throat.

His wife was suddenly standing by the kitchen door. It was as if she had materialized like a ghost. Through the white veil across her skeletal face, he thought he could see her eyes glowing.

Two days later, the group began the long track back to the shaman's village. Norainah wore a white scarf over her hair and the same white veil across her face. She continued her silent vigil but Rafiq was pleased because she would occasionally nod at him.

"I thought she wouldn't agree," said Rafiq to Zainab as they lunched beside a clear babbling stream on the verdant foothills. "It's madness what we're proposing."

"Your wife is desperate. This solution will give her back her life. She'll do anything for it. She can then be a wife to you."

Zainab delicately placed the last handful of rice, boiled egg and sambal into her wide mouth, then folded back up the banana leaf in which the meal had been wrapped, and placed it in a rattan basket.

Rafiq shook his head. "We don't even know if this whole thing is going to work."

"No, we don't. But we have to take that chance for your wife's sake."

"But ..."

Rafiq glanced at Norainah who was squatting some distance away beside a large rock and staring silently into the stream. Her lonely figure was draped in the gloomy shadows of overhanging trees.

"But what if this doesn't work? It would ... it would *devastate* her."

"She's already devastated, can't you see that? I really doubt it could get any worse."

"We don't know that!"

"Of course, we don't know for sure what will happen but don't you think it's a risk worth taking? For her sake?"

Rafiq glanced at the scattered dead leaves on the ground, before eyeing his bare feet and the hot sunlight that crept surreptitiously between his toes. They showed no answers but raised a hundred questions.

He sighed.

"I suppose it is. I just hope it all goes well."

"I'm sure it will," said Zainab as she struggled up to join Amin who had come up to them. "Don't worry so much."

Rafiq thought that Zainab, his fat eldest sister, and Amin, who was tall and thin, made an ideal pair.

As they prepared to continue their journey, Rafiq turned to Norainah and held out his hand. To his surprise, she took it and he was sure he glimpsed a flicker of a smile behind her veil. His heart momentarily soared. But what would happen if the solution the shaman proposed didn't work? He didn't dare think of the consequences.

Amin twisted an ankle during a steep descent and this slowed their progress. Complaining of a searing pain, he clung onto his flabby wife who hobbled along with him. Rafiq thought it odd that this shaman had not offered to help him with any of his occult charms. What did this mean? Perhaps he was no more than a charlatan who had fooled everyone in the district?

Because of the delay, they arrived at the shaman's village in the late evening. Insect shrills loudly engulfed them and kerosene lamps flickered like watchful eyes from the houses. Rafiq thought these dwellings seemed different from the village houses he was used to. Not only were they smaller but their roofs curved at a steeper angle and ended at long sharp points which reminded him of curving blades.

They followed the shaman past the surau, and then they followed a narrow track away from the village. They went past an occasional orchard and just as darkness fell, they found themselves at the end of the track, with a large house peering down at them.

The shaman called out as he approached. He was greeted by his daughter and two grandchildren. He asked them to prepare a meal for their guests, then invited the men to lodge in his house while the womenfolk would stay in his cousin's smaller house next door.

The next day, Rafiq awoke to a morning blanketed by a dark gray foreboding sky, and soon after the rain fell in torrents. The trees in the surrounding jungle quivered in the drenching, their branches flung from side to side by a howling wind. It rained all that soggy day but by evening the clouds had exhausted themselves and dispersed towards the sunset.

This suited the shaman perfectly for he had planned for the group to leave only after the night prayers. Amin would stay behind because of his injured ankle. After rolling up the prayer mats, the group wended up a steep muddy track behind the house. The night embraced them with its cold clamminess. All around sprang rowdy whooping animal calls and incessant insect shrills.

They arrived at a jungle clearing with Zainab breathing heavily beside Rafiq. Once everyone was seated, the shaman's assistant, an obese middle-aged man with particularly bad skin named Hamdan, gathered dry timber which he placed on the remnants of a fire at the center of the clearing and lit it. The flame, though smoky at first, soon sprang fiercely to life. It crackled and set off sparks that swirled like frightened fireflies; these drifted up beyond the dark canopy ... up, up towards the peeping stars. Its heat chased away the night's chill and warmed their faces.

The shaman sat cross-legged in front of a small cave surrounded by quivering undergrowth. He chanted in a low voice behind a charcoal burner, moving his muscular body rhythmically from side to side, his long white hair flitting about. His neck arched grotesquely in several directions as though he was wary of spirits or demons hidden in the looming trees above.

Shadows leapt across his face, throwing light and darkness across his sharp features. He would occasionally pause, clap his hands twice, and continue his pulsing chant. Hamdan joined in, sometimes adding his voice to the intonation, but more often, yelling out his agreement with the words "Benar!"

But what is true here? thought Rafiq. *Is it all just a show? A theater for the gullible?*

He glanced at Norainah who sat stiffly, stick-like legs tucked to one side, between him and Zainab. Rafiq had at first been worried for his wife but as the proceedings went on he became more and more fascinated. The shaman seemed lost in a trance and his chanting became faster and louder.

It seemed to shake the pressing leaves themselves. Leaves which were like thousands of dark warning eyes, making them blink as if they had dirt in their sockets.

But surely, Rafiq mused, *it was just the wind?*

He glanced again at his wife. If she was anxious it didn't show beneath her white veil. Flames cast shadows against her thin features. Her eyes were transfixed on the shaman and every movement he made, from the jerking gestures of his shoulders to the hideous expressions that leapt like rats across his face.

When the shaman had stopped chanting, he suddenly opened his eyes and his dark hand quivered towards Norainah. Two curling fingers slowly beckoned.

"Come," he said, eyes wide. "Come sit beside me, child."

Norainah stumbled forward and sat beside the shaman. He floated one hand over her forehead, her hair and the back of her skull, mumbling softly to himself.

Norainah's eyes began to flutter. Then, without warning, she collapsed to the ground. Rafiq jumped to his feet, leaping around the fire to his wife.

"You and Hamdan must carry her," ordered the shaman. "Take her into the cave behind me."

Rafiq nodded.

Hamdan and Rafiq carried Norainah towards the cave, her one foot dragged on the ground as they did so.

Zainab bounced along beside them.

"Be careful," she called as she lifted Norainah's leg. "Carry her gently."

"Of course I will," whispered Rafiq. "She's my wife!"

"Watch your heads, both of you," said Hamdan. "Come in, slowly."

They lowered her just inside the mouth of the cave. The fire outside dimly lit up the cave's interior: its rough walls, its jagged ceiling just above head height and a stack of branches in one corner.

Coldness engulfed him. Rafiq rubbed his arms to warm them up. A faint dripping echoed deep inside the grotto. He breathed in a heavy mustiness and felt his uncertainty grow. Kneeling before his wife, he wondered if snakes and scorpions lurked close by.

Norainah lay unmoving like a corpse.

"Is she, okay?" asked Rafiq.

"She's fine," replied Hamdan. He scratched his cheek and it wobbled horribly in the shadows. He grinned but his eyes were grave.

Rafiq stared at him.

Is he hiding something? Why does he seem so worried?

Hamdan turned and scampered out of the cave. He returned with the charcoal burner which he placed a couple of feet away from Norainah. This brightly lit up the interior and Rafiq could now see the worried countenances on every face. It seemed as though the rocky walls themselves were staring eagerly at his wife.

Then the shaman entered. He delicately removed Norainah's veil.

How thin she looked!

The burn mark, like a pale dried-up toad, clung horribly to her right cheek. He had once seen amphibians hanging from a Chinese medicine shop. There were also all kinds of dried specimens for sale: seahorses, three-horned beetles, centipedes and even a monkey's foot. Rafiq, given a chance, would have tried any of those remedies for his wife before attempting this risky cure.

As he gazed at her, he realized how beautiful she was. Her hair was long and flowed past her small shoulders. But her face was skeletal. If only she would eat properly. None of this charade was necessary to him. But it mattered to Norainah. She wanted it done. She couldn't live with the scar.

The shaman placed a piece of cloth on the ground. With one finger, he inscribed a symbol in the air over it. Then unfolding the thing, he revealed what was hidden.

In the dim flickering light, Rafiq saw nothing at first ... but then his eyes latched onto something small lying there.

A needle.

Rafiq was shocked at its size. More than an inch long. The thing was made of gold, shimmering hard before his eyes.

He heard Zainab breathe in sharply beside him.

Susuk, thought Rafiq and shuddered.

He had heard of how such practices could enhance a woman's beauty, but how it could it remove such a terrible scar from his wife's face? He could still stop this now if he said something ...

As though answering his thoughts, the flames from the charcoal burner suddenly flickered then dimmed. It was as though the needle had sucked in the light and, with it, the protest he was about to voice.

The shaman gripped the needle and drew it over the diminished flames several times. He inspected it closely, his lips tight and quivering. Then, slowly, he circled it towards Norainah's pale face. He placed its pointed end delicately on one side of her left nostril, just touching her flesh.

He swiveled his white-haired head towards Rafiq, eyes blazing.

"Are you sure?" he whispered, his voice thick as if he had dust in his throat.

Rafiq wanted to say *no*.

He had so many questions about this susuk.

Would it work? And what if it did? What were the risks? The questions trembled in his brain. But nothing, not a syllable, not a single breath of air spluttered from his mouth.

From the corner of one eye, he glimpsed Zainab slowly nodding.

"Very well," said the shaman. "For all that is right. For all that is wrong. Nothing can change the curses or blessings of this night."

Rafiq shivered. *What kind of spell is that? What does it mean?*

But before he could object, the shaman, with a single deafening shout, pushed the needle into her flesh.

Norainah screamed and suddenly bolted up. Her eyes wide open.

Blood trickled from her nose, around her lip, down to her jaw.

"Wipe it," said Hamdan. "Quickly!"

Zainab hurriedly did so with her handkerchief.

Norainah stared into space. Her face stone cold.

There was no sign of the needle. No sign of a wound or any more blood.

But still her eyes stared emptily. Her lips were parted but said nothing. It was as if her life's essence had been dragged from her.

The shaman took hold of Norainah's hands and helped her to her feet. He placed the veil back over her face.

"Time to go home," he said. "It is done."

Norainah slept silently that night.

The next morning they began their journey home. The day after they returned to their village, Norainah's appetite improved and she even said several words to Rafiq. On the third day after the ritual, he entered the house and couldn't find his wife. He stepped back onto the terrace and saw a figure beside a clump of banana trees. It was his Norainah.

She wore a sarong and a simple white blouse. He stepped into the blazing sunlight, crossed the dusty compound, passed the chicken coops and found her stroking the trunk of a banana tree. Its leaves were brown and drooping. All around the insects seemed to laugh.

She turned to him before he could open his mouth. "Remove my veil, Rafiq," she said.

"You ... you want me to remove your veil?"

She nodded.

"Are you sure? Out here in the open?"

She nodded again.

He stepped up to her and held the silky material between his trembling fingers. A bead of sweat dripped down his forehead. Then very slowly, he drew the veil away.

He blinked, hardly believing his eyes.

Sunlight shone on her face.

The scar, although still there, was hardly prominent. Its roughness was almost gone and it was not as pale as before.

The susuk worked!

But it was not just that ...

Norainah seemed healthier. There was a glow. Her entire face smoother and without even a single blemish. Even the small birthmark above one eye was gone.

How could this be?

Was this just his imagination? Rafiq didn't think so. Then she smiled at him. His heart soared. Everything would be fine from now. Surely?

Norainah did not wear her veil that day. She spoke often, ate well and even laughed. She was the way she was before the accident.

When no one was looking, Rafiq did a celebratory jig beneath the house.

As the days passed, the scar further diminished. Ten days after the ritual, it was gone for good.

So let me ask you again: is a gorgeous woman nothing more than flesh, blood, sinew, marrow, bones, phlegm, urine and excreta?

It would have been a perfect ending to a woeful beginning. Yes, my parents did live a mostly contented life. Then just a month before my father turned sixty-eight, he succumbed to his pancreatic cancer. So Mama moved in with me.

Nothing extraordinary about this. Death is a natural consequence of life.

Except that sometimes it isn't.

I found this out early on, when I just turned twenty. It was before I left home to board at a technical college.

My parents had sold our terrace house. They would end up living in different parts of the country. Never settling down.

As I packed my books, my father entered my room, sat on my bed and, with a weary face that held this secret, this burden for so many years, told me what had happened. About the ritual, the needle inserted into Mama's face and how she became better. It fixed her in the head. He didn't care about the scar, he told me, as he sighed and wiped sweat from his forehead.

It was hard to believe his story. I just nodded. But when he whispered about what the pawang then later said, I found I could no longer believe him.

How could I even contemplate such a thing? Even if it were true, what I had to do, if I ever had to, was in the distant future. A future in the reckless optimism of youth that would never arrive. The thing is, no one tells you how fast time runs away from you. And if anyone did, I wouldn't have believed them.

I was thirty-six and still single when my father passed away. By this time, I had no doubts about his story. The veracity of it pounced on me on one of those lazy Sunday afternoons.

We were sitting beneath plastic blue umbrellas at a hawker stall when my friend from the squash club tapped my shoulder. I was sipping my glass mug of kopi cham, an old-timer's drink I had taken to simply because it was so bizarre.

"Is that your sister waving at you?" he said, his Arsenal cap slanted on his head.

It was Mama. She had driven up in her Kancil looking for me. She knew this was my favorite stall.

"It's my mum," I said.

"Your mother! I always thought she was your sister!"

"I don't have one. I don't have any brothers and sisters."

"Well, your mother ... she looks so young. You sure you're not kidding me?"

From that day onwards, I realized that people often mistook us for brother and sister. My mother was then in her mid-sixties.

Of course, it was the susuk. That needle that was inserted into her cheek. It not only made her beautiful but it gave her youth.

"You okay?" she asked when I got into the car.

Her eyes were bright. Her skin smooth and radiant.

"Fine, Mama," I said, staring at her dark lush shoulder-length hair which she'd once told me she didn't dye. She was slim and wore a long-sleeve blouse and ankle-length skirt.

"I knew I'd find you here," she said with a smile. "I thought we could go to the movies. If you're not doing anything." There were hardly any wrinkles around her eyes. She looked in her mid-forties.

"A movie would be great," I replied. "Which one shall we watch?"

I wondered if other moviegoers would take us for brother and sister or husband and wife? Perhaps in a few years, I would look older than her.

Yes, my mother did age, but slowly ... very slowly. It was as though the lives of we normal mortals followed the minute hand while hers clung to the slow-moving hour.

Now I understood why my parents moved so often. It was to avoid the inevitable question:

Why doesn't your wife get old?

That's what they would have asked my father. New acquaintances would just think: *He's got a young wife.*

Some enviously. Some disapprovingly.

This problem could be dealt with if handled well. Like never staying in one place for more than a few years.

But the main glitch was what the shaman told my father. It was the day after the ritual when they were getting ready to set off on that long walk home.

"You must do it before you wife is too old," he said that early morning as fog drifted through the surrounding green hills. "Do it well before your wife dies."

"What do you mean?" my father asked. "Do what?"

"You must ..." the shaman inclined his frowning long-haired head, "... remove the needle!"

"Why do I have to do that?"

"Because if you don't ..."

My father, on being told the consequence, must have staggered backwards into Hamdan for the shaman's assistant caught him and spun him around.

"You must follow our instructions," said Hamdan. "It is necessary. Everything has a cycle. Nature cannot be permanently changed."

"You didn't tell me this before," blurted my father.

"I told your sister," said the shaman, staring hard. "Didn't she tell you?"

My father shrank towards a stand of tapioca plants, shaking his head. Insects viciously called from the surrounding jungle.

"It's an awful thing to keep secrets," sighed the shaman. "But you must know the truth."

He then repeated in detail what would happen if his instructions were not followed. The thought of it, when my father first told me the story, had made him want to remove the needle immediately. But when he realized how that would devastate his wife, he knew he couldn't do it. In any case, he didn't fully believe the shaman. He didn't even know then if the susuk would work.

But it did. And, believe me, my friend, all that the shaman said is true ...

For I have pushed the door open.

Barely able to breathe, I have stepped in.

Here I stand in an empty bedroom in a high-rise condo in a booming Asian metropolis where such things are not meant to happen. Although the curtains are drawn, the afternoon sun still burns the windows. There's the dueling voice from two mosques.

One new. One old. And the droning traffic below.

In the stifling heat, dust motes dance.

A rotting smell drapes itself like strangling silk around my skull.

In the half-light, the curtain beside me shudders.

It ripples up to the pelmet.

A hand ... *her hand* is drawing it open.

I stagger back.

It reveals a figure crouching on the parquet floor. Its head jerks up at me.

Sunlight slants upon two empty eye sockets.

One eyeball still clings to her cheek, suspended from the socket by a sliver of flesh. Whatever hair is left, is white and tangled. The face, the skin, every feature upon it is hideously old.

No ... much more than old!

She has decayed horribly. This is a body that should have been months in the ground. The rotting stench leaves no room for doubt.

"Ahhhhhh ..." she groans. "Eaaahhhhh ..."

Her gaping mouth reveals black rotten teeth.

Two fall out and spin like tiny dice towards me.

Her tongue, *its* tongue, repeatedly licks the foul air.

This thing, whatever it is now, is not human ...

... It's a slab of putrid meat.

Maggots crawl out of its eyes, its nostrils and ears.

But still, I recognize her ... I don't want to ... but I do.

This is Mama!

It can't be.

But what son can deny his mother? But I have to as I stare in repulsion at this decomposing creature.

Did I not tell you that a woman is nothing more than flesh, blood, sinew, marrow, bones, phlegm, urine and excreta?

This ... this is living proof of that!

Then there is ... a *trickling* sound. A thick brown puddle grows around her clawing bare feet. She squirms.

I gag, almost throwing up.

I step back.

This is a mistake. To the creature, that creature that was once Mama, it is a signal.

This thing like a praying mantis lightly gets to its feet.

It makes a guttural chuckling sound as it advances on me. Its gnarled hands reaches for my neck, the bony fingers quivering in anticipation.

I hear grinding teeth beneath its low ugly breath. For some reason, it reminds me of wreckage scraping on a beach, in a muddy sea filled with toxins, rubbish and hundreds of dead bodies after a tsunami.

Oh, to be swallowed up now and to never breathe again!

"Stay away!" I moan.

I back out of the bedroom. It follows me, staggering down the corridor.

I edge away, my legs hardly able to move. My eyes are transfixed on hers. But hers are just eye sockets, glowing like twin moons in a filthy night sky ...

Still she advances. Still I try to get away.

Then I realize, to my horror, that I've backed into the small bedroom.

I'm trapped!

It advances with that guttural chuckling, fingers quivering, head rocking dementedly from side to side.

My back is hard up against the built-in cupboards.

It leaps forward with a bellowing cry.

It falls upon me, its cold bony fingers like pliers upon my throat.

I slip and fall to the floor, knocking my head on the cupboard.

The foul thing laughs as it follows me down.

Its nauseating breath swamps me. The smell of feces and rotting flesh fills my head. Vomit swims up my chest.

Its sharp fingernails bite into my throat.

I cry in pain. But nothing comes out.

I cannot breathe!

I try to prise its bony fingers away but to no avail. Then I see it!

A dark mark just beside its putrefying nostril. It wasn't there before but I can clearly see it. It's even growing bigger.

The needle!

It has to be the needle!

I push my hand against its face.

But the powerful pressure on my neck doesn't ease. My vision swims. I slide my finger down its damp forehead, along one side of its spongy nostril and ... *I feel it!*

I grasp the cold hard thing.

Then I jerk the needle out.

The creature shrieks.

I yell in triumph as the gold needle glimmers before me.

Then the creature grabs my hand, flips it around and—still screaming—drives the needle into my eye!

Two voices cry out as one in that desolate apartment twenty-two floors above the earth.

This monstrosity, that was once my mother, then splutters, chokes and collapses to the floor. I feel its corpse-like body behind me, convulsing coldly against mine. Then, slowly, very slowly, like a wind-up toy reaching its end, it stops.

This is followed by a horrid sighing and a long wheezing. Followed by a cracking of bones. And a dripping, tapping sound ...

It reminds me of that sulking servant ... squatting in the corner of the kitchen, licking her lips. Her nostrils flaring in the heavy darkness.

Now you know ... now you know.

She whispers it over and over.

I think I hear her giggling.

Then there's silence. An awful dead silence. I lie there, unable to move.

The pain in my eye slowly fades.

I'm not sure how long we are there together, mother and son. Even if I could move my body, I dare not turn to look.

Of course, Mama is dead. As she should be. Nature must take its course, that was what the shaman said.

I lie there, cheek against the parquet floor until the light begins to fade.

If a woman is nothing more than flesh, blood, sinew, marrow, bones, phlegm, urine and excreta, then is it not the same for a man? Of course, it is.

Eventually, control of my limbs returns. Slowly I get up and, head spinning, stagger down the corridor to the bathroom. In the dust-covered mirror above the dirty basin, I examine my eye.

It feels gritty. But other than that it seems fine. I wipe off a trace of blood with a handkerchief. Warm tears trickle out. But there's no sign of the needle.

It's gone deep within me. Perhaps even into my soul. Yes, it must have gone there, for my skin already seems smoother. The susuk will keep me young.

I never wanted this. But now I have it, I will keep it. But will I jerk the needle out when the time comes? For my face will then reveal its true age. That's why my mother kept it in.

One can never underestimate a woman's vanity. Or a man's.

In death though, the needle turned her into a living corpse.

In the bedroom, Mama's skeleton, all in pieces, is sprawled on the floor. Not a single piece of flesh, tissue, phlegm or excreta remain. The phalanges on one bony hand nudge a dead cockroach.

I open the window and peer down the air well. The air is hot and damp as always but it is a relief from the rotten stink.

It is almost dark.

Again there echoes the voices from the two mosques. The evening call to prayers. They're filled with despair. Remorse. Even pity.

I gather the bones. Gather them so carefully, for they are Mama's.

One by one. I go to the window. And let them fall. There's a faint cracking as each one hits the concrete far below.

Lastly, Mama's skull rolls from my hands.

It spins.

Once. Twice.

For a second, the pale eye sockets spring up at me. Bright they are. Like twin moons in the ever-night sky.

Mama!

The crash echoes like distant thunder up the air well.

There follows, a shuffling noise far below.

Claws clicking on concrete.

Perhaps it's a rat. Or another creature to haunt my dreams.

"Goodnight, Mama," I whisper. "Goodnight."

I leave the condo, needle in my eye, claws clicking in my skull.

WEDNESDAY:
CLEAR BLUE SKY

HER FATHER'S BREATHING is deep and ragged. He crouches next to her on the kitchen floor. The power stopped working weeks ago and often there's no water in the taps.

Her belly squeezes vice-like and she wants to groan. The last thing they'd eaten was a can of baked beans yesterday.

But it isn't the lack of food.

It's fear.

Meegan is eleven and her brown hair which she used to proudly brush feels greasy and gritty. She's been wearing the same pair of shorts and T-shirt for weeks. Her dad, normally clean-shaven, now sprouts a messy beard with tattered gray streaks. Shadows of thick hair curl over his neck and the lines of his face are deeply edged in the shuddering light.

In one hand, he clutches an ax which he normally uses to chop timber which he would pile next to the fence in the back garden. Its blade glints darkly on the white-tiled floor.

"What are we going to do?" Meegan says.

"Shhh," he whispers, He places a hand on her shoulder. "Just be quiet now. They may just go pass."

Meegan shivers despite the lingering heat of the day.

The kitchen cabinet presses hard against her back.

From outside it grows louder: the sound of shuffling feet. Death comes in many forms, it says. There's a low muttering sound, like locusts feasting.

Light from their torches flicker sharply against the wall.

There's an evil laughter outside. It grows louder, echoing from the festering innards of insanity.

A horrible chill rises up Meegan's neck. It clutches her skull.

There's a loud crash. The kitchen window shatters. Glass falls into her hair.

"Run!" yells her father.

New model cars still rolled off assembly lines. Restaurants and cafés remained crammed with diners. People visited cinemas. Many were glued to their TV sets. People still worked.

Meegan's father told her that everyone was numb those first few months. The world carried on as normal, on autopilot, ignoring the inevitable.

Terrible news takes time to sink in.

Meegan still remembered that day. She had just come home that boring Wednesday from school and had flicked on the television. Every channel had the same thing: the US President announcing that the asteroid his government had previously said would miss Earth by 35,000km would, in fact, hit us. Her father had said that they wouldn't have admitted it if it wasn't for the Russians who were going to announce it first. They knew because their space agency had been monitoring space ever since an asteroid exploded over Chelyabinsk, injuring over a thousand. Two rockets with nuclear warheads had been shot at the rock to change its course but these proved futile.

So the world discovered that in twenty-six months, an asteroid six times larger than the one that killed off all the dinosaurs would hit the earth. It would end civilization, snuffing out all humans and animals. Perhaps some insects would survive but that was all. If the earth was lucky, things might be able to start again, but without us.

There was no room for doubt. Eminent scientists had pored over the data, looking for a glimmer of hope. Some mistake in the calculations, perhaps, or a possible gravity pull from some other source. But no, the best they could jointly come up with at the conference in Beijing was a 96 percent certainty of the asteroid hitting. The consequences, they agreed, would be complete annihilation.

"Why's it all gone bad?" Meegan had asked. "It was okay before. Why have people ..."

"Changed?" completed her father as he scratched his new beard. "I don't know. There must have been some sort of catalyst. Maybe it was when the banks stopped giving home loans. Or, who knows, maybe it was when the stock market soared then crashed or when the Internet slowed to a crawl. Or maybe people just realized there's no point working when they can stay home planting vegetables instead or twiddling their thumbs for the next couple of years. It's like an early retirement, I suppose. That's why I stopped working. But I carried on until most of my colleagues decided to stay home. There's not much point going to the office when you're the only one there. There's no point working when it's meaningless, when you know nothing will come of it. Two years and it's all gone ..."

He rubbed his hands against his temple as if he had a headache. As if all of it was becoming too much for one man trying to raise a daughter in a world gone wrong. If it was ever right to begin with.

"Plus there's no point in earning money either," he continued with a sigh. "No one has to pay the mortgage now because the banks are all closed up. And what's the point of earning money if you know it's coming to an end in a couple of years anyway? And what's the point of money if it's becoming more and more worthless? As soon as people figured that out and stopped working, well, guess what happened?"

Meegan shook her head. Her dad knew, of course. He had the answers. He was an engineer at the local council.

"The factories, farms, transport, shops, none of it could function as before. There's just less and less to buy. Everyone's hoarding food. Remember when I had to pay a hundred bucks just for those eight cans of peaches? Money's not going to be worth anything. So why bother working? With fewer people in the factories, in the farms, there's even less to buy. It's just a vicious cycle. A self-fulfilling prophecy."

"A self ... what?"

"Never mind, Meegan. It just means like that if you keep thinking you're going to have a bad day, then you will have a bad day. Or if you think civilization's going to end, and if enough of you think so, then it will end."

This was six weeks ago. She thought it had all gone bad. But she didn't know what bad really was until she had seen them.

She called them the marauders.

In the purple light of one early evening, Meegan thought that the neighboring houses looked just the same as in the old days. Just that no one had turned on their lights yet. No one did, because there was no power. She could, if she wanted to, fool herself into thinking that nothing had changed. Except, she knew, that somewhere above was a hurtling large rock and it had altered everything on earth.

Just as she was about to turn away, she saw flickering flames at the end of the street. There were perhaps twenty figures with several lit torches between them. Silently and slowly, they roamed up the road as if they were trick-or-treating. But no, they were not dressed up, although their overly casual gait was threatening enough.

They carried clubs, knives and chains. Then, without warning, like a swarm of hornets, they crowded around a house she could just make out down the street. Someone started yelling.

Then her father grabbed her hand and pulled her into the bedroom. But that was before she heard the faint sound of things smashing, screaming ... and laughing. As they both hid under his single bed, she could still hear the laughing, a horrible evil laughter, whispering in her head.

"Who are they, Dad?" she asked as she trembled next to him.

"I don't know," he replied. "But it's bad ... very bad."

They waited in the darkness. Only time and their anxiety, creeping slowly past.

Later they heard more noises and what sounded like a bellowing. Or a pig squealing.

They stayed under the bed that night, catching whatever sleep they could, worried that the marauders would return.

As dawn crawled in through the curtains, they went out through the laundry room into the cool morning air. They slid past the bare-looking vegetable patch, her tattered blue trampoline, the overflowing dustbin surrounded by bulging rubbish bags, the cobwebbed washing line dripping with fresh dew and into the car porch littered with piles of dead leaves. Their Nissan was covered in dust and hadn't been used for weeks.

At first her father wouldn't let her follow him out into the street but she said that she didn't want to be left alone. Her father, of all people, understood this. He suffered from sleep anxiety and couldn't sleep by himself. Since the divorce, Meegan kept him company through the night. He had dragged her bed into the corner of his bedroom. Her mother and older sister had moved to the mainland. She missed them. Especially so after losing all contact ever since the Internet and the phone signals went dead.

It felt weird being out of the house. Meegan hadn't left it for days. The blue sky seemed so wide, clear and infinite. It was hard to imagine a huge rock up there falling towards them. She clutched her teddy bear as they stood in the deserted street. Her father carried an ax which swung beside his leg.

It was quiet as if all the neighbors were now decaying corpses. Even the birds were silent.

Curtains flickered in the house opposite. The Chongs must have been worried too. They must have seen or at least heard what happened last night. People rarely came out of their houses nowadays. They didn't stop for a chat like before. They would nod and slink back into their isolated dwellings. People kept to themselves, perhaps with death crawling through their hearts.

Meegan didn't want to die. But two years was a long time. Especially if there wasn't any school or athletics training, which was three times a week. She could do a lot with her time. But the grown-ups acted as if they were already dead. This was bad for the kids because none of her friends would come over anymore. No more jumping on the trampoline or cycling around the streets, through the park or down to the beach.

They were all trapped in their houses.

Meegan and her father started down the road when they saw Phil Henry who lived with his wife Pam across from them. He was standing outside his front door wearing a purple sun hat, gardening gloves and holding a trowel.

His front garden was the only one with neat cut grass while the other houses had overgrown, unkempt lawns. His roses in a circular garden bed were bright red and cheerful in the slanting early morning light.

He waved at them.

"Morning, Phil," said her dad.

"An awful one," replied Phil. "Terrible night too."

He had thinning gray hair, a roundish face and smiled on one side of his mouth. This was due to a stroke several years ago which left one side of his face paralyzed.

"Do you know what happened?" he continued. "Those people. The bastards. They went to number 6 and number 11 last night. Smashed the whole place up, took what they wanted."

"Oh Christ," said her dad. "What about ..."

"Mr. and Mrs. Blake are dead. Heads smashed in. As for Mrs. Taylor, she and her three kids are gone."

"Gone where?" asked Meegan, feeling a coldness in her stomach. "Where've they taken Joe, Pete and Alice?"

"Oh my," said Phil, staring, his right eye blinking. "You don't want to know. There's evil things going on these days. Terrible things none of us could even imagine. Awful, awful."

"We need to do something," said her father. "We need to get together. Arm ourselves. Do what we can to keep these bastards out."

"If only we could," said Phil, shaking his head. "We're mostly old around here or have young families. Some have already left their houses. Gone where, I can't even guess, cos there's nowhere to go to. What can we do against these night raiders? That ax of yours isn't going to do much good. Hopefully they won't come back. As for me, I'm just going to get on with my gardening. I've weeding and pruning to do. I've tended my garden these past twenty-six years. Planted some olive trees a few years back. They're looking beautiful now. Sure, it'll all be gone in a couple of years and me and my Pam with it. But I've got to do something with my time. Now, I've got some tomatoes, would you like some?"

Without waiting for a reply, Phil slipped back into his house and brought out two bright red tomatoes. He gave them to Meegan.

"Thanks," said her father. "We really appreciate it. I'm afraid our vegetables aren't doing so well. I never learnt how to. I grew up in a big city."

"Oh, that's where it's gone real bad I hear," said Phil. "Riots every night. Everyone's joined gangs. There's all-out wars in some places. We've been lucky here. But I think that's gone now, after last night. You've got to take care of that daughter of yours. The little ones, that's what they're really after. But I don't think we've got too much to worry about. I doubt they'll return for a while. There're so many other neighborhoods to go to."

But Phil was wrong.

Four nights later there once again came the sound of shuffling feet and Meegan froze as lighted torches and long twisted shadows came reaching out for her. They were now more than halfway up the street.

"Come on, Meegan!" yelled her father.

She raced under the bed, followed by her father. From there, the smashing and screaming echoed like raging banshees. It was so much louder than last time and she shivered, her face quivering against the carpet.

She covered her ears trying to keep out the shattering sound of breaking glass. A door being kicked in. More screaming. But most of all the horrible laughing. Then that awful sound again, like a pig squealing.

Then silence.

Followed by a dreadful shuffling.

Again, Meegan and her father stayed under the bed that night.

When dawn finally came, they crept out into the street. They eyed the houses, the trees and gardens carefully in case the marauders were still around. Her father held his ax and Meegan her teddy bear.

"Oh no," she gasped as she stared across the street. "Phil, not him …"

The kind old man had given them tomatoes. The couple's possessions were scattered all over the garden including bits of furniture, books, magazines, CDs and a vinyl record player, its black electric cord trailing like a long twisted tail.

She glanced at her father. His lips were curled down and his beard trembled in the soft early light. A drop of sweat dripped down his forehead despite the cold morning air.

"I need to see what's happened to them," he whispered. "I need to see if they're okay."

But Meegan knew they were not okay. She shook her head.

"You can go back home, Meegan. I won't be long."

She shook her head again. "I'm going with you, Dad."

He stared at her, blinking in the glare of sunlight, and, for a moment, he looked so vulnerable that Meegan wanted to hug him and hold him close.

"As long as you do as I say, okay?" he said.

She nodded and clutched his hand.

Together they walked over to Phil and Pam Henry's house. As they approached his front door, where they had chatted four days ago, Meegan glanced back at their own house which sighed sadly at her from below its iron roof.

Except for the mess on the lawn, the Henry's looked like a normal suburban house on a normal morning in a year like any other. The red roses glinted with dew. The pavers neatly swept. The windows clean and shiny without a single cobweb.

When they got to the front door, Meegan's father turned to her.

"Wait here, I'll just take a quick look inside."

Meegan nodded, biting her lip.

He pushed the door open and entered.

She quietly followed.

The hall was the same. The shelves with porcelain teapots hanging on the wall were as she remembered.

She had been here only a few months ago to sell school raffle tickets. Pam had bought three and handed her several coins which she kept in a glass jar. She had worn black tracksuit bottoms and her white hair was tied in a neat bun.

She had peered kindly over her reading glasses and said: "I hope I win that bicycle. I'll give it to my grandson."

Yet Meegan now detected a faint smell that was never here before. A bad smell that doesn't come through your nostrils but one that leaks into your brain.

A stench of sickness. Or of the dead and the dying. There was a gasp.

It was her dad.

Meegan hurried into the living room.

Pam Henry sat in a blue dressing gown on the sofa.

Her arms were by her side as though she was having a quiet conversation. Her legs were open, which was not at all how a lady's legs should be in polite company. Her head was arched up at the ceiling. She may have been inspecting a stain above except for a large black gash around her throat. Dried blood clung to her white neck and spilled down the front of her gown.

Around her, the furniture had been tipped over, the display cabinet splintered, its wine glasses shattered, curtains ripped off the rails. The TV had been thrown onto the dining table. Books, trinkets, cushions and papers had been flung everywhere. Even the beige floral wallpaper had been ripped in places.

The marauders had come in through the verandah sliding door. The glass was smashed in, leaving a gaping hole and a clear view of a neat garden lined with olive trees. The door itself hung on a precarious angle on a single roller.

Meegan's father was breathing hard as he stumbled towards the kitchen. He was swearing to himself.

She followed him but not without first seeing Pam's one dead eye staring at her. Perhaps even following her.

But no! That couldn't be.

Meegan rushed away and stood by the kitchen door.

Phil was sprawled on the white tiled floor in a matching blue dressing gown. Thick dark blood pooled around his skull. One of his arms looked broken.

The kitchen had been ransacked. The cupboards were thrown open. Broken plates, mugs, dishes and empty packets covered the floor. Spilled flour had turned the kitchen bench white.

"Oh Christ," said her father, as he knelt over the old man. "Are you okay?"

"You must leave," whispered Phil. "Get out of your house. Go anywhere."

"Why?"

"I had to tell them. They beat it out of me."

"What did you tell them, Phil?"

"They wanted to know where the children lived. So I gave it to them. All the numbers of the houses I could remember, which weren't many. They didn't come for you last night because they'd just been to number 18. Took the two boys ... They'll come again. It's their sport. They like them young and fresh. Their leader, spiky blond hair and tattoos all over his arm, said he prefers lamb to mutton. Said it's all a free-range farm and they'll come and go as they please. I'm sorry ... they made me tell."

"My God!" gasped her father.

Then he turned and saw Meegan. His face quivered and his eyes were filled with despair.

"Get some towels and a blanket," he said.

When she brought them back, he used one towel to wipe up the blood and propped Phil's head beneath another. Then he covered him with a blanket and brought him a glass of water. But

Phil only coughed it back out. Meegan's dad bandaged the wound on his head and sat beside him.

Phil died an hour or so later. But Meegan was already back at home, sobbing in her bed. Before she left Phil's house though, she had made sure that Pam's one eye was truly not following her.

"Run!" yells her dad.

The marauders have finally come. Not for them. But for her. They're after the children she now knows. Their leader prefers lamb to mutton.

Meegan rushes outside through the laundry room. She runs into a huge shadow blocking her way. It's a big grinning man with wild eyes, spiky blond hair and bulging tattooed arms. He laughs as he tries to grab her but she ducks and slips past him.

Her father, who is right behind her, splits the man's skull with his ax.

There's a crunching sound followed by a piercing scream.

And the sound like a pig squealing.

"There, you bastard!" cries her dad as he yanks out the ax, drawing with it a clump of blond hair. "You're never going to touch anyone again!"

Meegan glances back and sees a pig with a black collar bounding after her. The leader's pet pig rolls crazily in the long grass.

Still shrieking, the leader falls to his knees, then collapses on the pavers.

Three men, one with a flaming torch, another yelling, rush at her father.

"Run, Meegan!" he shouts.

Her father swings the ax but misses.

One man grabs him and wrestles him to the ground.

"Run!" her father yells again but it comes out muffled.

Her father had said that this might happen and that she was to flee, no matter what. But for a second she stands there, desperate to help him.

Then she sprints away into the garden, past the pig that's now greedily munching the grass. She steps on a pile of timber logs and vaults over the fence into the house behind theirs.

She hears someone chasing after her. But then there's the sound of the pile of timber collapsing beneath him.

He cries out in pain. Perhaps he's twisted his ankle. *Good*, she thinks as she races along.

She sprints alongside the neighbor's house and is in the next street, then she goes down it, turns right, then left. She glances back several times, breathing hard. She's sure that no one is after her but she doesn't stop running until she reaches the beach.

She knows this route well, for this is her preferred way to school. She used to walk along the beach most days. If she was lucky she would see dolphins or sometimes a seal. But she's never been here at night. Gravel crunches under her shoes, so, despite the heavy darkness, she knows she's almost there.

Her blouse is covered in sweat. Her hands are trembling. Her throat dry.

The sound of waves breaking presses hard against her ears.

The beach is draped in a heavy blackness.

Then the moon slips out from behind the clouds.

That's when she spies black hillocks on the sand. In various heights and widths, they stretch out as far as she can see.

She gasps. She wants to curse the moon for revealing this.

She knows they are not people sleeping.

These are corpses.

The sea rushes up and down their legs and ankles. The white foam lingers on the bodies as if to coax them to join the living. Some are already floating like debris in the water.

She doesn't know where they've come from or what it means.

She cannot begin to understand. But she decides to stay here among them. For who would look for the living among this congregation of corpses? She thinks they must be freshly dead for they don't even smell. Or perhaps the sea breeze draws the stench away?

She sings softly as she sits between two huddled figures, cross-legged on the soft sand. She will keep vigil with the dead, these bodies that lie scattered as though in a war zone. Tears drip from her tired eyes but still the words and melodies slip softly, ghost-like, into the coolness of night. These are songs from the radio. Songs from long ago, fit for another place, another time.

When the sun peeks from the horizon, turning the clouds a bright crimson and exposing silhouettes of distant hills, pale faces emerge from the corpses. She gets up and walks among them. She gasps for she recognizes some of the faces. A neighbor, her PE teacher, even the dark-haired woman from the post office.

Then she leaves the beach, glancing back only once. Through the labyrinth of deserted streets, she cautiously treads her way back home. After watching the house and making sure the marauders have gone, she climbs over the fence and finds her father collapsed beneath the washing line.

His T-shirt is soaked in blood. Much of it has leaked on the concrete.

His face is untouched. His eyes are closed.

He may even be sleeping.

At least he'll never sleep alone now, she thinks, *for there're thousands of people in heaven*. There'll be no more moaning in his sleep or crying out loud and waking himself. He never told her what happened but she can guess it was from his boyhood. Someone coming at night, just like these marauders.

She stands there frozen before him. She finds it hard to breathe.

There's no sign of the leader her father killed. Sliced his head open with his ax. They must have dragged him away. Perhaps fed him to his pet pig. After all, the marauders only ate lamb, not mutton.

Her father seems so lonely lying there. He is her hero. He was so brave. He saved her life.

Dew from the washing line drips, tapping onto his face and sliding on his cheek as though it's his own teardrop.

Then she falls on him, holding him and sobbing. Her tears trickle into his beard.

"Why did you have to be a hero, Dad?" she whispers. "Why did you leave me alone?"

The only answer is a light breeze upon her face.

"I love you, Daddy. I love you."

Her cheeks are wet with tears.

She doesn't know how long she's been lying there, trembling against his cold body, wishing that he'll wake up, grin and say he's fine, that it was just a concussion, that all will be okay now. But he's unmoving ... quite, quite still and no amount of time will change that.

Later, as the heat of the day blazes onto her back, she gathers what she can from the house. She can't stay. The marauders know she lives here.

She moves into an abandoned house four streets away. It has a large vegetable patch that's gone wild. It has a basement as a hiding place, its entrance from the garden covered by overgrown shrubs.

The neighbors band together to fight against these marauding cannibals. Without their leader, they flee. Then they begin killing each other.

Meegan survives quietly for weeks. Weeks turn to months. And a year passes.

She often looks skyward as she stands in the garden, a thriving vegetable patch at her feet.

But nothing comes.

She wonders if her mother and sister on the mainland are okay. She doesn't know but she has to carry on.

The years slip by.

The boy from the next street moves in with her. Their vegetable garden is now huge. He's good at catching birds and the wild rabbits that have taken over the park. They have a baby. She's pregnant with another. She thinks she must be at least eighteen or nineteen now.

And still from the sky nothing comes.

Not when it's gray and pouring nor when it's clear and blue and goes on forever.

Thursday:
In the Village of Setang

I WAS NINETEEN when my mother died of fever which she contracted after her labors in the soggy paddy fields. Soon after her white shroud was swallowed by the crumbling earth, I received word that my aunt, Mak Ina, wanted me to move to Setang, the village where our territorial chief resided. Mak Ina worked as his head cook in what she called his "palace" and, as she was already seventy, she needed help in her daily duties.

Setang was half a day's walk from the village of my birth, but because of my club foot, it took me all day to get there as I hobbled down the track between jungle, gambier plantations and tin mines dotted about the scarred limestone hills. I arrived with my body aching, staggering with my bundle of clothes just as the insect voices mounted a shrilling octave. Then the Maghrib azan came, echoing like a wind and descending upon the valley.

At the village checkpoint, two Japanese soldiers leaning lazily against a coconut tree, with their khaki leggings half undone, asked me what I was doing here. I told them my business and the one that looked sulkiest and half-sick spat on the ground before waving me through. I hobbled past wooden houses on stilts, perched above their small dirt compounds of weary fruit trees and empty chicken coops. An old man, smoking a cigarette, fiddled with a wreck of a bicycle. Beside him a scrawny monkey sat, tied to a wooden post, tearing up a rotten papaya while its mournful eyes stared at me.

About fifty families lived in Setang, the most important of which was Dato Nan's. The territorial chief's house, I had heard, was five or six times the size of a normal one. Even as I followed the track alongside several getah perca trees, I could see its timber, the color of burnt umber, spanning across the hillside like a monstrous crow nestled on a verdant landscape.

I had never seen such a huge house before and my mouth widened as I drew closer. Its sturdy dark planks, its looming walls seemed to hold up the purple sky. Sloping up steeply was a thatched roof and, above it, the evening star was winking. Was it warning me or welcoming me? I didn't know. After my mother died, I felt I had nothing to live for, but here, no matter how unpromising, a new life was beginning.

I hobbled around to the back and found Mak Ina chopping pungent-smelling onions in the small building that housed the kitchen. She was a small and round gray-haired woman, who moved with great deliberation. After warmly greeting me, she passed me a drink of water mixed with lime juice and sat me down on a mengkuang mat.

"Any trouble with the Japanese?" Mak Ina asked, speaking slowly in a sing-song voice. "You shouldn't have come alone, you know."

As she spoke, my aunt's lips and tongue were dancing flames of orangey red for they were stained from a lifetime of chewing betel leaf filled with areca nut. She once told me that sireh gave her not only the energy but the inspiration to cook delicious food. But that was a long time ago.

"There were some along the way. But they left me alone."

"That's good," she sighed. "Well, Yan, you're lucky to be working here, you know."

"I know that, auntie."

"I didn't really need extra help in the kitchen. I can get help from the other servants. But you needed looking after. Luckily, Dato Nan agreed."

"I know. Thank you." I rubbed the sweat off my forehead and retied my long hair.

"After your mother died, I knew there was no one to look after you. You and I know that marriage is out of the question …"

Mak Ina didn't elaborate and so I simply nodded, indicating that I understood.

She was, of course, referring to my club foot—and to the black birthmark, the size of a guava on my cheek. No boys from my village had ever shown an interest in me. Perhaps that is also why the Japanese soldiers left me alone. There was once a boy though, but he married someone else. That too was long ago.

Mak Ina continued with a cursory description of the household duties that was expected of me.

"Another thing," she said, turning to me in almost a whisper. "Don't venture out of the servants' quarters after we've turned in for the night. Even if you can't sleep."

"Why's that, auntie? Is it the Japanese?"

She shook her head.

"Then why?"

"Just don't, Yan." She shrugged her small shoulders. "All we have tonight is tapioca. Now let's see you slice that one up. I want to make a boiled salad of it."

A few days later, well after Mak Ina had extinguished the kerosene lamp and we five servants were all lying on our mats, I realized my necklace was missing. I had carelessly left it hanging on a delicate branch of the frangipani tree beside the old well.

Though not expensive, it was my mother's and she gave it to me a few months before she succumbed to fever. Other than the bundle of clothes I had brought with me from my village, it was all I had.

Two of the other servants were already breathing heavily. Carefully, I got on my feet. Moonlight crept in through the gaps beneath the wooden shutters and this was sufficient for me to pad my way to the main door.

"Don't go out, child," a voice said.

It was Mak Ina.

"I forgot my necklace," I whispered. "I'll be very quick. It's just by the well."

"Get it tomorrow," she insisted.

"It might be gone by then, auntie. I'm so worried …"

I heard her sigh.

"You're a careless one, Yan," she whispered back. "Off you go then. Get it and come straight back."

The door creaked open and insect shrills suddenly filled the air. The dirt compound outside was bathed in eerie moonlight. A breeze swept through my hair and rustled the leaves of the trees.

The stone well was perhaps a hundred feet away and beside it stood the silhouettes of two frangipani trees. To my left loomed the long main building. Its curving shadows reminded me of a parang.

I crept down the wooden steps and hurried across to the well. The wooden bucket attached to a rope was cast carelessly to one side. A pool of dark water like freshly drawn blood floated beside it. I quickly searched the two trees, my fingers running along the small branches, feeling the rough knobbly bark.

But the necklace was gone.

Perhaps I was mistaken. Where else could I have put it? I was sure I had left it hanging on a branch, its silver chain glinting in the blazing sun.

Just as I was about to hurry back to the servants' quarters, I heard a sound. It was the snap of a twig. It was almost masked by the gushing of the stream behind the orchard but I had definitely heard it. I stared hard between the tree trunks and branches of the fruit trees but saw only shadows.

Then came another sound.

Something scratching the ground. I should have fled then. Instead I foolishly crept forward. Perhaps I thought it might be someone who had found my necklace. Or perhaps I was just curious. My heart pounded in my ears as I moved cautiously from tree to tree.

Beyond the orchard, the stream shimmered. It made a loud cascading sound as water flowed over small rocks which appeared remarkably white in the moonlight and resembled large eggs, some of which were broken. Then I saw it, crouched on the bank was an unmistakable muscular shape.

A tiger!

Perhaps the stream had masked the sound of my footsteps and the beast did not hear my approach. But now I was afraid to turn back, afraid that it would chase me as I retreated to the servants' quarters. So I hid behind the trunk of a rambutan tree and watched.

I saw the rhythmic movement of its body as it breathed the night air. Its ears twitched as if it was bothered by insects or perhaps, more worryingly, listening for prey. Occasionally, it would stare up at the jungle across the stream. Then, I must have glanced away for a second, for when I looked up, the tiger was gone.

I swallowed hard.

What if the beast had seen me? Smelt me? Perhaps right now it was circling behind me, stalking within the shadows of the fruit trees, getting ready to pounce?

Barely able to breathe, I stared at their misshapen silhouettes, listening hard, ready for the animal to charge. What I would do, I didn't know. I picked up a large stone from the ground as a weapon and held it close to me, between my small breasts. As I waited, the moon peeped between the branches, the stars glittering in the foliage. When I was sure the tiger was no longer waiting for me, I crept in the direction of the well.

Just as I reached it, I heard a sound. It seemed to come from beneath the steps that led up to the kitchen building. I knelt behind the stone work and then, suddenly, a figure stepped from the shadows. He was tall, muscular but slightly hunched. As he turned to climb up the steps, moonlight gleamed upon his long white hair that fell upon his broad shoulders. Even at this distance, I could make out his dark and angular features.

It was Dato Nan!

He was the reason we were all here. He was the chief of this district. This was his "palace" and he was perhaps the most powerful man in the state, second only to the sultan.

Dato Nan was wearing his bed clothes—a sarong and a light blue pajama top. At the top of the stairs, about six feet from the ground, he pushed open the kitchen door and disappeared inside. Pulling up my sarong, I raced around the side of the building soundlessly in my bare feet just in time to see him leave the kitchen building and stride along the timber bridge that led to the main house.

It could only be him!

His white beard caught the light of the kerosene lamp inside the entry hall as he entered. But that was not before he hesitated and glanced behind him. He stood there for a long moment. Then he turned away and firmly shut the door.

The next morning, when I was hanging out the clothes behind the servants' quarters, Mak Ina pulled me aside to ask me why I had taken so long to get my necklace the night before. She said she must have fallen asleep as soon as I had left and when she awoke I had not returned.

"I was about to go out looking for you, Yan," she chided in a slow sing-song voice. "Then the door opened and you came in. Alhamdulillah you're safe!"

"I saw something strange," I said. "I didn't want to tell you last night. I didn't find my necklace but I saw something else ..."

I then quickly told her what I had seen.

Mak Ina shifted her small round body beneath the scorching sun. She pursed her lips and scratched her gray hair as she listened.

"You mustn't tell anyone else about this," she whispered. Her face was grave and beads of sweat peppered her brow. "You shouldn't have seen what you saw."

"But why?"

"It's a secret. A dark secret."

"Tell me about it, auntie. Please!"

She glanced behind her towards the house whose timber shutters stared ominously back at us.

"Long ago, child," she whispered, "there was a dispute between Dato Nan's great-grandfather and a cousin-in-law of his. It was over who would become the next territorial chief. As you know, it's hereditary but governed by customary law."

I nodded, encouraging her to continue.

"Anyway, one day when this cousin was bathing in a hut made of palm leaves beside the river, a tiger leapt in and killed him. The villagers found his torso floating down the river. The palm leaves were smeared with blood. A village boy saw the tiger wading across the river."

"Where's this river?"

"I haven't taken you there yet, child. You'll need to follow the stream until it flows into the river. It's called the River Setang. It'll take a bit longer than the chewing of a betel nut to get there. It's quite normal for chickens, goats, even cows to be killed around here," she continued. "If traps or hunting parties are organized by those who are ignorant, they are quickly ordered to leave the tiger alone. Many think it's some sort of sacred creature that cannot be touched. But those closer to Dato Nan's family know better. The tiger legends have always been with us."

Her orangey red lips and tongue were fiery in the bright sunlight, then her eyes stared right into mine. "You know, this has nothing to do with your father. That was a terrible thing. But there is no connection between Dato Nan and your father's death. You must know that."

I slowly nodded. I did not want to speak about my father. Not now, anyway. He used to kiss me on the forehead, then gently touch my cheek. It made my heart soar.

He would tend to our small orchard, his dark back gleaming in the hot sun. His thin mustached face, the drooping narrow eyebrows spoke of his hard labor to feed and sustain our family. But he always made time for me, showing me games with polished stones on a wooden board he had crafted.

"You must know, Yan, that his death has nothing to do with our legends. That was seven years ago. It's all history now. We learn to forgive and forget. For instance, the British were our enemies seventy years ago but today we want them to save us from the Japanese... Yes, I was only a child when the British soldiers marched up the hill into our district. They looked so fine in their hats and red uniforms. After they had left the paddy fields and marched into the jungle, our men ambushed them. We attacked them with spears and parangs, keris and guns. Oh, what a shameful day that was for the mighty British and their empire! The thing is, some of their soldiers were also killed by tigers. There were two of them! This was all when Dato Nan's grandfather was still alive... But these British returned, this time with artillery and ten times more soldiers. They came on two sides and we were defeated. Many of us Malays died. That's how we came to be under British rule. Then, of course, the Japanese came with their planes and tanks. We thought they were liberating us—but they're far, far worse. As for those British, they did conduct a tiger hunt but never found their man-eating tiger. So you see, our village has a reputation for tiger attacks. Always has. But no one has ever killed or captured a tiger. Except for that one time ..."

"When was that, auntie? What happened?"

By this time, Mak Ina and I were sitting beneath a banana tree that held on tenuously to its dead brown fronds. A black-and-white moth flitted over the wild grass, then disappeared as though it was never there.

"Ah, you see, child," she said. "There was this one time when a man moved in from another district. He had never heard of the legends. So one early morning, when he came across a tiger eating the carcass of his goat, he raised his spear and flung it at the beast."

"What happened then?"

"Well, the next day, Dato Nan's father returned to the house with a deep cut in his thigh. Nobody knows how he got it. But everyone was whispering the same thing!"

"Are you saying, auntie, that Dato Nan's father was a weretiger?"

"Yes, a shapeshifter!"

"That can't be!"

"And Dato Nan is one too," she whispered, her eyes blazing. "It passes from father to eldest son. That's the story anyway."

"But it's just a story, right?"

"Yes, yes, child, just a story. But Dato Nan has five daughters. No sons. So when he dies, his position as territorial chief will go to his younger brother. Then we won't have any more problems with tigers around here."

The next day, as I helped prepare the evening meal, I received word that Dato Nan wanted to see me. So, from the kitchen, with my heart thumping, I followed the narrow covered bridge which connected it with the main house.

We servants used it several times a day to bring food from the kitchen. It was mostly curried or fried tapioca, sometimes with other vegetables, rarely with meat. The Japanese helped themselves to all our supplies. The reason the kitchen was kept separate from the main house was in case of fire. The kitchen had been ablaze twice in the palace's hundred-year history and the separation of the two buildings was what saved it. Of course, we servants only whispered the word "palace", for only the sultan was allowed to call his home that.

I pushed open the back door and entered the main building. I stood in a narrow dark hall. Mak Ina had told me that its walls used to be decorated with family heirlooms which included Chinese porcelain, pewter plates and silvery cutlery. Under the Japanese occupation, all of these had been hidden and only a painting of Dato Nan's father hung here.

From the hall, the building divided into two. To the left was the reception room where Dato Nan would receive visitors. Beyond the reception room was Dato Nan's bedchamber.

The other half of the building was to the right of the hall and it was reserved for family members. The first room was a dining area where mengkuang mats were spread out for meals. This was followed by two family chambers shared by Dato Nan's two spouses and children.

Instead of turning either way, I continued through the hall and out to the balcony at the front. The balcony was expansive and stretched out on both sides, like wings. This space was used for family activities and it often caught a cooling breeze from the jungle. From here, a set of stairs led to the main entrance at ground level.

At the far end of the balcony, three of Dato Nan's granddaughters played a dextrous game of hand-clapping. Dato Nan was lying casually on a mat at the other end, just outside his bedchamber. His gaunt-faced gray-haired massage lady, in sarong and white blouse, was rubbing his feet. She nodded when she saw me. As I approached, stooping my body to show respect, I smelt a mix of coconut oil and herbs.

Dato Nan wore a loose sarong. He was bare-chested and his nipples black. His long white hair was like sand over a small pillow while his white beard and thick eyebrows floated like clouds above the umber timber floors. Deep lines ran through his dark angular face.

"Ah, it's you, Yan," he said when he saw me approach. "Come, come closer. No need to be afraid."

Although Dato Nan was in his sixties, the muscles on his biceps and chest were firm under his dark leathery skin.

"I want you to learn to massage," he said in a voice that echoed deep inside his chest. "No use spending all your time in the kitchen. I'm getting old and my body needs more and more attention."

Then he laughed. It reverberated up in the dusky timber rafters, sending a sparrow fleeing from the balcony rails.

Without warning, his hand flashed up and grabbed the air. He was so fast, I hardly saw its blurring movement.

"Mosquito," he said. "They spread disease and must be killed."

He showed me the striped body of the insect before rubbing the blood off on his sarong. For the first time, I noticed his long, sharp fingernails.

"Now, come here, Yan. You can start by rubbing my neck and shoulders. I've had too many discussions with those troublesome village chiefs today."

I used to massage my father before he died, so I knew the various pressure points. Dato Nan, smelling faintly of vinegar and strongly of clove cigarettes, was a lot older but a lot more muscular than my father. His skin was tough and strangely warm beneath my fingers. He sighed as I pushed my thumbs into the tissues around his neck. I could feel the tension in the knots in his sinews.

As I massaged Dato Nan, I wondered if he was a were-tiger. But mostly I thought about my father, how he died and how unfair it was.

A crow cawed incessantly close by, its lonesome voice shuddering an awful darkness in my head. It sounded like a warning.

✕

One night, not long after I began massaging Dato Nan, I heard a deliberate scratching in the dirt beneath the timber floor of the servants' quarters. I opened my eyes and listened. There was hardly a sound. Even the insects had gone quiet.

There it was again. Something dragging its sharp claws against the earth.

I could hardly breathe.

Then I heard it. A low growl of a large beast.

The thought of the thing stalking just beneath me sent my heart beating like a kompang. But what events were unfolding this awful night?

I heard footsteps now—very slowly—climbing up the wooden steps. The timber creaked. It groaned as if in fear. There was a loud scratching, right against the door.

Then suddenly, silence ...

All was quiet, moment by terrible moment.

This soundlessness went on for so long, I felt like screaming. I dared take a step forward, my club foot rolling on the floorboard. Suddenly, there was a great crash as something heavy slammed against the door. It roared like thunder.

But the door held!

Then it struck again. This time, the door crashed to the ground.

A flash of white leapt in. It stood facing me, its sinewy body occupying almost half of the space in the servants' quarters. I edged away towards the far wall. I wanted to scream but nothing came from my mouth. There should be four other women sleeping here, including Mak Ina.

But I was alone.

An incandescent glow spilled in through the broken door. The tiger's fur gleamed. It was almost white in the moonlight and shimmered like some divine being. The animal's eyes shone as it padded forward. One paw delicately touching the timber floor, followed by the other. It seemed to know exactly what it wanted.

Sweat dripped off my forehead. "What do you want?" I whispered.

Now I could see its orange fur. Its black stripes. The white long whiskers. Its eyeballs, small and black, peering deep into mine.

"Leave me alone, please!"

Then it leapt.

It pushed me backward and toppled my body to the ground. It pawed my bare legs. I tried to crawl away on my back, using my elbows. But it clambered on me. It was heavy and smelt of blood and raw meat. Its teeth were large, sharp and dripping. I thought it was going to tear out my throat.

It growled and with the swipe of its front paws, flipped me around. With several jerking tugs, it tore off my sarong.

I do not want to describe what the tiger then did to me.

But, after several nights of the same nightmare, I had to tell Mak Ina about it.

"You should not have such dreams," she said.

But I did. And the same dream continued.

I began to enjoy the animal's visitations. I looked forward to it. There was always fear. But fear was followed by pleasure. Pleasure I had never known.

Little did I know that these dreams were a prelude to something more for one night, just before we turned in to bed, there was a knock on the door. It was one of the servants that slept with Dato Nan's grandchildren in the main building.

"Dato Nan wants you," she said. "He has back pain and needs a massage."

I yawned and rubbed my eyes.

"Come quickly," she said.

I pulled off the sarong that I used as a blanket and followed her. We went up into the kitchen, then across the bridge and entered the house.

"He's in his bedchamber," she said as we entered the hall which was lit by a single kerosene lamp. Then she disappeared.

I opened the door on my left and entered the reception room.

This was where Dato Nan would sit on a large mat for his meetings with village officials. I knew that a collection of keris and spears hung on the walls, but these were now just shadows. Beyond this reception room was Dato Nan's bedchamber.

I knocked on the door.

"Come in," he answered.

I entered, putting my right hand forward and stooping low.

"Ah, it's you, Yan," he said in a deep voice. "Come over here. My back is sore."

"Yes, Dato Nan."

He was lying on a bed. It was the only bed in the house and was a gift from the British many years ago. He turned onto his stomach as I approached. I knelt on the floor and began to massage his back.

"That's good," he said. He gestured towards the kerosene lamp beside the wooden shutters. "Blow it out. It's too bright."

I did as asked and returned to kneading his back.

Then, he turned over and took my hands in his. His were large and very warm.

"You're mine, Yan," he said. "All mine."

He stared into my eyes, before drawing me to him.

His hands slid beneath my blouse and he caressed my small breasts. Then he undid my sarong and pulled me on the bed.

That night, I knew that Dato Nan and the tiger were one and the same. It was not so different from my dreams.

Fear and pleasure merged and mingled as he changed his form over and over in the deepening shadows.

There was endless cooking in preparation for our wedding. Such events were usually held in the compound outside where mats would be spread for guests attending the dinner.

There were no chickens to slaughter as the Japanese had taken them long ago. Instead, the kitchen staff chopped coriander and galangal, they pounded tamarind, turmeric, garlic and ginger, all for a tapioca curry. The smell of cooking scented the air. As the bride-to-be, I was not among them, even though I had offered several times to help.

That night, to the sound of kompang drums, about a hundred or so villagers, mostly relatives, sat in groups of six around the meager dishes we offered. It was a small affair because the Japanese Occupation turned everyone frugal. For the same reason, there was no traditional cock-fighting contest that day.

As I sat on a timber dais next to Dato Nan, I could not fathom why such a wealthy and powerful person could be bothered with this club-footed, birthmark-faced girl. He could have anyone he wanted in the village. I wondered how many of them knew that he was a were-tiger.

There were rumors about the family, but who knew for sure? Was it only me, or did his other wives know his secret?

Dato Nan's ex-wife resided in the village with her grown-up daughter. As for his two current wives, they and their girls would continue to live in the two sleeping chambers at the other wing of the house.

Dato Nan insisted that I share his bedchamber.

"Now I can be at peace," he whispered to me one night after the wedding. "Now that I have a son, at last, growing in your belly."

I spun around to face him in bed.

"What?" I whispered, staring wide-mouthed.

"I know these things," he chuckled, stroking his beard. His white hair was draped flamboyantly over the pillow. "It's one of the instincts we were-tigers have. The other instinct I had was that you were the right one for me. Ah, to have found you so late in life."

He stroked my long hair and smelt it.

"You know, you're the only one I've appeared to in my true form. I was born a were-tiger. It's something that is passed from eldest son to eldest son. You've been very brave. I knew it that first night when you saw me by the river. You didn't run away. You stayed and watched."

His dark face, etched with deep lines held a knowing smile. In his stern eyes, I saw a kindness I had not seen before. Then he reached under his pillow and pulled something out.

It was my necklace!

"Thank you!" I said.

"I found it hanging on a tree beside the well," he said. "I didn't know who it belonged to. But when you came out looking for it, I knew it was yours. I had already changed form and I was watching you from behind the trees."

"I didn't know that," I whispered. "I've always heard stories of were-tigers. But my mother, she told me they weren't true."

"Well, now you know that we're real, don't you, Yan?"

He scratched his beard and stared up at the beams beneath the roof, as though mesmerized by its structure. "This magic is passed down through the generations. My great-great-grandfather came here from a village in Sumatra. He came on a boat, across the sea, then up the River Setang. He was a were-tiger. But he was not alone; there were many… There was a village deep in the jungle where all were-tigers lived together in human form. But when they stepped out of the village, they would turn into tigers. But my ancestor, for some reason I know nothing of, was forced to flee the village. And so he fled across the water to this land. It was a good thing too. For years later, all those were-tigers were hunted and killed. The jungle was burnt and, with it, our tiger village… My great-great-grandfather could take on human form whenever he wanted. But because he could only mate with humans, this gift, his magic, is only passed from eldest son to eldest son. With no sons of my own, I thought it would end with me and for many years I was happy. This gift is in so many ways a curse. I've tried so many nights not to succumb to the instinct deep within me, but the desire to stalk and kill is so strong. I cannot resist it! So for many years, I was content, knowing that this curse would not be passed. But then, as time went by, as my body grew old, I realized that what a loss it would be not to have were-tigers in this world. And that is why I asked Mak Ina to get you."

"What?" I blurted. "Me? You mean Mak Ina knew all along?"

"Yes, she did. She told me about your family. She told me about you. You know, my father had a club foot too. So I just knew that you would give me a boy."

"How? How could you know that?"

"I just knew, but it's so much more than that, Yan. Your family is from the same tiger village my great-great-grandfather came from in Sumatra. The magic is strong in us. Your family was descended from were-tigers too but the magic was never passed on because your grandfather didn't have sons. Now, finally, we can start our tiger village again!"

Somewhere in the building a gecko called out.

"Ah, there," he said. "The cicak agrees."

He then turned over, rocking the bed, and was soon snoring.

A night bird wailed from far away but, for me, sleep would not come.

Three months after our wedding, I heard shouting and a loud commotion outside. I leapt from the mat in the dining area and rushed out to the balcony.

Three villagers were carrying Dato Nan towards the house.

"Open the door!" I shouted.

A servant rushed down the steps and pushed open the front door at ground level. The villagers hauled my husband up the steps and onto the balcony.

Blood dripped from his body.

"Put him over there," I ordered. "Be gentle!"

I ordered the servants to bring water and towels. By this time the rest of the family, including his other two wives, had congregated around Dato Nan.

His body was splayed outside our bedchamber, at almost the same place where I had first massaged him. There was a gaping wound in his chest. His wives, including myself, tried to give him comfort, fanning him and wiping his forehead. He drank water, then coughed it out. His breathing was ragged, his beard shuddering as his body shook.

I held his hand and it trembled in mine. I knew then that I truly loved this man even though I had been manipulated, even though he was older than my father. For doesn't love transcend all things?

I looked into my husband's eyes. They blinked and were filled with despair. We bandaged his wounds but could not stop the blood from flowing. It spilled on the floorboards and trickled down a gap between them, falling far down to the earth below.

"Take care of our son," he whispered to me. His eyes were watery and pleading.

"Yes, of course," I said, and caressed his limp hand.

I stared up at the rafters, feeling terribly helpless.

Then my husband closed his eyes and I thought I heard a quiet growl.

Not long afterwards, he was dead.

He had been out hunting the night before and had stumbled upon a camp of Japanese soldiers. They had heard the stories about tigers in the area and had come in search of trophies. One of the guards had fired his machine gun in the dark. Two bullets struck my husband in the chest. He had spent the rest of the night trying to get back home.

The day after his funeral, on an early Thursday morning, I stood in the kitchen and stared at the dirt compound. The well, frangipani trees, the orchard beyond were covered in heavy mist.

"How are you, child?" said Mak Ina as she boiled some water in a dented old pot.

"I'm fine," I said. "It's Allah's will."

"Yes, it is, Yan. They'll find you a house in the village for the whole family. Dato Nan's brother will move in here."

"I know," I said. "That's how these things work."

"They say the Japanese will surrender soon. A huge bomb exploded in their homeland."

"I hope so. We need peace. All of us. I think I'll go for a walk now. Down to the river."

"Why there?"

"I like to see the water flow. Always moving. To some other place. To some other time."

Mak Ina stared curiously at me and then sighed.

I brushed against the gnarled branches of the frangipani trees as I drifted past the well. I glanced back at the long, umber-colored house. The wooden shutters seemed to shy away from my gaze.

Then I followed the track behind the orchard. It wended its way beneath the jungle trees, beside the gushing stream. It may have been saying a thousand things, but I heard none of it. The rocks that looked like large eggs in the moonlight, now resembled blood-covered fists or even giant bullets.

Insect calls led me on even as the sun glinted from behind the tumultuous foliage. There was a rustling in the branches. Monkeys perhaps. But I did not stay to look at them. Eventually, I found myself where the stream spilled into the wide River Setang. It was wreathed in thick drifting mist.

It was here that my husband's ancestor had killed his cousin-in-law over the succession of territorial chief. The bathing hut made of palm leaves was long gone but I guessed it was located somewhere along the shore I was now passing, which was filled with wild grasses and several hovering dragonflies. A small boat was pulled up on the bank but there was no one around.

I sat on a rickety timber jetty, my feet dangling over the muddy waters. The timber was cool and coarse beneath my soft sarong.

I placed a hand firmly on my belly. It had grown but was not huge yet. I felt the stirrings of my son in the amniotic fluid. I felt what must have been his elbows pushing slowly, rhythmically against my stomach.

My son, who would one day be a were-tiger.

As I too was descended from them, all my son's offspring would be were-tigers. This was my husband's wish. He wanted a tiger village again, perhaps somewhere hidden deep in the jungle.

What did he say?

What a loss it would be not to have were-tigers in this world.

I wiped away my perspiration with my sleeve, drew back my long hair and stared at the insects darting above the fast-flowing waters. A kingfisher swooped through the air and picked up a small fish. Then it was gone. Perhaps I had only imagined it. Like the trees, the river, the wild grasses before me that were so misty-veiled.

What were were-tigers? Humans who turned into tigers? Or tigers who turned into humans? I didn't know. I didn't care. All I knew was that tigers ate animals and often humans too.

That was how my father died.

I was twelve and sick with fever and he had ventured out to the jungle that evening to gather camphor needed for medicine. He had collected some but needed more. He had almost reached the waterfall when the tiger attacked. They only found his severed head. It was nestled above, stuck in the aerial roots of a ficus tree.

Did the man-eating beast play with my father's head as though it were some kind of ball?

In my child's mind, I had vowed I would find the tiger and kill it, this animal that had stolen my father from me. It was a vow I had never forgotten.

What a loss it would be not to have were-tigers in this world.

Would it be such a loss?

Disfigured shadows now hid in the mist. Were they the ghosts of were-tigers emerging? My lips trembled. I watched my bare feet swaying beneath me.

Forward. Backward.

Was that a drop of rain or a teardrop?

Forward. Backward.

They had no right to exist.

Not now. Not ever ...

My feet seemed too tiny.

They were falling into water.

There was a splash and coldness gripped my body.

Bubbles shot to the surface. Except for my sarong drifting like a net, all was cloudy before my eyes.

But my mind was clear.

There will be no more were-tigers in this world.

Not a single one.

I opened my mouth and drank the river.

Drank life from my body.

My husband's ancestor had sailed up this river. Together with my unborn son, we now floated down it.

Away forever.

Friday:
Midnight

THE ONCE-GORGEOUS WOMAN waited, staring through the verandah doors at the lawn, its neatly trimmed shrubs and the early moon, rising in the still-bright sky.

She barely said a word to the maid, to her girls, aged four and five, when they came home from kindergarten. Barely able to attend to the baby. *It just couldn't be true ...*

The late afternoon sun slanted upon her yellow dress, her shoulder-length hair, her roundish face, the almond-shaped eyes. But perhaps her dress was light blue ... *for memories are never certain.*

Frowning, she called the office but it went unanswered. The old clock in its dark timber casing pointed to 6. She never liked the boxy thing, its ever-moving pendulum, its noisy chimes but when they had come across it at an antique shop, he insisted on buying it.

She sat on the rattan sofa mending the girls' blouses while the sky turned purple over the town. Soon, tormented insect voices crept in through the open windows. The breadman hooted on his overloaded bicycle, his urgent calls fleeing like a wailing child into the distance.

She asked the maid to turn on the house lights. The maid was a lithe, long-haired girl of twenty whose immunization scar on her left arm was big and brutal. She did her job well enough but in a surly manner and was always dabbing her forehead with a pink handkerchief as though she'd been worked too hard.

Once the maid had gone to put the girls to bed, the once-gorgeous woman got up to look at herself in the mirror. She winced at her reflection. There were too many wrinkles for someone of thirty-four and her lipstick seemed too dull.

But there was something else.

For behind those eyes were shadows.

Flickering, hidden shadows. A dark mist she'd often seen, no ... *imagined*, surely just imagined, beneath the iris, shades of someone or something else whom she didn't dare meet. She shivered as she'd always done when such thoughts crept into her skull.

How can you be afraid of yourself?

Breathing hard, she quickly turned to the black telephone. With a finger trembling on the rotary dial, she called his office again. Still no answer. Where was he? He always came home early on Fridays. She wasn't going to have dinner until he arrived, even if he'd already eaten.

She stared resentfully at the old clock. It continued ticking in its timber casement, hands circling, pendulum rocking back and forth.

Passing time ... time passing.

Moving on relentlessly, unhindered, while everything else changed in its wake.

She sighed.

Still no sign of him. He usually got back before eight. She wasn't hungry yet. It was almost ten. Where was he?

She wasn't sure whether to be worried or angry.

Ding ... ding ... ding ...

Just as the clock finished its chimes, she heard tires scrunch the bitumen. She stepped outside into the sound of insects.

The Austin rolled casually up the driveway. Her husband hopped out in his crisp white office shirt, his new tie loosened, a briefcase swaying in his hand. The car door thudded behind him. Beneath his slicked-back hair, his handsome face smiled.

His lips tightened when he saw her.

They stood, the two of them, beneath the porch light, small moths flitting about their frowning faces as if daring them.

Daring them to do what though, on that warm breezeless night?

"Hello, where are the girls?" he said.

"Already in bed."

"That's early."

"It's past ten."

"Oh, I didn't realize the time."

He bent over and kissed her cheek. She stiffened.

"What's wrong, darling?"

"Where were you tonight?"

"A meeting. We were discussing the government tender."

"You're lying. Where have you been?"

He ignored her and swaggered past the metal accordion grilles, into the bungalow.

She followed his footsteps through the lounge and into the bedroom. His aftershave smelled too strong for this late hour.

"Where were you tonight?"

"A meeting. As I said."

He dropped his briefcase, undid his tie and draped it on the dressing table beside her wooden hairbrush. He slid off his watch and nestled it into his neat drawer, beside his cufflinks, handkerchiefs and comb.

"Don't you believe me?"

"I got a phone call this afternoon. A friend told me all about it. About *her*."

"Which friend?" He turned to face her, his jaws stiffening. "I don't know what you're taking about."

"So, who've you been seeing? Tell me the truth."

"No one. Don't listen to silly gossip."

"Tell me what's going on. Are you having an affair?"

"Oh, don't believe such nonsense!"

He shook his head and strode into the bathroom. The lock slid roughly into place. The sound of the shower echoed.

He came out later, a towel around his waist, a smaller one flopped around his shoulders. He raised his eyebrows, surprised that she was still outside the bathroom waiting for him.

He spun away from her towards the wardrobe, drying his hair with the towel. Drops of water splattered on the timber floor.

"Don't you dare turn your back on me," she snarled.

And so the couple raised their voices, like knives cutting flesh. It reverberated up to the ceiling and sliced through the house.

"What's wrong, Mummy? Daddy?"

Two girls stood at the bedroom door in their white nighties. Their faces gripped with worry. Hair falling dismally to their shoulders. A teddy bear dangled from their younger daughter's arm like a hangman's noose.

"Why are you two shouting?" the older girl said, a book of fairy tales cradled in one hand. "Please, please stop …"

"Everything's fine, my darlings …"

She shooed them back to their bedroom. *They must not see this.*

She gave the maid instructions. Told her to take care of the baby when he woke up for his midnight feed. She folded the girls' blouses which she had been mending and went back to the bedroom.

He was brushing his teeth, pretending the altercation had not occurred. Her mind in a haze, she got changed for bed as if everything was fine. But nothing was fine.

Neither saying a word, they got into bed as usual.

With the lights off, the silence between them began to shudder and shriek in her head, blotting out the rattling ceiling fan, the insects outside and his heavy breathing.

She knew he wasn't asleep. Knew it was all pretence. Was it just like their marriage of seven years?

"Who ... have you got ...?" she whispered. "Who are you seeing?"

Somewhere, in a hidden corner of her brain she hoped he wouldn't answer. Hoped that he was asleep and all this would go away. The morning would bring another day, a new clarity ... and they could perhaps start afresh.

For a moment, there was silence.

Then he grunted: "No one. No one at all."

So there it was: *the lie again*.

"Tell me the bloody truth!"

The bed groaned like a too-heavy coffin as they turned to face each other.

Two ill-formed silhouettes in the dark.

"I'm telling you the truth. I'm not having an affair. So stop asking."

"Don't lie to me ..."

"It's late. Go to sleep."

That could have been the end of it. She could have lived with his unsatisfactory answers, his denials and always have that doubt in the back of her mind. His infidelities. His unfaithfulness. Some wives accept it.

But she did not.

When she was nine, the once-gorgeous woman had sold cakes on the street where Japanese boots stomped, where decapitated heads were displayed on poles. She had endured her narrow-eyed, skinny mother who caned her legs and regularly locked her for hours in the bathroom to get the demon out of her. Yes, her half-crazy mother, whose wrinkles trembled as though earthquake struck whenever she spoke, believed in such things. In creeping creatures that stalked the night, that killed babies and ate small animals.

"You know you're not my child, don't you?" her mother often raved as she brushed her gray hair in her tight shorts and loose blouse. "That's right. Yeah, yeah, it's a big shock to you, isn't it?"

No, it wasn't, for her mother had told her this demented tale countless times.

"We were wondering why all those crows were sitting in the trees making an awful noise. So that's how we found you beside the railway track by the squatter houses. What an accursed day! Yeah, yeah, you were using the soil from the ground to clean your mouth. Rubbing it like chocolate all over your face. Why were you doing that, huh?"

"I don't want to hear this rubbish again!"

"Oh no, it's not rubbish. It's all true. Ah yes, beside you was that dog. A black one whose jaws hung wide open and its pink tongue hanging out to dry in the sun. Yeah, yeah, its belly torn open. Flies buzzing all around. The intestines all flopped out. Some already eaten. Blood everywhere, leaching into the ground."

"Please, I don't want to know ..."

"But your father, what a weak man he was. He said we needed to take care of you. You were only four or five and from the rags on your back, he knew you were a homeless orphan. And now that he's long dead, I have to raise you on my own. Yeah, yeah, a thankless task! So go out now and sell more cakes. I hope the Japanese soldiers rape and kill you!"

Her insane mother and her filthy lies!

That woman wasn't even her mother, if the story was true. But how ridiculous it was. One day her mother went out to buy cigarettes and never returned. Maybe the Japanese had raped and killed *her*. Or taken her for a conspirator and skewered her head on top of a pole somewhere, displaying for the masses to gawk at. This raving woman would never tell her mad stories again.

Nor did she have to accept her husband's lies either. She didn't have to accept anything.

She switched on the bedside light. It pierced her eyes. She stared hard at him.

"Tell me the truth!"

She grabbed his arm and refused to let go. She felt his muscles, the rough hairs on it.

"Tell me the bloody truth!"

She may have struck his head then ... but it was a detail that never came to mind. In the recounting of the story over the next thirty years, she would say he had beaten her up.

It is this incident that would mar the rest of her life, it would desolate her, define the bitter person she would turn out to be. It would haunt her until, in the end, it was only the disease that slowly wastes away memories that could steal it from her.

Perhaps mercifully.

"Tell me the truth! What kind of whore are you seeing!"

"No one! No one at all!"

She sprang up and darted to the window. It was late. A breeze like a still-warm corpse caressed her face. There were no lights on, other than the street lamp glowing upon the trees in front of the government bungalows across the road.

In sarong and pajama top, her husband sat cross-legged in bed staring at the tangled sheets. His hair fell over his forehead. He lit a cigarette and puffed on it. The walls of the bedroom swayed and hummed. She stumbled to the bathroom, hardly feeling the floor beneath her bare feet.

Blood pounded her head.

She sat on the toilet, thinking about what to do, what to say. The incandescent glow of the lightbulb throbbed in her eyes.

Then he came in. His shadow like a guillotine hung over her.

He raised a hand.

She drew in a breath.

His palm, like her raving mother's cane, struck her across the cheek.

Yes, it certainly did ...

But it may or may not have happened. Yet it was the truth to her. And it would endure through time, for memories are never certain. Our memories, no matter how fictitious, become our own truths.

Our own realities.

For a long moment, she just sat there trembling, staring at the wretched face of her husband. Only after he had left did hot tears flow.

Then, slowly, she staggered back up. She washed her face and dried it with a towel.

Her head was clear. There was a slow pulsing, a strange heat—or was it horrible coldness?—growing in her stomach. Her breath deepened, drawing up a strange swirling energy. It felt like someone else, or *something* else, was breathing.

When she stepped back into the bedroom, he was there, standing beside the bed, eyes on her, leaning awkwardly against the wardrobe.

"How dare you hit me!" she screamed.

She clawed at his face. He grabbed her arm and wrestled her to the bed.

Still she struck at him. At his shoulders. At his ears. "You bloody bastard!" she cried.

He yelled something incomprehensible.

It included the word *love*.

What about love? It can go to hell!

She kicked out and flailed her arms. She felt a nail scratch his cheek.

Then something fell and crushed her face. It turned hard, as he pushed it down hard.

The pillow ...

... it covered her mouth.

She couldn't see.

He was telling her to shut up.

She yelled for her girls to help her. It came out muffled.

Where are you? Where are you, my girls?

Still he pressed.

Help me ...

Her mouth was blocked. She couldn't breathe.

She pushed the pillow, but he held it down.

Just as she thought she was going to die, the pressure eased and fresh air filled her lungs.

Just breathe now.

In ... out.

In ... out.

Nothing else matters.

Just breathe.

She lay there in a broken silence.

Body shaking. Weeping and weeping.

When she finally managed to pull herself out of the tangled bed, she realized he had fled the house.

But did that really happen?

For as he pushed the pillow into her mouth, she felt IT ...

A burning vibration down below. Right in the coils of her stomach. Something she'd felt before, long, long ago ... further than memory could go.

It was fiery, a new consciousness ... old, angry, *hungry*. She could barely contain it. Then a heaving heat raged into her head and spiraled into her limbs. It tore through her like wild flames.

Her body shook violently. Then it stopped.

"What the—" he cried.

She only had to touch the pillow and it flew from her face. And there he was, kneeling on the bed before her. Except his face was pale and quivering. She hardly recognized him.

He was mouthing things she couldn't hear. Or couldn't understand. She didn't know which.

Then in his eyes she glimpsed it. Her own reflection. Small and dim but, yes, it was there.

Something she'd often seen in her own eyes. Shadows within the iris. A foulness that almost made her gasp.

But then why was she smiling?

Ah yes, her unfaithful husband, of course. The one who tried to suffocate her to death. The one whose tears slid down his cheeks and who was babbling stupidly ...

She raised a hand up high. Just like he had before he slapped her on the toilet seat. Except it was not her hand. It was covered in black scales. From long tapering fingers sprang sharp, ebony claws.

With a whistling swipe, the flesh tore off his once-handsome face. Blood speckled the walls.

Before he could finish screaming, she raked her other hand into his belly. It tore his pajamas and the warm flesh waiting within. Glistening intestines spilled out over the bed, tumbling out in spongy coils. Blood soaked the sheets.

His head fell back.

Followed by his body, over the bed. She heard his skull crack.

He was screaming no more.

Then she heard a sound.

She leapt over him.

Outside the bedroom, she found the snooping young maid. In a single movement, she grabbed her throat and smashed her skull on the wall. She had always wanted to do that. The once-surly maid and her immunization scar slowly slid down, raggedly like a discarded puppet.

Then the creature tore open the stomach and hungrily devoured warm, succulent intestine. Yes, it was well past dinner time but it had been worth the wait.

She glided past the hall mirror, not daring to look. For what had been hiding in her eyes had now transformed the obedient, once-gorgeous wife. Turned her into an unspeakable thing.

Just as it was about to push open the front door, that old clock began to chime.

Ding ... ding ... ding ...

Midnight.

The witching hour.

When things go bump in the night. When all good girls should be asleep. Ah of course, they were crying in the bedroom. The baby too. Must be feeding time.

She chuckled, stepped into the garden, ambled down the driveway and disappeared into the warm, starless night.

Or maybe she didn't.

For memories, no matter how unreliable, become our own truths. Our own realities.

Perhaps she then pivoted around and padded, grinning all the while, into their bedroom. The two girls would wail no more as the door was flung open and stomachs torn apart, their intestines flopping like fat worms from their guts. Oh yes, she would truly feast again. Perhaps on the baby too?

Or maybe, just maybe ...

She never left that matrimonial bed that night. Never raked her husband's handsome face or clawed out his stomach. It was her husband who fled the house cursing, driving off in his car, never to return. Leaving her curling and weeping beneath a pillow.

Leaving her to her stories and broken memories to tell anyone who would listen. Leaving her divorced and desolated, a once-gorgeous woman, bitter and haunted for life. Her grown-up children, two girls and a boy, would abandon her as soon as they could. What then but a life of misery and only dementia waiting with open arms? Mr. Alzheimer, her lover and only friend.

Except for the nurse, on a late shift, who spoon-feeds her medicine, drool ever-slipping down the old woman's trembling chin.

That surly nurse, who sits there with one eye on a television show, the other on an old clock and its ever-moving pendulum. The nurse in a neat white uniform and her wondrously warm intestines waiting within.

It is, after all, just gone midnight. And the chiming, ah ... it begins.

JURIAH'S SONG

INTRODUCTION

ONCE UPON A TIME, a long time ago in a galaxy far, far away—well, not really, only a few years back in the crawl of another Kuala Lumpur traffic jam—a friend and I decided to escape the city. Just two guys off on a weekend out on the road. We decided to be adventurous. In this predictable world of so many routines we wanted to be unplanned and see where we'd end up. The expressways would be our driver. But when it rained heavily that afternoon, turning the city into a swimming pool and blocking our exit, we had no alternative but to head south.

Our route led us to Seremban. Was that it? To us, this didn't seem particularly adventurous. Although it was past six in the evening, we needed to move on. So we turned off to Port Dickson. We arrived at nightfall only to find all the hotels, from the rumah tumpangan to the five-star resorts, full. Perhaps being unplanned wasn't such a good idea!

Never mind, we would have better luck in Melaka. So we took the old dark winding road past the small kampungs, with the occasional goats suddenly appearing like ghosts in front of the car. Arriving at the historical city, we were dismayed to find its hotels again fully booked. Our dear neighbors, the Singaporeans, had packed the city. Why? It was a Labor Day weekend. We spent the night restlessly in the car beside the river, a stone's throw from the red Dutch building, the Stadthuys. Later, I wrote a short story based on that experience.

On our second night, much to our relief, we checked into a hotel. Ah, the joys of air conditioning! There was a band playing in the lounge that evening. They were good. The singer was tall, skinny and garbed in black. I requested the Bob Marley song, "I Shot the Sheriff." By sheer coincidence, that number was in the band's old repertoire and so they did it magnificently. During the break, the band members joined us for drinks. When the lead singer found out I was an author, he seemed genuinely interested in my dark tales. I flippantly said that I might write one about a rock band. He suggested a tale about a haunted guitar. I thought that was a good idea. But a more tantalizing fancy came to me a few days later. I would write a story about him. I gave him the name Akri. I found him a past and a future. I dragged his loyal band members into the tale. This was the start of *Juriah's Song*.

But a story, particularly a novel or a novella, has many fathers and mothers. Another good friend once told me about his own unsettling experience. One night, as a student in London, he awoke with a start. He realized something dreadful had entered his room. I won't spoil it for you by revealing what happened next. That wasn't the end of it. A few years later, this thing visited him again at his home, one of those old and long shophouses in Melaka. Evil doesn't restrict itself to the dark hours, for this happened one early morning. My friend, despite his all-consuming fear, could hear his nephews' footsteps in the courtyard, leaving for school. I have no reason to disbelieve him.

I had always wanted to write about his ghastly experience. *Juriah's Song* was the perfect place for it to happen. Coincidentally, both key events influencing this book are linked to Melaka. I've been told that there are lots of awful spooks in that historical city. Spirits roaming free. Who can doubt it after the thousands who have died there through the centuries, attacking and defending the city founded by Paramesvara?

At just under twenty thousand words, *Juriah's Song* is not quite long enough to be a novel. Or short enough to be a short story either. So it falls into that no man's land called the novella. A strange 'in-between' place. Some sort of a twilight zone. Neither here nor there. Neither friend nor foe. Neither dead nor alive. That 'in-between' place can be a strange, perhaps uncomfortable, location.

Someone once called *Juriah's Song* a "horror love story." That surprised me as I never thought about the novella in that manner but when I re-read the narrative, I realized she was right. Love features strongly. I had not set out to write a horror love story. It just turned out that way.

It's hard to know where a story is going once you start. New forces, new ideas, new characters are born and sometimes even try to take over. Writing is always an adventure. Like two fools hitting the road with no plan, you never know where it's going to take you. You never know which part of your inner self will rise to the surface. There's no mistaking it though. Your inner self, some part of you that's been buried for years, will rise. Like love, I suppose. The words forming on screen or paper are the catalyst for your subconscious thoughts to spring out. It doesn't matter whether it's genre, literary or mainstream fiction. This does happen.

I've written two other long works. These are my novels *Dark Demon Rising* and *Vermillion Eye*. In *Dark Demon Rising*, the main character's father is a bomoh and the question is: will he follow in his father's magical and mysterious path in the village? And if he does, what are the horrific consequences? In *Vermillion Eye*, a simple spell goes terribly wrong and the bomoh unknowingly unleashes a powerful shaman's wrath followed by a terrible curse.

Evil, in its many ghastly forms, flourishes in Australia decades later. Both novels involve a bomoh.

You'll also encounter a shaman in the pages of *Juriah's Song*. This time the shaman is female. Coming from the kampung, she overindulges in the delicacies offered at five-star hotel buffets. More vitally to our rock star, she has a deep and painful secret to reveal.

So that's three long works for me and three bomohs. Could that mean anything? Perhaps not. The writings just turned out that way. I don't think I've got to lie on a psychiatrist's couch and reveal my inner need to write about bomohs. Or as Bob Dylan says, "I've already confessed, no need to confess again."

Yet, the shaman—the traditional healer, the medicine man, the village shaman, the pawang—they have been a vital part of kampung life for centuries. So maybe it's only natural for a Malaysian writer like myself to write about them. Anyone who seeks the extraordinary from the ordinary, the spiritual from the material, the meaning from the humdrum, will be interested in shamans. As for me, maybe I'm just bomoh-obsessed!

Juriah's Song was previously included in my short-story collection *The Woman Who Grew Horns and Other Works*. As Benjamin Disraeli once said: "An author who speaks about his own books is almost like a mother who talks about her own children," so I'm proud of this particular child but I don't want to brag. Let me know if I do!

Juriah's Song is a quick read. If it's a Labor Day weekend, be sure to make your hotel booking. Otherwise, who knows, you might have your own story to tell!

I hope you enjoy *Juriah's Song*. And stay safe always.

TUNKU HALIM

1

AKRI sat on a log. Sand between his toes.

He wore a pair of Raybans which hid a scar under one eye. Through these black tints, the sea crashed like hideous mouth-foaming stallions. So it was with life—what was wondrous became woeful. What was right became wrong.

With leather trousers rolled up at the ankles and new Nikes perched on the log, a gleaming Gibson guitar lay poised on one thigh, the wood cradling an image of the sunrise. His thumb swiveled beneath its neck and his fingers flew around the metal strings as he strummed chords in quick succession, his voice leaping through the balmy air.

The song had showered him with success. He still couldn't believe that he'd only recorded it six months ago and when his debut album, *Eyes Dancing*, was released it became the all-time top-selling album by a local artist. His record company now pestered him for a CD in English to launch his career internationally. But Akri wasn't so sure.

He would rather hang himself than come up with such a song again. Within a few short months of the release of the album, everyone wanted to know him. He was invited to the grandest parties at the poshest hotels, the VVIPs shook his hand and his fans queued for hours to greet him at shopping malls. He was the pride of the country. In two days, he would be at the stadium playing at his largest concert yet and it had been sold out weeks ago. So why was he not rehearsing but instead sitting here on a log playing a guitar to the running crabs and scattered shells?

Black clouds swallowed the sunrise and now swelled over the coconut trees. He thought of ducking into his new Alfa Romeo which he had just driven through the night. But despite the coming storm and the waves wetting his feet, Akri strummed another opening and bellowed out the first line of a song long written but unrecorded called "Space and Time". How could he play it to anyone but sea and sky?

A drop of water splashed on his nose. Lightning flashed. The leaves of the coconut trees swayed. Yet he sang on.

The lyrics were obscure. To the uninitiated they could have been about anything, but to Akri it was about her. It happened ten years ago, when he was seventeen.

Juriah.

She had happened …

And nothing could ever be the same.

2

JURIAH'S PARENTS objected to their sixteen-year-old daughter seeing a youth with no prospects. Yet Akri and Juriah continued seeing each other in secret, embracing in shopping centers and her father's luxury four-wheel drive. They realized that these fleeting trysts were a prelude to something beyond themselves. And so Juriah, the more plucky of the two, invited him to her bedroom. "Come back to my place tonight," she said.

Akri didn't want to. He didn't dare. Her parents were in the house, sleeping only two rooms away, yet Juriah wanted him there.

"Okay," he said, but inside he quivered.

So when his Casio watch finally flashed two a.m., Akri left his brother's Proton beside some shophouses at the top of the road. He drifted down the slope toward her like a meteor being drawn by gravity with no will of his own. He yearned to be with Juriah but what if he was caught?

There were houses on one side of the road and on the other side stood a high concrete wall where a new condominium block towered, making Akri feel as small and insignificant as an ant. He scurried by an old banyan tree with its swarm of roots dropping from the air like the tentacles of a monster. He slid past a battered graffiti-covered telephone booth. The shadows and bushes beside the monsoon drain cloaked him as he surveyed the houses. When he reached Juriah's house he paused for breath. When he was sure it was safe, he crossed the road and opened the gate.

In shorts and T-shirt, Juriah sat hidden on the front doorstep beside her father's four-wheel drive and the smaller car her mother drove. With a gleeful smile, she waved him in.

He managed a grin as he crept beneath the porch. Taking off his tattered Bata shoes, he entered the house.

She got up and silently closed the door.

In the glow of the streetlight streaming in through a window, her warm eyes, small nose and curving lips gave her the semblance of the perfect Malay lady, the attentive hostess at her husband's Hari Raya open houses in the years ahead. A wife who would support her spouse in all matters. A friend, neighbor and relative who would seek consensus beyond all else. Yet this façade was broken not only by her unconventional straight hair which grew to her waist, but her refusal to use a handbag in whatever shape or color, and also a shattering smile, one full of joy and recklessness, which Akri knew was reserved only for him. For a moment, he forgot all fears.

"Come on," she whispered and floated up the stairs.

He followed.

Juriah waited on the first floor, eyes sparkling.

She nodded toward the closest room and whispered, "My parents' bedroom."

Akri froze. What if the door suddenly opened? What if her father or mother, hearing voices, came out? He hated her for being so daring.

She slid into her bedroom. Once they were inside, Juriah closed the door and turned to him.

Their lips merged in a warm, warm sea. In that moment, as he swam its unchartered depths, all fears and worries were swept away by its turquoise waters.

After the hurried kisses and caresses in shopping complexes emblazoned with neon-lit McDonald's, KFCs, MPHs, Guardian Pharmacies or in her father's leather-seated oversized vehicle with its clutchless gearshift and windscreen covered in club badges, this was the first time they could fully give themselves to each other.

Akri pulled off her T-shirt, fumbled with her bra and kissed her breasts. Then he tugged his shirt and trousers off. She undid her clips and her hair fell over her shoulders. Their lips and bodies met. Skin on skin. Bodies on fire.

"Only when we're married," Juriah whispered as they caressed, as they lay warmly entangled within the sheets.

Akri turned from her and stared at the ceiling layered in shadows. Making love wasn't important. Her very presence breathed life into him.

She placed her head against his chest and Akri was surprised to hear an almost inaudible sigh. Juriah tried to hide many things but she couldn't always conceal her feelings—yet exactly what they were, he couldn't guess. But when she sang to him, which she often did as they wandered the shopping malls holding each other, he was sure she loved him as much as he did her. Her voice, although soft and tentative, burnt with passion like the flame of a candle that could light up a city. "I only sing for you," she once told him and Akri didn't doubt it. Sometimes when Juriah couldn't see him, he got through his day imagining her hands clutching his and singing and so his loneliness, his tireless yearning would end. Now, as he embraced her, he knew he had everything he could ever want.

The window hung open and the night dripped its warm stickiness against their naked bodies. A motorcycle sped by. A gecko's shrill echoed around the room. For a forlorn instant, the odor of incense drifted by only to be replaced by Juriah's familiar perfume which reminded him of the smell of rain in the morning and steam rising from the road and coconut leaves glistening fresh as if the world had just been born.

He wanted to marry her. He would wait if he had to—if it would take forever, let it be so. He didn't ask for much in life. A steady job. A good secondhand car. A modest house. Perhaps three or four children. And, of course, Juriah.

He turned to her nakedness. She gazed at him, her hair tangled down one smooth cheek toward her parted lips.

"What about your parents, Juriah?"

For a second, her eyes clouded over, then a smile rose like the sun upon her face and it seemed that no worry or mournful refrain could touch this girl.

"You're a good-for-nothing," she said with a giggle. "That's what abah calls you—a good-for-nothing. I'm his only child. He wants the best for me. He hopes I'll marry some rich guy with a degree in business or accounting or something. Maybe a Datuk or Tan Sri's son. We'll live in a big house with a Mercedes and a Lexus. We'll holiday in Europe every year. You see, he only has my future in mind. But I want you. You, you, you, my good-for-nothing."

She slid one smooth leg between his thighs.

"Juriah," he whispered.

He pulled her to him, his lips finding hers and again came the currents of a hot swirling sea. He ploughed through its misty depths and if his heart had been broken a thousand times, here it was mended and renewed a million times over. He dived headlong into the turmoil of passion. A bright light, like an exploding sun, tore through his head.

And everything was Juriah.

3

AKRI SANG ON THE BEACH with waves lapping his shins. The sky swelled darkly like a giant prowling octopus and the leaves of the coconut trees swayed in the dance. As Akri strummed the last chord, the clouds burst open. A million minute explosions hit the sand. With rain lashing his face, Akri ran toward the empty fruit stall across the track.

He stood beneath the shelter of the zinc roof in his soaked clothes, with his wet guitar, watching the downpour. He could see the gray shadow of his car in the distance. There was no hope of getting to it now. The rain fell on the sea, the beach, the kampung houses. It drummed a staccato on the roof.

Oh Juriah.

How his heart ached for her.

He recalled the first time he went to her house. It was in the daytime, on a bright civilized Sunday afternoon. Overwhelmed by the size of the dwelling and its many fine ornaments and religious plaques in gold frames, he had sipped tea and politely forked at the pandan cake. He told her parents how he admired a particular vase, one which bloomed pink carnations on white china, sitting prettily, almost priggishly, on a hexagonal mahogany stand by the staircase. Her plump mother, with large plastic spectacles and a scarf of leopards and tigers which covered half her hair, told him with a big smile that it was a Wedgwood and very mahal.

Juriah sat beaming at the other end of the coffee-table, occasionally slipping between the kitchen and the Balinese chair from Janine's with more tea, cakes and cream biscuits from Marks & Spencer. Her mother teased her for fussing so much.

Juriah's father sat poised in a leather single seater and moved his shoulder from side to side as though he had a neck ache. A dark muscular man in a T-shirt and purple sarong, he spoke in a deep voice about the ministers and senior servants who were with him at Malay College, all the while smoking a carved wooden pipe which billowed smoke about his dusty hair.

"I went into business," said her father, sipping his tea. As he did so, the sinews in his throat trembled powerfully. "Government contracts, some import-export."

He rattled off the names of three Tan Sri he had close contacts with. He relit his pipe, shook his head and complained about the stock market and exchange rates, all the while stabbing the air with one crooked finger like a claw.

Akri nodded in feigned agreement. Juriah's father was not a man you argued with. He was sure that this businessman could rip him apart with his bare hands.

"And I hate these bloody loafers. Wasting their time in shopping complexes. What are they doing for the country? We should have military service—bring back some discipline. Then we'll have no drug problem."

Akri continued nodding as he tried to keep the Noritake cup from trembling in its saucer.

He knew the shopping complexes only too well. In the cool, bright air, with techno music pumping softly, Akri and friends would wander its tiled corridors and metallic escalators, eyeing the shoppers. That's where they got to know girls. That's where he met Juriah sitting in the food court next to a crowd of schoolgirls in their light-blue tops and white tudungs. His friends egged him on.

He didn't waste time with the usual kissing noises, which when he really thought about it, sounded like a gecko being strangled, but rather just sat next to her and her mee bandung and refused to leave.

"The youth of today are the future of our nation," said Juriah's father, tapping his pipe on a crystal ashtray. He could have been a judge with a gavel or a politician with a truncheon. "What we've produced so far is pure rubbish!"

Akri squirmed in his seat.

Then, as though both of them were part of some big conspiracy, Juriah's father turned his ruddy dark face close to Akri's and asked him what subjects he was taking at college. For a second, Akri said nothing. Then the words came gushing up his throat and between his trembling lips.

"Nothing."

Akri stammered as he told Juriah's father that he had left his school in Klang years ago, that he didn't even do his SPM. That he didn't have a job at the moment.

Before he could fully discern the man's reaction, he found that the fine cutlery and the Queen Anne silver serving dishes were removed and, before he could say that he dropped out from school because of his mother's death from leukemia and that his father had disappeared when he was three, he found himself outside the gate and Juriah rushing up the stairs into the bedroom, crying. The last thing he heard as he scampered up the road was her father shouting:

"Get out of here! Come back and see what I'll do to you!"

The memory was like watching a movie in his head. It allowed him to witness, in a sober, detached manner, that first encounter with Juriah's parents. Perhaps he should have lied then. He could have said he was studying some subject that would help him get a good job. Perhaps Business, Accounting or Law. But Akri was just seventeen then, and he hadn't caught on to an adult's propensity to divulge untruths and to layer his real self in fabricated imagery.

But imagery, no matter how dishonest, no matter how ineptly manufactured by the glossy magazines and newspapers, was everything to him now. The international market was ready for his music and he would crack it in a year or two as his manager had promised.

By now the rain had stopped. The tropical storm, as always, was fierce but short-lived and left a cleansing coolness which Akri breathed in, making him smile. To think that he had swapped such soul-reviving air for KL's pollutants.

Akri left the shelter and turned down the muddy lane. He kept to the side and avoided the puddles, the half-buried plastic wrappers and crushed cans of Fanta and Coke, the mud and slime and chicken shit, as he made his way between the rickety wooden houses with their rusted zinc roofs and thin faded curtains.

He turned a corner. Behind a mountain of cigarettes displayed in a perspex case, hid a stall selling drinks and cakes.

"What will you have?" said the old man with thick black spectacles and white haji skullcap. He squatted majestically on a stool, a cigarette dangling from his lips, his dark toes peeking out from beneath his faded sarong.

"A packet of Kents and a black coffee, no sugar."

The proprietor slotted his gnarled feet into his slippers. He motioned to Akri to sit down as he leisurely got off his perch and attended to the order.

"Thank you, Pak Alif," said Akri when a glass with steaming coffee was slid on the red plastic table.

"I knew it was you," said Pak Alif, a grin brightening his face. "Even with your ponytail and dark glasses." He stuck a toothpick in his mouth and chewed on in before pulling a chair and sitting down. "I wasn't sure if you wanted me to recognize you now that you're a rock star."

"Come on, Pak Alif, it's me, Akri. Did you think I'd change so much?"

"You never know. People from the big city always seem to change for the worse. They get so big-headed with their expensive cars and grand houses. They look down on us here in the kampung."

"I would never do such a thing. After all Pak Mansur taught me everything I know."

At the mention of his late brother's name, Pak Alif's eyes moistened.

"If only he could see you now," he said in a soft voice as he shook his head.

Yes, if only he could see me now.

He first met Pak Mansur in the water ten years ago. When Akri fled KL, he took the first bus out of Pudu Raya and ended up in Mentakab where he languished for a few days before moving on, staying in several small towns and by the time he had reached the village, his money and his will to live had run out.

Just before sunset, with the sky a hazy purple, Akri took off his shoes, trudged through the sand and waded into the pounding sea. His clothes floated around him as the water lashed at his face. Salt burnt his lips and the wind howled around his ears. He closed his eyes and then plunged his head into the salty water. He opened his mouth so death could claim him. His arms and legs seemed to fall away and a shimmering lightness came to his head.

Oh Juriah ...

He thought he saw her shadow fleeting in the waters. Yearned to behold her eyes, eyes that held another world. Of kindness.

Gentleness. And love.

She swam to its depths.

And Akri followed.

Into the darkness.

Away from this heart-breaking world.

Into sweet everlasting darkness.

4

THEN HE PUSHED THE THING ASIDE and opened his eyes.

Juriah's hand fell back over his lips.

"Be quiet," she whispered. "You were muttering in your sleep. My father's awake."

She huddled against her bedside table clutching a large teddy bear over her naked body.

Then he heard it.

Footsteps.

Moving around downstairs.

My shoes!

Her father would surely find them at the entrance.

Akri recalled the tall dark muscular man, smoking his pipe beside him at that fateful tea. The man had hands that could rip him apart.

Get out of here! Come back and see what I'll do to you!

He bolted up in bed. "I've got to go," he whispered to Juriah.

She nodded. Her hands were pressed against her temples. In her nakedness, she looked scared and vulnerable. Perhaps she now realized that this rendezvous was too risky. It tempted fate too much. That glee and cheekiness in her face were gone.

Akri glanced around the room. The grilled-up windows were of no use, his only hope was to rush out the door, surprise Juriah's father, then make a run for it.

He got off the bed almost knocking over her Hello Kitty clock. He edged it back on the bedside table, next to a photograph of her parents in a Snoopy photo frame. Her father stared back, eyes filled with hidden violence. Akri quickly slid into his clothes.

Footsteps thudded up the stairs. In the quiet of the night, they seemed unnaturally hollow and loud, like chickens on a chopping board being beheaded.

Akri tried to take a deep breath but the air just got caught around his lungs. He glanced back at Juriah. She too had scrambled into her clothes.

Akri had trouble breathing.

Something covered his mouth.

He gasped for breath.

He nodded and tried to smile. But it must have come out wrong, for Juriah crossed her arms over her breasts and her face looked all skewered.

Akri placed a hand on the doorknob but couldn't stop its trembling. The sound ...

... it was coming nearer ...

... stomping on the landing.

Slowly and dreadfully they came. Like the footsteps of an executioner. Hanging. Electrocution. Gassing. Lethal injection. It didn't matter what form it would take.

Death was here.

Akri shuddered.

Then his head cleared and he realized that this was only Juriah's father and he surely wouldn't have murder on his mind.

Get out of here! Come back and see what I'll do to you!

Akri tried to push the words out his head.

The footsteps were just outside Juriah's door.

They stopped.

Akri was about to push the door open and run when he saw them.

Two wonderful silhouettes under a calendar, messily strewn beside Juriah's dressing table covered in soft toys.

His shoes! He *had* brought them up with him!

Tattered though they were because they were all he could afford, he suddenly had a great affection for them. So Juriah's father couldn't have found them and instead must have heard some noise and was just checking the house.

Akri almost sighed with relief except he was sure the man, the beast, now stood outside her bedroom.

For a long time silence reigned.

What was her father doing there? Why was he waiting? Was he going to come in?

Akri didn't dare to move. Didn't dare to breathe.

Juriah's father made no sound. Yet Akri could almost feel the beast thinking. He imagined the man breathing a low, rumbling breath, as he pondered going into his daughter's room.

Her father had only to open the door and they would be discovered.

Akri glanced at the doorknob and his eyes widened when he saw his hand still clutching it. What if the thing started turning now? Would he resist?

But the doorknob remained still.

And turned cold.

And a chill seized Akri's heart.

Yet her father still didn't move.

For a long moment, they stood there. Akri and the beast divided by only two layers of plywood.

Then the doorknob began to turn.

5

JUST AS AKRI THOUGHT the ocean would claim him, his neck was grabbed. His head flew out of the sea and he was gasping. Water poured from his mouth as he spluttered and coughed.

He was dragged through the churning water like a log, as though he was already dead.

Amidst the splashes, the shoreline rose in his eyes.

No! No! No!

Juriah was there. Swimming in the water below. That's where he belonged. Not this cruel world.

He tried to struggle. To plunge back into the sea. But he was too weak.

And so he was hauled out of the water, retching and spluttering.

"So you want to die?" said the man as he knelt in the sand panting.

Akri said nothing but instead wept into the crook of his arm. Why had he been saved? Fate was so against him it wouldn't even let him die.

The man with a thin face turned dark by the sun got up. His white mustache bounced toward his hair which was even whiter, like condensed milk poured straight from the tin. He pulled the wet sarong down from across his shoulder and tied it about his waist. He dusted sand from his fisherman's hat, its coconut leaves frayed and torn, and placed it back on his head.

"I'm Pak Mansur," he said. "I was beside the bushes over there with my guitar. I saw you go into the water. Luckily for you I wasn't playing, otherwise you would have found some other spot on the beach to kill yourself."

"Not lucky," Akri said, shaking his head. "Very unlucky. Couldn't you see I wanted to die?"

"Oh, that I could certainly see. Don't worry, your time to die will come. That I can guarantee. But not this evening."

"Why not?"

"Because this evening you will join a lonely old man and his wife for dinner. You can choose to die some other time."

With that Pak Mansur laughed. He offered Akri his hand and pulled the youth from the wet sand.

"That's better, isn't it?" Pak Mansur said, his eyes glimmering with good humor. "Come with me and we'll get some dry clothes on you."

Perhaps Pak Mansur was right. Today was not the time to die. After all, he had little choice in the matter. There would be some other time with no busybody fisherman watching the beach.

Akri followed the old man to some tall wild grasses where the fisherman retrieved an old guitar with one string missing. He struck a chord and sang the chorus of a familiar Malay song.

"Like it?" asked the old man when he had finished.

"Yes," Akri said truthfully.

"Good," said the old man. "So there's no need to die so soon. There'll be many more songs in your life." He slung the guitar over his shoulder. "Okay, time for us to go. Mak Halijah will be getting worried."

Akri's clothes dripped. The sand was still warm and Akri felt his feet sink tiredly into it. Crabs, hundreds of them, scattered in all directions.

Once he glanced back and noticed his footprints in the sand trailing into the distance, then, just as he was about to turn away, a large wave crashed and as the sea swirled around his shins, he saw his footprints had been washed away. One minute they were there and the next they were gone. As if he'd never walked there. As if he never existed.

"Come on, young man," called Pak Mansur. "The sea isn't all that interesting. What are you staring at?"

"Nothing much," said Akri. He turned and hurried after the old man.

By the time Pak Mansur took a route that led away from the beach, night had fallen and insect voices floated like a mist through the darkness. The two men followed a trail through clumps of dune, rocks and wild grasses. These gave way to muddy mangroves and small trees and soon they came upon a modest wooden house on stilts tucked into the side of a hill. From the lighted window came the sound of cooking.

Akri sat quietly on a mat of dried coconut leaves with a plate of rice, sambal and fried fish while Pak Mansur told his wife about how he had rescued the youth. Mak Halijah, in her glasses and a billowing white tudung, said Subhanallah several times while shaking her head. In one corner flickered an old black-and-white television with the volume turned off.

Later as the hour grew late, Mak Halijah showed Akri to a narrow room at the back of the house which was dimly lit by a single lightbulb covered in dust. She unrolled a thin mattress and placed it beside a window, all the while telling him that the room belonged to their teenage daughter, their only child who was not only the prettiest girl in the village but collected stamps and had once won a Quran-reciting contest. She had recently gone to Shah Alam to study Economics.

Mak Halijah struck a match and as the flame lit up her face Akri was surprised to see her eyes were moist. Was it pride or sadness? Akri wasn't sure. Then, as if she realized his eyes were on her, she smiled at him before lighting a mosquito coil and leaving the room with a single draw of the curtain.

It took a long time for Akri to sleep. The whooping sounds from the trees and the endless stream of insect calls kept his thoughts fluttering around his head like a butterfly. He tried to kill himself today. Would he do it again? And why did he choose suicide? Then, without warning, Juriah came leaping from the sea, fists clenched, screaming at him with fire in her eyes and the water boiled with her fury. The image told him everything. She didn't want him dead or alive. Perhaps she had sent Pak Mansur to haul his monkey-arse out of the sea and back on the muggy land where it belonged. But, finally, as the whooping became the sound of waves and the insect voices ceased their cursing, sleep like drifts of sand came over him and buried him in dreams. Not one of which he remembered when the sun peeked through the trees and the cockerels woke him with a start.

After a breakfast of bread and Planta margarine sprinkled with sugar, Pak Mansur asked him to stay to help mend the nets. Akri agreed, after all he was stuck in this heart-wrenching world with nothing to do and nowhere to go. He agreed to stay a few days.

He ended up staying three years.

Other than helping Pak Mansur harvest lemongrass and plant kangkong and onions at the back of the house, he sometimes took to the sea. Here in the salty air with the wind in his face and the chugging and belching of the smoky motor, Akri found a certain calmness, an acceptance of all that had happened.

The work was hot and sweaty but, as he pulled the nets and brought out the catch, he told Pak Mansur that he didn't think he would ever leave.

Pak Mansur shook his head and stared deep into the water. He said that although his was only one of the four fishing boats left in the village, there still wasn't enough fish left in the sea to sustain any kind of life. Then later, as he slit the bellies of two small mackerels and washed out the bits of entrails, he declared that he didn't much like the water anymore. There was an oily taste to it that wasn't there when he was a boy. In those days, the sea supported thirty families with nets bursting with gleaming wide-eyed fish. But now his wife had to help at the songket cooperative to supplement their income.

One day when Pak Mansur decided that the sea was too choppy for fishing, he asked Akri to join him behind the house near the chicken coop. Pak Mansur picked up his guitar, the missing string now replaced, and with three gnarled fingers showed him a C chord. Then he handed the instrument to Akri. Akri sat cross-legged and leaned against the flimsy structure where the chickens were supposed to live but never did, and followed what the old man taught him.

By the end of that afternoon Akri could move between three chords. By the end of the week, the youth from the city was strumming and singing old Malay love songs and, although he did it awkwardly, Pak Mansur beamed with pride. Within a few months, the youth from the city could play almost as well as Pak Mansur. Akri didn't know he had truly mastered the instrument until one day, just before Hari Raya Haji, Pak Mansur called him over and said with a sigh that hung long in the air: "My guitar days are over." He handed his old guitar to his protégé, and left in search of his boat.

6

AKRI JERKED his hand away.

He almost cried out in terror, eyes fixed on the turning doorknob. *Allah! What am I going to do!*

At any moment, the door would be flung open and the beast would be standing there, his mouth opened in a roar. Akri wondered if he would be able to run fast enough. And what would the beast do if it caught him?

Juriah was beside him, trembling while she clutched his body, breathing in panic.

The doorknob horribly creaked as it dreadfully turned.

Then it stopped.

Before snapping back into place!

There was a pause followed by the sound of Juriah's father walking away.

The thumping got softer.

The sound of a door opening. And shutting! The beast had returned to his bedroom.

Akri allowed the breath to spill from his lungs and, slowly, he crumpled to the floor. Juriah came to him and, for a long, long time, they held each other.

Why had her father changed his mind? Akri had no idea. Perhaps it was an answer to his prayer. Or pure luck. It didn't matter why. They hadn't been caught.

It was still dark outside the house. Akri's watch flashed twenty past four. They decided to wait for half an hour and then Akri would leave; by then Juriah's father would surely have fallen asleep.

That was what Akri prayed for as Juriah stole out of the room.

She crept across the dark landing and Akri followed, shoes held safely in one hand. He kept an eye on the door of her parents' room, expecting it to be flung open at any moment, feeling a sense of reprieve with every unmolested step he took. He thought he could hear her father breathing, the air flowing up and down his trembling throat, low and slow as though it belonged to a prowling man-eater, poised for the kill.

Just my stupid imagination, he thought, trying to console himself.

He bit his lip and edged across the parquet floor. It felt unnaturally cold—like the blade of a knife. He made his legs move, taking slow deliberate strides, careful not to make a sound.

He reached the staircase. Juriah glanced back at him, gave him a half-smile, then slipped away—a fleeting shadow that quickly disappeared. Akri followed with one hand tightly gripping the rail. Breathing deeply, he realized that if he tripped and fell it would be a disaster. The noise was bound to wake Juriah's father.

But Akri was careful, taking each long breath and with it each deliberate step, one at a time as he made his way down to the living room. He still remembered vividly the first time he came for tea—the pandan cakes, Juriah's shyness, her proud mother, the arrogant father—but mostly how he was thrown out like a lump of shit. He was almost at the bottom of the stairs and soon he would be back in the Proton and driving home to his brother's house. He felt tension leave his body. He vowed never to do such a recklessly stupid thing again. To think that both of them were almost caught naked!

Juriah glided through the lounge and opened the front door. She turned and, through the window, the streetlight fell on her face and it glowed. The most beautiful person Akri had ever known. A voice, Juriah's mellow singing, soared like an eagle in his heart, up and up it went, gliding on the updrafts toward the billowing clouds and the unrepentant sun. He could easily spend forever with her.

Through space and time.

So melodious were his thoughts that, as he came off the last step, he failed to see his hand stretch from the railing, lifting in triumph.

He failed to notice its awkward reaching motion until it was a couple of inches from the ornament. And that was too late. The mental command from brain to arm took just a split second too long.

And so his fingers brushed against the ornament. How cool it was. Like the flesh of a statue.

That vase.

The white china, circled by ever-so-pretty pink carnations, sitting so priggishly on a mahogany stand. Even in the living room buried in deep unchartered shadows, Akri could see its ceramic whiteness float like a vengeful ghost through the air. Juriah gasped, eyes wide, and perhaps Akri could have leapt to save the thing as it seemed to slowly tumble, spinning and somersaulting, to the floor.

If only he did.

For the crash was like a gunshot.

Porcelain flew everywhere.

"Nooooo!" Juriah cried.

Before Akri could skirt around the pieces of broken porcelain, fumbling to put on his shoes, the lights blazed.

"Who the hell is that?" Came the roar from the top of the stairs. "What are you doing here?"

Juriah's father wore a white singlet and a checkered sarong. With his dark face and disheveled gray hair, he was a man-eating beast in a human body.

He thumped down the stairs, legs splayed wide, muscles taut. Eyes burning.

A strangling twist in his lips.

A long object in his hand.

A parang in a wooden scabbard. Its handle wrapped in plaster as though the thing had suffered a vicious wound.

"Tell me who you are!" the beast barked. And then recognition struck monstrous creases into his forehead. "So it's you. I told you never to come back!"

"I ... I ..." was all Akri could manage.

"Yah ..." Juriah cried, then she turned to Akri, mouth trembling. "Stay with me, Akri. He won't touch you, not if we're together."

"Touch him?" the beast growled. "I'll kill him!"

Akri staggered back. "Please don't," he whispered.

The beast was almost at the bottom of the stairs.

Then suddenly, with a yell, he grasped the handle of the weapon.

Akri ran.

Behind him Juriah cried out for him to stop, but the sound that sang in Akri's ears was the unsheathing, a long high-pitched singing as the blade flew from its scabbard.

The beast roared as he chased Akri out the gate into the street.

Akri ran uphill. And if he had a tail it would have been between his legs. He cursed himself for parking the Proton so far away. But mostly for being a hopeless coward.

The banyan tree conspired with the beast, as it tried with its tentacle-like roots to snare his feet. He leaped over them and as he ran beside the monsoon drain, the concrete wall and the dark condominium above, he glanced back.

The beast wielded the weapon high in the air while his other hand held up his sarong as his bare feet ripped up the road.

The beast screamed, "Stop, you molester!"

Akri knew he couldn't keep up the pace for much longer. Sweat poured down his brow. He was never one for sports, whether football, hockey or the baton shuttle relay, and if he slowed down the beast would be upon him.

As he took the curve in the road, his hopes soared. The silhouette of the shophouses appeared and the shadow of the Proton in the empty carpark under a street lamp was less than two hundred yards away.

Not far to go.

Just have to keep running.

"Come back, anak setan!" the beast roared.

Just as Akri fumbled for the car keys in his pocket, the sound of an engine filled the air.

He glanced back and was blinded by light.

He shielded his face.

But the beast, a raging muscular silhouette, carried on running and grabbed Akri's shirt.

Akri pushed the hand away and stumbled backward.

The blade flashed in the explosion of light.

Akri leaped away, but not before he felt a burning under one eye. He fell on the road clutching his face. Through the mist of pain the headlights hurtled at him.

He screamed.

Followed by an ear-piercing screech as the vehicle swerved. The four-wheel drive ran over a monsoon drain and slammed into the wall with a dreadful crunch.

Akri rose to his knees breathing hard. Blood dripped on his shirt. He pressed a handkerchief to the wound. The ground swayed beneath him.

The vehicle was a wreck. The front section was crushed. One headlight still worked, throwing a misshapen glow like a hideous face on the stonework. One wheel spun uselessly above the drain, a black Ferris Wheel of hurt and anger. There was the nauseating odor of smoke and petrol.

Akri stumbled toward it on shaky legs.

The beast was beside him breathing hard. He dropped the parang. It fell noiselessly on the grass.

"Allah," the beast whispered.

Akri saw the registration number. He had been in the four-wheel drive countless times with Juriah. They had taken long drives in it, not going anywhere in particular, but just to be together. They had kissed and caressed with it parked late at night beneath the angsana trees a couple of roads from here. In it they held their breaths as some voyeur on a motorbike peered through the condensation-covered window with a blazing torchlight on their faces.

And here it was now—the front section all mangled, broken glass on the dark blades of grass, on the hard unforgiving bitumen.

"No!" Akri screamed.

7

AKRI RAN to the four-wheel drive and tried to haul the front door open.

The beast pushed him aside and grabbed the chrome handle. In sarong and singlet, he tugged hard, the muscles straining like pliers upon his arms and neck. In the glow of that one surviving headlamp, he looked like an enraged lion battling against a mechanical monster.

The beast screamed in frustration.

It was no use. The door was stuck.

Through the shattered glass, Akri saw that the airbag hadn't worked. Juriah lay slumped on the steering wheel as though bent hideously in prayer. One hand lay twisted and limp on the dashboard. Her hair covered her face but through a gap in the black veil he could see that her lips were parted as though yearning for a kiss. A cold, cold kiss with a single icy drop of blood like a tear poised on her lower lip. He saw these things at five in the morning, even with dawn two hours away, right now at a time ruled by darkness and desperation.

"Juriah! Juriah! Juriah!" shouted the beast. Except he was no longer the beast, the terrified face belonged to a desperate man. Juriah's father, trembling and shaking, looking everywhere and nowhere, hoping for a miracle.

"An ambulance," Akri cried. "I'll call for an ambulance!"

"No, I'll go," said her father and, before Akri could say anything, the older man was running downhill toward his house.

Akri tried the passenger door but it too wouldn't budge. But the back door did and he climbed in. He was greeted by the stench of blood.

His heart was like a bird in a cage ferociously attacking the bars. He dropped the soaked handkerchief and, with his sleeve, brushed the blood pouring from his own wound under his eyes, not wanting to believe that this was happening ...

Why didn't she put on her seat belt? It was easy to guess. She didn't think to do so, not when she was chasing after her father and boyfriend—the two people she loved and one was wielding a parang.

"Allah, Juriah," he whispered, "please don't die." Akri had seen enough movies to know that he shouldn't move the victim. Arnold Schwarzenegger, Jean-Claude Van Damme, Mel Gibson, Jackie Chan, Chow Yun-Fat, even Bruce Lee—he didn't know why these actors piled into his head all of a sudden with their muscles and meaningless bravado. Not now when he needed to think straight. He couldn't be an otak udang. Not now.

Through the shattered windscreen, a few lights in the condominium came on. He took a deep breath, leaned over the front seat and stroked Juriah's hair, all sticky and clumped together.

On the leather seat surrounded by broken glass like a scattering of useless diamonds, lay Juriah's hand. Akri reached for it and held its softness, its compelling smoothness, hoping, praying for some sign of life.

Was it going cold? No! It couldn't be! This couldn't be happening to her. They had a lifetime ahead of them.

Not this! Not this!

He dropped her hand and spun around desperately, hoping that someone had heard the crash and was coming to help. Perhaps her father had already called the ambulance and was running back uphill. But no, he'd left only moments ago.

He turned back to Juriah and hit his head against the ceiling lamp. He flicked it on.

In the newly-lit chamber Juriah, without warning, pushed one arm against the steering wheel, slumped back on the car seat and turned to him.

Akri cried out.

Her face was a mask of blood.

A breeze swept in through the open door and her white T-shirt stirred. Four large drops stained it, so that she still looked alive, perhaps sleeping with a nose bleed. Except that a nose bleed didn't drench your head in blood. There it coagulated, turning sanity into madness, turning love to fear.

She made a noise.

A moaning. Soft at first and barely audible. The moaning grew louder into a shrill.

"Juriah!" he cried.

The sound stopped.

One of her eyes opened. "Akri," she whispered.

"Juriah, you're alive," he said, trying to control the shaking in his voice. "Don't worry, everything will be fine. Your father's calling an ambulance."

"Akri," she whispered again. "Oh, Akri."

Like a corpse impatient with the confines of its coffin, she turned her bloodied head from side to side before stopping it just short of Akri's face.

He gasped.

A two-inch piece of glass poked from one of her eyes, the eye that was closed and puffy. With her other eye, she blinked and stared mournfully at him.

"I don't want to ... to leave you. I don't ... want to go."

In that one look, in the whiteness of her eye, in the dark world of her eyeball, he saw her pain. But, beyond that, he beheld a helpless yearning and with it her knowledge that it would never be fulfilled.

He clutched her hand.

Please don't let her die ... please!

Juriah groaned, her mouth drooped and out came a stream of blood that curled onto her chin and slowly dripped onto the seat.

"Everything will be fine," he managed to whisper. "You'll be okay. Your father's called an ambulance, it'll be here soon. It'll take you to Pantai. They're going to mend you."

But his heart didn't believe a word he said. Why did people always lie to the dying?

Dying?

No! She's not going to die!

"Akri, I ... I want to stay with you ... always." Juriah's eye never left his. Everything she was and everything they shared was in that one unfaltering gaze.

Gently, he stroked her cheek, her sticky blood covering his fingers. "We'll always be together, Juriah. Through space and time."

"We are one ..." she gasped and squeezed his hand. "Forever ..."

Then her head jerked back as though she had remembered something awful.

She let go of his hand, looked hard at him, and said nothing.

"What is it, Juriah? What's wrong?"

Her stare turned cold.

Then she said the words that haunted him to this day.

"But ... but ... why did you ... run?"

With a single gasp, her accusing eye fell shut.

8

ONE AFTERNOON, after mending fishing nets, Pak Mansur and Akri climbed down the creaky steps of the house the old couple had lived in for forty years.

They waved to Mak Halijah who sat on the floor with two neighbors, dipping squares of Jacob's cream crackers into their cups of tea, eyes glued to a rerun of *Ali Baba Bujang Lapok* on television. Mak Halijah giggled like a child every time P. Ramlee chanted his cave-opening magic words.

But sometimes at night when the sea was calm and the insects hushed, Akri could hear a whimpering. Mak Halijah in bed—was she awake or asleep? he had no idea. But he knew why she sometimes cried in the twisted folds of her blanket.

For the first few months in his new home, he often wondered why their daughter didn't visit or sent a card or letter. Other than that first night when the old lady showed him his room, no mention was ever made of her. He once asked Pak Mansur but the old man just walked away muttering something about Hari Raya. But when Hari Raya came, no daughter materialized.

One afternoon, Akri visited Pak Alif at his stall by the beach. Pak Alif, perched on his stool with toes peeking from his slippers, chatted about some young civil servant who had just taken a third wife. Akri was enthralled by the gossip and wanted to know more, but he had come for a reason: he wanted to know about Pak Mansur's daughter. Finally, after his second cup of coffee, he managed to broach the subject.

Pak Alif stared through the thick lenses, then he removed his spectacles and wiped away his tears with a large handkerchief.

"You know my brother and Mak Halijah married late in life, don't you?"

Akri nodded solemnly.

"Their only daughter. So talented."

"Where is she, Pak Alif? Why doesn't she visit?"

"She's dead."

"What?"

"Gone to heaven." Pak Alif shook his head and put away his handkerchief. "She was studying in Shah Alam. One morning, after breakfast in the cafeteria, she coughed blood and an hour later, while lying in bed in the dormitory waiting for the doctor to arrive, she died."

"What ... what was wrong with her?"

"Some disease. A blood clot or something like that, the doctor said. That was five years ago. Pak Mansur and Mak Halijah never got over it. They talked to everyone as if she was still alive. She was their entire world. They were so proud of her."

"Allah, I didn't know she's dead."

"But Akri, since you've been staying with them, I have seen a big change. They both seem so much happier, especially Pak Mansur. It's like he has a son."

"I treat him like my own father."

"I know, Akri. I can see that."

And so, with these thoughts in his head, Akri left the house with Pak Mansur. Mak Halijah and the neighbors waved cheerily before returning to the movie, their crackers and tea. Akri strolled under the coconut trees, avoiding the occasional puddles and chicken droppings. He glanced at the old man and felt a great warmth surge in his chest.

"So what do you think, Akri?"

"Sorry, Pak Mansur?"

"A guitar? Getting you a new guitar?"

"I'm happy with the one you gave me."

"What—that old piece of rubbish? Huh, you should hear a proper guitar. Especially the way you play. It'll sound wonderful. We can slowly put money away for one."

"There's no need, Pak Mansur."

The old man turned to him and smiled, his mustache bright in the afternoon blaze. "One day, in a couple of years maybe, when you come home you'll find a new guitar waiting for you."

"But ..."

"Don't argue, Akri. I'm an old man and there're only so many things left I can do. Better hurry up or we'll be late."

It was a sweaty climb up the dirt path and they arrived at the gold-domed mosque just in time for zohor prayers. They took their ablutions from a tap beside a drain as the electric pump in the new marble fountain had broken down. They left their slippers on the blue-tiled steps.

Datuk Kamal's Bally shoes stood aloof on the top step unmolested by other more mundane footwear. As the local UMNO strongman, Datuk Kamal had promised a new mosque for the village during the last elections and, when he thrashed the opposition candidate, the Indonesians from the abandoned beachfront holiday apartments thirty minutes away arrived in their dusty trucks and finished the mosque in less than six weeks.

There were only twenty people in a hall that could easily accommodate two hundred. They joined a couple of middle-aged men near the front. Above them, gleaming ceiling fans on long poles clicked like mechanical insects and threw hot air around the stout pillars.

The gathering stood as the prayers began. Akri raised his palms to his ears and lowered them to his waist. As he recited the verses in his head, Akri saw himself plucking the guitar and thought he heard Juriah's voice, singing from beyond the grave.

He heard her a few times when his mind was quiet, when he walked alone on the beach with the sunlight fleeing the sky, when he dug the moist warm soil with his hands among the worms and onions, but mostly when he cradled the instrument, fingers meandering on its strings, plucking the delicate notes, thoughts lost on her. A voice filled with neither love nor anger, but sorrow. He still remembered how she stared at him. That look in her eye, was it anger or disappointment? He didn't quite know. All he could tell was …

The loud crash came from outside the mosque.

All heads turned to see a black bicycle lying at the entrance, heaped on the steps like a sacrificed goat.

A bare-chested man leaped over it and bounded in.

He held up his checkered sarong with one hand while the other wielded a long object.

The scene had played in Akri's mind a thousand times.

Juriah's father!

Thoughts rushed at him like a four-wheel drive with lights blazing. But that was three years ago and this man looked nothing like Juriah's father. He was young and clean-shaven except for a plaster on his neck. The shadows of the circling fans cut up his thin tall figure so that he looked like a man walking in from another dimension. Another space. Another time.

The man's mouth was open. His tongue slithered like a snake's. His eyes were so wide, they threatened to pop out of his skull.

The parang gleamed as he strode in.

A mad man, Akri thought. *A mad man running amok.*

But this man was not running, he was strolling. Walking in so confidently, like a VIP at a wedding.

While some of those attending prayers scrambled away like frightened monkeys, others broke ranks and shouted at the man to drop his weapon.

A man in a songkok, whom Akri identified as the local mechanic with a wife and two young sons, tried to grab the parang but the assailant sidestepped him.

The weapon flashed.

Blood splattered across the tiled floor and the mechanic grunted and fell to the ground holding his stomach. His entrails, gray and glistening, slipped out like worms between his fingers.

The assailant leaped, rising over the dead man's body as he sliced the air above his head.

"Die! Die! Die!" he screamed. "All of you will die!"

The men tried to surround the attacker but the parang flew at them. They tried to grab the man as the assailant danced out of the way. He spun his body and lashed out. A man in a white kopiah fell in a spray of blood.

Akri, heart beating rapidly, sweat pouring down his brow, was on all fours, crawling toward the far wall. He was not alone. Datuk Kamal, the UMNO man, was trembling on the ground, mouth wide open, glasses clutched in one hand. Three other men crouched in one corner, babbling on their hands and knees, faces filled with terror.

The assailant leapt at Akri and, just as Akri thought he would be killed, he saw hands and a flash of white hair.

Pak Mansur!

The old man struck at the assailant's arm and blocked the blow. The blade struck the floor.

"Leave him alone!" shouted Pak Mansur, standing over Akri, his legs splayed in a silat stance, fists clenched. "You're not well, Roslan. Go home."

"Why?" growled the man.

"I'm sure your wife is waiting there for you."

"My wife?" said Roslan.

"Yes," said Pak Mansur. "Your wife. I came to your wedding last year, remember?"

Roslan laughed. "Yes, you did. But I didn't know then that my wife is a demon from hell and all of you are her followers."

"We are just here to pray. Now go home."

Roslan said nothing. His eyes fell to the floor. The strength seemed to leave his arms.

Pak Mansur signaled the other men to keep their distance. "Now give me the parang," he said in almost a whisper. "It's okay, believe me. You'll be all right."

Pak Mansur stepped up to Roslan and placed a hand on his shoulder.

Roslan looked up. He had a pitiful expression full of sadness and remorse while Pak Mansur's face was filled with kindness. The same kindness that had brought Akri to his home. Yet it was etched in courage too. The courage to face the assailant. The courage to rescue Akri from the sea.

"We'll look after you," said the old man.

"Yes," whispered Roslan. Then his lips parted in a grin. His eyes shone with madness. "And I'll look after you too."

He stepped back, mouth open, tongue flickering, and then leaped forward. Pak Mansur raised his arms.

But too late!

The blade flashed.

Followed by a dull crack.

"No!" Akri screamed.

Pak Mansur made no sound. He fell like a tree cut down. His shoulders landed heavily on Akri's legs.

The parang lay half-buried in the old man's skull. Gray matter splattered on the blade.

Pak Mansur's mouth was wide open. His eyes wide and unbelieving.

His arms were splayed out as though begging for an embrace from above. Or perhaps from his wife who was still giggling in front of the television at home. Or perhaps his dead daughter who he pretended was still alive.

Pak Mansur's body lay still except for one foot that struck the tiles repeatedly. The soft tapping sounded like rain. Black acid rain.

Akri's shirt, covered in Pak Mansur's blood, was warm and clung to his chest and his nostrils were filled with a thick metallic smell. A fly landed on Akri's ear. He brushed it away and it landed on the old man's clotted hair. Two others joined it, their bodies shivering in the feasting. Pak Mansur's hair should have been white like condensed milk but now it was red like undiluted rose syrup.

Akri crawled away from the still-warm corpse, the parang still quivering in Pak Mansur's skull as though the weapon had a life of its own. Akri looked to see if it was bandaged in plaster but no, the wooden handle gleamed proudly. It had done its job. It had killed three good people that day.

Roslan screamed and kicked as he was dragged out of the mosque by the crowd of men. The corpses he had created were quickly covered in white bedsheets which just as quickly turned thick and red.

Later, the sirens came. Men in white poured in with stretchers. Men in pale blue asked questions and wrote into their notebooks. Lightbulbs flashed.

A crowd gathered. Shouting. Tears. Questions. More shouting. More tears. But Akri couldn't see Mak Halijah anywhere.

Akri followed Pak Mansur's body in the ambulance. It sped, sirens blaring, to the nearest town. As they reached its outskirts he could see the abandoned holiday apartments sadly staring like broken giants at the empty sea.

Akri couldn't believe Pak Mansur was dead. But the young doctor in Emergency told him that the old man had died instantly when his skull was cleaved in two. Akri muttered his thanks, then wondered what he had been grateful for. He couldn't take the words back and so turned away from the hospital.

He walked out in the noonday sun. He should have turned south, a two-hour walk would take him back to the village and Mak Halijah waiting with a hundred burning questions. He turned north and went as far as his legs would carry him. Eventually a bus came along. He slumped into its torn plastic seat and stared out the window, at the white heat that smothered the dust and trees. He wanted to go home. Wherever home was.

9

AKRI DIDN'T THINK he would ever return to the village, yet here he was standing outside the mosque, with sweaty back and armpits, new guitar slung over his shoulders. It hurt breathing and his head throbbed.

The crowd of slippers was there again, lined up on the concrete steps. It was time for zohor prayers. He didn't dare go in. What if there was a crash of a black bicycle? What if a mad man came striding in with his parang raised? This time it would be Juriah's father.

You killed my daughter! You bloody rock star!

He'd scream, mouth foaming from his beast-like head.

Akri turned from the mosque. He would not be praying today.

He followed the path which wound its way down between houses on stilts past four boys kicking a football, shouting at each other with big grins. He saw a Milo tin on a window sill, a Twisties wrapper in a puddle, a crushed Orangina can beside a discarded bicycle wheel.

A crow, black feathers glistening, hopped on a rusty zinc roof before fluttering, wings beating, toward the green hills. A gray cat sat curled on the steps of a house, staring at him.

If he had not sauntered up to Juriah in that food court while she forked at her mee bandung, she would still be alive. Happily married to the son of some Tan Sri or Datuk and her only worries, other than how to deal with her impertinent driver or lazy new maid, would be whether to wear that sequined dress or the Italian silk baju kurung to tonight's dinner function.

He kicked a stone in disgust and watched it roll down the slope.

How could he have been so careless? Why did he hit that vase of carnations on the mahogany stand?

And he had fled that night. Juriah had asked him to stay but he ran, tail between his legs. He still felt her one cold eye on him.

... why did you ... run?

Her words bubbled corrosively in his head.

Sweat trickled down his forehead. He wiped it with a handkerchief.

From between two houses, past a mound of wild grass and bushes, he glimpsed the sea and an island like a broken skull in the distance. He wished he could get into a boat and sail away and never come back. But there on the beach beside a patch of black sand, surrounded by a stand of leafless coconut trees, was his shining red car. And then there was the concert in two days. And there was Juriah ...

What did a youth with no prospects think he was doing with a rich man's daughter? What was he thinking of when he kissed her and felt her breasts in her father's four-wheel drive? That vehicle full of club badges that would send her crashing into a concrete wall.

A door to a house opened and out came a white-haired lady bearing a wicker basket. A white tudung over her head and shoulders, glasses winking in the noonday sun. At first Akri thought it was Mak Halijah, but this woman was a lot younger. She smiled and Akri said hello. A stern-looking bearded man with a green cap followed her out and the two hopped on a scooter which disappeared with a snarl.

Akri sighed and adjusted the strap of his guitar. It wasn't the four-wheel drive that killed Juriah. He had done it by his cowardice. He killed Pak Mansur, too. If he had not been groveling on the floor of the mosque like a frightened dog, Pak Mansur would still be alive.

He reached a junction. A right turn would take him to Mak Halijah's house but Pak Alif had said she died two years ago. He regretted not having seen her after Pak Mansur's death, to apologize for his cowardice in the mosque. She was in many ways like a mother to him. Why did he stay away from the village for so long ...

Akri turned left and wandered down the path.

He followed the track until it reached the muddy banks of the river. He turned upstream until he came to a shack, made of a rotting pile of planks and a collapsing thatched roof, which seemed in danger of tipping into the water. Two chickens stared at him before scooting away.

Akri took a deep breath, then knocked on the door.

"Come in," came a muffled voice.

He pushed the door, which creaked on its hinges. The dark that greeted him was dusty, hot and clammy. "Hello," he said.

"Come in," came the voice again.

At first he couldn't see her and then, as his eyes adjusted to the gloom, he saw a large crouching figure.

Light spilled onto what he mistakenly took to be a slab of old meat with thick worms lashing about, but it turned out to be hands wrestling then pausing, wrestling then pausing, upon the figure's ample lap.

From a sagging face, as dark as the confines of a toilet bowl, sprang long withering white hair. Thick lips like old tires munched fastidiously under eyes that bulged and seemed to glow.

"What are you waiting there for?" she said, while still chomping. "You want me to send you an invitation?"

Akri took off his shoes and in three steps was in the center of the shack. He was surrounded by broken furniture and what seemed like bits of other people's lives. Hanging from the wall was a rosewood clock with the long hand missing and the second hand going backward. A television with a cracked screen lay tilted on a floor scattered with empty plastic bags, their contents dried up long ago. On a table with its green veneer peeling off were more plastic bags but these were tied with raffia and filled with black clumps—and surely the tiny movements within had to be maggots at work?

"Sit down," she said, pointing to a mat on the floor. Her eyeballs were huge like black marbles as they rove up and down his body.

Akri shifted uncomfortably. The smell of fresh urine and a faint smell of feces wafted up his nostrils.

"Don't worry, young man, I won't eat you," she chuckled, low and deep. It held a murky quality as though her voice had come from a corpse deep in the river. She brushed her faded yellow dress, then spat red betel nut chewings into a white chamber pot.

She turned to grin at him.

Akri sat down and crossed his legs. The soles of his white socks had turned black.

This was a mistake. What the hell was he doing here? This woman could not help him. But Pak Mansur, he had …

"Now, what troubles you, my son?" The woman, with her munchings dispatched, now spoke in a less obscure voice. She leaned forward and sipped from a metal mug, shuddering as she did so. Then as she slumped into a plastic chair, Akri saw the woman had one leg missing.

"I'm Akri. Sorry I don't know your name, Makcik. Pak Mansur said that ..."

"You don't need to know my name," she said loudly. "Pak Mansur? Oh yes, I remember him. He's dead, isn't he?"

Akri nodded. Head cleaved in two. But he said nothing.

"But that's not why you're here, is it, my son?"

"No. Once Pak Mansur and I passed your house and he told me you were a shaman. A very good one."

"He did, did he? Did he also tell you that I'm completely mad?"

"No, no he didn't." Pak Mansur had in fact told him that the bomoh had many screws missing but Akri wasn't going to mention it.

"Hah, you don't have to be polite. And I know who you are, my son. Seen your face in the magazines. Don't they call you AK47—Malaysia's answer to Bono of U2?"

Akri couldn't help but grin. "I suppose the press have said that. I didn't know you like rock music, Makcik."

"Rock music? I hate it. But doesn't mean I have to be ignorant." She pointed to a waist-high pile of magazines and yellowing newspaper next to a broken cupboard. "Always important to know what's going on. So now tell me young man, Encik Akri, also known as AK47, the machine-gun man, Malaysia's answer to Bono. Tell me what troubles you. What brings you to my palatial home? Is it love or lust or money or revenge? People only want these things nowadays. Tell me, what help do you need?"

"You think you can help me?"

"Of course I can. Now tell me everything."

"Everything?"

"Yes. From start to finish. From A to Z. From one to infinity."

"You see ... it ... the whole thing ... happened about a year ago. Before anyone had ever heard of Akri or AK47. We were playing at a cocktail bar in Penang. One night ..."

10

AKRI STOOD ON STAGE, garbed in black, strumming an old Fender guitar. In a voice that barely hid his boredom, he spewed out one of the new soppy songs from the US. Patrons all over the country, keen to show they were connoisseurs of the very latest—whether the newest BMW, handphone or golf clubs—requested these bank-balance-inspired numbers without fail— scribbling on swatches of paper: the song, the even more feeble dedication.

Through his dark glasses, Akri could barely make out the faces of the audience. They lounged around their paper coasters and tall drinks, smiling lazily. A bespectacled man in slippers, who Akri guessed must have made the request, mouthed the words between gulps of beer. Two middle-aged women in miniskirts parleyed in a corner. A group of businessmen yakked as they poured from a bottle of Chivas Regal, slapping each other on the backs and shoulders in a big show of camaraderie.

Monday nights were quiet and less than a third of the tables were occupied. Akri didn't care. When he sang he felt at peace and nothing, not even the indifferent audience, not even the mundane lyrics of the song, could touch him.

With it out of the way, he struck an E, grinned and belted out an old Springsteen number.

The guys from the slapping and whisky drinking crowd turned and frowned at him. The two middle-aged women edged closer together as if for mutual protection. The bespectacled man stared open-mouthed, then vigorously wiped his glasses.

Akri, pleased with the response, roared into the mike.

Melissa, playing bass, pouted her bright red lips while her small slim body, garbed in a black leather waistcoat, swayed from side to side. Occasionally she would toss back her shoulder-length hair and beam at the audience, her mascara-lined eyes shining. Zain, her husband, ran his fingers across the Yamaha keyboard. His head, topped in an Afro hairstyle, bobbed up and down, nostrils flaring, silver ear stud winking, large white teeth flashing beneath the spotlights. In a baseball cap, shiny shorts and a singlet, Choy pounded the drums, his round metal glasses strapped to his head. He closed his eyes and let the sweat pour down his round face as he twirled the drumsticks and attacked the drum kit.

The hotel management was sure to complain about the ruckus but Akri didn't care. He shook a defiant fist as his voice carried out into the corridors and lobby of the hotel. He would only be too happy if the chandelier there broke into a million pieces. When the song was over, Akri took an exaggerated bow to the muted clapping.

Rohaini, the waitress in a long skirt and checkered waistcoat, slipped him three scraps of paper. More requests.

Akri sighed. He wanted to take a break but, with another ten minutes left, he supposed he could quickly rattle off the requests. In the next set, they could do a few of the new numbers they'd been practicing.

Somewhere in the middle of the second request, as Akri declared for the umpteenth time that no love could be as good as this, his eye was drawn to the bar.

Maniam, the thin-as-a-lizard bartender was in attendance, flamboyantly shaking a cocktail, displaying his white teeth in a captivating grin. Three men in ties lay huddled under an array of twinkling wineglasses, probably discussing import-export or other meaningful stuff.

Beside a wall, a female figure stood alone. Watching.

Akri shuddered.

Her height and build.

They're the same!

She had similar hair too.

Straight and falling to her waist.

A sick feeling like a thick and bloody worm writhed in his chest.

He stared hard, trying to capture her details, details which he already knew, facial features which blazed in his mind. But this woman's face was buried in smoke and darkness.

Yet her eyes—and he knew how dreadful they would be, if he could only see them—were surely fixed on him.

... why did you ... run?

For a second he saw red eyeballs swimming in her dark head as she crawled from the grave, pushing the tufts of grass aside. Thought he could feel her cold heavy breath upon his skin. Her razor-like nails running along his throat. And if she opened her mouth, there would be white glinting fangs ...

Akri turned away.

No! Can't be!

It had to be his imagination. She was just some woman in a nightclub listening to the band. The fact that she stood alone and had no handbag like Juriah meant nothing. And the sick feeling in his chest, that was just indigestion. Surely ...

This is bloody madness!

He was crazy to think the woman was Juriah's spirit, here to haunt him.

Akri forced himself to take a second look. The figure stood.

Glaring back.

A corpse shrouded in black.

But this time he thought he saw movement.

Right ... right there!

Her hand—no—her fingers. They tapped against her thigh. Beating hard.

Were they following the band's rhythm? They seemed to be but Akri couldn't help thinking that her fingers drove the band's music, as though she was the conductor.

Her movements, although small, filled the cocktail lounge.

Filled it with hate.

As though she was tapping nails into his bleeding skull. Why did ...

Allah!

He had stopped singing right in the middle of the song!

Akri turned from the figure and tried to grin at the perplexed audience.

The band members stared at him with a hundred questions.

He tried to grin and gave them an unconvincing thumbs up. He managed to pick up where they were in the number, strumming the chords and allowing his voice to lift out of his throat.

Soon he was back twisting his legs across the stage.

When he felt that his heartbeat had returned to normal, he turned to the figure.

But she was gone. As though she had walked through the wall.

The bar was empty except for the three men in ties and Maniam grinning as he filled a jug of beer.

Akri looked into the crowd. He saw only the waitresses balancing trays and customers huddled in sofas and smoke curling and unfurling in the darkness.

11

ALTHOUGH it was almost one in the morning, the band always went for a drink in the coffeeshop opposite the hotel. They were much too energized after a performance to go straight to bed.

"What happened there?" asked Zain, putting his Milo down. "Why did you suddenly stop singing?"

"I forgot the lyrics," said Akri, shifting uncomfortably in his chair. Two men lit cigarettes at a table beside them. The young waitress in shorts and skimpy blouse brought out a couple of plates of fried noodles.

"Oh, like hell you did, Akri," said Choy. "You never forget lyrics."

Akri feigned laughter. "Sometimes I do. It depends what I'm doing. Who I'm seeing."

"Who you're seeing?" said Melissa, digging into the noodles. "You can't mean girls. I don't believe you're interested in girls. I've never seen you with one. Are you sure you're not gay?"

"Oh yes, Melissa," Akri said. "Choy and I are great lovers. I just love his Chinese ass."

Choy sniggered and punched Akri on the shoulder.

"Wait till I tell my girlfriend that I'm getting a Malay dick every night!"

"Oh, quit it you two," said Zain. "People might think you're serious."

"It's you that's too serious, darling," said his wife, taking his hand. "Relax. There's hardly anyone here."

Zain grinned sheepishly at her and stroked her hair. The two were getting on much better now. A few months ago, Akri was afraid the marriage was going to break up.

Choy yawned. "Time for bed I think."

With that, the band trudged back to the hotel.

But Akri couldn't sleep and so, at four in the morning, he stole out of bed.

The night was humid but, thankfully, the streets were empty. He walked down the streets toward the sea. As he sat on a wall watching the dawn creep into the sky, one endless thought cast a shroud upon his mind.

Juriah! Juriah! Juriah!

12

"AND EVERYTHING would have been fine," Akri said, hands on the steering wheel of his Alfa Romeo. "Except this woman came back the next night and the night after that."

"You already told me that," the bomoh said, raving white hair springing up to the ceiling. She gripped the leather seat with her dirty fingers, sweat beading her forehead even though the air conditioner was turned right up. She shifted her bulk as though trying to get into a comfortable position; finally she reclined her seat and propped her stump on the door handle.

"I thought that maybe she was some weirdo fan who liked our music. But nobody comes three nights in a row. And she only stayed for two, sometimes three songs."

"Maybe she's like Cinderella," sniggered the bomoh, except it came out in a toad-like croaking. "Has to get home before midnight or else she'll turn into a pontianak."

"That's funny, Makcik," Akri said. He shuddered, not at all appreciating her humor. If she knew the whole story perhaps she wouldn't be so flippant. "I saw her three times in Penang. Then our contract ended and we went to Johor Bharu."

"And what happened there?"

"We were playing at another five-star hotel. The crowd was younger. I got them to dance and sing. Some of them even came on stage. Then I saw the dark figure in the corner. She just stood there staring. Fingers tapping. I couldn't see her face. But I knew who she was."

The bomoh yawned and made a strange gurgling sound in her throat. She slid one hand beneath her faded yellow dress that ran to her ankles and scratched her good leg.

Akri continued. "I felt cold all over. Like a ghost was dancing with its arms around me. I felt like ... like hands of ice were on my throat."

"Like she wanted to kill you, my son?" She continued scratching.

"Yes, that's right! I fainted then. Fell right off stage in front of everyone. They had to call the doctor. That was when I knew for sure that this was no ordinary woman. This was a spirit. A bad spirit!"

"Very, very interesting," the bomoh said, hair flying as she turned to look at him. She placed her dark fleshy foot on the seat and examined a hairy toe. "But, now you must tell me, my son, the other band members of yours, did they see this spirit?"

Akri didn't answer until he had overtaken a large log-carrying truck. The car sped past an old man on a bicycle laden with green coconuts, cycling beside a slope where two large earth machines ploughed the clay. The road crested a hill covered in rubber trees. Above them the burning sun followed.

"Melissa's blind on stage because she never wears her glasses. Choy's spectacles are always steamed up. Half the time his eyes are closed anyway. Zain said he didn't see any strange woman. He told me I was crazy. Makcik, are you sure you need to come with me back to KL?"

"Yes, yes, I have to see where you live. Feel it out. See what lurks there. There might be evil charms full of bad, bad magic. You know, my son, I think you're driving much too fast." The bomoh began picking her toenail while her other hand dug her nose.

"Probably," Akri said under his breath.

If there was one thing he was sure of, it was that he wanted to get to KL as fast as possible. The bomoh had a tendency to slip into some Indonesian love song which she'd sing as though she had cockroaches in her throat. Nor could he take the bomoh's sour body odor much longer. And twice, he heard a deep rumbling from inside her and, sure enough, out came a trumpeting boom followed by a noxious odor that wrapped its slimy tentacles around him. Even with the windows down, the pestilence seemed to coagulate in the leather seats.

"Have you told me everything?" the bomoh said, placing her one foot, now with a peeled toenail, next to the air-conditioning vent. She wiped one slimy finger on the leather seat.

"No, there's something else." Akri didn't want to reveal the rest of the story to this detestable bomoh but he had no one else.

"What is it, my son? You must tell me everything if you want me to help you."

"It happened a few months after the woman first appeared. We were in PJ ...."

13

THE BAND was doing a stint at the Holiday Villa and Akri lodged as he usually did in his brother's single-story terrace house in USJ. He muttered in his sleep on a mattress beside the cracked louvered window, sarong down to his knees, blanket strewn against a wall.

He woke with a start.

Turning on his back, his eyes flew open.

Beside him, the clock radio flashed two thirty-three. He rubbed his eyes.

The glow of a street lamp dropped misshapen shadows on his bare body. The silhouette of a single lightbulb coiled down from the ceiling. His guitar was still propped on a broken filing cabinet where he kept his clothes. A towel stand laden with underwear and T-shirts leaned crookedly against a wall where tattered posters of Jimi Hendrix and Bob Marley eyed him and, for a second, he thought he heard them snigger.

But it was just the insects. Akri closed his eyes and listened to their secret shrills. The smell of the mosquito coil mixed with tobacco smoke clinging to his clothes could easily have been the odor from a crematorium.

The Mitsubishi box fan hummed. Perhaps a ghastly machine weaving evil through the humid air, for a poisonous feeling trickled down his throat. He shuddered.

Am I on the edge of a nightmare?

A precipice on the way to hell. Did he still dwell in that frightful dream world?

He wriggled his fingers and toes just to make sure he was awake.

He was. And this knowledge brought sweat to his brow.

His breathing came in ragged spurts and his heart thumped in his head.

And then he felt it.

A presence.

That shifted in the kitchen. It made no sound. But it was there as surely as the moon watched from behind the clouds. As surely as the pots and pans lay soaking in the kitchen sink.

And it edged to his room.

Stood outside his door. Thinking. Evil thoughts circling.

The doorknob creaked as it was slowly twisted. The door groaned.

Although Akri had his eyes closed, he knew with a terrifying certainty that Juriah stood there. She had trailed him from Penang to Johor Bharu and now she had followed him home.

He was horribly aware of her presence creeping into the chamber. Her straight waist-length hair brushed the wall, bare feet sticky on the concrete floor. Her breath drew in as she saw him lying shirtless on the bed. She padded across the room.

Akri felt as though he was in an electric chair.

Would she now flick the switch and electrocute him?

Or would it be something else? Fingers on the throat? Pillow over his head? A hungry bite on the neck so his bed would be warmly soaked and sticky in his own blood?

It didn't matter how. He deserved it.

He was a fool to think he could make it in this world with his own songs. To think he could exorcize his sorrow, his shame through music. Put the past behind. But here she now was.

Living. Breathing.

And vengeful. That much he had felt on stage when he saw her standing as still as a corpse. Knew the burning, angry eyes that were hidden in the shadows. Felt violence in her tapping fingers.

The bed creaked.

Something cold and soft like blood-soaked meat held his ankles. Akri could only manage a moan.

He wanted to scream but his tongue was coiled in his throat.

And there came the odor of what once could have been Juriah's perfume but the smell had gone rotten, it reminded him not of rain in the morning but a puddle in a steaming alleyway where rotting rodents floated.

Hands—yes, he was sure they were hands—slippery and drenched in cold blood, moved up his bare shins and across his thighs.

Something silky brushed his legs.

Hair?

Before he could tell, a weight like a disused mattress fell on him.

He gasped.

The bed groaned.

Breasts squashed his chest. Smooth ankles against his shin. Cheek against his cheek. Dusty hair upon his mouth!

Juriah slithered against him.

Skin on skin.

Their bodies freezing as melting blocks of ice.

Again he tried to scream but nothing came. His voice was a toad struggling in his throat.

He wanted to open his eyes but was afraid of what he would see.

A shard of glass poking from one eye. A decomposed head filled with worms and maggots. A mouth filled with broken teeth and a blackened slug-like tongue. Or perhaps something more hideous?

Outside, rain splashed the pavement. It fell and fell. He heard it filling the drain.

Juriah shifted her weight on his chest. And then, as though she had read his mind, sharp fingernails pushed his eyelids, as though trying to prise them open.

No! No! Noooooo!

He forced his eyes to stay closed.

"I don't want to see you!" he cried. "Please don't kill me."

I'm not here to kill you, she whispered. It sounded more like a breeze in an empty well than a voice.

Surely the words were just in his head? But it was real. He could feel the cold corpse's infected breath caressing his ear.

Open your eyes.

"Never," Akri managed to whisper.

He wasn't going to let her trick him. He remembered her staring in the nightclub. The rage. The fury.

If I open my eyes, she'll rip my throat out!

Or perhaps just the sight of her decomposed head would kill him. The head that now hovered a couple of inches from his face as though eager to kiss him with its slithering tongue.

"No," Akri whispered. "Go away ... please!"

But she remained on his body. Skin upon skin. Bodies cold. Using his body as her bed.

The smell was now a damp stench from the mangrove. Her weight shifted like a slithering iguana upon him. Draped over his body for what felt like hours.

Akri felt a thousand things. Revulsion. Anger. Hatred. Even love.

But mostly fear.

Somehow, perhaps through tiredness, perhaps through a madness that caressed his brain, he fell asleep.

When he woke, with the sunlight shafting upon his body, he thought he heard a voice singing.

Was it a nightmare?

He pushed the faded curtain aside and peeked through the louvers. The pavement was wet with rain.

And the voice sang like a hurricane through his skull.

14

"JEALOUSY," the bomoh said and roared with laughter, sending spit flying onto Akri's shirt. She propped her crutch against the wall and leaned against a window which framed a sparkling view of the city's skyscrapers. "People jealous of you are casting spells. Fame and wealth can cause a lot of problems. This thing that lies on your body is no doubt an evil spirit sent by people envious of your success."

Akri had driven as fast as he could and, four hours after leaving the village, they hit traffic on the outskirts of the city. Akri felt ill as they crawled along the car-infested highway but he had managed to tell the bomoh most of what had happened, finishing the story as they entered the underground car park.

They had just arrived in his newly-built three-room condo on the twenty-third floor and the first thing the bomoh did was urinate in his bathroom with the door wide open. Without flushing or using the tap, she headed for his bedroom while casually wiping one hand on her dress.

"I'm not rich, Makcik," Akri said, screwing up his face. "I'm just comfortable. I can buy most of what I want. The record company, my manager, they're all rich because of me. Yeah—I'm famous here in Malaysia. But that's all."

"That's enough to make people envious, my son." She leaned heavily against her crutch and threw his cupboard door open, her hair bouncing about her shoulders. "Look at your shirts, can't you see your shirts, full of faces!"

"Faces! What faces?"

"Can't you see? Some are crying. Some laughing. Some screaming. You must throw them away. Better to burn them."

"Who is casting this spell?"

She didn't answer but instead hobbled down the corridor, her crutch tapping on the parquet, before making a bounding hop and landing like an elephant in the dining room.

"And your furniture!" she cried. She pointed to his new dining table and Italian chairs. "Ghosts in them. Haunted. Can't you see the spirits sitting there?"

"No, I can't."

"Someone has cast a terrible spell. Jealousy, I'm sure. Envy at your success."

"But ..."

"There are wicked people out there."

"But this spirit that visits me ..."

"What about it?"

"It first visited me when I had no money, Makcik. Before I had a single album."

The bomoh plonked herself down on the sofa, which Akri decided meant the thing wasn't haunted. She reached under her dress and scratched.

"Then something else," she whispered. "Some other sinning motive. Some other reason for this presence."

"Like love?"

"Maybe."

"Or hate?" Akri thought of Juriah's father. Surely he blamed him for her death. But Akri knew better.

"Yes—love, hate, envy, greed—wicked people will cast spells for any of these reasons. We need to know why or how."

"I think it's love."

"Why?"

"The spirit, it's not just any spirit. It's Juriah!"

"Who is this Juriah?"

Akri had hoped to keep the story to himself. It was a pain he carried all these years, a pulsing gem he kept deep in the coils of his gut. He had never told anyone about her, not even Pak Mansur. But now it came out. He managed to keep his voice steady, to keep the tears from his eyes as he slowly told the bomoh about how Juriah died.

The bomoh fished out a clutch of leaves from a cloth bag and stuffed them into her mouth, nodding throughout, occasionally exploring her nose with one finger as she chewed. He didn't care what she thought. He already knew he was a coward. Juriah was gone forever. Nothing could change that.

When he finished his story, Akri who had ended up sitting on the floor and nervously rocking his body to and fro, stared hard at the bomoh looking for a reaction. There was none. She seemed preoccupied with her toenail.

"I know Juriah will come again," he continued. "Sometimes nothing happens for months, then she might come three nights in a row. I don't know why. And always lying on me, trying to force my eyes open. I'm afraid one night I will open my eyes and see her decomposing head, that glass poking out of one eye, worms crawling out of her face."

"How do you know this?" The bomoh dropped her foot and grimaced at him.

"I ... I just know." He looked away and for a second he could see Juriah's one cold accusing eye on him.

... why did you ... run?

He turned to the bomoh. "Makcik, please help me. Please get rid of the thing."

"How often do you see it at your concerts?"

"Sometimes it's there. Sometimes not. When I do see it, I get so scared ... I just know it's going to do something bad. I feel it. I know it. I ... must be going mad."

"My son, you should have told me all this earlier." The bomoh sighed. "Now I understand. There is no question that this is Juriah's spirit come to visit you. A very powerful spirit from what you've described, created at the point of the car accident, but there is something else ... Something else that created such a powerful presence, something you didn't know or something you're not telling me."

The bomoh's bulging eyes seemed to go unnaturally red.

"What is it?" The bomoh whispered in that muffled, chewing voice that came from deep within a river.

"I don't know."

"Don't worry, my son, I'll find out."

"Don't you need to cast a magic spell?"

"That's not necessary. I will know in time. But right now I'm getting so very hungry. Where shall we go for lunch? How about an expensive five-star hotel!"

15

THE WAITRESS at the coffeehouse led Akri and the bomoh to a table by the window which had a view of the snaking LRT track and the shimmering swimming pool many floors below. The bomoh let her crutch fall but instead of taking her seat on the rattan chair, she gently hopped toward the buffet table.

At twice the size of any of the office workers whether dressed in a tudung, shirt and tie or skirt and blouse, the crowd parted as she entered the fray. Akri quickly followed her elbowing bulk but by the time he had negotiated past several tables, the bomoh had already armed herself with a plate and was attacking the roast lamb.

On top of the hunks of meat and fat she scattered fingers of petai. The white rice was piled on before she slopped it back on the serving tray and replaced it with huge mounds of Cantonese fried rice. Then came the rich spoonfuls of fish head curry, followed by the entangled legs and wings of ayam masak merah, the worm-like orgy of oily mee goreng and the mass slivers of cold roast bovine-flesh. Next came a modest dollop of mixed braised vegetables which was topped off with a scattering of achar and prawn crackers.

She bulldozed into two middle-aged ladies babbling in Hokkien at the desert table and completed the edifice with two servings of cheesecake which shook precariously as she hopped back to the table.

By the time Akri joined her, the bomoh had scoffed the cheesecakes, her white hair leaping about as she did so. With eager fingers, she shuffled wads of mee goreng, roast beef, vegetables and achar into her mouth.

"Delicious, very delicious," she said in that familiar river-like voice. She let out a booming coagulating fart and grinned.

"You must be hungry," Akri said, his appetite gone. A few heads from the other tables turned in their direction.

"A bomoh's work is hungry work," she muttered as she tore into a drumstick.

"Especially if I'm paying for it."

"It's a buffet, my son. Doesn't matter how much I eat. Or do these people still weigh all the unfinished food and charge you? Huh, with me you don't have to worry about that!" She paused for a moment and her thick red tongue came out to lick the sauce off each of her fingers. "Ahhh, I just love the towns. I love the buffet breakfast, the buffet lunch, the afternoon tea, the high tea, the buffet dinner, and then supper. It's so wonderful ... we are seduced by food!"

She downed the iced water, some of it dribbling down her chin, before shoveling rice into her mouth.

"It's not the money I'm worried about, Makcik," said Akri.

Akri could feel everyone in the restaurant staring. A girl of fifteen or so in a school uniform stood close by with a pen and paper, her mouth wide open. Akri knew she wanted an autograph but was stopped dead in her tracks by the sight of the bomoh's fearless gluttony.

"I'm more worried about my reputation."

"Small price to pay," the bomoh said, now squatting rather than sitting on the chair. She stuffed the last hunks of greasy lamb into her mouth. "After all, I'm helping you with Juriah's spirit."

Then she laughed, tossing her large head backward, and sent a spray of rice over the table, some falling into Akri's iced water.

"I don't see how you're helping me, Makcik."

"Oh, but I am helping you. I'm finding out why Juriah's spirit still roams this earth."

"It's because she's angry at me. My stupid cowardice caused her death. She asked me to stay but I ran with my tail between my legs! She wants revenge, don't you see? I felt those accusing eyes of hers when I was on stage. And I remember how she looked at me before she died."

"But there's more to it, my son. There's something else that has given her the power to haunt you."

"What is it? Tell me!"

"You really want to know?"

"Yes, tell me!"

"Then look, my son."

"What? I don't see anything."

A small mound of fried rice sat on the bomoh's otherwise empty plate.

She picked up her fork and started pushing the grains to the edge of the plate until there was nothing in the middle except for a ...

"What is that, Makcik?"

"Look carefully."

At first Akri thought it was just a big grain of rice. But it was dark red and it ...

pulsed

Akri couldn't believe his eyes and so edged closer. His head was but a few inches from the plate.

It still ...

pulsed

Closer still. His nose almost touched the plate.

The grain was so small, he shouldn't have been able to see it.
But he did!
He couldn't believe what he was seeing.
A tiny, tiny head ...
... and a round, black eye.
Staring back at him!
Within the body, a red heart was beating.

"An embryo," whispered the bomoh. "Only a few hours old. Yours and Juriah's!"

Even as Akri stared at the thing with his mouth wide open he knew she was right. Although Juriah wanted to wait until they were married, nothing could hold them back and so they had made love that early morning. The first time for both of them. Then he had fallen asleep and the embryo formed in the warmth of her womb. Cells dividing. Breathing. Growing.

And those tiny round eyes. What worlds did they hold?

The bomoh reached for her plate. She plucked the embryo, placed it on her tongue and slipped it into her mouth.

Akri leaped from his chair.

"How could ... how could you!" he shouted.

The bomoh grinned, her thick lips quivering. Eyeballs big and quite insane.

"Don't worry, my son. The embryo, this pulsing grain of rice you and Juriah made was never there. Just a vision."

"What do you mean a vision?"

"I fashioned it from knowledge deep within you. You and Juriah created life. He would have been a darling little boy who would become a strong, handsome man with a wonderful life ahead of him. But your girlfriend, Juriah, was killed yet somehow his life-force brought out her spirit to roam this earth!"

"I don't believe it!"

"He, your son, is made out of that powerful, unquenchable love you had for each other. So her spirit feeds on his energy and haunts you. There is only love here!"

"But she hates me! I feel it when she stares from the crowd. That horrible tapping on her thigh ... it's filled with anger and ... and violence."

"That I can't explain."

"And the ghosts on my clothes?"

"I don't know, they're just there. Maybe using the same energy."

"You have to help me, Makcik."

"I've done all I can."

With that, the bomoh picked up her crutch and hobbled out of the coffeehouse. The staring crowd parted to let her through.

Akri was left alone with her empty plate and the view of the snaking LRT track below.

16

IN A RED LONSDALE SINGLET and a baseball cap, Choy pounded the Zildjian drum set, clashing the cymbals and twirling the drumsticks high over his head, sweat pouring down his glasses. Zain leaped about the keyboards, Afro hair bouncing, silk shirt shimmering in the spotlights. Melissa swayed in a corner in her black waistcoat and tight black jeans, eyes closed, striking the strings of her bass guitar as if in a dream.

In spite of their rhythmic vigor, Akri's mind was somewhere else. He couldn't concentrate on the song. His thoughts were still on what the bomoh had shown him two days ago.

An embryo ... a bloody embryo!

He pushed the thoughts from his head. He needed to focus tonight.

But what did she mean by "There is only love here"?

AK47! AK47! AK47! Screamed the crowd in his largest concert yet.

Every seat in the stadium had been sold. A sea of shadows. Clapping. Bopping. Cheering.

He pushed the thoughts of the bomoh aside.

They're here for me. Every one of them. I mustn't let them down.

The band had performed three fast numbers. Now they would play what the crowd wanted to hear.

Akri put away his electric guitar and picked up a tattered acoustic. Zain, Choy and Melissa stared at him, surprise on their faces.

He plucked a few strings, then opened with a slow riff, alternating between a C and a G7. He drifted toward the crowd, Pak Mansur's trusty guitar in his hands. It was his silent tribute to the old fisherman.

If only he could see me now.

With the remote microphone fastened around his neck, he sang the first line.

The sun hollows the depths of my eyes.

The crowd roared.

Akri's fingers flew over the strings and his voice filled the darkness and the night sky.

Boats dancing on midnight waters for you
Is the moon a man when it waxes
And a woman when it wanes?

The crowd sang along.

This was the song that made him number one. Played in all shopping centers and available in all good record stores, said the adverts. The one on everyone's lips.

The song Juriah sang in his head after that first night she used his body as a bed. A soaring yet pitiful voice that nearly drove him mad, and it only stopped after he had recorded it.

When he first played it to the band, Melissa had tears in her eyes and Choy insisted they record it straightaway. Zain was speechless and finally said that he wished he could write so beautifully.

Why had Juriah given him this song?

This song of the dead? If his fans knew it was a spirit song perhaps they wouldn't be cheering. Perhaps they'd run home and pray feverishly for protection.

He turned to his sea of fans. A sea of people under a dark clouded sky.

In the front row faces were yelling, shouting, singing. Everyone stood and waved their arms as one and the security guards couldn't get them to sit back down. Lighters came on and from the galleries to the stalls it seemed a thousand stars filled the night.

Akri sang the chorus.

Eyes dancing, eyes dancing
Love is a timeless melody
The beholder of sacred destinies
Eyes dancing, eyes dancing
You're the first of my love
And the last breath I'll ever take

Akri had to fight to keep tears from his eyes. *Juriah.*
She had come and nothing could ever be the same.

As the pace increased, Choy struck the drums like a mad machine over the roar of the crowd. Zain tossed his head about as his fingers danced like spiders on speed across the keyboards. Melissa swayed in a blue spotlight, smiling sexily at the crowd.

Akri drove the plectrum up and down. For a second, he was back in the village, leaning against the chicken coop with Pak Mansur proudly watching him practice, the sea softly echoing through the coconut trees. Then the thumping of the drums brought him back to the stadium, its pounding sent shockwaves through his heart as though it was trying to break it apart. The words rushed from his throat like fire.

The stream moistens my lips to kiss you
I'll cradle our love deep into the sea
Is the moon a man when it waxes
And a woman when it wanes?

In this tumult of waving arms, a couple of girls with painted faces and AK47 T-shirts tried to climb on stage but were pushed back by the security guards.

Eyes dancing, eyes dancing
Love is the timeless melody

Arms were flying. Heads were shaking. Yet, even as he sang, Akri felt something wrong.

Then he saw in the front row of the leaping crowd, a figure standing still. Like a gaping hole. Like a mouth caught in a scream.

A motionless body.

Straight hair down to her waist. *Juriah!*

It should have been no surprise that she was here.

Akri struggled to continue singing. He should have gotten used to her appearances by now. But he wasn't.

Eyes dancing, eyes dancing
The beholder of sacred dreams

A red spotlight flashed on Juriah's face and the words got caught in his throat.

She had the same straight hair to her waist. The same height. The same build.

But …

... that's not Juriah!
He staggered forward.

Eyes ... da ... dancing
You're the first of my love

He now screamed the words.
His hands fell from the guitar.
It had never been her at all.
The figure reached into her pocket.
The spotlight flashed at the gun in her hand. Pointed at him!

And the last breath I'll ever take.

Her arm moved.
And Akri knew.
She fired just as the rock star leaped.

17

THE PARAMEDICS scrummed around Akri. Their crisp white uniforms gave them a ghost-like quality in the glare of lights.

"Why?" screamed Zain.

The paramedics had trouble pulling the guitar from Akri's body without lifting him, and finally cut the straps to get the instrument away.

Akri could barely smile as the heat of the stage lights fell on his black-garbed body. The police and security guards had formed a line between him and the fans. His fans. And they were deadly silent.

They lifted the stretcher and he felt he was floating. A drop of water splashed on his cheek.

It had begun to rain.

The woman who shot him was being hauled away by three officers. She was also in a stretcher. He wasn't sure if she was still alive. His fans had given her a savage beating.

Rain splashed all around them.

"Why did you do it, Akri? Why did you take the bullet? It was meant for me." Tears ran down Zain's cheeks as he stumbled beside the stretcher, his Afro collapsing in the rain.

Melissa's fingers squeezed Akri's hand. Choy yelled at the photographers to get out of the way as he rushed ahead of the stretcher.

Akri turned to Zain. He wanted to ask him a thousand things but all he could manage was: "Who was she?"

"We were having an affair. I broke it off a year ago. I knew all along who she was, but I didn't say anything. I didn't want Melissa to find out."

Akri blinked. His head spun. The spotlights seemed to fall into his eyes and lift him away.

"I'm sorry, Akri!"

"Look after my old guitar," he whispered and managed a smile.

Zain nodded. Relief on his face.

A flash of lightning cut through the sky, illuminating the stadium and the bewildered crowd. Some of them had put up umbrellas, many emblazoned with the AK47 logo. The merchandisers had been hard at work.

Akri was pulled down the corridor out of the rain. His clothes were soaked. The stretcher almost tipped over in the scrummage. The doors opened and they rushed out of the stadium into the torrent again.

The crowd surged around them. Some shouting. Some pleading. Some crying.

A girl with dripping hair pushed a pen and paper in Akri's face.

A security guard dragged her away.

They slotted the stretcher into the ambulance.

"Please be okay," Melissa cried.

"We'll be at the hospital," shouted Choy, droplets splashing off his baseball cap. "You hang on, okay?"

Akri wanted to say he'd try.

The ambulance doors slammed shut.

The whining of the vehicle filled his head as it shot down the highway.

His clothes were wet but also warm and sticky. He tried moving his fingers but couldn't. From the pain, he knew he'd been shot somewhere in the chest. Why did he take the bullet meant for Zain? He didn't know. Perhaps it was for Pak Mansur. Perhaps for Juriah.

One paramedic dried his face with a cloth and covered him in a blanket. The other gave him oxygen and then inserted something into his arm. He heard a machine softly beeping. His heartbeat, he guessed. He was a fan of *ER* and *Chicago Hope*.

Part of him wanted to laugh. Shot on stage in front of his fans. He wasn't John Lennon. Or JFK. Or Martin Luther King. He also wanted to cry.

He closed his eyes. He felt very cold. The whining seemed to slip away but the beeping became louder. The paramedics were talking but Akri couldn't quite hear what they were saying. His breathing got in the way. And the rain kept drumming the roof of the ambulance.

Through the corner of his eyes, lights flashed outside.

So what do you think of your situation now, my son, the bomoh whispered in that deep-river voice which meant she was chewing betel nut or slating her fearless gluttony. *Has Encik Akri, also known as AK47, machine gun man, Malaysia's answer to Bono, really learnt his lesson?*

Was there a lesson to learn here? He didn't know.

Blackness like a flock of hungry crows flew into his eyes. He saw his parents. His father before he disappeared when he was three. His mother on her deathbed, wrinkled hands in his. Pak Mansur, with hair like condensed milk, showing him a C chord beside the chicken coop. Lying naked in Juriah's bed as she slipped her leg between his thighs.

The ambulance hit a pothole in the road and he was jolted awake.

The vehicle stopped, followed by honking and scooters revving. Windscreen wipers clicking.

Slowly, the ambulance crawled through the traffic. Stopping and starting. Stopping and starting. One wheel climbing the pavement.

He heard its sad whining and the beeping of his heart, his rapid breathing and the paramedics still talking. But wasn't there a hushed sound out there? A whispering that weaved its way between the droplets of rain bouncing off the bitumen? It wasn't the bomoh. He knew this voice only too well. It sounded like a breeze through a cave.

He could feel her coming through the door. Sweeping in from the dark wet streets and the lightning-cracked sky.

Soft warm hands clutched his ankles. They brushed the blanket as they slid up his shins, thighs and over his stomach and chest. Her hair fell against his cheek, her smooth lips against his ear. Yet that familiar crushing weight didn't fall upon him. She must have been hovering over his body. Not using his body for a bed.

But the ambulance men, surely they could see her? But they couldn't have: they carried on talking. What was it about? All this yakking? Football. Yes, now he could hear them.

He could hear everything now, especially her soft soft whisper.

Open your eyes.

Juriah didn't try to prise open his eyes. Not this time. She knew Akri didn't care what he saw.

We'll be together through space and time.

Yes, Akri thought. *Through space and time.*

He opened his eyes.
And smiled.
The machine beeped rapidly.
A great pain tore up his chest.
The paramedics made several attempts to resuscitate the rock star. But failed.

18

A DREAM. It must be a dream.

Akri finds himself barefoot and creeping. He must be careful. He knows this. And the darkness that once engulfed him is drawing away and leaving him in shadows.

And his clothes, they are dry.

He sees the floor, walls, and a figure in front of him.

There is something in his hand. He looks and sees the silhouette of his old Bata shoes and is surprised at how much he has missed them.

He knows that the figure ahead is Juriah. She disappears downstairs.

He is afraid. Why?

The door. It might open and out might jump Juriah's beast-like father with a parang flashing in his hand. A parang with a hilt wrapped in plaster as though the weapon had suffered a vicious wound.

Akri bites his lip and looks away from the door. He doesn't know how he came to be here and how he can walk with no pain in his chest. He follows her.

He is breathing hard, but not that rapid broken breath in the whining ambulance with paramedics talking about football. This time his breathing is low and deep.

He takes the first step. Second step.

Third step.

He continues his descent with bated breath. There is no angry shout from behind him. Not yet, anyway. He is now halfway down the stairs. His breathing comes easier and the tension begins to leave his body.

Juriah reaches the lounge, glides across to the front door and, through the window, the streetlight falls on her face and it glows. Juriah looks up at him, straight hair falling to her waist. She smiles. His heart soars.

Akri has almost reached the bottom. The white vase of carnations is sitting there on the mahogany stand. Ever so priggishly, even in the dark.

It is right in front of him. There's something about it he should know about. But right now, he can't recall.

He takes another step and is now standing beside it. Juriah turns and smiles. He feels a sense of great relief. They've made it to safety.

Akri raises his hand to wave at her. His arm leaves the rail.

Rising upwards and sideways.

A thought jumps into his head.

The vase!

He had once seen it flying across the room like a vengeful ghost. He had heard it smash on the floor like a gunshot. And everything had changed.

He pulls his hand back to the rail just in time. He takes a deep breath and looks at the vase. The shadows of the pink carnations seem to move in the darkness as though caressed by a breeze. It is daring him.

Pak Mansur, Choy, Zain, Melissa, his thousand of fans—none of that will be if the vase isn't sent shattering to the floor.

He doesn't even need to think.

He reaches the bottom of the stairs and pads across to join Juriah. They kiss.

He can almost feel the new life growing in the warmth of her womb. Cell by cell in that pale light of her uterus. That grain of pulsing red that will never find its way onto a bomoh's tongue.

"Things are going to be very different now," he whispers.

"What do you mean, Akri?"

"I'll tell you tomorrow."

She nods. He slips on his shoes.

"I'll pick you up in the morning," she says, holding his hand. "At the shopping center."

He grins and kisses her forehead.

She gently closes the door.

Akri creeps past the four-wheel drive, slides out the gate and disappears into the night.

The song in his head long forgotten.

EARLIER STORIES

╳

Something Called Mamsky

THE WIND IS STRONG TONIGHT, blowing off the Tasman sea and the pitter-patter of desolate rain splatters my window. It's damp, cold—the kind of winter's night when I just want to curl up beneath woolen blankets and never rise again. How I long for sunny Brisbane.

Why Tasmania, Robert? Mother asked as she brought out the steaming hot pies, wearing those disgusting green oven gloves given by Aunt Josy last Christmas. *To get away from you*, I could have shouted in her plain, pale face. Could have watched it crumble beneath that cheerful smile, pies falling to the linoleum floor, the brown filling of meat and sauce spilling out in dark puddles around the cracked crusty pastry. *How dare you say that Robert, how dare you*, she would have said with hot tears springing from her eyes, her curly gray hair disheveled as if she'd just crawled from bed.

But I'd said nothing and the pies remained on the oven tray. I waited and held that anger. Only when it had fully dissipated did I open my mouth. And the words were soft and sweet like caramel. *It's a good university, mum. I'd love to be somewhere close to home but the course in Tassie's just right for me. And I know how you and Dad have always told me to put my studies first.* She smiled weakly, reassured of my love, although only slightly.

Dad had heard none of it. He just sat watching telly adverts with his unbuttoned shirt, his almost-empty can of beer and blissful TAB dreams. "Where the hell's my bloody job!" he had shouted at the newsreader one evening, flinging his beer can against the wall. Foreman of a textile factory with fifteen years of experience and no factories open. So he bought the TAB whenever he had spare cash, hoping, just hoping to strike it rich. He'd lost all his other dreams. His one pride was me. I was going to university and as far as he was concerned I could go anywhere I damn well pleased.

Mum, with her damn churchy friends. *Hallelujah, thy kingdom come, thy will be done!* Dragging me off to church each Sunday. It would've been all right if wasn't for Bible readings on Tuesdays and Thursdays. It was destroying my life. Not to mention choir practice on Friday nights. I resisted every move, every little piece of persuasion. Fought all her tantrums, her tears, her emotional blackmail. Heated arguments. So many we had. All about church. And I lost every one of them. So there I was three or four times a week with the Fanatics.

Damn Fanatics. Speaking in tongues. Not a pretty sight. Holding hands in circles. Singing and dancing round and round. Tongues flicking in purple mouths, in time to a crazy clicking sound.

... paka bante rine sokintare mare pake tore moti shalmari damere pakashara merime ...

Praise the Lord!

I felt like a bloody hypocrite. Did it just to please her. And she would smile so sweetly. But when her anger was raised, with the fury of the Lord brimming in her, she was like an ugly demon. She would switch without warning, from angel to Satan. It was dangerous. So I watched and waited. I'd endured her hell all my life. So I ran. University was my savior. Or so I thought.

Tonight with a cold wind blowing up the Derwent, snow on the caps of Mount Wellington, I yearn for home in Brisbane with the sun warming my skin ... even with the Fanatics, even with mum ... even with clicking tongues. Maybe I should have gone to Sydney or Perth, hell even Melbourne. But Hobart with its isolation and wilderness had called and I had willingly come.

Tonight we too had done some calling. A different type of calling. And something did come. Dear God, it really did come. It was all right when we were all together. Safety in numbers. That safety broke as each bedroom door closed. One by one. An occasional *good night* spilling out. Everybody's in their rooms. Sleeping peacefully beneath warm blankets. Can't imagine any of them shivering in bed like me. *Open your Bible and read*, Mum would say, *and ask God for heavenly mercy!* I freeze, almost thinking that this time, this one awful time, she was painfully right.

Bible or no Bible, I know the others are sound asleep. To them this would just be something that happened. Something they could maybe use as interesting conversational material over dinner. During dessert and coffee, somebody might just start it off by asking: "Do you believe in ghosts?"

One of tonight's participants would obliquely reply, "Well, one cold dark winter's night we met something strange ..." Yes, it would be an interesting tale. When you've seen or met a ghost, you instantly become more interesting. And I'm sure they've become more interesting for it. Character-building, you might say.

It's been three hours since I turned off the lights. The wind outside is now a distant howl. I feel a tingling underneath the plaster on my forehead. Feel the gash on my skin. The blood still clotting. The plaster feels cold, damp, like some slimy creature that will soon crawl all over me.

I push the thoughts away but others start to echo around my brain. I see the damn thing moving. I hear that scraping. I feel vibration in my bones. I'm afraid to close my eyes. Afraid to sleep. In case. Just in case.

Somehow I must have fallen asleep. The alarm startles me. I turn it off and it falls to the carpet noiselessly. Feeling an emptiness in my body and a throbbing in my head, I drag myself into a sitting position. Shafts of sunlight break through the mist and play on my blanket.

Morning. What a relief! Yet the light is too bright for my eyes. My blanket is twisted, my pillow flung to the floor. Must have had a nightmare. Last night was a nightmare. Waiting without sleep. Getting ready to scream for help. Thank God, morning has broken. Cat Stevens. Ha, ha. I fall back onto the bed. Bloody idiot. Coward. Afraid of ghosts and creepy-crawlies. Mum would have laughed. She'd laugh like an angel or shriek like a demon.

Hope I'm not ill. I hardly eat breakfast. I force down spoonfuls of cereal. Coffee smells good, tastes good too but it doesn't take away the sick feeling in my throat, in my stomach. Alex is spreading margarine thickly on toast. We exchange greetings. I hear myself tell him I need to rush. He doesn't mention last night and I'm relieved.

I step out into an English winter's morning in Hobart, cold and gray, dark clouds coming in from across the sea. Maybe it'll rain again; I adjust my scarf and zip up my jacket as high as it'll go. I stroll past dull, gray, narrow terrace houses with windows like watchful eyes. See a couple of kids getting packed off to school. Spy a couple of young girls with nice legs on their way to work at the supermarket. Watch an old man sprouting a dirty gray beard, muddy clothes, trotting toward a garbage bin. See a cat ...

No. No, it wasn't. Too quick to see properly. Some furry animal. Maybe a small dog, not a cat. Why would a cat follow me? Getting paranoid. Nothing's following. Nothing. Nothing at all. Must think of something else. Not last night. All a big joke.

I hurry and arrive at the bus stop. When I first got here I loved the cold. Loved the romance of it. The mist drifting down the river. Huddling underneath my coat watching the drizzle speckle the frosty pavements. Loved the windswept, luscious trees. Like being in an English movie. Fog, snow, hale, black ice: loved it all then. It's all too cold now. Especially at night. When things creep out and ...

The bus is coming ... thank God ...

The university buildings aren't too far from where I get off. I shiver as I step out and briskly head toward the computer labs. Computers are the present and the future. It is science: powerful, god-like, rational, logical.

I need to finish my program before the end of term. Mr. Brice was already assessing some of them ... but ... last night ...

Shit. Why can't I stop it? Can't seem to stop thinking. Keep wandering back. I see, I hear, I feel it on that damn table. It's alive and ticking in my brain. Feel like I'm falling. Being swallowed up. The scratch on my forehead is like a wound in my mind. I feel the creeping plaster there. It's a mark of madness. What in God's name is wrong with me?

The computer screen is a sea of crawling green and black, all out of focus. Been sitting here all day. Thinking ... about nothing ... but ... it. Repeating itself over and over. Can't think of nothing else. There is nothing but ...

"Are you okay, Robert?"

I look up at Mr. Brice. He sports thick plastic glasses. "Yes ... yes, fine."

"Are you sure? You look quite pale." He takes a seat beside me and glances at the screen.

"I'm fine ... just a touch ... of the flu ..."

He turns to me, his eyes magnified like burning orbs. "You know, you've been staring at that database design all day and you haven't done anything. You don't look well."

"Maybe it's worse than I thought."

"Your eyes—they're pretty red."

"Didn't get much sleep. I feel a bit under the weather, maybe I should go."

"Good idea. Come back when you feel better." He pats me on the shoulder and wanders off to the next student.

In a daze, I follow the winding path to the bus stop. The image, the noise, filling and emptying, filling and emptying my mind.

Getting dark. Hate these wintry days. The skeletal trees stand naked without leaves, like an army of limbs reaching out of the ground. Reaching for me. The mist hangs over the trees and drifts through the twisted branches. Reaching fingers. The gray of the campus buildings stand gravely in the chill. Like monuments. Like tombstones. Can almost hear the groaning creak of the hinges as the caskets slowly open. I shudder, quickly glance behind me and hurry on. My thoughts have become my worst enemy.

I return home. Home is a house in town shared by five. Chris and Alex are having bread and soup for dinner. I wave to Jane as she comes in. She smiles, her blonde hair falling over her sullen face. She looks anorexic. I feel exhausted. Maybe I really am ill.

Hardly eating dinner, I stumble to bed. So cold tonight. It's good to be in. Good to be beneath warm blankets. I reach for a novel. I can read the words. It works a little. I feel better. More in control. I read awhile and doze off. A few hours pass ...

Christ! I'm awake again. Sweating. It's hot. A sharp throbbing hammers my head. A wind howls outside. Rain splatters my window—rain or blood? Too dark to see. Breathing hard, don't know why. As if I've been running. Running to get away. From what? Hunted. Being hunted. My mind filled with one thought. The damnable events of last night.

Last night the five of us sat at that wooden creaky dining table in the lounge. Naturally varnished with scattered dark stains like undiscovered islands from meals eaten long ago. Eaten by people whom we had never met and God knows how many years of them there were. The last owners had most likely decided to replace the aging table and so, after many years of dedicated service, it was packed off to some used furniture store in town and sold for scrap. It had only cost us twenty dollars.

Used plates with potato, fat, gristle, shreds of spinach swirled in brown sauce sat one on top of the other. Could have been a Henry Moore. Half-filled mugs of tea dotted loyally in front of each of us university students. Energetic, full of life and expectations for the future. We were poor (or acted like we were) and shared this house together to keep our weekly rents low.

Strange tonight. No boisterousness or horsing around. No mad jokes, no political discussions or on-the-spot film reviews. And Jane's black-and-white television was off.

Tonight there was something else. There was energy. Like after a thunderstorm or just before a hurricane. A keenness edged everyone's faces. Though I tried to hide it, I was sure it showed on mine. That look of expectation. As if waiting for someone. As if Mel Gibson or Nicole Kidman was about to step through that door at any moment. We were waiting for someone. Someone special. But at the back of my mind, somewhere way back, I wondered whether that someone could have been a something.

"Hey Rob, it can be real exciting," Chris exaggerated a yawn and stretched out his lanky arms behind his head. He had dark hair and a twinkle in his eyes. Half French, half English—a combination across the English Channel. Not so difficult now with that Eurotunnel. "You know what it is?"

"No, what?"

"Well, there's five of us." He leaned forward and examined the face of each person. "We could get a Ouija going." As he said the word "Ouija" his expression turned serious.

"A Ouija?" Jane asked, a frown rising beneath her strands of blonde hair. I never liked walking next to her. She was taller than me. A home-grown Tasmanian from Devonport.

"Oh, you know the game," Chris said. "You ask spirits lots of questions, it's quite fun if it works. Any of you tried it before?"

"Well, I've heard about it," I replied. "But I've never tried it. Does it work?"

"Maybe, maybe not," Chris answered mysteriously. "Let's try it and see."

"Yeah, should be exciting," Alex chipped in with a grin. "How does it work?"

That was all it took to get us going. Chris tore bits of paper into two-inch squares. He scribbled a letter of the alphabet from

A to Z on each one, then took two pieces and scribbled the words "Yes" and "No" on each. While he did that, we cleared the dishes and wiped the table clean.

Chris placed each bit of paper in alphabetical order in a circle. The "Yes" and "No" scraps were placed at opposite positions within the circle.

A shiver ran through me when the circle was completed. It laid there waiting at the center of the table, measuring about a meter in diameter but looked much bigger. Not only bigger, but vibrant. Breathing a life of its own. It seemed to focus us into it. Bringing us together to serve something. A calling.

I tried to dismiss these thoughts. It was, after all, nothing but a circle of scrap paper. I was apprehensive but attracted too, not able to resist. Somehow it seemed forbidden. Dangerous. Yet drawing me. The others didn't appear concerned, it was no more than a joke ... a game.

"We need something for all of us to put our fingers on," Chris remarked as he looked around.

"Like what?" said Alex excitedly.

"Something light with enough space for our fingers." Chris surveyed the lounge, eyes darting from corner to corner.

"What about this?" an excited voice rang out. It was Dave, a Physics undergraduate with untidy ginger hair and scruffy clothes to match. He waved a plastic beer glass in the air, schooner size.

"That's perfect." Chris took the glass. It was transparent, with no handle and stood six inches in height.

I surprised myself by laughing. It seemed ridiculous to use that receptacle of intoxication for this purpose. Dave loved his beer. I felt better and thought we ought to start before I lost my nerve.

So the plastic beer glass was turned upside down and positioned at the center of the circle. One by one, our index fingers were placed on it. A meeting of fingers, a meeting of minds. Jane giggled. This could actually be fun.

"Ohh ... it isn't working," Jane said, breaking the silence. "Chris, are we doing it right?"

"Yes, Jane, but it won't work if you keep interrupting."

"But it's been twenty minutes! And my arm is getting tired."

"Maybe we should go for a beer instead," Dave volunteered.

"Be quiet, Dave!" Chris snapped. He rarely did so. "It'll work," he said in a quieter voice. "We just have to be a little more patient."

Ten minutes later, the plastic glass trembled.

Chris looked around at each of us to make sure we had all noticed. Everyone had. We leaned forward. Something was happening at last.

Slowly. As if dragging a heavy weight. The glass moved half an inch.

Then paused as if resting. It moved again. Then stopped. I almost felt pity for whatever was moving it. It moved a little further, about two inches. Doing better now. Getting the hang of it. Getting stronger.

"Read out each letter to me," Chris said as he took out his notepad and pen to write down the letters.

The glass continued moving slowly, making a dull scraping sound on the table. It headed toward the S, T, U, V, W part of the circle.

"V!" cried Jane excitedly. The glass paused, as if catching its breath, then moved away. At a faster pace. It was coming toward me and I shivered with excitement.

"J!" we chorused.

"P!" The glass was moving fast, the scraping sound more insistent. It seemed to vibrate my flesh.

"S!" The glass continued to move, dragging our fingers with it. It was going fast now. Moving powerfully. I was certain it was not being pushed by anyone of us. Nobody was playing tricks. It moved much too fast and too deliberately. The strong force came somewhere from the bottom where it scraped against the table. I felt its presence.

There was something else here with us. "L!" Chris was writing each letter down. "A!" Dave had a fixed look of amazement. U came next followed by D, R and B. "N!" The glass started to slow down.

"F!" The glass moved slowly away and came to a stop. We took our fingers off the glass.

"It worked," Jane said softly, her eyes dazed. We sat quietly, staring at each other in disbelief, mesmerized by what had happened. Chris passed me the paper he'd been writing on. It read: 'VJPSLA-UDRBNF.'

"It doesn't mean anything," he said with a frown. "We should try to communicate with it."

We took a break. Everyone was excited. We'd made a strange discovery. Something different, beyond the realms of the ordinary. An eerie communication. No mobile phones here. No optic cables. Just a plastic beer glass, scraps of paper and an old junky table. Even though the message we got back was utter nonsense, we'd got a response. The glass moved! It was incredible. Something was here with us and we were now going to try to talk to it!

We were back at the table. Our index fingers meeting. Chris told us what we were going to do. We waited for two minutes.

"Is anyone there?" Jane asked timidly. The glass remained still, holding all our fingers together, binding us as one.

"Is anyone there?" Alex asked, a little louder. No movement.

"Is anyone there?" It was my turn to enquire as we went round the table. The glass stayed still. As if waiting.

"Is anyone there?" Suddenly there was the familiar sound. The scraping. The glass had moved an inch. It was Chris. Somehow he seemed to be more involved. Seeming to draw it.

"What is your name?" I asked, pronouncing each word carefully. The glass slowly moved as before. Like a very heavy object being dragged along.

"M!" we instinctively chorused together. This seemed to encourage it as the glass moved a little faster and with more confidence.

"A!" The mover of this glass built up speed much faster than the last one.

"M!" It also moved differently. But there was something else.

"S!" It felt different.

"K!" I shivered, the scraping sound seeming to vibrate deep within my bones.

"Y!" The glass stopped as if it had hit a red light.

It was suddenly quiet but for the wind outside. Our fingers remained tethered to the glass. Chris, looking pleased with himself, lifted up his notepad and showed what he had written. It read "MAMSKY".

"We've got his name," he said. "It's Mamsky."

"Do you think it's a spirit of some dead person?" whispered Dave.

"I don't know, but you can ask."

Dave looked intently at the glass crowned by our fingers. We held our breaths in anticipation. "What do you do?" he asked.

Jane looked at him with a frown. It wasn't a great question. But the glass was already moving, heading toward Alex.

"F!" We chorused.

"Q!" The glass was moving rapidly.

"S!" It darted off without stopping.

"K!" Our fingers were being dragged furiously.

"Z!" The letters didn't make sense.

"J!" What was it trying to say? I had no idea.

"V!", "N!", "E!", "P!", "G!", "U!", "T!"

It stopped.

"FQSKZJVNEPGUT."

Made no sense to me. We looked at each other, puzzled. We could hear the rain on the window.

"What is it saying?" Jane asked.

"It's just nonsense," Chris said, shaking his head.

"Maybe it didn't understand us. Let's ask another question." It was Dave.

"Like what?" asked Alex. "You're the one with the clever questions."

Dave gave him a glare.

"Mamsky is a funny sort of name, isn't it?" Jane asked.

"Sounds sort of Polish, I think."

I stared at the glass. "What sex are you?"

The glass trembled. Moved.

"A!" We chorused faithfully.

"N!" It moved off again in the opposite direction.

"A!" The scraping of the glass on the table filled the room.

"M!" Chris wrote the letters down.

"A!" This didn't make sense.

"L!" It stopped.

Chris was excitedly pointing at his notepad. His eyes were wide. "Look," was all he could say.

"What is it?" I asked and looked at the pad. "A, N, A, M, A, L." I stared at a lost. And then I got it. "My God! It's an ANIMAL!"

The room lay in complete silence. Everyone staring blankly at each other. "You mean we've been talking to the spirit of some animal?" Dave asked.

"I suppose so," said Alex, "but what kind of animal is it? I mean …"

A sudden scraping. Our fingers dragged along the table.

"C!" We responded.

"A!"

Jane cried out, "Are you a cat?"

The glass moved to "Yes". And stopped.

There was silence. The wind howled outside, the rain hitting the window in regular waves. Somewhere a car sped by through the puddles.

The door to the house burst wide open. It swung on its hinges and slammed against the wall. A shattering of glass. The glass panel had broken and fragments flew everywhere.

The wind and rain blew into the living room, and before anyone could do anything, the pieces of paper from the Ouija were blown everywhere in a confetti of white. A wedding. Or funeral?

All that was left on the table was the glass. The pieces of paper with letters we'd faithfully been calling were scattered all over the carpet. It was a mess. Our Ouija had come to an end.

Alex closed the door and the wind and rain disappeared. I realized that there was an irritation on my forehead. I touched it and felt something wet.

"My God!" Jane cried. "You've got a cut on your forehead."

"Must be from the broken glass." Chris frowned. "A stray piece must have flown here."

Alex got out some plaster and antiseptic. After washing the wound, he put the plaster on. "Don't worry, Rob, it's not a deep cut."

I stared at him. "I'm bloody worried," I said. "Do you think the door blew open by accident?"

Everyone looked bewildered. There was silence. Nobody, it seemed, had linked the door being blown open and the breaking glass to anything more than the wind.

"Mamsky's with us," I said and felt the plaster on my forehead.

I'm lying in bed and feel fingers around me. It's like a sauna. My head hurts. Too late to regret playing that wretched game. They're all asleep peacefully, Chris, Alex, Jane and Dave. Unaware of my torment. Probably told the whole world of their night of excitement. But why me? Why choose me? No answers come. Just a realization that the game has not yet ended. That the glass is still moving and the hunt is on. I almost laugh at the stupidity, the irrationality of that thought. Thoughts of a mad man.

My head is pounding. Pounding hard. Sometimes it's like a sledgehammer at the walls of sanity. Sometimes it's like a meat tenderizer with serrated edges, like teeth, loosening up my mind.

I try to get up. Can't seem to rise. My limbs like lead. The outlines of my room edged in the dark. Study desk with scattered papers. Books untidily arranged. Pin-up board filled with outdated reminders. Van Gogh poster, bright yellow sunflowers. The ordinary world. Ordinary, simple, beautiful, rational. How I long for it. I'd do anything to put an end to this torment. As if in reply, the shadows of trees outside play on my walls. Swaying, searching—reaching out. Playing, telling me, *there's more to come my friend. Much much more.* I fall on my pillow, a dryness in my throat.

It's the sledgehammer now. A pounding pain. Harder. Sharper. Coming from the cut on my forehead. My body shaking, vibration softening my bones. Mercilessly, the sledgehammer continues its wicked pounding.

No science here. No rationality. No computers. Just things that move in the crazy darkness. Things forgotten from long ago. Like God. Like good and evil. And things that come when you call. Visions of Mum flood before me, in feverish prayer, tongue wagging holy gibberish.

... paka bante rine sokintare mare pake tore moti shalmari damere pakashara merime ...

Wet with perspiration. The shadows alive. Wind howling madly. The damn glass moving. The awful Scraping. Scraping to and fro. To and fro. Endlessly. Endlessly. The plastic beer glass moving. Dragging slowly like a great weight. Getting faster. More confident. More powerful. Faster and faster. At an incredible speed. Can barely see it move. Letters screaming. Boiling in here. My breath getting louder, spilling out in great heaves.

The scratch on my forehead bleeds. Warm. Wet. The cut ... the scratch! From the Feline Fiend! Feral Feline Fiend! I did see it near the bus stop. Been following me all day. My mouth is open. I'm babbling away. Don't know what I'm saying. All I can hear is The Scraping.

It's so loud it's bursting out my brains. Except it doesn't sound like scraping anymore. It's a *Scratching!* Oh, Jesus, it's here for me! Been prowling, hunting me all day. Now it's here. Scratching my mind to shreds. Help me, somebody!

Through this mind-paralyzing sound I see the door. It's opening. Very slowly. Very slightly. But definitely opening. Revealing the cracking slant of inky darkness beyond. Like the jaws of hell opening. Slowly getting wider. Just enough for something furry to come through. Oh God, I see it. A black shadow leaping in. It's here, it's come for me! It's Mamsky! *HELP ME, PLEASE ...*

I remember blood. A sharp, liquid pain in my mouth before passing out. I'm safe now. Yes, quite safe. The faint beeping of a machine. The smell of anesthetic. Plastic curtains on rails. Clean white walls. A row of beds. Nurses and doctors moving. Footsteps clicking in the corridor. Someone coughs. Bright fluorescent lights. Hurts my eyes.

Chris, Jane, Dave. They're looking over me. Concern etched deep in their faces. I try to speak to tell them. To warn them. But nothing. Nothing comes out.

"Don't try to speak," Chris says, his eyes mixed with pity and fear. "You need plenty of rest."

Jane takes my hand. "We've called your parents, they're flying in this afternoon."

I don't understand. Why are my parents coming? I came here to get away from them. Why are they coming?

"Everything's going to be fine," she says, her eyes moistening.

Running footsteps in the corridor.

Alex rushing in, alarm on his face. "They still can't find it. Looked all over the place. Turned his whole room over!"

What is he talking about? Can't find what?

"His tongue. The doctors say he must have bit it off then swallowed it!"

My tongue! Bit off! Swallowed it! Gone! Gone where? I'm trying to scream. Nothing comes out. Chris and Alex are holding me down. I'm fighting to get up. To scream.

The Scratching! The Feral Feline Fiend! Got my tongue! Damn cat got my tongue!! I'm trying to scream. Trying to scream *MAMSKY!!!*

✕

A SUMMER QUARTET

IT'S ONLY SINCE I'VE RETURNED HOME that I've been able to look back at that summer and not seize up.

That was five years ago. I'm married now. We want a child and we'll take that plunge into buying a house soon. Life for me, you see, is progressing.

But how can it? If I'm still standing in the mire of that summer? Of what happened to me, to Jason and mostly Bob.

Their faces dance before my eyes. Jason, with blond hair like sunshine, blue eyes like the sea—clean-shaven, lean and muscular. And Bob with plastic glasses and beard like a white Ayatollah.

As for me, I was Shamsuddin, in my fourth year in England. I left Malaysia at sixteen to do my A-levels. Instead of missing my family, I missed the hawker stalls we went to after football, sitting on stools beneath fluorescent lights, drinking coconut water, scooping up white flesh with metal spoons.

It was therefore strange that I was pulled into the circle of Jason and Bob. Like so many Malaysians studying overseas, I expected to cling to other Malaysians as I had done during my As. This was only natural, you stayed with what you were familiar with, taking refuge from this alien culture. And, of course, your head spinning from the way they spoke as if they had marbles in their mouths and then having to admit that in their country you were the one who spoke strangely.

Jason, Bob and I just happened. Perhaps it was our various personalities melding, perhaps it was my quiet disposition which they found gave their rowdy nature a chance to shine. This I'll never know. But being accepted by Jason and Bob opened up a new country for me.

We chased women, or "*wimmin*"—as Jason would say, sloshing down pint after pint of Bishop's Tipple, a particularly heady beverage, dark like stout and tasting like strong beer, and this would inevitably lead to us singing rowdily through campus.

At the insistence of my wife, I no longer touch alcohol, and pray five times a day. I fast all Ramadan too. Pretending's not for me. But sometimes, late at night, I can still taste Bishop's Tipple on my tongue. And the rancid sweetness of that summer.

At the beginning of the summer term, the university took on exchange students. That was how we met Deborah.

We were waiting for Jason when I saw him ambling along the river with a new girl on his arm. This one had curly brown hair, but was not thin and rake-like as usual. Instead, she had great curves and big hips. Pretty, as Jason liked them.

As they reached us, a cloud drifted by and the summer sunshine fell away.

"Hi boys, sorry I'm a bit late. This here's Deborah." They sat on the tartan blanket. "Deborah's from Massachusetts, she's here on exchange. Damn Americans, flooding our country!"

"You big joker!" She said and turned to us. "I hear you all study History."

"Yeah," said Bob. "I have to put up with their ugly faces every day."

"You mean pretty faces, don't you?" She turned and pinched Jason's cheeks. "All of you together. The best of friends, huh?"

"I suppose so," I said. "We must be pretty desperate."

Deborah laughed. "And where are you from?"

"Malaysia."

"Sounds nice," she said. "I'd like to visit it someday."

A cloud moved. Bright sunlight fell on us, throwing a dark shadow on her face, and that was when I perceived that behind those curved lips, behind the darkness in those eyes, thoughts were deliberately hidden, twisted thoughts I could not guess at ... I pushed the foolish image aside.

She glanced at me, for a second her smile fell, as if she knew what I'd seen.

Deborah changed our lives. It had always been the three of us at the pub, discussing music, guzzling Bishop's Tipple and sometimes even talking History. Girls came second. But now Jason and Deborah were inseparable.

Jason still appeared for classes and afterwards we would ask him for a pint. But no: *sorry boys, got to meet Deborah*. Of course, Deborah, always Deborah. And on those rare occasions when he did come along, it was always *Deborah this* or *Deborah that*.

"Bet he's with Deborah," I muttered.

"I know what you mean." Bob slurped his bitter, getting foam on his beard.

"We should be happy for him," I said. "For both of them. Deborah's a nice girl after all."

"Yeah, nice girl," said Bob with an expression I couldn't read. He stirred his beer with his finger, then sucked at it. He was a strange one.

Once after a lovers' tiff, Bob sent his girlfriend a dead rat by DHL. She called him a raving lunatic and left. He came to my place, completely disheveled, mud all over his clothes. He had been running all afternoon in the fields like a madman. To him, real music was heavy metal and his favorite T-shirt showed a two-horned creature crucifying a naked girl with blood dripping down her breasts.

Bob sloshed down the rest of his beer and got up. "I've got to go. There's an essay on Marxist Germany I've got to finish tonight."

"I'll stay and finish my drink," I said. I didn't feel tired and it was only nine o'clock.

"Okay, see ya tomorrow ... and don't go talking to stray girls in my absence."

I laughed and waved to Bob as he left the pub.

I sat alone watching a couple of guys at the dart board.

"Hello, Sham, what are you doing here alone?"

I turned to see a figure wearing a sleeveless T-shirt and shorts.

"Deborah ... I was just here with Bob, but he had to leave to finish an essay."

"Poor Sham, so he abandoned you?" she said, pouting. "I'll tell him off next time I see him."

"Where's Jason?"

"Oh, he's in Surrey, visiting his parents. He asked me to go, but I didn't feel like spending time with the old fogies. Want a beer?"

I shook my head.

She made for the bar. A few admiring heads turned as she walked past. It was hard not to stare at those legs.

Deborah came back a minute later and placed a pint of Bishop's Tipple before me.

"But I didn't want another drink."

"I know, but I thought you might like it anyway, it's a sort of peace offering." She sat beside me and crossed her legs, revealing flesh high up one thigh.

"What do you mean, peace offering?"

She lit a cigarette and blew smoke over the wooden table. "Come on, I know you don't like me. You think I've taken Jason away from you guys. I've seen the way you look at me."

I stared at her brown eyes, then decided to come clean. "Well, you did take Jason away from us, that's a fact. And I don't like you for doing that."

"But I didn't want that to happen. We fell in love and wanted to spend all our time together. I suppose it's selfish of me to want him all to myself. I'm sorry."

"Don't apologize, Deborah, you've done nothing wrong. I shouldn't be resentful."

"Well, I am sorry for not thinking about you and Bob. Can we be friends?"

"Sure we can," I said and grinned. Then she pecked me on the lips. I sat back for a moment, not knowing what to say.

She gulped her wine, disappeared and came back with more. She sat close to me and, occasionally, her bare legs brushed mine.

We spent the evening drinking and talking like we'd never done before. I felt envious of Jason.

"I knew you were my friend," she said and hugged me. I felt the softness of her breasts against my chest. I wondered what was happening but one part of me said not to bother thinking, to let whatever was happening happen. Yet another voice was saying that this was not good. It was bad.

All too soon the bartender was calling out for last drinks, and rang a bell.

"It's so boring here," Deborah said. "Pubs close just when you're starting to have fun. Let's go somewhere else ... how about drinks at your place?"

We bought a couple of bottles of red and took the short walk to the house. There were several houses on campus where each student was given a room with a desk, bed, wardrobe and bookshelf.

We sat on my bed, our backs against my wall covered with posters, taking swigs from the bottle.

What happened next fills me with shame, but it has also left me with a feeling I never wanted, yet cannot be erased—the thrill and pleasure of kissing Deborah, of slipping her T-shirt off, of unhooking her bra and kissing her naked body all over. It shouldn't have happened, couldn't have happened. But it did. And nothing I can ever do now can erase what I did. The betrayal of my friend Jason.

I could blame it on the drink, blame it on her seduction, say it was all her fault. But it was me, I was the weakling, I knew it was going to happen, yet allowed the events to take over. I could have easily pushed her away at any time but I just fell on her, my brown skin on her pale flesh, and let the world slide away. I had no friends. No loyalties. My world was nothing but Deborah.

The next morning, I woke to the sound of a lawnmower, blanket tangled around my feet, pillow on the floor. I reached out for Deborah and felt only crumpled sheets. She had left my door wide open.

That evening, I went to Deborah's lodgings. I entered the building and knocked on the door. There was no answer. I left, wondering what the hell I would have done if she was in.

A few days later, I was on the late bus back to university when I saw Deborah walking arm in arm with another guy. I jumped off the bus and saw them go into the Queensgate Hotel.

Peering through the window, I saw her—but the man's face was blocked by a pillar. They entered a lift with the sliding grilles which hid them from my gaze.

I ran across the road to the park and looked back. A light came on the third floor and two figures embraced, kissing and caressing. Then they fell away from the window and the lights went off.

I waited for a long time not knowing what to do, wondering if I had the right to do anything. I felt a mixture of hurt, anger and betrayal, for myself and for Jason. It only compounded my feeling of shame. In the end, I decided there was nothing I could do but go back to campus and drown myself in beer.

I went back to my room to find that even this was denied me.

Jason stood there waiting. "I managed to hire a car from a friend," he said with a grin. "Got me a great rate."

"I see."

"What you looking so morose about? Term ends this week and we're off on Monday."

The trip! I forgot all about it. Jason, Bob and I had planned a camping trip to France months ago. It was before Deborah came along but it seemed we were still going ahead.

"That's great, Jason. Did you manage to borrow that tent?"
"Got that last week …"

Jason discussed our holiday animatedly. It was like the days before Deborah. I looked at him and felt ill.

With great relief, I thought the trip to France was going to be called off because the next day Deborah broke up with Jason. We all found out that she had been sleeping around on campus. I wouldn't have believed it if I had not seen her at the Queensgate Hotel. Why she had to do it at a hotel, I had no idea. I felt a fool—just used and discarded—one in a queue of many.

As for Jason, Bob told me he trashed his room, then forced his way into seeing Deborah. *I'm leaving you*, Deborah screamed. *Over my dead body*, cried Jason as he flung her books across the room. The security guards were called and he was almost suspended.

Bob managed to persuade Jason that the trip was the best thing he could do. It would take his mind off her. It was not the best for me. I didn't want to see Jason. Didn't want to face my betrayal everyday. But Bob persuaded me to go.

So we arrived at Calais. I sat next to Jason, reading an AA map. Bob sat behind, his legs sprawled over the seats. We avoided the motorways and used the back routes. Our camping gear was in the boot. Cooking stove, eating utensils, corned beef, canned soup, torchlights, matches, sleeping bags. Bob had packed them all.

When we got to Reims, a dark cloud fell over Jason. We managed to chat with him in the car but at the campsite his manner became more silent, more rancid. This fanned my flames of guilt. Irrational as it may be, I felt Jason knew what I'd done.

Jason and I hardly spoke and it was only Bob's incessant voice that kept away the silence. Jason turned off his torch and we said goodnight to one another. I curled uncomfortably in my sleeping bag, wishing away the memory of Deborah's brown hair on my cheek, her lips on mine, our bodies warmly entwined. For a long time I didn't sleep, listening to the sound of Bob and Jason deeply breathing and the wind rustling the leaves outside like an unwelcome stranger.

The next morning, we set out early after bread and boiled eggs cooked on a rusty gas cooker. We headed for Chaumont, and then followed the winding road up the mountains. The sun hung over the snow-covered rocks and the car wound around the bends, climbing its way through the huge trees and escarpments. Though we took no photographs, as none of us remembered to bring a camera, when I close my eyes today I can still see those mountains covered in pure white.

On our way down from the French Alps, we picnicked on a hillside overlooking a green valley. None of us wanted to leave here, it was beautiful, but beneath it was a feeling of rot. This beauty we didn't share, we kept it to ourselves, hoarding it greedily with our eyes. This is where our friendship truly ended. We feasted on the scenery and the friendship became nothing. Our conversations empty and the laughter forced. I was sorry for Bob, he was the innocent one. I was snared in my shame, while Jason was buried deep in himself, reliving his memories of his lost love.

Ironically, the campsite we arrived at that evening was all we could ever want. It was set in the lower parts of the mountains. A stream burbled nearby and a small hill filled with fir trees stood behind us. The fresh air was delicious and nature blossomed everywhere: yellow speckles dotted the slopes and birds chirped on wooden fences. But I was too poisoned to be a part of it. If real beauty was inside the heart then Deborah had entered mine and corrupted it and I, of course, let it happen. All I had to do that night was say no.

The three of us sat on the ground sheet below a clouded sky that occasionally opened to let us glimpse the stars. The only source of light was from Jason's torch, hung from the tent pole, casting shadows on the ground sheet. The roast chicken was bought from the village and Jason carved it between us. We ate our meal, rinsing it down with cheap red wine.

I don't know why I decided to talk about pontianaks. Perhaps there was nothing left to talk about.

Bob seemed intrigued. "So it's some kind of vampire, this ponti ... ponti ..."

"Pontianak," I said.

"Right. It's a vampire, right? Created when a pregnant woman dies at childbirth?"

"Sounds like rubbish to me," Jason said.

"We Malays believe in it. It's our folklore. It may even be true."

"Yeah," said Bob. "Like Dracula."

Jason threw a chicken bone on his plate. "That's only some damn 19th-century novel. It's all bullshit to scare the peasants."

I ignored him. "Anyway, I was saying that to say the word pontianak aloud is actually an invitation for it to appear."

"So it likes its name, huh?" Bob grinned.

"You probably think she's a pontianak," Jason said. "Well she's not, she's a wonderful person."

"You talking about Deborah?" asked Bob. Bob and I already knew the answer. This was the first time during our trip that Deborah was mentioned.

"Of course, I'm talking about Deborah," Jason said. "Who else?"

"Well, you did break up with her, didn't you?" Bob scrunched his beard in his large hands and looked at Jason expectantly through his glasses.

"No, she broke up with me," Jason said, staring at the black blades of grass. "Don't you know what the hell's going on?"

"Don't worry about it," said Bob. "You'll be glad she's left you." Bob continued talking about the ins and outs of love but Jason was getting more morose. Bob was not doing a good job. I tried changing the subject several times but Bob, never one for reading the situation, always steered it back to Deborah.

"Forget her, Jason," Bob said flippantly. "She was the campus bicycle."

"What the hell do you mean by that!" Jason rose, eyes burning.

"She slept around, everyone knew that," Bob said, inching himself away from him, as though suddenly realizing what he'd done. "Don't get so upset, will you?"

"I'll get bloody upset if I want to, okay?" Jason shouted.

"Calm down, Jason," I said entering a conversation I didn't want to be part of. "Bob's just telling you the truth."

"Don't bullshit me, Sham. You ... you don't believe those stupid rumors too, do you? Well ... do you?"

"Maybe they're true," I said. "You could really do better for yourself."

"Deborah's not that kind of girl." Jason paced up and down on the grass. "Prove to me it's true," he yelled, pointing at me.

"You've drunk too much, Jason," I said. "Let's call it a night, shall we?"

"No!" he yelled, continuing to pace. "Prove to me it's bloody true or shut your damn mouth!"

To this day, I don't know why I said it. Perhaps I was so infuriated by his pig-headedness, or perhaps the wine had loosened my tongue.

"I slept with her."

Jason stopped in his tracks. We stared at each other for what seemed an eternity, then his features crumpled.

What happened then was a blur. Jason grabbed the carving knife, drawing it from the dismembered fowl, and rushed at me. I rolled to the side, shielding my body with my arms. Jason lost his balance and he fell on top of me. His knee jammed into my guts. I yelled.

Bob grabbed Jason from behind and both of them fell over me. I caught hold of Jason's legs. There was a scream—a cold, ugly shriek—and their bodies fell to the ground.

Bob got up and stumbled backward. From the tent pole, light beamed from the torch to the knife sticking from Jason's throat. Bright blood gurgled from the wound. His mouth opened and closed as if he was trying to say something. His face pale, frightened, uncomprehending. Blood foamed over his neck dripping onto the canvas. His hands reached up toward us. I stepped back, horrified. Then his limbs fell silently to the grass.

Bob stumbled over to Jason and put his ear to Jason's heart. Then he stood up, stared into my eyes and said: "There's no heartbeat. Jason's dead. We killed him."

As if in reply, the sound of engines came out of the night and two pairs of headlights meandered toward us. Two caravans were turning into the campsite. They would call us murderers.

X

"Quick, get the body into the tent," Bob yelled. I rushed over to Jason. This couldn't be. It wasn't happening. Jason was not dead. But he was. He was dead and we had killed him.

"Hurry up Sham, or we'll get caught." Together we wrapped the body up in the ground sheet and dragged it through the tent opening. Just as we put the bundle down, the caravans stopped in front of our tent.

"*Bonjour*, are you still awake?"

"Yes, we are," Bob called out in fluent French. "Have you just arrived?" I stood in a daze by the entrance, in the shroud of darkness.

"Oh yes," said the burly Frenchman in his fifties. "We're come quite a distance today, that's why we're so late. Sorry to have disturbed you with the noise."

"That's all right," Bob said. "We're just about to turn in."

"Have a good night then, and to your friend there too," he said glancing at me before trotting back to his caravan. Luckily, we didn't shake hands with him. Our hands were covered with blood.

I followed Bob into the tent. Neither of us dared turn on the torch. Bob slumped himself at the entrance. I sat opposite wishing the last five minutes hadn't happened. I tried not to look at the bundled shape at the end of the tent.

"I ... I don't know how it happened," Bob finally said. "I pulled him from behind and grabbed for the knife, then he fell ... he must have fallen on it, pierced him right through the throat."

Bob buried his face in his hands and I thought I heard a sob.

"I think it was me," I whispered. "I killed him."

"No you didn't," Bob croaked between his fingers. "I did it. Why the hell did I grab him?"

"No, Bob, it was me. If I didn't grab his legs, Jason would still be alive."

Bob raised his head, his eyes burning into mine. "Then we both did it. We both killed him."

I sat in the dark with this thought. They would call us murderers. No one would believe it was an accident. This was my fault. I blurted it out and Jason lost control. I glanced at his canvas coffin and shivered.

There wasn't much we could do that night, so we decided to wait until morning. We laid down by the entrance of the tent. I tucked my knees against my chest and closed my eyes, rocking my body. Bob was breathing deeply; I wasn't sure if he was awake or asleep.

Hours passed ... I thought of many things ... of my home in Johor Bahru close by the sea ... of Mak running excitedly out into the garden to tell me I got the grades for university ... of when I scored a hat trick for the school ... of my dead friend clawing his way out of the canvas bundle, his hands gone green with rot.

Jason grabbed my throat, his eyes red, his fangs open wide.

Why did you do it! he yelled in my face. *Why did you betray me? Why did you kill me?*

I screamed.

"Get up, wake up, you're having a nightmare!"

I opened my eyes. It was Bob.

I looked out at the grass outside awash in sunlight, breathing heavily. "Was it all a bad dream?"

"No, Jason's dead—we killed him."

I turned to see Jason's body wrapped in the ground sheet, so stark, so real in the daylight. I recognized the shape of an arm beneath it.

"What are we going to do, Bob?"

"Don't know. I need to think."

I crawled out of my sleeping bag. "I've got to get out of here." I left the tent and walked across the grass. The sun blazed in the sky, another hot day coming.

By ten o'clock the temperature had risen to the high thirties. We took refuge under a tree, leaving Jason's body alone in the tent, now like an oven.

In the afternoon, Bob went to the village and brought back a large spade. When our neighbors were not looking, we went into the forest and he found a spot behind a tree.

I dug first, shoving the spade into the earth and shoveling it out, on and on, until my back hurt. Still I continued digging. Anything to not have to think about Jason. We took turns until the grave was ready.

By the time we returned to the tent, night had fallen.

"We'll have to bury the body tomorrow," Bob said. "Don't think we can find the grave again in this light."

We slept outdoors. I didn't think I could sleep in the tent again. I tossed and turned in my sleeping bag, confounded by the shrill of the insects, and when I looked skyward the stars were like a million watching eyes.

The next morning, the body was still with us. We dragged it to the forest and the gaping grave. We placed it in a half-sitting position as the grave was not long enough. Our friend Jason could have been sitting down for a meal or a pint of Bishop's Tipple.

It was too hot. I returned to the tent. Later, Bob came back and said that he hadn't completed the job.

"It's a stupid idea," he said. "Should've thought it through. We can't just say that Jason went missing can we? They'll just search for him with dogs and they'll find the body here. Got to think of something else."

I spent that afternoon under a tree. Each time our French neighbors approached, my heart skipped a beat. They never entered the forest, though. All they did was fish, dragging out glistening bodies that thrashed about in the searing sun.

Bob and I did nothing all day but sweat in the heat.

The next morning, the second morning after Jason's death, Bob said we were leaving. Bob drove the car close to the forest. We pulled Jason out of the grave, his body still covered in the ground sheet. After checking that we would not be observed, we brought him out of the forest into the open.

"*Monsieur*, may I give you a hand?"

I almost screamed.

The Frenchman stood smiling with a mug of steaming hot coffee in one hand.

"No, thank you," Bob replied. "We're quite all right."

"Are you sure? It looks heavy." He stepped forward and rested a palm on the canvas.

"No, no," said Bob. "We'll be fine, really." He pulled the body toward the boot, away from the man's hand.

"Thank you anyway," I added, using my French for the first time.

"As you wish," said the man. He continued to watch us, sipping his coffee.

Just as I got Jason's legs into the boot, an arm fell out of the canvas and dangled between Bob's legs as though it was going to grab his scrotum. Bob's eyes widened. I was about to confess everything when I realized that the Frenchman was looking away. I quickly helped Bob shove the upper part of the body into the boot and slammed it shut.

"What was that big thing?" asked the Frenchman.

"Oh, just another tent," Bob said before I could open my mouth. "A spare one, we pitched it in the forest."

"I see, must be a big tent," he said doubtfully.

Bob and the Frenchman chatted politely until Bob told him that we had to leave. He bade us a pleasant and safe journey. Then, without looking back, we drove off.

"You know we can't go to the police." Bob glanced at me as he drove. "It's too late to do that anyway."

"What ... what can we do, Bob? We have to do something."

He turned the car onto the main road heading south. "I know, I know." His forehead creased into a frown. "We have to get rid of the body somehow and call it an accident. Trying to bury it was stupid. We must lose his body."

"How are we going to do that?"

"I don't know yet. Let me think."

We drove on and on, past small villages and open fields with rolls of hay like massive wheels, up winding passes and down narrow tree-lined roads. I crazily hoped that just by going somewhere, anywhere, Jason would no longer be dead. The sun was high in the blue sky, and like the past two days, it became hot as hell.

Finally, Bob said we should head for Marseilles and he told me his plan.

I looked at the green hills speckled with white clouds. "Only the location's changed?"

"That's right," said Bob. "Everything else is the same."

By mid-afternoon Jason's body began to smell. It was only a slight whiff to begin with, but when we stopped for toilet or food, the stench was unmistakable. The petrol station attendant stuck his nose in the air, made a face, and looked at us questioningly. Bob pretended not to speak French and motioned for him to hurry up.

By evening the stench was like a rotting dog in the back seat. It came in nauseating waves. Even with all the windows down, the fetid odor still filled our nostrils. This was Jason's retribution.

Once Bob had to stop the car so that I could vomit my lunch. Dinner was out. Somewhere near Grenoble, Bob spotted a junk yard where he bought an old Citroën car engine.

Night fell and on we drove. We changed drivers a couple of times and by midnight we arrived in Marseilles. The town was still noisy with locals walking about arm in arm, and the sound of laughter and merry-making spilling from the bars.

Bob was worried about the body and the smell bringing unwanted curiosity. So we left the car in an alley and walked to a cheap hotel. While I had a shower, Bob called home. We each took the single beds and due to sheer exhaustion, sleep claimed me quickly.

The alarm clock woke us up before dawn. We had to get to the car before anyone got curious about the stench. It was still there. Bob drove it to the pier and, because of the suspicious odor, he parked it at a distance. An elderly man, with a black cap and large white eyebrows, was in charge and Bob told him three of us were going fishing for the day. After agreeing on the price he said the boat would be ready in half an hour.

It was the longest half hour I'd ever known. The fishing boat, when it finally arrived, was old and noisy and smelled of rotting fish. To me that was a blessing. It would mask the other smell. When no one was looking, we pulled the bulky canvas on the deck and pushed the oily throttle toward the open sea.

We'd been ploughing through the waves for about thirty minutes. The sun was tucked behind the clouds but the cabin felt like an oven. I stood out on the deck and allowed the cool wind to wash over me.

Bob was at the wheel. He looked questioningly at me. I glanced around. There were no other boats about and we were far enough from the mainland. I nodded to him and he cut the engine. The boat slowed and bounced on the waves. The anchor splashed overboard.

Under Bob's directions, I had prepared Jason long ago. I fastened his body to the Citroën engine. Oil and grime got all over his T-shirt. His skin was an awful color. One eye looked as if it was about to slide down his cheek and hang there like a ghastly pendulum.

I gagged at the stench. I tied the engine to his stomach. As its weight pressed on his stomach I heard a squelching noise come from within and I smelled something even more horrid and foul pour from his mouth.

Together we dragged the body to the side of the boat and sat him against the rail. We lifted his shoulders up and heaved him over. His head dangled back upside down, mouth open, eyes bulging, as if surveying the waters. With a heave we pushed his torso up and then the weight on his upper body dragged the legs over. Jason's body fell, hardly making a splash, the engine pulling him down to the depths. For the first time in three days, I felt I could breathe again.

"Please forgive us Jason," I whispered as the waves crashed against the boat. "For what we've done to you. You were our friend and we killed you. I don't know how … how it happened and I don't know if you'd ever be able to …"

I stopped. For that was when I saw Bob smile. A smile of satisfaction, even pleasure. Yet so much more. I shuddered, dreading to think what it could have meant.

"Well, let's go!" said Bob.

As the boat approached the pier, I saw a figure standing there looking out to sea. I knew who it was.

Her white top gleamed in the afternoon sun. Her hair danced in the salty breeze. Legs, long and smooth against the wooden rails. What was she doing here?

Bob smiled as he gazed at her. "I called her last night," he said.

I said nothing but watched the boat pull up beside the pier.

Bob jumped from the boat, hurriedly tied the rope and bounded up the steps to Deborah.

They embraced. They were still kissing as I approached along the wooden planks. Could it be that part of my mind had caved in? I didn't understand this. Bob and Deborah? This was all wrong.

"My darling," Deborah whispered in Bob's ear.

"My love," said Bob. Neither seemed to care that I was standing there.

"He's truly gone?" Deborah ran her fingers through Bob's hair.

"Gone for good, my love. He'll never come after you again."

"What the hell are you talking about!" I yelled.

They turned to me, surprised. And then I knew. Seeing the two of them together brought the memory back. That night at the Queensgate Hotel. The man with Deborah. It was Bob.

"Don't worry about it Sham," Bob said. "Your part's over."

"What part? What the hell do you mean?"

Then I caught an eye looking at me. Deborah's eye, behind her brown hair. Then I knew.

"Bob ... no ... I can't believe this. You planned it all. And Deborah, you were behind this, you wanted him killed just because he was hounding you!"

"Oh Sham, how could you say that?" Deborah smiled seductively.

"Go to hell! You were with Jason, then you were with Bob and then me. You're a bloody whore!"

"Shut the hell up!" Bob punched me in the stomach and I fell back against the rail, gasping, falling to one knee. "You leave her alone, Sham. It was all an accident."

"Accident?" I said, trying to catch my breath. "You knew Jason had a temper. You provoked him, you knew he'd react that way. It was no accident. You killed him!"

Bob clenched his fists and came toward me.

"Bob, no!" It was Deborah. "Don't make a scene. Someone might see us. Leave him."

She turned to me. "Sham, if what you say is true then you're an accomplice. Just as guilty as we are. And you'll go to jail, do you want that?"

She reached out to help me. I brushed her aside and got up.

"Bob," she said. "I think it's time to report the accident. You should go with Sham."

Bob looked at me. "Coming?"

I stared at him. He was a murderer. He stuck a knife in Jason's throat.

"You coming or not?" Bob stared back at me.

But I had helped in the struggle. I helped with the body.

"Well, are you coming, Sham?"

Deborah was right.

I was an accomplice. It would be jail for me.

I nodded. And despised myself for doing so.

Deborah smiled.

And so Bob and I reported Jason's drowning to the French police. Boats went out searching but the body could not be recovered. Nobody would be looking for a body on the floor of the sea, a body with an engine tied round its stomach.

I returned to England and then campus. I never saw Bob again. He left university and followed Deborah to America. I helped pack up Jason's things and sent them back to his parents. The only thing I didn't send back was a photo of her.

I'm looking at the photo now. It's propped against the desk lamp. Deborah is wearing a short-sleeve top and a hat. Jason must have taken it a month or so before he died.

Next to the photo is a postcard from Massachusetts. Don't know how she got my address. She's coming to JB to visit, arriving tomorrow. She'd broken up with Bob a couple of years back. "Just to pay you a visit," the postcard read. "To relive old times."

I run my finger along the postcard. It trembles at the thought of her soft pink skin, the curves along her breast, the smoothness of her thigh.

The bitter flame of Bishop's Tipple flickers along my tongue.

My wife is most enthusiastic that an old university friend is coming to visit. She insisted that Deborah stay with us. I didn't protest. I'll pick Deborah up from the airport tomorrow. I wonder what plans she has for me.

For the three of us.

✕

BIRTHDAYS ARE DEATHDAYS

AH, I CAN ALMOST FEEL THE FRAGILITY OF HIS BONES! The gaunt features blotched with dirty freckles, the flimsy layer of silvery hair not quite hiding the skull below, the gray stubble like a contagious pox on the man.

Nothing, nothing in those downcast eyes, no glimmer of hope, no kindling of life. The bones, thin and hollow beneath the parched, wrinkled skin, are like dry twigs ready to snap should I push. And push, I'm oh so tempted. A skeleton holding that bag of nerves, dead muscles, tissues, spent organs for almost ninety years, is ready to break. A lazy twist to that old, flimsy neck would end his existence and he'd thank me for it, grovel on his knees in gratitude, head flopping, eyes cast at the oily ceiling, tongue lolling like a dog's.

"Think it's Monday," he says. "Monday morning, see you fucking." His lips twist raggedly into what could be interpreted as a grin. "Wish I were mad ... mad for a cup of coffee. Maybe it's Thursday; Thursday's child has far to go."

With Herculean effort he struggles within his stinking clothes, pulls himself out of the urine-stained armchair, glances at the dining table filled with pills and bottles, hardly smells the rotting fruit—black, powdery, wormy—and treads to a kitchen where the odor is unmistakably rancid. Unwashed pots, pans, plates at impossible angles, caked baked beans fermenting on forks and knives, spoons buried in primeval stew, decaying rubbish spilling over the edge, cockroaches scurrying eagerly over his shoes.

Banging and clattering, the kettle is put to boil.

"Polly put the kettle on, Polly put the kettle on," he hums, his body trembling as he looks out the window to the wild sunlit garden. "I never ... never knew such hurt."

The kettle whistles, long and jarring, tugging him back from that memory, across the years, from a small town wilting under the scorching sun, past rainforest, sea, desert, the weed-infested garden, over the funnel-web nest, in through the moth-eaten curtains, to the steam-belching kettle.

That small town. Close to the rubber plantations where Indians collected milk from open wounds, saw goats roaming the scanty streets where wooden shacks on stilts passed for houses. Here our young banker leaped up the echelons to branch manager, the youngest in the country—celebrating at the only decent bar Kuala Pilah offered, the one next to the Chinese chicken rice shop, air-conditioned with the widest selection of karaoke tapes. And here he was introduced to a soft-spoken Malay girl with the lightest of skins and darkest of eyes. They were the perfect couple—so everyone said.

The stool creaks. He cradles the mug of steaming coffee, hand-painted with the face of a crazy clown, resembling Chairman Mao: shiny, bald forehead, mounds of black hair like graves on each side, wearing an icy grin. A 34th birthday present from Sarah. He stares at its muddy swirls, listening to the clock tick; and tick it does, until he can bear it no more and tears stream across his coarse, dry face.

"Sarah ... Zain ... Norlisa. Anything. Just to see you."

He whimpers like a baby gasping for breath, hardly seeing the shattered remains of the mug across the linoleum floor. Cockroaches, feelers flicking, dart out of the shadows to the pools of brown liquid.

"I never meant for any of it to happen," he says in a dry rasping voice. He drags himself through a dark corridor of faded photographs to the bedroom.

How I've watched our man, from the day he disappeared from that small town, leaving the land of his fathers, to set foot in another country laced with hopes of a new beginning—the cool southeaster sweeping past the airport tarmac to his full, lengthy hair, cascading from a handsome, dark Malay face. Aquiline nose soon to breathe the gummed mountain air; lips to taste salty spray of waves from Sydney's harbor.

Those first few years were the best that ever were. Days of planting dahlias, of pruning camellias, of loving Sarah, nurturing Zain and Norlisa. Falling asleep under a sky of wine-colored clouds, on a Mickey Mouse blanket next to a basket of bread and cake, the toddlers' laughter behind the trees, Sarah nestled in his arms, rainbow lorikeets chirping from tree to tree, and the gentlest of winds rustling every shiny leaf. That was the best day in his life.

How could our oh-so-dear friend possibly know that two years later, on a beastly cold night of lashing wind and rain, he would be running for wife and children? Boot piled with bags and teddy bears, Sarah never once glanced at the rear-view mirror to see him slumped on a verge at the end of the road, panting, a mixture of cold rain and hot tears trickling down his cheeks, his voice hoarse from screaming out for her. She drove to Newcastle with a hard determined look on her face, blonde hair disheveled, fretting over how to tell mother of the bitter arguments, endless fights, black and blue tantrums.

He wandered back shivering to an empty house, and toward dawn with trembling hands, drank from that Chairman Mao mug given by Sarah, not knowing he'd never see his family again.

Since that night the years passed, grindingly slow with a bitter taste in his mouth, with eyes only seeing deceit, dereliction. Everything crumbled, everything broken.

Hiding in the squalor of his house, the ill-gotten sun scorching the garden brown, wilting dandelions; shivering alone beneath piles of unwashed bedding, the winter's wind clambering at the window. Never saw the falling leaves of autumn, floating gently, crisp and brown—or tiny leaves sprouting in spring, flowers bursting bright yellow petals.

The empty, desolate years crawled like a devouring funnel web on his thin naked body—needing Sarah, Zain, Norlisa, he dreams of life fleeing. But for the bottles—ah of course the bottles, in all shapes, colors, tastes, filling his cupboard, emptying his mind. Then came the cold pills and boiling injections which should have killed him long ago.

And today, his 88th birthday, our crying birthday boy, hardly able to stamp on the remains of a broken mug, Chairman Mao's eyes refusing to crack, had gone back to that humid town and known despair—not fleeting dark memories or pangs of guilt, but real shame, real regret.

A perfect couple—uncles and aunts whispered, parents met on both sides over sweet tea and banana cakes, marriage plans: well over two hundred to attend. But he, arrogant and ambitious, a month before the wedding, exclaimed over dinner that it was over. He was leaving this runty town—transferring to the big city, where a small-town wife would not fit, and Kuala Lumpur teemed with educated, sophisticated girls.

That night, this dark-eyed Malay girl, in the confines of her room by the shadows of her bedside light, hardly hearing the shrilling insect voices breaking the stillness beyond the spidery coconut leaves, slit her wrists with her father's razor blade and in fascination watched the clots of blood fall and stain the white bedsheet. Lying in its warm stickiness, thick with red, feeling life slipping from her body, she knew the fetus inside her was already dead.

So our birthday boy now for the first time truly feels, knowing what he did. Now, after years of hopelessness, after all he loves has left him, he truly painfully, feels.

And I, in a mixture of trepidation and delight, have always been there with him. My fingers mingling with soft brainy tissue, caressing his cerebrum, tainting thoughts, playing his emotions. Turning irritation to boiling anger, coaxing compassion to blank indifference, twisting Sarah's love and any affection that dare come his way, like a serpent against him.

His birthday and every following day are deathdays. An old man dead to life. There he lies on an unmade bed, watches the sea of cracks in the ceiling, listens to the distant hum of a lawnmower.

"Georgie Porgie, pudding and pie," he mumbles, "kiss the girls, please make him die."

He is barely able to smile.

Barely able to live.

Breathing deeply. Sleep creeps on him, muscle strands twitch and loneliness dissipates, finally. The eye of Chairman Mao watches him by his bedside clock that stopped long ago. A fly hovers, circling outside the window draped in silky spider webs.

I could wake him. Bring him back to hopelessness. But rest, rest to gather any remaining strength, for his waking hours will be filled with nothing. And lonely bitterness is all he'll ever have.

I'll be there in the shifting darkness, in the glare of daylight, floating in the giddying silence, to keep that old heart pulsing over these empty years. Squeezing, pumping the crimson fluid through leaky, clogged-up blood vessels, until it is dry like scrunched-up, yellowing newspaper. And still it will beat. The only way to end it is to take the final bow. I know its visions have speckled his thoughts, hand overflowing with Panadol, head in the gas oven, engine running in the garage. But he hasn't the will.

Perhaps it'll change, when loneliness breaks his back, when the sickness in his bones brings him to his trembling knees. Maybe then. Maybe then he'll slit his coarse, limp wrists, and in fascination watch the clots of blood fall like rain, like I did mine.

Maybe then I'll let him die.

HAZE

THE MAN WITH THE NEATLY-CROPPED HAIR GOT OUT OF BED, that scene of passion, scene of sweat. He buttoned his office shirt around his thin body, got the holes wrong and did it again. He rolled up his tie and slotted it into his shirt pocket, its end poking out like the tongue of a Maori dancer. She struggled from the sheets and slipped on a black nightie.

"It's late, I should go," he said in a room lit by dying moonlight.

"I had a good time," she whispered, not knowing why she said it, why she did it.

"I had a great time, too."

"Will you call?"

"Sure."

He kissed her lips, her forehead. She held him until, all too soon, he turned to the door. She led him through the darkened house, through the lounge to the front.

She watched the gate swallow his shadow. Heard his footsteps beating past the other terrace houses. She waited until the headlights of his car disappeared, then took to a rattan chair, her small body embraced by a large batik cushion.

She lit a cigarette; the flame fell upon a pale face, a delicate nose, a mole on one cheek, shadows under her eyes, her neat and carefully crafted hairdresser hair.

But this man ... this man ... she doubted she would see him again. He only wanted a one-night stand; that much was obvious from what he had said when she lay in his arms and disappeared into his eyes.

Don't get emotional on me.

The one-night stand. At twenty-nine she thought she was over such frivolities. She should find romance, a husband, children. She should get on with her life.

Lying tangled in the heat of this man, she wanted to talk like she had never done, but found solace in turning the fan on, listening to its rattling, both their bodies languishing in the warm breeze. She would one day buy a cool, silent air con, perhaps when she saved enough. Maybe then this man would listen to her talk about her father, but not now: he had closed his mind to her, his heart locked away.

She had not spoken of Father since the cremation. He had left the office one Friday evening. As he hurried down the narrow stairs of the shop lot, he stumbled and fell, smashing his head on the concrete. An ambulance came forty minutes later, by which time his blood had meandered five steps down and buzzing flies had circled the hot scented air, congregating on the rich globules that leaked from his broken skull.

She lit another cigarette. Placed her feet on the coffee table and toyed with the remote control, wanting something to watch so she didn't have to think.

She sat there hour upon hour, cigarette after cigarette, thinking about the man who had left her bedroom and the man whose shadow stood in the doorway all her life. She heard the mournful call to prayers from the mosque three streets away, she saw the sunrise beyond the curtains, coming up from below the car porch like a blob of an eye, watching.

She shivered. But hadn't she been shivering all along?

She rose, showered, soaping up her small naked body in the shower, put on her clothes and makeup and left for the hairdressers before her housemates woke up. She didn't want to face their questions about what happened last night after the bar, after they came back for wine, after he had put his arm around her in front of everyone. After she had stopped thinking of everything but the emptiness in the pit of her stomach.

A few weeks later, on her day off, she pulled a brown envelope from her letter box.

The television was blaring. She sat in the rattan chair with the batik cushion, lit a cigarette, placed her feet on the coffee-table and tore it open.

The cigarette slipped from her fingers, fell on an exposed thigh ... hit the floor ... sparks bounced across broken marble.

She did not yell. She did not scream.

A Chinese youth barked a rap number.

She stared blankly at the letter.

A Sunsilk advert. Benson *&* Hedges. Minum Milo.

There had to be a mistake.

Please let there be a mistake.

With it clutched in her hands, she found herself at the doctor's clinic.

The bench was hard on her bottom, the gray walls peeled, and behind the counter a sultry nurse called out names, gave out medicine and complained. The glass door opened, admitting old men, young coughing women, men carrying motorcycle helmets, babies crying and a white heat swept up from the baking, car-infested streets.

Finally, her name was called.

"Do another test, doctor" she said. "This can't be right. It was only for a stupid life policy."

The doctor adjusted his glasses, fiddled with his jade ring and shook his head. "No, it's correct. They have fail-safe procedures to prevent such errors. These blood test results are hundred percent correct." He rolled a pen between his fingers. "Young lady, you are HIV-positive, there's do doubt there. But you don't have AIDS. It may take many years before you get AIDS and so much is now being done for AIDS patients, there are drugs available and new research is being done all the time. And you ..."

"No, doctor, they must have made a mistake!"

He nodded. "We can test you again, if you like."

"No, I don't like. Just test me, okay?"

He drew the blood from her veins, dark red filling the syringe. She noticed the long surgical gloves he wore.

"Did you say something?"

"No doctor, just a prayer."

He reminded her of her father. Gray hair. Round face. Glasses. But the doctor didn't care. And her father, he cared too much. The metallic odor still wafted up her nostrils. Blood meandering down concrete steps. Black fat flies giddy from the feasting. One veined hand still clutching a plastic folder, a broken handphone beside a fallen shoe.

And the second test? It came back a week later. A week lived in a haze of caffeine, nicotine and alcohol. A week lived by a zombie, a hag, a bleeding menstruating whore. By anything but a fragile, feeling woman who would surely have gone mad from the burden of waiting with those twin agonies of helplessness and hopelessness.

Again it was positive.

HIV-positive.

She had AIDS.

She had bloody AIDS!

How, how could the vile thing have gotten into her? It had to be him! After all that wine, she didn't even think condom.

Don't get emotional on me.

What a fucking joke! She was emotional all right—she wanted to kill him. He had AIDS. The bastard.

With fingers massaging a tai tai's sodden head, she glanced in the mirror. The shadows were darker under her eyes, the pale face paler, the mole bigger, blacker. In her veins she felt the poison—saw its mark hiding beneath her powdered skin, ready to burst cold sores all over her body. What was she going to do? She wouldn't be able to work here anymore. Couldn't work anywhere.

She watched from the five-foot-way, carrying a pink plastic bag of mee soup, curry puffs and cigarettes. She was no longer one of them, those that sat happy in the air-conditioned offices, air-conditioned cars, air-conditioned restaurants ... laughing ... smiling ... cool and happy ... while this fire burnt inside her head ... knowing the virus surged in her blood ... just waiting ... and waiting ... For days she thought of killing herself.

Of slashing her wrists in the shower.

Of filling her mouth with pills and washing them down with wine. Far tastier. Painless too.

Then came the haze.

She awoke one morning and couldn't see the houses across the road. It was as if, while the people slept their air-conditioned dreams, a thick vapor had leached from the tarmac roads and grassless fields, rising like dead men's ashes to block the sun and sky.

Its breath choked the city, smothering hilltops, skyscrapers, cars, traffic lights, billboards, scarfed women with handkerchiefs over their noses, a parking attendant rubbing his eyes, two small coughing boys clinging to their parents on a motorcycle for dear life. She saw them all and felt their grief.

She was determined that this haze was to be her panacea. Her healing vapor. What else could it be? Why else did it come?

So every evening, she stood by her bedroom window, stuck her head out and inhaled its dust. Besides the angry traffic, barking dogs and prayers from the mosque, all she heard was her fan rattling.

She held the soot deep in her lungs, so its poison could seep into her blood, as if like a medicinal incense it would kill the virus.

It did not. Would not. Never did. Never will.

She must have been crazy to think it would.

But she continued breathing, knowing the haze carried no antidote but a pollutant. From her lungs it dissolved into her blood stream, and the carcinogens melded with the virus creating a chimera of illness.

After days of breathing corruption, after her body was truly fucked to bloody bits, one night she awoke and drove to find him.

It was past one but the bars were still full. She had a G and T and then saw him through the cigarette smoke—with a guy and two other girls.

He was laughing, an arm around the one with a skimpy miniskirt. An arm pulsing with blood filled with AIDS. He moved his hip to the pounding rhythm, hips ready to infect any careless girl.

And the bastard looked healthy. Too bloody healthy.

He was paying the waitress. She downed her drink and followed them out onto the street. The air smelt worse out here.

She tapped his back. "Hey!"

He turned. "Yes."

No. She had made a mistake.

"What do you want?" he said.

"Sorry ... thought you were someone else."

He glared and spun away.

She went home, barely able to keep the steering wheel steady. What would she have said if it was him?

You gave me fucking AIDS.

And then what? Watch him laugh?

Don't get emotional on me.

She wanted to cut his balls off.

And her father? He had left the office that evening. He wasn't in a big rush after all, lazily buttoning his trousers with one hand. She remembered now. It was coming back to her like incense burning in the back of her skull. And where was she? She lay like a broken doll on the carpet behind his black wooden desk, tears streaming down her cheeks.

The next night came upon her like a black ghost, stripping the sky of its remaining shards of light, leeching those heaving memories from her skull. The bubbling in her veins brought her to Bangsar again. The haze fell thickly as though expelled by some great smoke machine. She stared at the blackness above, expecting a giant mirrored ball to descend from the sky and, in time to the lasers, the crowd would dance to "Stayin' Alive".

A festival of the damned.

A Carnivale Macabre.

She carried on down the street, almost falling into a drain. A man coughed into a clenched fist. The signs of the bars and restaurants were smears of light upon the faces of these teary-eyed revelers. Cars looking for parking spaces squeezed between shadows of parked ones, their headlights unable to penetrate the gloom, the dust, the smoke. She came across a bar she had never been in, and entered. The fumes here were not as thick as outside but the noise crashed against her eardrums. Two expats, who looked liked Bosnians, were chatting up a couple of Filipinas—maids probably, not from the way they dressed, but from the hardship on their faces no make-up could hide. A group of locals scrummed around a table, perched on stools, some birthday maybe or a Friday night after a week at work.

She didn't have to wait long. A smiling mustached face came before her, offering to buy her a drink, then asking her to join his friends. They laughed. They drank. His arm around her, stroking the nape of her neck. At first she felt her body tense up but she forced herself to relax, she thought about the sea, the mountains, the holiday in Pangkor she once went with her mother when she was ten, anything but the hand that now caressed her breast.

And in her blood the mixture bubbled on.

She couldn't remember what he did for a living, something to do with plastic products. He lived in an apartment which he said would normally have a view of the city. But his bed was soft, perhaps like her heart once upon a time. He wanted to turn on the air con but she told him no, just leave the windows open. He barely protested and so the smoke filled their lungs as they embraced, as tongue met tongue and sweat met sweat. He came with a soft gasp, like a cork released from a bottle of wine and she filled him with all the delights of HIV.

She had been crying. Yes, she remembered now. She had been crying behind her father's desk, panties around one leg, while father was walking away, closing the office door. She silently followed, a warm trickling down one thigh, panties dragging along the carpet. His handphone rang, beeping urgently. He let go of his zip and reached for it, but before he could put it to his ear, he turned. And saw her.

His face turned cold, filled with rotting guilt, and a realization that she was no helpless six-year-old.

That first time when wet algae-stained tiles rubbed upon her back. The leaky tap, the shit-stained squatting toilet, the bare light bulb, bright and spinning on a water-stained asbestos ceiling.

Through the haze-filled, dreary, smoky nights she wandered the bars, looking for men. Sometimes she would not find her victim, but mostly she did. As she watched the ecstasy rush up their faces, she saw, with a great satisfaction, terror leap like wildfire in her father's eyes as she grabbed his shirt and pushed.

Then the haze lifted.

The skies cleared. The skyscrapers shone like diamonds under the sun. The advertising on billboards could be read once again.

And she forgot about Father. Forgot about her AIDS. It was time to find a husband. Raise a family. No more one-night stands.

MONKEYS!

TECK SANG TWISTED THE SHEET IN HIS HANDS. And although the new National Panasonic with its optional dehumidifier and new-technology carbon filter hummed at a temperature set at a sensible twenty-two degrees, sweat was boiling acid on his forehead. The clock radio flashed two-thirty and even though Mariam didn't make a noise— no—it was *because* she didn't make a noise, not even the slightest hint of breathing or the grinding of teeth, he knew she too was awake. Other than her hysterical account of what happened when he'd rushed home from the office, they had hardly said a word.

Of course, there were grilles on the windows. Which fool living in this Indonesian/Bangladeshi/blame-the-foreigner infested country would refuse to install this fail-safe security device? And it didn't matter that the metal bars would transform the dwelling into a smoking cage should an electrical fault cause a fire. It was a question of balancing competing risks. But the grilles, fixed only two months ago by Low Kang Contractors, weren't narrow enough. They were supposed to keep out thieving humans, not thieving monkeys.

At ten-fifteen yesterday morning, Mariam entered the baby's room, so soothing in its Laura Ashley borders and curtains, where she let out a soul-shattering shriek and dropped the milk bottle. A monkey, gray fur, white patches bristling, was halfway out of the grilles, its dark head, arms and chest outside, its lanky legs, swaying crotch and long curly tail inside. It held something in its big brown hands, that cloth she had bought at the Isetan sale seven months into her pregnancy from an unsmiling Malay sales assistant who herself was pregnant and busy munching a biscuit. She admired the design: white teddies on yellow cotton, so dearly soft like Daniel's cheek on her breast that first morning in the hospital. That was only a month ago. As the monkey pulled the bundle through the window, Mariam saw a flash of paleness. A flash of baby. She rushed to the cot.

Daniel was gone!

Inside the bedroom, the fan spun on number 2 while in the blazing heat outside, squatting on the top of the chain-link fence, three monkeys, all eyes and teeth, grinned wickedly as they fastidiously scratched their scrawny limbs. Then they ran with the bundle, scurrying across the road, leaping over the drain and into the jungle.

A dog barked. A car shot by. A telephone rang.

She thought she heard Daniel wail. A faint cry lost in the hot humid conspiracy of mud, leeches, mosquitoes, twigs, creepers, towers of leaves. Or was it a monkey hand over a baby mouth?

Shaking uncontrollably at the cot, she held his abandoned pacifier to her cheek, warm saliva still sticky on the nipple.

And Mariam blamed him, her husband. But was it his fault? He wasn't the one who didn't shut the window properly.

He kept his body still and prayed that the shadows on the ceiling were one of the gods or goddesses—any supreme being, it didn't bloody matter which one— bringing his baby back.

So much for prayers.

He coughed and wished he were drowning at the bottom of a swimming pool or had the guts to jump from a building, perhaps a brand new shiny one and fall on a tolled highway, causing the grandmother of all traffic jams. Instead, here he was lying in bed while his baby was out in the jungle, injured or worse. He wanted to cry but the tears refused to come. Why was that? Was his life so sterile that he couldn't even feel sorrow? Was it the 14-hour days at the office that had taken the life, the soul, out of him?

He turned and stared at his wife's back; his partner for the past twelve years. Those months before the wedding were difficult: a Chinese Taoist marrying an Indian Muslim. Not that it hadn't been done before. But trauma for both families was inevitable. Threats: financial, emotional, physical. Then denial. Finally, conversion, circumcision, religious lessons. A large multiracial crowd turned up for the wedding that went so smoothly. So what was all the fuss about? Of course, at Chinese New Year and birthdays his family was limited to the few halal Chinese restaurants in town. The food usually wasn't as good and more expensive too. But so what? Mariam didn't always come for she knew his mother loved suckling pig. And Dr. Raja's fertility program finally produced a baby. And now this.

And she, his wife, blamed him. He had insisted they move to this new housing estate. After all, he was foolish enough to work for the development company. Foolish enough to relocate because of the employee discount. Foolish enough to take that cheap Standard Chartered home loan. Foolish enough to stay in spite of the monkeys. "They steal bread. That's how it always begins," said the dull-eyed police officer as his team busied themselves with searching the jungle.

They had taken it from the gate as if they owned the place. When that avenue of sustenance was thwarted, they invaded the house scattering bread and plastic everywhere. Once they threw half-eaten papayas all over the kitchen so it looked like a cage in a zoo and their Filipina servant spent a whole afternoon cleaning it up. The neighbors complained and kept their windows closed, stifling though it was. But for Teck Sang, who was never home, his first encounter with them was at golf.

Teck Sang's ball had landed off the green. Hisham's shot ended up under a fledgling tree. "Don't worry," Teck Sang said, pulling his cart behind him. "You'll at least manage a bogey. Watch me par this one."

He checked his alignment, visualized the ball bouncing just before the hole—no—right *into* the hole for a birdie, then swung.

The ball leaped toward the flag and fell as he had visualized. As an engineer, Teck Sang had visualized many things: the BMW, the driver, the new house, working for Datuk Teh, the success of this development—the creation of the condominiums, houses, shopping center and golf course from virgin jungle. The ball rolled toward the hole, slowing down just as it should before ...

Black fingers.

A darting shadow.

The monkey leaped up and down beside the flag, the ball held high like a prized chicken egg in one hand. "I don't believe it!" cried Teck Sang.

The creature squatted on the center of the green, gave them a sly grin and proceeded to defecate on the manicured grass.

Teck Sang threw down his club and Hisham, the government officer, burst out laughing.

A laughter that soon stuttered and stopped. Teck Sang, very slowly, picked up his club. Both men backed away, eyes on the jungle beside the fairway.

In the shadows, scores of eyes glowed. Then they shrank back into the mass of trees. The monkey, still with the ball in its hand, gave a whooping cry before disappearing into the undergrowth, leaving behind a souvenir of soft steaming marbles.

Teck Sang turned in bed, his thoughts back on the baby. As the air conditioner continued its endless hum, fear turned to despair. Once again he contemplated suicide. Did calamity always produce such thoughts? Tragedy was in the papers every day. Teenage son succumbs to carbon monoxide poisoning from electric generator. Driver drunk on samsu sends a bus plummeting off a bridge. Fire kills six, trapped as the father in a panic couldn't open the padlock. Head-on collision kills the bride on the way to her wedding. It went on and on. He could lie here all night and conjure the newspaper articles from the depths of hell.

Teck Sang needed to urinate. Conspiring with his wife's pretence, he quietly, so delicately, slipped out of bed, leaving Mariam to the silent accusations of a mannequin. In the bathroom, the insect noises startled him. It was not its loudness nor its sinister quality but rather the implied threat, of creatures that could slip in through the grilles and wreck havoc, mayhem on a life so well-planned.

Why would the monkeys do such a thing? Was it revenge? With their metal monsters and projected P&L statements, humans had destroyed the jungle. But the stricken, homeless creatures didn't retreat deeper into the wilderness, for it was a jungle that was already being laid siege by other housing developments.

Monkey see, monkey do. You pay peanuts, you get monkeys. What other monkey sayings were there? Teck Sang wondered, as he tugged his pajama pants down and urinated, listening to its watery echo in fascination. There was something about a monkey and a typewriter. Once he had pewter figurines of the three wise monkeys: see no evil, hear no evil, say no evil. Where were they now? He didn't know. Why the hell did he lose them anyway? He washed his hands and wondered if he was truly going mad. Such recollections wouldn't help find Daniel.

Mariam was whimpering. A soft bitter sound. So she had given up the pretence of sleep. He didn't want to return to the bedroom, so instead he clutched the sink and stared at himself in the mirror. For a time that was all he could see, but as the minutes ticked by, the ball leapt toward the flag, the sparkling BMW, the new three-bedroom house materialized. But hadn't he, as he sat buried among the stacks of files, beeping phones, in-tray, out-tray, paper-clips, memos, Dell computer, yearned to hold Daniel before he grew up, to have more than this rat race, a life that didn't fly on autopilot until that very last minute when it plummeted to the sea, like it was doing now, and then everything, all the images, thoughts and regrets, resolved to the shadows buried in the trees— the monkeys staring back at him.

He was struck by the sudden realization that he hadn't held Daniel more than a dozen times since his baby was born, and he collapsed under a crushing blow, as though the roof had fallen on him.

Perhaps it was a minor heart attack. A minor stroke.

Or a major case of heartbreak.

With his cheek trembling upon the hard blue tiles, tiles that faintly smelt of bleach, he began to weep.

"Teck Sang," Mariam whispered, standing by the bathroom door in her nightie. "Are you, okay?"

"No," he said.

She went to him, both of them embraced on the floor. From outside, came the whooping call of the monkeys.

THE HIDDEN SHORE

IT WAS A BEAUTIFUL NIGHT. From where he stood, he could see the village lights to the south. Like little piercing dots, almost fragile, against the heavy, incessant pounding of the South China Sea. On a windy night, you could tell that the kerosene lamps were swaying on the beams of the wooden huts.

From this distance, the swaying translated into a twinkling of lights, like stars. Only a cluster of stars, for further south was darkness, nothing there but sandy shores and the dense pressing jungle—waiting to suck any careless wanderer into its entanglements.

And to the north was more of the same. Beach and jungle and darkness. So the village was but a cluster of fragile lights in the surrounding blackness— enveloping, all embracing. And the sea was always there. Crashing loudly, announcing its power.

More fishermen than usual were out tonight. Setting out just before sundown, returning after midnight. But many of the younger ones had turned from fishing and joined the oil company in town. Exploring, pumping and refining oil from far out at sea. Leaving their traditional ways behind, throwing themselves into the arms of the ever-waiting modern world.

Michael Robson breathed in deeply. The air was good and clean, and the wind was blowing, sweeping away the ever-stifling humidity. Rolling waves crashed onto the brown sandy beach and circled about his curling toes. His trouser legs were folded just below the knees, exposing his white skin to the white foam created by each breaking wave.

Despite that stupid incident with the boat today, Michael was able to smile.

To him, this was paradise. The view was magnificent. The stars, real stars, filled the entire night sky. His smile broadened. It was a fairyland stretching into infinity.

It was so vast that he was completely overwhelmed. He suddenly felt so small and insignificant. Just a speck in the wide, endless universe. And when you added the element of time, you became nothing. Absolutely nothing.

But here on this beach, he felt enormous. He felt greatness. His troubles disappeared and he felt only love. For he was in love with the most wonderful person. And with this love he felt the delight of life and living.

He laughed as he danced in the surging foaming waters. Splashing and spraying water with each step he made. But he didn't care. By the time he had finished his merrymaking and celebration of life, his clothes were completely wet. It was only then that he realized someone was watching.

"Tuan, what kind of dance was that?" asked Ramli, who burst into giggles without waiting for an answer. He clamped his small dark hands against his mouth, his body shaking in delight.

Ramli was not more than nine or ten. His body was thin and small, and he looked not unlike a monkey.

"Oh, that dance, it was an aboriginal dance from Queensland," lied Michael, hiding his embarrassment. "Have you heard of Queensland? Do you know where that is?"

"Oh yes, Queen land, it is somewhere in England, where your Queen lives." Ramli wore a deep wise look on his face and nodded to show that he understood what he was saying. The whiteness of his eyes were set like jewels in his tanned face.

"No, my friend, *Queensland*. It's in Australia, where I come from. Queensland's in the North."

Michael walked up to Ramli, the light from the Beachcomber Chalets lighting up his ruddy face which looked younger than his thirty-four years.

The Beachcomber Chalets were run by Ramli's father. It was set in about ten kilometers from the main road that linked the various towns and villages on the east coast of the Malay peninsula.

Ramli helped around with the chores and loved talking to the guests. Not that there were many guests here. There were only a few chalets and Ramli's father never seemed to get round to repairing those with the leaks. Many of the chalets were not fit to be let out.

"I would like to visit you in Australia one day," said Ramli as he walked alongside Michael. "I've been to Kota Bahru twice and next year I may even go to Kuala Lumpur. My aunty lives there."

"Well, Ramli, Brisbane's a lot further than Kuala Lumpur. But I'm sure you'll get the chance to visit me, one day perhaps, when you're a bit older."

They were walking along the path where it passed a row of chalets with kerosene lamps hanging from the rafters over the front doors. They swayed gently, casting moving shadows on the ground. Michael's chalet soon stood waiting in front of them.

"Good night, Mister Michael, I have to go home now, my mother will be angry waiting for me."

"Good night, Ramli, sleep tight," Michael called out as Ramli turned and scampered away into the darkness.

The sound of the ocean was further away. Its pounding on the beach broken by the coconut trees and surrounding undergrowth. The lights were on. So Zara was still awake.

Michael could see the white crest of the waves running through the darkness to the white sands like lovers blindly hurrying into each others' arms.

He gazed at the sun as it slowly rose out of the water to touch the clouds. There was nothing quite like a sunrise.

Michael made sure he saw it every morning with a cup of black coffee in his hands. Its aroma stirred his senses.

It was always cool and fresh and a light breeze would blow in from the sea.

He placed his bare feet on the wooden rail, crossed his legs and leaned back on the rattan chair. The cushion was old but comfortable. This was a morning ritual which he usually treasured.

But not this morning. Zara had been waiting for him when he stepped in through the door the previous night.

It was strange but sometimes he expected her not to be there. As if she would suddenly disappear. It was too good to be true. A dream come true. But now that dream was being sent back to the land of dreams, where it had belonged all the time. How foolish he had been to have wanted love in his life.

By some twist of fate they were brought together two weeks ago in that village just south of the Beachcomber Chalets.

His final soil samples were just being extracted when a pair of dainty feet in blue plastic sandals stared up at him from the sandy ground. The toe nails were painted cherry red.

"What are you doing, sir?" The voice was soft and almost melodious, the English surprisingly good for this rural outpost.

"Soil samples," he had said absent-mindedly as he looked up from his metal containers.

The hot afternoon sun was just behind her, high above the tall coconut tree whose outstretched branches clawed at the sky. The face from which the voice had emanated was shrouded in darkness but her silhouette disclosed a youngish female—probably in her early twenties—with a small and attractive shape. Her hair flowed down her shoulders and merged into the darkness of her body.

Michael blinked at the sunlight dancing on his face.

"Can you show me what you're doing?" she asked.

"Sure, come down here, and I'll show you." Michael was feeling bored anyway and he didn't think it would hurt being friendly. No, that was an excuse, he had to admit it. He was feeling somewhat down. Company would be good.

She knelt in front of him and Michael saw her face for the first time. It was perhaps his imagination then, but he was sure he saw her face glowing. Like the sunrise after an endless, sleepless night. A face so intense, full of beauty and life.

He must have stared at her for a long time, for she asked him if something was wrong.

"No, nothing's wrong. Everything's fine, just perfect." With hands that slightly trembled, he showed Zara how soil samples were taken.

He hated that. He hated to be so affected. Especially here, a million miles from home. She had stirred something within him.

What that was he couldn't tell for sure. Not at that fatal juncture in time anyway.

And this morning she lay asleep inside with the fan revolving slowly above her and as the mosquito coil made its last twist, smoldering itself into extinction.

Asleep, at peace, not knowing the crazy turmoil she had caused with those strangest words.

He had been happy last night on the beach and had managed to throw off the stupidity of the boat ride and accepted Zara as she was. The last thing he expected was to return to such disenchantment. Such despair.

He said no words last night but turned off the lights and turned away from her.

He lay there in the dark with his eyes open. It was warm and he pushed away the blanket. Zara was already asleep, softly breathing.

How could she sleep so easily? Was she not affected by what she had said? In a sonorous and mysterious answer, the insect voices came in through the mosquito netting. And beyond that, the surf was breaking.

The night was warm and Michael felt beads of sweat welling up on his forehead. They sprouted from the skin on his legs and crept along the hairs like globules of lava.

He pushed the blanket away and twisted his body away one way and then the other. After what seemed like hours, he slowly dozed off into the land of fitful dreams.

Now awake he sat alone in the early morning. Tired and washed up like a rotting log on the beach. Rolling with each wave as it pounded onto the waiting rocks.

And Zara was still asleep—undisturbed, like a child, her youthful face smiling in contentment, her small body breathing softly.

"I'm not going to Australia with you," she said last night as he walked in from the darkness. She flicked absent-mindedly through the magazine, her hair in a mess. The virgin white sheets were curled around her legs like a python about to slither up her delicate body for the kill.

Michael's heart fell. The python had strangled him, jumping across and winding itself around his torso. Suffocating him. Drowning every morsel of hope.

Michael said nothing but carefully sat down on the rattan sofa at the foot of the bed. His lips were pressed tightly together as he stared at her. He was good at controlling himself, to show no feelings, his hurt. She did not meet his gaze. She could have killed that python easily.

"I like it here. You'll like it here. I know I agreed to go back with you when you went home. I really wanted to."

She could have been talking about the weather. Could have been asking him about his day at work. She continued to flick through the magazine. There was a picture of an adolescent Malay model on the front smiling seductively. Michael felt ill.

The television was on and a man with a bright red tie and mustache was reading the news. The word MUTE in green displayed itself on the right corner of the screen. It was as if the same thing had been done to him. MUTE. No words, just listen.

He could see the thin and tall figure of Aunt Patty rushing up to him, the remains of the white china teapot scattered on the carpet and a huge stain growing. "It was—" he tried to say, as Aunt Patty slapped him hard.

"Shut your mouth, you wretched boy," she shrieked at him, her eyes wide and her white hair like a banshee. "You horrid child, you've broken my teapot."

"But it wasn't me," he said as tears welled in his eyes. His entire face stung as if it was on fire.

"Shut your damn mouth and don't give me any excuses!" yelled Aunt Patty as she stepped up to him threateningly. "Go up to your room and you'll have no dinner."

He ran up to his room as Antoine, the Pomeranian, yelped. "Oh Antoine, my little darling, did mummy scare you? Poor little thing." Aunty Patty's voice echoed up.

He had tried to tell her that Antoine had jumped up on the table and brought the teapot crashing down. But she wouldn't let him. Or maybe Aunt Patty already knew that it was Antoine all along. And it didn't make a damn difference.

Aunt Patty resented him. *Shut up, shut up, shut up*—she always said. Switched to MUTE. But televisions don't cry. Children do. And even grown-ups.

Zara was still talking about the weather, smiling and chirping like a bird. "So you see there's no need to go to Brisbane. We'll stay right here, you're going to love it, I just know. There's so many things to do. We can go sailing, swimming, sunbathing. You'll love all that—we're going to have a great life!" She looked up at him for the first time and smiled happily.

"But Zara, my contract here," Michael said as he approached the bed that seemed like a mile away, "it's over, we have to go."

He didn't bother telling her that she already knew he hated swimming, sailing and sunbathing. In fact, he hated the water; he didn't understand what the hell he was doing here by the seaside.

"You don't understand, darling," she countered as she gently held his hand and pulled him to sit beside her. "We don't need all that, we can live here happily together. On the Hidden Shore, we'll live there, we don't need anything else."

Zara stood up and padded lightly on the wooden floor. The bathroom door closed and he heard the tap turn on. He sat on the bed alone, confused and abandoned, surrounded by white sheets and pillows.

$$\times$$

Michael sipped his coffee.

The sky had now turned blue and a few cumulus clouds frolicked over the tiny silhouettes of a couple of fishing boats that were now making their way home.

The sea had turned a pale green. A few twigs, branches and dead leaves lay scattered on the beach. A black bird flew by and settled on a coconut tree.

Michael sighed.

It was so peaceful here but his heart was in turmoil. It was impossible to make sense of it all.

Zara would not go with him to Australia. He could understand that. This was after all her country. Her people.

Kelantan was her home. The east coast was her being. The village, her life.

But what was this Hidden Shore?

What did it have to do with them? With Zara? Why was it so important? He didn't understand any of it.

It was insane. This Hidden Shore!

That was why Zara wanted to go out on the boat yesterday. She was so insistent.

He didn't feel like it. It was hot and he was lazy, but Zara dragged him down to the creaky wooden wharf which stood ten minutes south of the Beachcomber Chalets.

Ahmad, who hired out the boats, was there listening to his transistor. It was a sixties pop song which reminded him of breezy days in Brisbane. It was out of place in this hot, humid country, surrounded by jungle, with Zara harassing him to go for a boat ride and the sun blazing on his face.

The waves were riding into the sweeping beaches on both sides. It was almost high tide. Zara passed Ahmad without saying a word. Ahmad slowly got up from the stool. He had a long white beard and his face was tanned a deep healthy brown with wrinkles that set themselves deeply in his face.

The radio was turned off and the unspoilt beauty returned.

"Hello, Mr. Michael," he said and smiled warmly, "want to go for a boat ride?" His grin displayed two missing front teeth and what remained were crooked or on the verge of falling out.

Ahmad led Michael to his small wooden boat named Sayang Bulan. Michael sat at one end next to the engine and Zara was already sitting at the front facing him. She wore a red T-shirt and around her slim waist was a batik sarong. She wore the blue plastic sandals that had confronted him under the coconut trees two weeks ago.

Now that he was in the boat Michael was determined. Ahmad started the engine and stepped back onto the wharf where he untied a thick and grimy-looking rope and set the boat free.

"Careful the coast over there," he called out as Michael pushed down the lever, "very dangerous there, many rocks."

The engine roared and the boat lurched forward and then they were heading out to sea.

Soon Ahmad was a distant figure and behind him there was nothing but the dense green jungle. Not even the chalets could be seen, for the trees and bushes from this distance had swallowed them up.

Michael could feel his heart thumping as the boat left the bay and the open sea spread itself in every direction. It was like the open hand of some giant which was so incredibly large that it was impossible to see. Its fingers ready to squash him into pulp like a helpless ant.

His breath became deeper, sharper, and his temple started to pound.

Almost involuntarily, almost without thinking, he pushed against the lever and the boat spun to the left, toward the coast.

As the trees came nearer, as the solid ground started to come within swimming distance, Michael's body relaxed and it gave way to normal breathing.

Zara's back was to him. It was only then that he realized that she was laughing. She undid her hair and allowed it to blow freely in the wind. She turned and smiled. It was a smile that Michael didn't recognize but would be very familiar with. It was a mysterious smile of complete confidence and satisfaction.

Was she laughing at him? No, there was no way she could know. She was just having a good time.

The waters were a bright green further out to sea. The hue graduated to blue along the coast where the waters lapped against the black protruding rocks. The jungle pressed against the coast and the sounds of birds and monkeys were clear against the sound of waves.

This was better. A lot better.

The boat continued to cut through the water as it followed the coast. Michael, heeding Ahmad's warning, didn't go too near the rocks; there were a few here and there but not too many. They passed the occasional sandy, deserted beach, each one welcoming, promising a delightful afternoon sitting on the sands and letting the waves wash over you.

"Go there," yelled Zara excitedly over the chugging of the engine.

Michael followed her index finger until he saw a clump of large dark rocks. They were large and jagged like a giant's incisors. The waters lashed against them and white spray rose up like fierce rain droplets toward the leaves on the hovering trees.

Alarm crossed Michael's face. "No way," he yelled back at her, "it's far too dangerous."

He had had enough. It was hot and he hated the sea. Hated it all. He had never been boating here and didn't like it one bit. And now Zara was acting crazy. He turned the boat around, away from the dangerous rocks, even though they were well clear of them.

A huge wave lashed the boat which rose up and then down and suddenly the rocks were a lot closer. Michael jammed down hard on the lever, and the engine roared, sending them away from the threatening rocks and toward the direction of the chalets.

"*No, no, no,*" shrieked Zara, despair on her face, "it's the Hidden Shore, *the Hidden Shore!*"

Michael ignored her and steered the boat along the coast back toward the wharf. He had enough for the day. Zara sat there toward him, her head in her hands, sobbing loudly.

"So you're not coming to Australia then," Michael said as they sat at a picnic platform on the beach that was part of the Beachcomber Chalets, yet set well away from it.

A small table with two stools stood on the wooden platform with thick branches that were tied all round acting as railings. Above them was a thatched roof of dried coconut leaves.

Michael hid his anger and pain. Last night, he danced in celebration on this beach. He was the happiest man in the world. Maybe he had even hit upon some form of enlightenment.

What a joke! He returned and Zara crushed his dreams. She refused to come with him to Brisbane and confused it all with that stupid incident yesterday on the boat and that so-called Hidden Shore.

He didn't know it was so important to her. Didn't know what it was. He thought all about it, all about her, while drinking coffee on the terrace this morning. Finally she had risen and acted as if nothing had happened. Maybe it was nothing to her.

Damn it, it was all so complicated. But he loved her. That made it all so difficult.

The wind from the sea blew in from the now-exposed beach and the occasional annoying fly buzzed around their faces. The remains of his spicy noodles, freshly cooked by Ramli's father, looked like an orgy of thin black worms. Zara didn't want anything. She rarely ate, if at all. She sat there tucking her knees up to her chest and smiling that same confident smile.

"I had a lovely sleep," she remarked, ignoring his question. "Were you lonely sitting on the terrace all morning? I would be with nothing to do. I suppose you were reading your novel. I don't really like reading, it's so boring. I like swimming and dancing on the sands. It's so nice here, isn't it?" Zara brushed back her long dark hair with her hand, her eyes were bright and almost sparkling.

"I'm so glad we met each other, Michael," she said as she reached out and took his hand. "You've made me so happy. That first time I saw you, I thought to myself: 'What is that man doing crouching under that coconut tree with all those complicated-looking things?' There was something in you that looked so lost and I wanted to talk to you. That's really difficult for me, to come out and talk to you. When you looked up to me I knew it, you were lost. You were looking for something in the earth under the coconut trees, but you couldn't find it, could you? You've been looking all around the world but couldn't find it. It kept running away every time you looked. So I decided that I'd find you. And when I bent down and you stared at me for so long, my heart started beating so fast that I almost fainted. For I knew right then that you would love me and I knew that I already loved you."

Michael, despite the hurt, could say nothing but stare into those wonderful eyes. She was right. He had been looking for something. He had traveled the world, Egypt, India, Europe, Indonesia and everywhere else. He had been running and searching for a long time.

He left as soon as he had finished university. Aunt Patty was glad when he went to university and she was even happier when he left the country. There was no love there, she didn't even like him. All it was, was a duty to his father. It was a mix of duty and dislike, maybe even hate.

And so he left at twenty-two to find his own life but he had not found it. Until now, twelve years later.

"Will you stay here with me, Michael?"

The answer was yes. *Yes, yes, yes.* He was so happy here. But it was senseless. He couldn't stay here, he knew that. What was he to do? What were they going to do in this remote part of the world? It was just so crazy.

"I really want to stay," he finally said, "but it's impossible, don't you see. There's nothing for me here. Why won't you come back with me to Brisbane like we'd agreed? It's beautiful there. I know you'd love it."

Zara's smile faded and she pulled her hand away. "This is my home. It's yours too if you only understood." Her voice grew louder, sharper. "I can't go with you to Australia." She stood up and threw out her arms for him to see. "All this is now our home. If you love me, you'd stay. There's nothing for you in Australia. Everything you want in the world is here." Her eyes blazed. "And you've forgotten the *Hidden Shore*."

Zara stormed off, leaving Michael alone. The beach, as always, was deserted and the tide was starting to come back in. His frown set deep on his brow.

Zara was acting crazy. He really had to talk sense into her. He'd never seen her this angry. He felt a pain rise up in his chest. It was hurt, anger and sorrow all mixed up and he didn't know what to do.

He felt an impulse to run into the sea and just swim into the distance. But he stopped himself with the thought that the sea would swallow him up. Like it did when he was eight.

They had been sailing for about an hour that afternoon. It was a Saturday; they had just had lunch at Pazzo's The Pizza Place and they did that almost every Saturday except when there was a big cricket match on. Then they would get Pazzo's to deliver. It would be cold and never as good but Daddy didn't complain, as he would be concentrating on who was bowling.

The boat was a thirty-footer and the wind was blowing just right, his father said. Michael looked forward to these sailing days when he could be alone with his parents and he loved watching his parents smile and say nice things to each other. Sometimes they even called each other 'darling'.

They couldn't go sailing too often for the boat was shared with two others of Daddy's friends. He wished that Daddy had his own boat. This boat was beautiful. It was clean and new and the white sails were large and taut against the southern breeze.

It would have been remembered as a wonderful afternoon. The sun was out and the sky was blue but for a few clumps of clouds. They seemed to have the sea to themselves. There wasn't a boat in sight and the shoreline was but a band on the horizon.

Seagulls flew in and ate bread from Michael's hand. His mother kept telling him not to lean too far out or he would fall into the water. And she wouldn't let him go barefoot either; it was dangerous, she said. But she did let him drink Coke and eat a big bag of crisps. That was a perfect culinary combination.

Michael saw his father's face change. It is difficult to imagine how somebody could chew on an egg and mayonnaise sandwich and smile at the same time, but that was what his father was doing at that precise moment. He was watching the birds gather around what must have been a shoal of fish, when he realized the sky was darkening rapidly to the south. First, he blinked, and then his smile evaporated as if sucked into his mouth and his brow furrowed deep.

"Looks like a storm is coming up, Lisa," he said as he threw the remains of his sandwich into the sea; almost simultaneously a seagull dashed by and pecked it from the water.

His father went for the steering and started to bring the boat around. "We better head back for shore right now."

"Will it be here soon, Andrew?" his mother called out to him as she started to pack the food up into the picnic basket. She knew that the situation was serious. Her husband's troubled face told her all she needed to know.

"Too soon, too bloody soon. Wish we had the radio on to warn us but I just didn't expect the weather to change like this."

Michael sat perplexed with his Coke and crisps. Suddenly, everything had changed and not knowing what to do, he followed his father's example: he threw the half-empty can and the remains of his barbecue-favored crisps into the churning sea.

The boat completed its turn in the direction of shore.

"It'll take us about half an hour to get back," yelled his father over the sound of the wind, "hope the weather holds until then."

But it didn't. Nobody said a word as the boat rode the large waves in the direction of safety. Both his parents gazed at the shoreline, wishing for it to get nearer, their faces grave and tight-lipped.

Michael shivered and clung to his mother's arm. He couldn't help but notice that the knuckles of her hands clinging to the rails were bone white. The seagulls had disappeared and they were all alone.

Everything was very wrong and the dark clouds were much nearer. Dark clouds of war. The wind carried a sinister chill like an albatross hovering over the sail.

Within five minutes the storm hit them. The sky was black and everything turned dark. A sudden gust of wind ploughed into the boat, sending them reeling to one side.

The sea rose up and sprayed icy cold water on their faces. Michael sprawled on top of his mother as she fell on the deck. She yelled out in pain.

Michael tried to get up but felt her arm pull him closer to her. He tasted salt on his lips. A streak of lightning cut through the sky, brightening the boat for an instant, and the loud crash of thunder echoed in their ears. Rain poured down in big heavy droplets.

"Don't get up," she yelled over the fury of the wind, "just hold on tight to the rails here." Michael quickly nodded to show that he understood.

His father miraculously was still standing steering the boat. "Got to bring down the sail," he said almost inaudibly as the waves crashed all around him.

He suddenly looked very vulnerable in his sports shoes, shorts and green sweatshirt. Despite being tall with broad shoulders and hard features, he looked lost. And scared.

He stumbled onto the deck as the boat jolted to the left, clung to the mast and started to quickly unwind the white ropes. He almost lost his balance a couple of times.

"Hold on tight now, Michael, I'm going to help your father." His mother, despite the bow lifting itself high above the stern and staying there for what seemed a long time, managed to reach his father.

Then the bow crashed down and it looked as if both of them were going to be swallowed by the raging waters.

But they held their ground with both of them battling against the wind, against the severe rocking of the boat. Lightning flashed across the sky, lighting up the streaks of pouring rain.

Michael clung hard onto the rails, shivering uncontrollably. He was soaked, his face wet with salt water, rain and tears. His heart beat loudly in his head, so loudly that his vision began to swim before his eyes. He felt faint but forced himself to hold on tighter.

And then he felt a churning in his stomach and a pounding in his head. Just as he vomited his crisps and Coke all over the white deck, the boat lifted high up and seemed to stay suspended in the air.

As it fell Michael felt himself turn upside-down and suddenly what was the black sky above became churning white waters. And he was falling into its welcoming arms.

Michael fell into the waves and deep into the murky water. He sank deeper and deeper, everything was bubbles and darkness.

He wanted to breathe in the water and become a part of the ocean but something said *no, kick with your feet, Michael, kick*.

Michael kicked hard and he felt himself stop sinking. As he carried on kicking, his sport shoes against the water, his body started to ascend. His lungs felt like bursting but he held his breath and kicked harder.

Just as he was about to give up and breathe in the water, his head suddenly splashed out onto the surface and he heaved, filling his lungs with air.

All around him the storm was raging, lightning and thunder blazed the sky, and the rain lashed upon his face. The boat was nowhere in sight. *Where was the boat? Where were his parents?*

He spun his head in all directions. He kicked off his shoes to lighten himself and kicked to keep afloat, turning his body one way and then the other. He couldn't see them anywhere. Panic swept over him.

"Mummy!" He yelled out as hard as he could. "Daddy, where are you?" He yelled again and again until he started sobbing hard and couldn't yell anymore.

His arms and legs started to hurt, trying to keep himself above the waves that lashed him from side to side.

He was alone. All alone, no one answered his calls. His whole body ached. A huge wave came at him, sending his body back into the water. He kicked himself up and coughed out water.

He was panting for air, struggling to keep his head above the water. He was going to die here, and where were Mummy and Daddy, why didn't they come to save him? He couldn't last much longer. He was exhausted.

Then out of the corner of his eye he saw a dark shape floating on his right. Without thinking he grabbed at it. It was hard and smooth. He pulled it to him and realized it was the lifesaver from the boat. That was unmistakable from the blue and white stripes on it.

He tiredly pulled the loop over his arms and over his head. Then he passed out.

"Mr. Michael, Mr. Michael—what are you doing?" It was a distant familiar voice. Michael didn't realize that he was bent over with his head in his hands.

He slowly pulled his gaze from the unfocused wooden floor and saw Ramli. He had a large smile on his dark, tanned face and wore a faded T-shirt.

"Oh ... just thinking ... that was all." Michael felt tired. Reliving the accident drained him.

A rescue helicopter came that evening. He remembered the loud whirling sound and, through half-closed eyes, saw it hovering in front of him, behind it was a most beautiful red blood-like sunset.

His parents had been caught under the boat when it overturned, that was what the police guessed, but they couldn't be sure. Both drowned. His mother was beneath the boat with her legs caught in the rigging. His father had been floating on the water with an arm missing, taken by a shark.

When he opened his eyes again he was in hospital and a tall, stiff figure stood there by the window. It was Aunt Patty with a scornful look on her face.

She strode up to him almost menacingly. "I promised your father I'd take care of you if anything ever happened. Why he said that, I don't know, maybe he knew something like this would happen, and it has. If you're going to stay with me you'd better behave!"

"Where's Mummy and Daddy?" Michael said tiredly, he tried to get up but hadn't the strength. Where was he and what was Aunt Patty doing here? He hardly ever saw her and he knew his mother hated her.

Aunt Patty's wrinkled and spotted face came up to him. "Dead, they're both dead, you wretched boy. And you're alive, aren't you? Going to have to live with me, aren't you? Always said your father was a loser and now look what he's done to me, brought me you to bring up. You're a spoilt, pampered boy, going to have to teach you how to behave."

Aunty Patty didn't wait for an answer but turned and walked out the room. Michael could hear her heels clicking down the corridor. He shivered in the hospital bed for a long time, hoping that she was lying. Yet deep down he knew she wasn't and death seemed the only place left for him to go to.

"I was thinking about what it was like when I was about your age," Michael said to Ramli as he got up and came out of the picnic platform. Ramli walked alongside him as they headed back for the Beachcomber Chalets. Crabs were everywhere as they came out, they ran a few feet and disappeared, leaving a multitude of fine trails in the sand.

"Did you have many toys?" Ramli quipped as he skipped ahead, ignoring the crabs as they alarmingly scattered in all directions.

"No, not many," Michael responded almost without thinking, the dreadful events still on his mind. "Do you have lots of toys?"

"My swimming pool," Ramli grinned, and then laughed as he pointed at the waves rolling in.

Not mine, thought Michael, *certainly not mine*. It was beautiful though, beautiful and dreadful.

The days after the accident were blurred. Maybe it was from the tears or tranquilizers. He didn't know. He had to be dragged to the funeral. Aunty Patty slapped him and warned him to behave and to stop sobbing like a spoilt child. He remembered many people, some came up and hugged him, others touched him lightly on the shoulders as if he was diseased or some kind of ghost that had no right to exist.

He remembered big beautiful flowers, the thudding of earth on the coffins, words he didn't understand. And a cold wind blowing. He didn't cry, didn't say a single thing. All he wanted to do was go back home and find out that it was all a stupid joke. His parents would be hiding there and would yell out "Surprise!" and he would rush into their outstretched arms.

They had arrived at the Beachcomber Chalets. Ramli saw two of his friends playing some kind of game on the beach and, waving to Michael, ran to join them. Michael wearily stepped up to the terrace of his chalet without realizing that something was wrong.

The door stood half open and as Michael pushed it open his eyes widened. "What the—"

It looked as if a tornado had swept through the room. The double bed was overturned with a pillow half peeking out, pathetically pinned against the floor; the painting of a Malay village hut lay in a corner, snapped in two.

A table lamp had been flung against the dressing table mirror, displaying a large diagonal crack; shards of glass lay broken on the wooden floor. The contents of Michael's Samsonite had been thrown everywhere, his clothes lay all over the room, and torn bits of magazines and books had become scattered debris.

Michael held on to the door frame for support. His first thought was a burglary. But something was not right about that. He had nothing worth stealing, maybe a hundred ringgit and credit cards, but nothing more, and a burglar wouldn't wreck the room like this.

It was Zara, it had to be.

Why had she done this? She was angry but surely not angry enough to do this. Unless she was crazy.

Michael spun round expecting to see her outside laughing at him, but it was deserted. *Why did she do this?* He would have to talk to her, to reason with her, to tell her that he cared and they would always be together. He would make her understand and calm her down, and they would kiss and it would be all right again.

But where was she now? He had to find her.

As if in answer to that question, his eyes were drawn to something on the sand. Whatever it was, it was surrounded by broken shadows of rustling coconut leaves. The sun was bright and glaring so at first he couldn't make it out, then he realized what it was.

They were letters written into the sand to form three words. He stepped off from the terrace and knelt on the sand to examine them. Though some of the letters were smudged by his own footprints, the words were unmistakable:

The Hidden Shore.

The Hidden Shore, the words shouted out at him, clawing for his mind. What the hell had the Hidden Shore to do with this? What did it have to do with anything?

She didn't want him to leave; the ugly state of the chalet told him that much. But this Hidden Shore business was crazy.

A clump of black rocks had wedged itself between their lives, and the damn shore wasn't even hidden! What was she ...

Then he knew.

He knew where she was going. She couldn't have gone long; if he hurried he would be able to catch her before she hurt herself. The currents there were strong and the rocks sharp and dangerous.

He had to hurry.

Ahmad was not there but Michael jumped into the boat anyway and somehow, by twisting and pulling the oily knobs and gadgets, managed to get it started.

The other boat was still there, he noticed; after wrecking the room, she must have slipped back past him and taken a boat from the village. It had been a crazy two days and it wasn't over yet.

Instead of heading for the open waters he brought the boat alongside the coast. It was a faster route, and it kept him away from the open ocean. The sight of its vastness sent a shiver through him. It was like a giant waiting, taunting him.

Michael, remember me from long ago?

You escaped that time. Why don't you join us now? Come to me, come on ....

Mummy and Daddy are waiting. We're all waiting.

Waiting just for you.

"No," Michael said out loud—surprising himself, "I've got to get to Zara, I haven't got time for you. You killed my parents and now you want to kill Zara."

He felt confused, angry and scared but the one thing he knew was that Zara was in danger. There was no doubt where she had gone and he had to get there in time. Why had she done this? Anger made you do stupid things.

And love too, a small voice said inside his head. He ignored it and concentrated on steering the boat toward the Hidden Shore.

The boat seemed to take ages compared to the previous day. He followed the coast leaving a white backwash against the blue waters.

The trees silently pressed against the coast above the rocks and sand. The monkeys and birds were strangely silent as if watching him in anticipation. Like the hush of an audience as the curtain opened in a darkened theater.

The sun stood off-center. It was about two in the afternoon and the sunlight fell directly on Michael's worried face, interrupted by shadows from the occasional passing cloud.

Sweat started to form on his brow and back. He took off his T-shirt and flung it into the corner that formed the bow. *It couldn't be too far*, he thought to himself. It had to be somewhere just ahead beyond that rocky point. She didn't have much of a head start.

The boat rounded the point a little too closely. The waves lashed at it and the rocks were tall, looming not more than twenty feet away. Michael nervously steered the boat away from the jagged coastline as he pulled away from the point. The water was rougher today. He had to be careful.

But where was Zara? He now had an almost uninterrupted vision of the coast and she was nowhere in sight. She had to be somewhere. *And where was the Hidden Shore?* It had to be just a little further on. He hoped he could remember where it was.

He cast his eyes around each inlet, each corner, but she was nowhere to be seen. The engine chugged on as the boat led him further up the coast. Had they come this far yesterday? He couldn't be sure. Where was she?

It then dawned on him that he may have been completely wrong. She might have just gone to the village and he had stupidly come here based on the writing on the sand which right now was being erased by the afternoon breeze.

Then he heard her voice.

"Michael, it's me."

He spun around and there she was, floating fully clothed happily on the water, rising and falling as each wave came in. She beamed.

"Zara, what the hell do you think you're doing?" he shouted. "How did you ...."

"Never mind that, darling. Come join me on the Hidden Shore."

Before he could say anything she turned and started swimming toward the rocks which he instantly recognized as the Hidden Shore.

The black, jagged rocks were unmistakable. There was nothing hidden about it. She swam slowly but a wave swept in and helped push her along.

"Zara, you can't, you'll kill yourself!" Michael yelled in panic. "Come back here now!" She was not more than thirty feet from the rocks.

Zara turned and floated on her back, crazily reminding him of a water lily. *"Come on, Michael, this is what you've been searching for all your life!"*

Michael's thoughts spun wildly, like shooting stars circling the endless night sky. And in that world he became nothing but a speck of dust while the universe continued its explosion into time.

This is what you've been searching for all your life.

He could hear thunder and lashing waves. His parents battling at the bow of the boat trying to get the sail down. The storm pounding at the three of them, the boat capsizing and the white waters becoming the sky, and the ocean, like a giant, swallowing him.

Aunt Patty, now five years dead, was yelling at him, her white hair and spotted face like a banshee's bearing down from above. *You wretched boy, do the right thing, this is what you've been looking for, you wretched boy! Go now!*

Then he heard Zara's voice, soft and warm. *You were lost and now you're found.*

She was so lovely, how she had made him laugh. And she was right. He had led an unhappy, lonely and stupid life. There was no meaning, there was nothing to it. *Until now.*

The water swallowed him like a long-lost lover as he dived into the pregnant waters after Zara. The momentum from his dive propelled his body forward just below the water's surface.

He surfaced for air and saw Zara, not more than fifteen feet in front, surrounded by the dark, angry rocks. She didn't look scared. She looked confident and happy.

She mouthed the words, *I love you.*

Suddenly a wave pushed him from behind and his whole body rose and fell forward with it. The wave continued and, in horror, Michael saw it wash over Zara.

He was sure she would have been pushed against the rocks but when the wave finally crashed, Zara was nowhere to be seen.

Michael had no time to think for a larger wave hit him from behind, sending his body hurtling toward the jagged rocks.

He was left not more than five feet away from them and his feet had still not touched the sandy bottom.

It was still deep here, with nothing to hold on to. Neither could he see Zara but he could see the sharp edges of the rocks like spears waiting, drooling trickles of salt water back into the blue green waters.

Drip, drip, drip.

This was paradise indeed, a deadly paradise. He waited for the next wave to come.

The man, who must have been about thirty-five, sat smoking his pipe at the foot of the steps that led to his modest wooden hut at the edge of the village. It was one of the better ones and stood close to the beach.

The water was calm today and there were children, almost black from the sun, splashing water and running away from each other in a game of endless tag.

He had just taken to the pipe about a year ago and took pleasure in the aroma from the tobacco. From the muscles on his arms and the darkness in his face you could tell he was a fisherman. But today was a day of rest; the fishing had been good the previous day. He had caught at least twice the amount he normally would have, and it had been raining. It had been a lucky day.

"He was a strange man," he now said to the two younger men sitting at the bottom of the steps.

One of them was mending a fishing net and the other wore a white skullcap which showed that he had been on a pilgrimage to Mecca. His name was Yusof.

Yusof was sharpening a parang, a long curved multi-purpose blade. It could be used for slaughtering chickens or cutting down sugar cane.

The man exhaled smoke which wafted up to the roof thatched with dried coconut leaves from which hung a large kerosene lamp. This particular tobacco was one of his favorites.

His eyes were bright and below them were the beginnings of wrinkles and he wore a long dark mustache that curled around his lips. "He spent all his time alone and I used to hear him talking to himself. It was all very strange."

"What do you mean strange?" Yusof asked as he tested the sharpness of the parang.

"He was a nice man, but strange. He would spend hours, maybe even a whole day in his chalet. Sometimes when I passed, I could hear him talking to someone, but there was nobody there with him."

The man mending the fishing net listened closely and nodded occasionally.

"One afternoon, we found his room completely overturned. He was seen taking a boat heading north along the coast. When he didn't come back the men went looking for him."

"Did they find him?" asked Yusof eagerly.

"No. But they found the boat washed up against the rocks. It was badly damaged. We never found the man. Not a piece of clothing, nothing."

"Maybe he drowned and was washed out to sea," offered the man with the fishing net.

"Maybe, maybe," said the man as he allowed the wisps of smoke to curl from his lips and be taken by the breeze. "Some of the old ladies thought that he might have met a spirit from the waters. You never know. They come looking for lost, lonely people. I don't know if he was lost or lonely, and I don't know if I believe in a spirit from the waters. But he was a nice man. He showed me an aboriginal dance on the beach over there." The man now pointed with his pipe.

The two men followed it to the beach well to the north. It was the beach belonging to the Pacific Resort Hotel.

The hotel was white against the surrounding dense jungle and stood fifteen stories in height. A couple of speedboats, the size of toys, could be seen racing through the water in front of the beach. A windsurfer was making his way along the coastline.

Many of their relatives worked there in different jobs. The work was easy and the pay was good and regular, and they had uniforms. But they had no boats, no fish and no wind in their faces. The men were not sure if the hotel was good or bad. It was just there. And they knew its story.

Ramli's father could not make ends meet and sold the Beachcomber Chalets many years ago. The land had then been sold a few times, and five years ago they built the hotel. In those five years, three tourists had gone missing while boating alone.

"Do you think the spirit took those three other men also?" asked Yusof.

"Maybe, maybe not. Maybe they were just careless and drowned. The currents out there can be very strong, you know."

Ramli took another puff from his pipe and again allowed the smoke to drift out through the corners of his mouth. "You never know with the sea. It can change just like that. It's the same with life, I suppose. You never know what's going to happen."

The two men nodded and said words in agreement. The one with the skullcap tied a knot into the fishing net. Yusof took out a bottle of oil and with a piece of dirty cloth wiped the oil along the blade of the parang.

Ramli looked into the distance and saw the fishing boats setting out for the night's work. It would be dusk in an hour or so and the stars would be out again, as always.

PIG HEART

THE ACTORS

IDRIS   An office worker and later trustee of the
               Khairul Heart Foundation
HUI LENG   An office worker and later trustee of the
               Khairul Heart Foundation
SELVA   An office worker and later trustee of the
               Khairul Heart Foundation
ANNA   A travel consultant and Khairul's fiancee
KHAIRUL   A former MBA student
HAMDAN   A member of the Abu Al-Jihad Youth Society
JOURNALIST #1
JOURNALIST #2
JOURNALIST #3
IMAM   The Muslim marriage solemnizer

Two other members of the Abu Al-Jihad Youth Society
Other journalists and photographers at the Press Conference
Guests at the Wedding

✕

I

Idris: Teh tarik satu, kurang gula.

Hui Leng: One Coke, no ice.

Selva: Give me soya bean, also no ice. My curry chicken, give drumstick okay? Eh, you two read the paper today?

Idris: About what? That man got rape in the KLCC car park?

Hui Leng: Yeah, terrible lah. Nowhere is safe nowadays.

Selva: Aiyo, I'm not talking about that. You didn't read ah, in the NST about that Malay fella with a pig heart?

Idris: What! What you talking about?

Hui Leng: A Malay fellow with a pig heart?

Selva: This fella on scholarship – studying Masters in London, MBA I think. This Rolls Royce come knock him down lah, on Bayswater Road, you know, next to Hyde Park, nearing Marble Arch,

	down Oxford Street, round corner from Piccadilly. I went holidaying there with my wife two years ago. Not Piccadilly but Marble Arch, we going shopping but, aiyoyo, too expensive now with the lousy exchange rate.
Idris:	And the fellow with the pig heart?
Selva:	Oh, ya, ya – doing MBA you know, London University I think, very prestigious. Family coming from Pahang, my brother knows his cousin. Only this morning he showed me the newspaper article, page two. My brother used to work with the fella in the Works Department.
Hui Leng:	With this pig heart guy?
Selva:	No, no, his cousin lah. Nice fella, my brother said. Live Datuk Keramat there. Three children. Drive new Proton, you know.
Idris:	Selva! What lah you! Tell us about this guy with the pig heart? I don't want to know about the cousin!
Selva:	Oh ya, ya, this fella with the pig heart. He was simply crossing the road, Bayswater Road, you know, next to Hyde Park, nearing Marble Arch, down Oxford Street, round corner from Piccadilly, when bam! this Rolls Royce coming knocking the poor fella down.

Idris: Yes, yes, yes, you told us that lah. But why he has a heart of a pig? Now, are you talking metaphorically, so that this guy actually is a greedy filthy person or has he got a real heart of a pig?

Selva: Oh no no, I'm not talking metaphorically. This fella really got pig heart, you know, made from swine. Living, beating and pumping blood in his chest.

Hui Leng: So this fellow with a heart of a pig was crossing the road and got knocked down?

Selva: No, no, no – before he crossing the road he had a normal human one. A human heart pumping blood through four pulsing chambers. Aiyo, what do you call them? These bloody chambers, eh? Atria and ventricles! That's right! Pumping rich thick blood through atria and ventricles!

Idris: And then? And then? Tell me lah!

Selva: Be patient, man! I was saying, after car knocking him down on Bayswater Road, you know, next to Hyde Park, nearing Marble Arch, down Oxford Street, round corner from Piccadilly, this fella had a heart attack, almost die one. So this English buggers, prominent, full-qualified doctors, Harley Street and all that, you know, they giving him a heart transplant. But, aiyo, instead of putting human heart they putting in pig heart. Bioengineered one, you know. Readily available and better rejection rate than inferior pathetic human ones.

Hui Leng: I'd rather have a human heart any day, and I'm a Buddhist! And I just love our delicious char siew pau, pai kuat, siew chee and my siew yoke fun. Mmmmm . . . char siew pau, pai kuat, siew chee, siew yoke fun.

Idris: What 'fun' are you talking about? This is terrible lah! How could those horrible mat sallehs do such a horrible thing! This poor, poor man. What is his name?

Selva: Khairul lah. My brother knows his cousin. From Pahang coming, you know. The cousin lives Datuk Keramat there. Driving new Proton. Nice fella.

Hui Leng: I've read about those pig hearts. The company that's doing it in the US is making lots of money. Aiyah! I wish I invested in it. It's listed on the NASDAQ. But how come this Malay guy agree to a heart of a pig? You Muslims don't eat pigs, right?

Idris: It's haram lah. We don't eat swine flesh, use it or even touch the damn thing. It's a foul dirty creature that eats anything.

Hui Leng: Aiyah! Not so bad lah! We Chinese eat it all the time – char siew pau, pai kuat, siew chee, siew yoke fun. Mmmmm . . . char siew pau, pai kuat, siew chee, siew yoke fun. And we don't get sick! See how strong I am! So, Selva, why this Malay man agree to a pig heart transplant?

Selva: This fella having a pre-existing heart condition. You know, born with the medical problem, but only surfaced after accident. If they don't operate, he die one, you know. The fella that knocked him down some English Lord – Lord James. Very kaya one, multi-millionaire, industrial products that kind of thing, own half the country. So he pay lah. Otherwise this Khairul give him law suit. So they put a pen in this Khairul's hand and he signing the consent form for heart transplant.

Hui Leng: Why he don't ask for a human heart, mah?

Selva: Aiyo, this Khairul he say he didn't read form properly, say he didn't see this thing about pig heart. Fella in hospital bed, on drugs and everything. So just sign lah, don't read.

Idris: So he was tricked into it! This is terrible! These English people are too much! Just because we were once their colony doesn't mean they can bully us. This is an insult to all Malays, all Malaysians and Malaysia! We must boycott their goods. Buy England last!

Hui Leng: Yah, you are right. Terrible people! That's why we must look East, not West. Buy British last!

Idris: Betul! These Westerners think we are inferior brown people. They lecture us about democracy, human rights, the environment and now they do something like this! It's all one big conspiracy to keep us in our place. They don't want us to industrialize, they don't want us to compete with them in the global economy. They've plundered our tin and rubber, they've sabotaged our currency and hijacked our stock market and now they insult us by putting a pig heart into a living, breathing Malay. We must stand up to them!

Selva: Aiyo, what can we do?

Idris: What can we do? I'll tell you! We'll remove this stinking pig heart from this Khairul's chest and get him a real human heart. A Muslim one! We'll set up a fund to do it. What do you two think?

Hui Leng: I agree!

Selva: I also agreeing!

Idris: To the Khairul Heart Foundation!

All: To the Khairul Heart Foundation!

11

There is the sound of a heartbeat which fades away.

Anna: [On the phone] I haven't seen him in two whole days. Not since the article in the NST. We tried to keep the operation quiet but someone leaked the news when Khairul got back from London. How is he? I don't know. I haven't been able to speak to him. His brother told me he's too upset to talk to anyone. Oh, his health? It's been three months since the operation. He's slowly recovering but all this commotion isn't doing him any good. Have you seen the paper this morning? Now it's on the front page! They are saying that this offends the dignity of Islam, the dignity of the Malays and the sensitivities of all Malaysians. They are calling in the British High Commissioner to explain. It's becoming an international incident. Oh, there's the doorbell. I have to go.

Anna puts down the phone and goes to the door. Khairul enters in a wheelchair.

Khairul: Hello, Anna. Surprised to see me?

Anna:	Relieved! So you've decided to come out of hiding?
Khairul:	I was torturing myself, thinking what people would say. I had nowhere else to go but here, to be with you.
Anna:	Why have you not returned my phone calls?
Khairul:	I don't know. I didn't feel like talking. Have you seen the papers?
Anna:	Yes, I've read them over and over. You're in the front page today. Oh how . . . how did they find out about the operation?
Khairul:	I don't know. I just don't know. It could have been anyone.
Anna:	But only a few people knew.
Khairul:	I shouldn't have told anyone in the first place.
Anna:	Including me?
Khairul:	Especially you. When I found out that it wasn't a human heart, I just lay in that hospital bed crying into my pillow. I couldn't eat. I couldn't sleep. I wanted to do my prayers, but didn't dare. Would Allah accept my prayers? Would he accept me? Or am I condemned to hell? I asked a thousand

times. A Muslim with a pig heart? I really felt like walking out of that hospital in my gown and then jumping in front of a double decker bus. What was the point of living? I'd become this foul, ugly, dirty creature which no one would want.

Anna: But I want you.

Khairul: Anna, it took you a week to get to London.

Anna: I couldn't get a flight! How many times do I have to tell you that! And you know I work for a travel agent. It was all booked out. Believe me!

Khairul: Perhaps you didn't really want to go to London.

Anna: But I did go. Even if you did pay for the flight. I did go, Khairul. Better late than never, right? I went for you. I flew to London because I loved you and still love you and will continue loving you. I want you. How come you're doubting me again?

Khairul: Lying there on that hospital bed with tubes sticking out of me watching the endless summer drizzle outside my window, I didn't think you'd want me if you knew about my pig heart. But I couldn't lie to you and tell you all was normal, even though you were thousands of miles away in KL. So I picked up the phone and told you.

Anna:	And I took that next available flight to London. Don't you believe me? I used all my contacts at all the airlines to get that flight. Please believe me, Khairul!
Khairul:	[Pauses] I do. I needed you there.
Anna:	And I needed to be with you. Remember how I wheeled you along the Serpentine that sunny day? We were throwing bread to the ducks and licking lovely ice cream. The sky was blue and there was a man with a hat sitting on the grass and playing a guitar. And there were squirrels running on the grass and climbing on the trees.
Khairul:	I remember only too well. We hadn't a care in the world. Our only worry was finding a halal restaurant for dinner, so we ended up in Malaysia Hall eating beef rendang and nasi goreng.
Anna:	And then a movie. They really had such a trouble with your wheelchair. You just loved all the attention, didn't you?
Khairul:	Yes, ah yes, I did. That was a beautiful day. I wished we didn't have to return to KL.
Anna:	So did I. I really cherished that freedom with no busybodies spying on us from the bushes as we held hands in the park and on the streets. I hate

that. You stare at these busy bodies and they stare back even harder at you. They make me feel so dirty with their eyes.

Khairul: That's how I feel right now. I feel the whole nation has its beady eyes on me. How did your parents react when they read the news?

Anna: Abah says it's a crime what those English doctors have done to you. He understands. He holds nothing against you. My mother . . . she needs some time to adjust to this. It's all a bit of a shock.

Khairul: Yes, it has been. My phone has been ringing non-stop for the last two days. My brother's going mad taking down the messages. I didn't read them until today. I couldn't believe it, they're all so supportive. They're even setting up a fund to pay for a new heart transplant. They call it the Khairul Heart Foundation.

Anna: The whole nation is behind you. They may be staring, some with fascination, some with curiosity, but all of them are behind you.

Khairul: Yes, I know. What a relief!

Anna: And our wedding next month? Will we have to postpone it? You know with all this media

	attention and all that? You never know what people might think, right?
Khairul:	As long as we love each other then there's no reason to do that.
Anna:	I suppose so.
Khairul:	Anna, I have one question.
Anna:	What is it?
Khairul:	Now that the whole nation knows that I have a pig heart, does that change anything?
Anna:	[Pauses] No, of course not. I love you for you. When you first told me that it wasn't a human heart, I was very upset and I cried all day. But that's only normal. Anyone would feel like I did. But I accepted it. And I still accept it.
Khairul:	So the wedding is still on?
Anna:	Why shouldn't it be? I want us to be together.
Khairul:	Are you sure?
Anna:	Why shouldn't I be sure?

Khairul: I have to go for Friday prayers now. My brother's taking me.

Anna: When will I see you?

Khairul: Tonight. Maybe tonight.

III

Hamdan: [reading the *New Straits Times* to the audience] "At the opening of a new Bukit Jalil medical center, Encik Khairul, who was one of the attending VIPs, told reporters that he had to swallow over forty pills a day as part of his medication and that his monthly supply of pills can easily fill a shopping bag. The side effects of these anti-rejection drugs include weight gain and mood swings. Fortunately, Encik Khairul has only put on six kilos since the operation and as for mood swings he asked reporters to interview his fiancee who he jovially said would be in a better position to know. When asked if he intended to enter politics because of his sudden popularity, Encik Khairul said that for the moment he wanted to get healthy again and finish his MBA in London."

[To audience] Who does this Khairul think he is? At first, I sympathized with him. But it's been weeks now and everyone is still treating him like some kind of hero. What has he actually done? Nothing! These British doctors put a pig heart in him and everyone says he's the rallying point for the nation. That all the political squabbles have suddenly stopped and now we as a nation have to fight the West to get our honor back. What rubbish! I, a member of the Abu Al-Jihad Youth Society, have worked hard for so many years for Islam and Malaysia and what recognition do I get? Nothing. Then this Khairul comes along with his pig heart and everyone is so sorry for him and treats him like a hero. Maybe they're even thinking of putting a statue of him next to Tugu Negara or maybe name a road or a building after him. For all you know, he might even have asked those British doctors to put a pig heart into him. What? You don't think so? I tell you this could very well be the case. As for me, I've had enough of reading this rubbish!

Hamdan tears the *New Straits Times* into shreds and drops the pieces off the stage.

IV

Idris: Teh tarik satu, kurang gula.

Hui Leng: One Coke, no ice.

Selva: Give me soya bean, also no ice.

Khairul: ABC satu. I'm sorry, I haven't been able to meet you earlier. Things have been very hectic for me.

Idris: No problem. We've been very busy too. Ah, let me introduce you to the trustees. This is Hui Leng and Selvarajah. I'm Idris.

Khairul: A multi-racial board of trustees. I like that. You guys should be on some government advert promoting muhibbah together with some catchy heart-throbbing song.

Idris: Heart-throbbing song? Nak gelak. No offence, eh? I suppose you're right. The three of us are what Malaysia's about. We are all good friends at the office and there's no polarization even at lunch time.

Khairul: That's good to hear.

Selva: So Encik Khairul, you okay now? Your health and all that?

Hui Leng: Eh, Selva, you mean Datuk Khairul. He got his Datukship last week. Didn't you read Friday's paper, mah?

Selva: Aiyoyo, I didn't know. I'm so so sorry lah and let me offer you my heartiest congratulations and felicitations and all the very best for the future, foreseen and unforeseen.

Khairul: Selva, there's no need for any of that. Becoming a Datuk was a surprise. I'm not even sure why they gave it to me, I haven't done anything for the country.

Hui Leng: Oh, but you have, Datuk. You have united us. The whole nation was getting so politicized with so much bickering between the parties and then suddenly you came along with your, err, predicament, and all of a sudden the whole country is united. You're our hero lah!

Khairul: It's nice of you to say that. I hope I can live up to the country's, the people's expectations. And please, don't worry about this Datuk business, just call me Khairul.

Selva: Oh, that's so very humble of you. Now Datuk Khairul, Khairul, I mean, your health, all okay now?

Khairul: Well, as you can see, I'm stuck in a wheelchair at the moment. It's not that I can't walk but I'm very weak. The doctors want me to conserve my strength. Also, I have to take a strict regiment of pills and injections to prevent rejection of the heart and also a whole load of antibiotics in case of infection.

Selva: I see, but otherwise everything okay?

Khairul: Yes, I'm fine now. As good as can be expected, I suppose.

Selva: Oh ya, my brother he knowing your cousin, Amin. Lives in Datuk Keramat right?

Khairul: Oh yes, my cousin Amin. Actually, he's my second cousin, I haven't seen him in years.

Selva: They working together in Works Department. Your accident on Bayswater Road, right? Next to Hyde Park, nearing Marble Arch, down Oxford Street, round corner from Piccadilly. I go there holiday with my wife two years ago. Not Piccadilly but Marble Arch, lots of shopping but, aiyoyo, so expensive with the lousy exchange rate.

Idris:	Eh Selva, I'm sure Datuk is a busy man lah. Datuk, you got any questions about the fund we set up for you.
Khairul:	Oh yes, I have. You know, I was very excited when I heard that you three set up a fund. I wanted to personally thank all of you.
Idris:	We wanted to do it lah. These English doctors are too much. How could they do this type of disgusting, horrible thing. We set up the fund so that our own local doctors can replace your, err, [points to Khairul's heart] heart with a human one. We'll find you a Muslim one!
Khairul:	How much has the trust collected so far?
Hui Leng:	I'm the Treasurer. I tell you eh, we started the fund a month ago and now have forty-five thousand. The public very supportive you know. Contributors come from all races: Malay, Indian, Chinese, Eurasian, Iban, Kadazan. Everybody wants to help. You know the Minister launched the fund, so a lot of publicity. Aiyah, you been in the papers many times. Our hero, what?
Khairul:	Oh, there's just been too much publicity. It's all a bit embarrassing. It's getting a bit out of hand. I have school kids coming up to me asking for my autograph and even a public company approached

	me to join their board of directors. It's all getting a bit much. Anyway, this forty-five thousand, is it enough for a new operation?
Selva:	I'm speaking to Pantai, Gleneagles, Damansara Specialist, Tawakal, IJN. All very good hospitals. All falling over themselves to do the operation. All want to give good discount. So the money collected is more than enough, no problem one. All you need doing is set the date for your operation.
Khairul:	Actually, I've recently spoken to my doctors, both here and in London. They've said that I should wait at least twelve months before another heart transplant. So I can set a date, but it's just not as soon as everyone expects.
Idris:	Oh, macam tu. In twelve months time, huh?
Khairul:	Yes, in twelve months time. Is that a problem?
Hui Leng:	I can't see any problem with that. In fact, the fund may have grown very big by then. By that time, all your medical bills will be covered and maybe even pay your expenses for a year. This fund can collect lot of money, you know.
Selva:	Datuk, if you agreeing, we can set aside extra money for other charitable purposes. Our

	Khairul Heart Foundation can be helping other Malaysians with heart problems.
Khairul:	That's wonderful news! Yes, yes we must do that. But we should change the name of the foundation to something else.
Selva:	To the 'Datuk Khairul Heart Foundation', eh?
Khairul:	No, no, please no. I don't want my name to remain at all. You know, I'm only a beneficiary of the foundation, not the founder.
Selva:	Aiyo, so very modest of you. I'm sure we can be working something out.
Khairul:	And the funds are in a single bank account?
Hui Leng:	Ya, ya, at RHB Bank.
Khairul:	And all three of you are signatories?
Hui Leng:	Ya, ya, any one of us can sign. But maybe later we change that, right Idris?
Idris:	Boleh, boleh. We set up the whole thing in a hurry. We were all so shocked about what they've done to you Datuk. I couldn't believe it lah. A bloody insult to Islam, the Malays and all Malaysia.

Khairul:	Actually, I really think the whole thing may have been blown a bit out of proportion.
Idris:	No, no, they did a terrible thing. We must fight this neo-colonialism. These Western countries think they are so bloody big lah. Who they think they are lecturing us about democracy, human rights, the environment?
Selva:	All one big conspiracy against us.
Idris:	Betul! The Western countries don't want us inferior brown people to succeed. That's why what has happened to you has united the nation against them. So we set up the fund, bukan to give you, to give the whole country back its dignity.
Selva:	To the Khairul Heart Foundation!
All:	To the Khairul Heart Foundation!

V

There is the sound of a heartbeat which fades away.

Khairul: I'd like to thank you for coming to this press conference this afternoon. As you all know there's been a lot of speculation going on since the news of my heart transplant first came out a few weeks ago. I'd like to read a short statement and then I'll take any questions.

Journalist #1: Excuse me! Before you start, is there any truth in what Sir James has alleged.

Khairul: What has he alleged?

Journalist #1: His statement via the British High Commission is that after he knocked you down on Bayswater Road you had two heart attacks because of your pre-existing heart condition. You were given the consent form to read and his secretary drew your attention to the paragraph about the bioengineered pig heart. You were told that because of the urgent need of a transplant . . .

Khairul: That's rubbish! I only found out after the operation. Do you honestly think I'd agree to a pig heart?

Journalist #1: We don't know what you thought. But the British High Commission has faxed us a copy of the consent form. I have it here in my hand. And it says right here, bold and underlined: 'The heart to be transplanted will be that of a bioengineered heart of a swine. The patient agrees and irrevocably consents to the use of such an organ and has no moral or religious objections to its use.'

Khairul: I didn't read that! I was too sedated! I was in a hospital bed!

Hamdan: Liar! You read the consent form. You didn't care what kind of heart was on offer. You didn't dare risk waiting for a human heart. The pig heart was available and so he took it! You're a murtad! You've renounced Islam!

Anna: Who the hell are you? Which paper are you from?

Hamdan: I'm not from any paper.

Khairul: Please leave! This is a press conference for journalists only. You're not welcome here!

Hamdan:	I won't leave. I'm from the Abu Al-Jihad Youth Society and have every right to be here. You'll have to throw me out if you want me to leave!
Journalist #2:	Excuse me eh, Datuk Khairul, I'm from The Star. Can you please tell us about the goings on at the Khairul Heart Foundation?
Khairul:	The Foundation collected enough for another heart transplant in the first few weeks.
Journalist #2:	This was to replace your pig heart with a human one?
Khairul:	That's right. But my doctors said I'd have to wait at least twelve months because I underwent the first operation only a few months ago.
Hamdan:	That's nonsense! We know you can do it straightaway. But you don't want to take the risk of another heart transplant, do you? You'd rather keep your pig heart! Not only do you have a pig heart, now you have a brain of a pig!
Anna:	Please be quiet! This is supposed to be a press conference not a shouting match. You don't belong here anyway.
Journalist #3:	Datuk Khairul, I understand you and your fiancee are getting married next week.

Khairul:	That's right, I wish I could invite you all, except for that extremist over there.
Hamdan:	You go to hell! Pig Man! You're an insult to Islam!
Journalist #2:	I understand, Datuk Khairul, that the Khairul Heart Foundation has lost all its money.
Khairul:	No, that's not quite true. All will be okay, if we can find one of the trustees.
Journalist #3:	So what happened to the money?
Khairul:	One of the trustees, Idris, has withdrawn all the money from the account and disappeared. No one can find him at the moment. The other two trustees, Selva and Hui Leng claim they didn't know what Idris was doing. I can vouch for their innocence.
Journalist #1:	So with no money, you can't have the operation?
Khairul:	No, not unless we find Idris or start a new fund.
Hamdan:	This makes you very happy then, doesn't it, Pig Man? Now you can't have the operation and you can keep your stinking pig heart!
Khairul:	You're talking rubbish! Get out of here!

Hamdan: We've made a police report about you. You're a threat to Islam, to Malay unity and the stability of our government! Just you watch out! We'll put you under ISA!

Anna: Please leave! You don't belong here! What's wrong with you people? Only a few weeks ago, all of you were supporting Datuk Khairul. Now all we get are insults and insinuations!

Hamdan: Talk about insults? Your Datuk Khairul is an insult to Islam, an insult to the Malays, an insult to Malaysia! If he's not careful I'll tear up his stinking pig heart with my bare hands!

Khairul: I don't have to take your abuse! Get out of here!

Khairul, in his wheelchair, tries to run over Hamdan. Hamdan throws Khairul out of the wheelchair.

Khairul: You're a mad man! A bloody mad man! When you die, I'll bury you with a pig! That's what I'll do. Put your naked body in the earth with a filthy rotting pig! Then we'll see who's an insult to Islam!

Hamdan: How dare you! How dare you say that? You're an evil bastard! Get him! Get the pig man!

Two others from the Abu Al-Jihad Youth Society jump up from their chairs and, together with Hamdan, punch and kick Khairul. The journalists do nothing to help. The photographers take photos of the beating. Anna is restrained by one of the society members.

Hamdan: How dare he insult me! He is one big sham. One big lie. Tell your boyfriend, if he's not careful, I'll come back one day, rip out his stinking pig heart and stuff it into his mouth!

The lights dim. Everyone exits the stage, leaving Khairul on the floor and Anna beside him.

Anna: Khairul! Are you okay? Please tell me you're okay. What have they done? What has happened to love and compassion? How could they beat up a man in a wheelchair?

Khairul: They didn't beat up a man in a wheelchair. Can't you hear the thing beating so horribly in my chest? They beat up a man with a pig heart.

Anna: What do you mean?

Khairul: A man who is an affront to Islam, to all Malays, to all Malaysia.

Anna: You're not that! Don't listen to those people.

Khairul: Oh, but I am! How the country, how the people have all turned against me. Only a few weeks ago I was their hero and now I'm a villain. It's in all the papers and TV. Didn't you hear what that bastard said? I have a pig heart and I have a pig brain. To them my hands and feet might as well be hoofs. I might as well have a curly tail and mud on my snout. I have become a pig! One they can slaughter!

Anna: Please don't cry.

Khairul: I'm a monster! A loathsome demon they must destroy. They'll not stop hounding me until my blood soaks deep into the ground. And it doesn't matter, because it's just pig blood. I . . . I am the Pig Man!

Anna: You're overreacting. I'll…I'll get an ambulance.

Khairul: I don't need one. I need an imam. To tell everyone that I'm still a Muslim, still a man who deserves some dignity, some respect. All I want is to be left alone. Not to be some repulsive freak to be poked and prodded or made fun of or beaten up!

Anna: Let's get you home. You'll need a doctor.

Anna helps Khairul into the wheelchair and wheels him away. She has forgotten her handbag and comes back for it. She sees the scrap of paper on the ground. She picks it up and reads it.

Anna: It's the consent form. That journalist must have dropped it. The words, they are in bold and underlined: "The heart to be transplanted will be that of a bioengineered heart of a swine. The patient agrees and irrevocably consents to the use of such an organ and has no moral or religious objections to its use." Khairul! Oh, how can I believe that you didn't read this! Oh, Khairul!

V I

Hamdan is sitting cross-legged on the floor and sharpening a knife.

Hamdan: [to audience] Yes, I'm here sharpening my knife. What did you expect me to do? Didn't you hear what that Pig Man said to me? What? You didn't? Are you deaf? Can't you listen? Don't you know what's going on here? His words, oh they're burning in my ears and it hurts like a rusty skewer twisting through my brain. He said . . . he said . . . he said when I die he'll bury me naked with a pig. A pig! A pig! A filthy rotting pig! Oh, I can feel the filthy animal, sweaty and warm, embracing my naked body and stroking my thigh with its hoof and licking my ear with its rough tongue even as dry soil falls upon my dead eyes. How dare he! How dare he! He will burn in hell for this! I cannot sit here and do nothing while his insult is screaming away in my brain. He is an affront to Islam, to all Malays and Malaysia. And he dares to insult me! To insult me! At night, when I try to sleep, I see his grinning face and he's pushing up his pig nose at me. And when I finally fall asleep I dream of him. There's a hole in his chest and the pig heart is there, all bloody and beating away,

pumping blood through his veins. And then he
pulls the glistening organ out and offers it to me!
He asks me to lick it. He tells me to take a nibble.
And I do! I can't help myself! I chew on the thing,
my hands covered in warm pig blood. And I
swallow slimy chunks of it. Then Datuk Khairul
starts laughing. Yes, that's right he starts laughing
at me. Louder and louder until I know that he is
the devil! A shaitan on this earth. When I pray
at home, but especially at the mosque, I can hear
him oinking. That's right, oinking! Far away at
first and then he's right next to me. I can feel his
warm smelly breath on my ears. And you expect
me to do nothing? This devil, this pig, is an insult
to everything I believe in. My race, my country,
my religion. No Muslim can stand aside and do
nothing. The Exco members might ask us to wait
and be patient, but others in the Abu Al-Jihad
Youth Society, oh yes they feel like I do. So I'm
sharpening my knife. Sharpening and sharpening
and sharpening. And that pig heart is beating
and beating and beating. And don't you act so
surprised.

VII

A Malay wedding. The akad nikah is taking place. The crowd is sitting cross-legged on the floor and talking. Khairul is dressed in baju melayu. His wheelchair is set to one side. The crowd goes quiet as the Imam and Khairul, sitting cross-legged opposite one another, clasp each other's hands in a prolonged handshake.

Imam: Saya nikahkan Datuk Khairul bin Haji Abu Samad dengan Anna Iznarin binti Haji Maroof dengan mas kahwinnya tiga ratus ringgit tunai.

Khairul: Saya terimalah nikahnya Anna Iznarin binti Haji Maarof...

Anna, in her wedding clothes, rushes in.

Anna: Khairul! I'm sorry!

Khairul: [Releasing the hand shake.] Anna what are you doing out of the room?

Imam: The bride is not allowed to come out. You must go back and wait there until we are done here. When he finishes the sentence in one breath then you'll be married. So don't be so impatient.

Khairul:	Anna, you should go back to the room.
Anna:	No Khairul, I can't! I'm so sorry!
Khairul:	What is it, Anna? What's wrong?
Anna:	I'm sorry, I can't do it!
Imam:	Can't do what, young lady? Go back and wait. Soon you'll be married.
Anna:	I can't go through with it.
Khairul:	What do you mean?
Anna:	I just can't go through with the wedding? I'm sorry.
Khairul:	I . . . surely we can . . . was it something I said?
Anna:	No, it's isn't. Don't you know why I can't marry you?
Khairul:	No, I don't! But I can guess. It's this foul thing beating in my chest, isn't it? You can't marry a man with a pig heart! What do you want me to do, Anna? Rip out this filthy rotting thing from my chest?

Imam: I think all of us should go. We should leave the couple alone to sort out their problems.

Everyone leaves except for Anna and Khairul.

Khairul: So tell me why you changed your mind? Anna, why this change of heart?

Anna: Change of heart? Ha, ha. I like that.

Khairul: I wasn't trying to be funny. Why have you changed your mind? You've now decided you can't marry the pig man?

Anna: It's not that at all, Khairul. It's not that!

Khairul: Then what is it? What's made you destroy our future together? Tell me!

Anna: It's this, Khairul!

Khairul: What's that?

Anna: The consent form. The words are bold and underlined. "The heart to be transplanted will be that of a bioengineered heart of a swine. The patient agrees and irrevocably consents to the use of such an organ and has no moral or religious objections to its use." How could you not have read it? It's so clear on this form.

Khairul: I've told everyone a thousand times that I didn't read that part. That I was sedated. I was in the hospital bed.

Anna: But you weren't sedated enough to sign your name here so clearly and legibly?

Khairul: I just signed it like I normally do.

Anna: I don't believe you. You had to be wide awake to sign your name so perfectly.

Khairul: So you don't believe me? You think I, a Muslim that prays five times a day, a Muslim that gives money to charity, a Muslim that fasts all Ramadan, a Muslim that's been on Umrah, agreed to the English doctors putting a pig heart in my chest? Do you honestly believe that?

Anna: I do. But I understand, Khairul. Believe me, I understand. You had little choice. I know your life would have been in danger if you waited around for a human one. It could have taken weeks, just waiting, and you could easily have had another heart attack. So you put life before religion. You went with what was readily available. You took the pig heart. There was little time or opportunity to think what that pig-heart transplant would mean.

Khairul: Or perhaps I didn't care. Perhaps I just hoped no one would find out.

Anna: What? You didn't care? You agreed to a pig heart with no thought of your own race and religion? I can't believe that!

Khairul: I wanted that pig heart. I wanted it glistening and throbbing here in my chest. I just hoped no one would find out.

Anna: I don't believe you! So why then did you tell me and the rest of your family?

Khairul: Guilt! I felt guilty a few days later, so I told you.

Anna: I don't believe you! You're a good man. A good Muslim.

Khairul: Am I? Just because I pray and fast and have visited Mecca doesn't make me a good Muslim. Who do you think got Idris to abscond with the money from the Foundation?

Anna: You?

Khairul: Yes, me! We split it half-half. My money's collecting interest at the bank. He's gone to spend his.

Anna:	Why Khairul, why?
Khairul:	Do you really think I want to go through another operation? Put my life at risk again? Do you know how risky a heart transplant is? Why should I do it just to satisfy all those people who are more righteous than thou, all those religious fanatics, xenophobes, chauvinists and fascists! Why couldn't they just let me be!
Anna:	You got Idris to steal the money so you didn't have to go through with the transplant?
Khairul:	Yes! And the money is pretty good too. I thought it would give us a good start in life!
Anna:	I don't want that tainted money.
Khairul:	Or a tainted husband, I suppose. One with a stinking pig heart beating in his chest. An oinking husband with a curly tail and mud on his snout!
Anna:	No, you're wrong. I would've been happy to marry you, with or without your pig heart. But I don't want to marry a liar. You said you didn't read the consent form. But I know you did. And now I know you got Idris to steal the foundation's money, I don't want to marry a thief! It was donated by all good Malaysians for a good cause. If you don't use it then it must be returned or used

for some other charitable purpose. But I suppose you're not going to do that, are you?

Khairul: No, I won't.

Anna: Then you're a thief. I never knew you were like this. That pig heart has changed you. It has taken you over and made you a greedy filthy swine. Good bye and don't bother to see me again. I hate you. Good bye.

VIII

There is the sound of a heartbeat which fades away.

Anna: That filthy lying swine! He knew all about the pig heart before the operation. I caught him out with that consent form, didn't I? He signed the damn thing so perfectly he just had to have known about the pig heart. There, there's the signature. Signed so perfectly. Signed . . . so perfectly? But . . . but how come it now looks more like a scribble under the light. Just an awful scrawl? An awful accusing scrawl. Could . . . could he have been sedated when he signed it? Just . . . just like he told me? But he admitted everything! He even admitted getting Idris to abscond with the money. Yet I know Khairul's no thief. I was so ready to believe the pig heart had corrupted his soul, made him a greedy filthy swine. Could I have been wrong? Could I have really been wrong? I have to talk to him. [Picks up the phone.] Hello! Can I speak to Khairul please. What? Gone out for a drink alone? He doesn't do that kind of thing. He did? Which bar did he go to? I see. Thank you. [Puts down the phone.] Oh Khairul! What have you done? What have I done?

IX

Khairul is sitting in the corner of a bar drinking alone.

Selva: I thought it was you. I was sitting there at the bar minding my own business when I saw you there.

Khairul: Go away, please. I'd rather be a alone.

Selva: Aiyo, what happen to your wheelchair? Why not using it? You lost the thing on the way here? You must conserve your energy.

Khairul: I can get by without it. I'm not a cripple. Just a person that's destabilizing the country. An affront to Islam, all Malays and all Malaysians. Anyway, people recognize me if I use it and they shout or spit on me. I know I shouldn't be exerting my body but I don't care. If death finds me, so much the better.

Selva: Come now. Things are not so bad lah. I read about the whole shameful incident in the paper yesterday. That girl no good, you know, walking out on you at your wedding.

Khairul: That girl was everything to me.

Selva:	Don't you worry, you'll find another. The river is full of bright-eyed, succulent fish ready for the taking and tasting. [laughs] Maybe not our Klang river but other better ones lah, I see them all the time on National Geographic. Aiyoyo, you drinking beer? Idris said you're a religious person and, like him, you never touch alcohol.
Khairul:	Screw religion. And this beer, it tastes horrible. But I'm sure I'll get to like it in time. As for Idris, he can go hang himself for all I care. A religious person doesn't steal.
Selva:	Right lah. All religions say stealing is no good. But, this Idris is only seemingly religious. All form, no substance. Religious in appearance. But all surface only. Inside all lowya one, corrupted like stinking rotting meat.
Khairul:	And a religious person isn't supposed to lie.
Selva:	Oh yes, that Idris is a lousy fella. A bloody liar. A big fat liar.
Khairul:	I was talking about myself.
Selva:	You lied? No good to lie, you know. Who did you lie to?
Khairul:	To Anna, my girlfriend.

Selva: Oh, lying to your girlfriend. That's understandable. We men have our secrets. Must be a white lie. What did you lie about?

Khairul: I knew it was all over from the first time she set eyes on me in the hospital in London. Her eyes, normally glowing with life and love were dull and forlorn like decrepit shutters had fallen over them. She wouldn't admit it to me, but mostly she wouldn't admit to herself: she couldn't marry me, not with this thing beating in my chest.

Selva: Ah, love it comes and goes. We have much sorrow and joy in life. Two years ago, my marriage was also in trouble you know, three miscarriages, so I took her to London for holidays. After that all okay and now we have a baby boy. Nine months old now and very cute. But how can you tell your fiancee no longer want to marry you from just one look?

Khairul: Oh there's more. It took her six days to get to London. She said she couldn't get on a flight. And she works for a travel agent! My parents came two days after the operation. There were lots of flights available. She just wasn't sure about coming, she wasn't sure about me, she wasn't sure about us.

Selva: All the love in the world sometimes can't beat the conventions, the culture, the religions. They cage us lah, and we don't even know they're there.

Khairul: Oh yes, she was in a cage from the moment I told her about the pig heart. From then on I could see her trying to escape, yet not knowing how. All that publicity made it even more imperative that she break off with me. But she didn't know how to do it. Not until she got hold of that consent form. I scribbled my signature on it while sedated on a hospital bed with tubes sticking out of me. She convinced herself I signed it so perfectly.

Selva: Now you told me you lie to her. What about, eh?

Khairul: I told her I'd read the consent form and knew they were going to give me a pig heart. She'd convinced herself of that fact anyway and I just confirmed it for her. I only told her what she wanted to hear.

Selva: Why did you lie to the poor girl?

Khairul: So she could pull out of the wedding with dignity. So her guilt wouldn't destroy her. Now, in her mind, she'd think I knew about the pig heart before the operation. That I accepted it to save my own life. Now she can start anew and forget about me.

Selva: You really love this girl, eh? Poor, unfortunate girl. Ah, what love is. The things it makes us do. It challenges everything. Everything turns upside down.

Khairul: But it was still a shock when she broke the wedding off at the last minute. I went half-mad and told her I convinced Idris to abscond with the money from the foundation.

Selva: Aiyoyo, you told her that? If only she knew the truth. Idris was slowly siphoning money from the account before he even met you. The fella was also taking money from work you know, falsify expenses and all that. Maybe he set up the foundation in the first place not to help you but to help himself.

Khairul: Maybe. I really don't care. It's all over now. I'm going to disappear. I've had enough of all this publicity. I get abusive phone calls, piles of hate mail and ugly-looking magic charms thrown over my fence. No one wants to know me in this country. I have no friends. My relatives won't see me. Everyone believes what's in the papers and on television. I write letters and hold press conferences but nothing gets printed. I'm a pariah here. A bloody freak!

Selva: Aiyo, only a few weeks ago you were our hero. Everybody wanting to know you. And now this.

Khairul: The media is fickle. They glorify you one moment and despise you the next. And the people, they're just brainwashed by what they read in the papers and see on television. They've forgotten how to think. This country, with all its sensitivities, has broken my heart and this organ isn't even mine. It belonged to a slaughtered pig. And as for religion . . .

Hamdan: There you are, betrayer of Islam! Now we've found you!

Khairul: Who are you? What do you want?

Hamdan: Don't you remember? We gave you a nice beating at your press conference. We've been following you for days. You claim to be a Muslim and here you are getting drunk with your Indian lover boy!

Selva: Eh, I'm not his lover boy! What you people want?

Hamdan: What do we want? We want compensation. We want retribution. We want an apology for the treacherous things he has done to Islam, all Malays and all of Malaysia.

Khairul: Hey, then I'm sorry, okay? Sorry for everything. Sorry for getting knocked down by that Rolls Royce. Sorry for coming back to this country. Sorry to still be alive with this filthy ugly thing beating in my chest!

Hamdan: Your sorry's not good enough. Your apology cannot erase the terrible offence to all of us. Don't you know you're a living, breathing insult? I can

> hear your snorting and baying in my head even as I try to pray in the mosque, as I toss and turn in my bed trying to sleep. No Muslim can rest while you're still alive!

Khairul: I'm not the one whose drunk, you are! You're drunk on religion!

Hamdan: I'd rather be drunk on your blood!

Khairul: It's pig blood and it's haram! [Khairul laughs]

Hamdan: You bastard! Get the pig man! Get his lover!

Hamdan and three others from the Abu Al-Jihad Youth Society raise their knives and attack Khairul and Selva.

Hamdan: My knife for your pig heart!

Khairul and Selva fall to the floor. The attackers flee.

Anna: Khairul? Khairul? Khairul?! Who is that man beside you? Tell me you're just sleeping. That all that blood is just red paint. That all this is some sick joke.

There is the sound of a heart beating.

> An act of revenge for the stupid, selfish woman I've been. You didn't know about the pig heart.

> You're not a liar! I convinced myself of all of that. I am a foolish woman. A blind bird in a cage. Trapped by convention, culture, religion. And it was not love that blinded me. It was our so-called sensibilities and sensitivities. Listen to me, Khairul. I was the one! I told the papers about your operation. I wanted to get out of the wedding!

The heartbeat gets louder.

> Please forgive me. But I'm free now, Khairul. Free from all that has held me back! I'm pushing you along the Serpentine and we're feeding ducks, licking ice cream and holding hands. No one is staring at us. No one is dirtying us with their beady, greedy eyes.

The heartbeat slows down.

> I belong to you. No matter what organ beats in your chest, your heart is filled with nothing but goodness. I'll gladly exchange my human heart for your pig heart just to understand the misery I've caused you. Forgive me for everything. I love you!

The heartbeat stops.

> Wake up. Please wake up! Khairul! Khairul! Oh, Khairul!